When We Touch

When We Touch

SHANNON DRAKE

ZEBRA BOOKS
KENSINGTON PUBLISHING CORP.

ZEBRA BOOKS are published by

Kensington Publishing Corp.
850 Third Avenue
New York, NY 10022

ISBN 0-7394-4013-6

Printed in the United States of America

Chapter 1

Maggie, Lady Graham, daughter of the late and renowned Baron Edward Graham, felt an odd foreboding as she approached the town house, seeing the carriage with the emblem of her crest emblazoned on the door. No hackney, the conveyance that had arrived at her doorstep. It meant that her uncle Angus had arrived, and since he seldom came without sending a note of his intentions to call, there was certainly a dire problem somewhere within the family.

She swore softly beneath her breath—something she quickly assured herself that no lady would do. And, yet, of course, that was her title, despite the fact that her late husband had been a commoner. As the daughter of a baron, she was entitled to be called "lady" until the day she died. Not that it mattered so terribly to her. But then, beyond a doubt, she was the black sheep of her family—sooted and grimed, she was certain, in the eyes of her oh-so-social-conscious uncle, aunt, and cousins.

Angus, she thought, with a twinge of humor entering her tired mind, *must surely regret his older brother's marriage*—and the fact that, after several childless years, her mother had produced not just one child, but two, in the form of twins. In the great scheme of legal matters within Great Britain, her own birth mattered little. But seconds after her arrival, Justin had entered the world. And thus ended Angus's hope for her father's title. Actually, it was all quite amazing. Justin was hardly a boy any longer, and Angus still swaggered about as if he were head of the family.

"The ogre is here!" Mireau said softly from behind her.

"You mustn't refer to Angus as an ogre," she said, flashing a quick smile to her friend. Jacques Mireau had come into her life at a far happier time. Since then, he had decided that he must be her defender. Also, as he was an aspiring author, he needed patronage while he penned his golden tomes. Theirs was, therefore, quite a beneficial friendship, though she was certain there were others who saw far more into the relationship than what existed. She didn't particularly care. Illusions of grandeur were not a part of her existence. She felt blessed to have had a short piece of magic in her life that had taught her the beauty of what might be in truth, and the suffering to be found in the hypocrisy of so much that was done in the pursuit of a life that was customarily no more than image and mirage.

"You refer to him as an ogre," Mireau reminded her.

"Only when we're alone."

"We haven't yet walked in the house," he said. "And

your footsteps are slowing, as if you are loathe to do so."

"I shall admit, to you and you alone, that Uncle Angus is not my favorite person."

Mireau's hands fell softly on her shoulders and his powder blue eyes widened, as if with dire dread and alarm. "We must face the firing squad quickly! The longer one lingers in the agony of doubt . . . the deadlier the pain!"

"What nonsense—facing a firing squad would make it all over, wouldn't it?" Maggie said, forcing a note of impatience. But at his teasing, she quickened her steps. Angus was there. Might as well find out why, and endure whatever lecture he now had to give.

At the top step, she suddenly swung on Mireau. "I can handle any ogre!" she assured him, drawing closed a small parasol as they entered the house.

Clayton was at the door, as if he had known of her arrival just outside. As if he had been waiting, and watched her pause. She inclined her head slightly at the skeletal old dear who doubled as their butler and her brother's valet, brows knitting into a frown.

"Lord Angus is here, Lady Maggie," he announced, though the announcement was surely not necessary. Still, quite correct.

She smiled. "Thank you, Clayton," she said, undoing the tiny little buttons at her wrists and removing her gloves as he took her cape from her shoulders. "Have you offered my dear uncle tea as yet?" She gave Clayton her gloves and the small reticule she had carried.

"My lady, we have just been waiting your arrival so that you might serve," Clayton told her.

She delicately arched a brow. Was she being tested on her ability to serve tea—at this late date?

"How delightful and courteous that Angus has waited," she said, certain that her uncle could clearly hear her every word. "We shall certainly hasten ourselves right into the parlor, then."

Clayton blocked her path and whispered softly, "The family only!" A wiggle of his eyes back and forth informed her that she was to leave Mireau behind.

"I'll be in my attic garret, when you need me," Mireau said quickly.

"Coward," she said with a smile.

"Indeed. He might well be here to inform you that I must be out of the house."

"Rubbish. He hasn't the right."

"Lady Maggie, may I suggest that you not keep Lord Angus waiting?" Clayton prompted softly. He cleared his throat, taking a liberty. "Your brother has kept him sole company quite long enough, under the circumstances."

Maggie frowned again, nodded to Mireau, and approached the parlor. For once, she wished that she were better dressed. But she had spent the morning on charity work, a cause near and dear to her heart, so much more so because she had learned from Nathan of the poverty and squalor to be found just beyond the opulence of so much of London. She was very simply dressed in black linen from head to toe, her outfit devoid of lace or decoration of any kind. Dirt and grime were the only adornments on her skirt. She had two great passions in her life then—easing the lives of the ragged and starving orphans to be found in the East End, and unmasking the charlatans who claimed to be "mesmerists" and cheated rich and poor alike out of their livelihoods while promising to contact their deeply mourned departed.

"Uncle Angus!" she said, sweeping into the parlor. Even as she did so, her voice perfectly modulated, her every move that of the lady born and bred, she couldn't help but notice the genteel poverty of her own homestead. The divan was growing threadbare at the edges, as was the one-time exquisite Persian carpet on the hardwood floor.

"My dear." Angus had been sitting at one of the high-backed chairs around the divan. A stiff chair, and his posture was equally as stiff. He had known she had arrived, of course. He had waited for her arrival in the room to stand.

He came forward, tall and imposing, white-haired, muttonchopped sideburns, small mustache and goatee perfectly groomed. His waistcoat and jacket were elegantly tailored, and she could see the shimmer of his sterling watch bob. Angus cut quite a figure, she had to admit. And in looks, he reminded her of her father, though that dear man became more of a wisp of memory as the years since his death passed by.

He caught both of her hands, then kissed each of her cheeks, as if he had spent most of his time on the Continent. He had not. He worked for the Queen's household, though in just what capacity, she had never quite known.

"Maggie," Justin said softly, rising as well. She glanced quickly at her brother. He looked ghastly.

They were twins, and certainly bore a resemblance. From their mother they had inherited an unusual shade of hair—a true reddish blond, gold in the light of the sun, light, and yet, very rich. Nathan had once told her that it was like a shining halo—not the halo of a soft or silly angel, but rather that of an avenger, out to bring Almighty Justice. It was part of her temper, he had teased. And part of the fighting spirit that he'd vowed he so loved.

In his memory, she would never cut it.

Justin, too, seemed quite fond of his, wearing it a bit longer than the fashion. He was clean shaven, which suited him, for his features were cleanly cut, and decidedly strong, very handsome. Today, however, her handsome sibling looked not only ashen, but bent, as if holding his own frame erect was a terrible effort. He offered her a weak smile, looked sicker still, and sat again.

"Ah, the tea!" she said, as Clayton entered, bearing the tray. She went about the business immediately of pouring, telling Angus, "Uncle, I believe you prefer it with just one lump and a bare touch of cream?"

"Indeed, my dear."

"Molly's scones are beyond delight, sir. You must taste one."

Angus accepted his cup of tea, but waved his hand impatiently at the offer of a scone. "Pour your brother his tea, my dear. And find a perch for yourself, for the business at hand is serious."

She couldn't help a quick glance at Justin. He refused to catch her eye. He didn't look one bit like Lord Graham, a grand baron of the Ton. He looked like a stricken invalid.

She passed him a cup of tea, noting that his hands were trembling and the fine china service clattered dangerously in his grip. She pretended to ignore his state, keeping her composure as she poured tea for

herself, purposely adding fuel to her uncle's fire as
she took her time, then found a seat in the straight,
wing-backed chair opposite him.

"So, Uncle, this is not a social call," she said at last.

"Hardly social," Angus said, and she thought she
detected a snicker to his words.

"Pray then," she said, slightly hiking a brow, "do
enlighten us."

Angus leaned forward, setting his cup on the Oriental
table before him.

"I can no longer afford the behavior of this branch
of the family!"

She was startled enough that her own cup clattered upon its saucer. "My dearest uncle, I am offended. For though we would never fail to bow to
your wisdom—or forget that you are the brother of
our dear departed father—it is my brother, Justin,
who bears the family title."

"And has made waste of all that the family has
gained!" Angus said angrily.

Her eyes flew to her brother at that point and sick-
ness fell to the pit of her stomach with a walloping
thump. Justin would still not look her way.

"Justin has gambled away all but the title, I'm
afraid. I've kept this home afloat—and your brother
from his gambling debts—longer than I am able.
Your cousin Diana is due to make her first appearance in society this season. You and Justin must now
bear responsibility for your own welfare."

"But—but—!" Maggie stammered, then grew furious with her own lack of composure. "We were left in
secure finances."

"You were—you are now in deep debt—to me,
and not just to me! God knows what other creditors

there are who have not been paid," Angus said contemptuously.

Justin suddenly came to life, and whatever he had done, Maggie was proud of him in that one moment of righteous anger he showed. "My lord uncle! It was you who suggested that I spend my nights following in the party of our dear royal Eddy, and it is thus, sir, that I have come to these lamentable circumstances!"

"Lamentable, indeed. If you do not change your ways or find some means of salvation, you are likely to find yourself in the debtor's section of Newgate!"

As she had heard far more than anyone really wanted to know about the prison, Maggie was instantly horrified.

"Uncle," Justin said quietly, "I believe you're being a bit dramatic. The new prison for debtors is in Pentonville, if I'm not mistaken." He looked at his sister dryly. "It's considered quite a model prison. There's good ventilation, and it's solitude they put you in these days, hours and hours alone to contemplate your sins. Truly, the building is supposed to be a gorgeous example of the genius of Victorian architecture."

Angus was furious. He wagged a finger at Justin. "Let me tell you, my worldly young lord! You may still be hauled into Newgate until your trial takes place, and believe me, the rats and the stench remain! Along with many of those hardened criminals awaiting execution."

"They don't execute men for debt," Justin said coldly.

"This cannot be true!" Maggie said. "I knew that we were rich in the sense of family and title if not in vast estates, but there was a trust!"

"There *was* a trust. No more."

Maggie stared at her brother again. Now, his eyes, as rich a blue as her own, stared back. "I'm afraid it isn't easy keeping up with the Prince, or his companions," he said.

"There should be a rich marriage in the offing for your brother. In time," Angus said. "I have been quietly making inquiries, intent upon finding the proper bride."

Maggie could well imagine. Angus would be looking, certainly. He would be seeking an aging dowager with properties and monies in abundance. However, she would be far beyond the age when a child might be produced, and therefore, the title would fall to Angus and his heirs.

"Now, I may suggest first that you cut down on your household—starting with the chaff," Angus said.

"Jacques Mireau."

Angus grimaced in a fashion that made his lips very slim. "The man is a leech."

"A friend, a poet, and one day, a famed writer, I am certain," Maggie said.

"There are whispers about you," Angus said.

"I'm sorry, Uncle, as I know how very much the opinions of those in your strata matter to you. What is said about me is not important."

"For your brother's sake, it is highly important." Angus's fingers were all but white as he gripped the arms of his chair. "As if you have not embarrassed the family enough already—marrying a policeman!"

"Well, then, thank God that he died so young, rather than embarrassing us further!" Maggie cried, unable at that point to restrain her fury.

She wasn't at all sure herself why this argument seemed to be so much between her and Angus—she wasn't the one who had gambled away the family fortune. But then she realized suddenly that she was under personal attack, and she knew that she was about to discover why.

"There is a solution," Angus said.

"And that is?" she demanded.

"Marriage."

"Well," she said, glancing at Justin again. He was to be wed to an old dowager. However innocently he might have fallen into vice, he was the one who had done so.

"And, pray, what marriage might you have negotiated in my brother's behest?"

"Your brother's marriage, my girl, is still under negotiation."

"I'm sure she's rich and charming—and certainly, sir, with your wisdom, you've chosen someone with a definite measure of . . . maturity," Maggie said politely.

Justin let out something that sounded strangely like a snort, not at all becoming a baron. Nor did he seem to care—it was a sound of self-loathing, and disturbed Maggie greatly.

"There is surely a way out of this rather than a hasty and unhappy marriage for my brother," Maggie informed Angus sternly. "This is, after all, the nineteenth century."

"Maggie!" Justin protested, forming words at last. "It isn't my impending marriage that brings such a searing sense of pleasure and satisfaction to our dear uncle's face."

His sarcasm did not go unnoticed.

"Ungrateful whelp!" Angus said angrily, almost rising.

"Ah, but titularly, he is the head of the family," Maggie murmured.

"Others of far greater magnitude have rotted away in Newgate," Angus reminded her.

"The marriage he has planned—and, oh, yes, certainly to a person of wealth, charm, and *maturity*, is for you," Justin said.

Stunned, Maggie gasped aloud. "Me!"

"Why so surprised, my dear niece?" Angus asked. He wore a look of feigned distress, while she knew that he secretly relished her amazement and discomfort. She shuddered within, wondering what manner of man her uncle might have found for her.

Angus stood, hands clasped behind his back as he paced around the chair. "Frankly, I'd not have thought of such a happy remedy for your plight on my own, I fear." He stopped and stared straight at her, shaking his head with dismay. "You had such a brilliant season in your youth, my dear! You dazzled the Ton, and you had the credentials to bring about a splendid marriage. But you chose to disgrace the family and take up with a commoner!"

She thought wryly that he might have been less disproving had she opted to commit murder.

"I know, Angus, that this is something completely beyond your realm of understanding, but I married Nathan because I fell in love with him." She was standing herself, and realized that her fingers had knotted so tightly into her palms that she was digging holes into her own flesh. "In fact, sir, I remember your kind, sympathetic, and so completely understanding words at his funeral. That I was somewhat young still, and though tarnished, I might still have some redeeming value!"

He didn't notice mockery or reproach in her words; he found in them a note of her own understanding. "Aha! There, you see? What I said was true. The time has come. I was at the club the other day and a most remarkable thing happened. Charles, Viscount Langdon, approached *me* about you. He had heard about your unfortunate marriage, and the death of your husband, and was quite concerned for your welfare. He remembered you, and believes still that you are the most beautiful young woman ever to walk the earth. Beautiful—and available, I fathom. But that is far beyond the point. The marriage portion he has offered would pay off the gambling debts and allow Justin an opportunity to redeem himself, and the family name. Money means nothing to Lord Charles. He has properties throughout the known world and made quite a fortune to add on to his family inheritance, which includes vast stretches of land in Scotland as well as on the Continent and in the Caribbean." He glared at Justin, indicating that the nobleman in question knew how to responsibly handle a family fortune while Justin most assuredly did not. "Well, my dear? This is a rare opportunity for you. Society would accept you once again."

"Uncle Angus, surely this cannot come as a vast surprise to you—I have attended those 'society' teas, balls, and parties that have had any appeal for me for the past several years. This, I know, will surely shock you, but the opinions of dandies, fops, and braggarts do not mean a great deal to me. When Nathan died, I said that I would not marry again."

Angus waved a hand in the air impatiently. "A sweet sentiment, voiced by many a young widow, and certain to be changed."

Justin cleared his throat. "I believe that Lord Charles is looking for a companion, rather than a bride in the way that a man does in his first youth."

She glared at her brother. He flushed, and looked away. Then he stood, as well. "Uncle Angus, the idea of this marriage is repulsive in my sister's eyes. I incurred the debts. If it be Newgate, sir, then I shall go as the Crown commands."

"The pair of you will likely rot with the rats!" Angus said impatiently. "I was stunned and greatly relieved to entertain the offer of such a man, especially when I certainly could not offer a young lady of good reputation and sound family."

"The family you speak of is yours as well, Uncle," Maggie said. "And I do beg your pardon! I hardly walked the streets of Whitechapel propositioning laborers, nor did I tease the married men of the Ton, which others you would consider to be of excellent value have done."

"You married a commoner, and you are past your first youth. Like it or not, my dear, that, indeed, lessens your value in the marriage market. Not to mention the fact that you bring no fortune, indeed, one is needed to salvage you both from the dank cells of debt."

"Sir, do you realize that this very conversation is *common?*" Maggie demanded. And so it was. Yet it was blunt, and she was shaking because she knew that he was speaking a certain amount of truth. *Common, yes, it was all quite common. She had married a commoner. She had never once regretted her decision, not even when she had laid Nathan to rest. The two sweet years they'd shared before a cutthroat's knife had brought him down had still been worth whatever agony of loneliness was left to bear in the years to come. She hadn't minded not being rich—the very concept of true wealth and elegance had died with her parents. She had a mind and a spirit for causes, and she had certainly thought that they were living well enough on their allowances.*

She looked across the room at her brother, and for a moment, fury raged through her. Then she knew that he was not at fault. Angus had instructed him after their father's death. And Angus had taught him that society was everything, winning the friendship of the Crown, being among the most elite of the Ton. She had known that he ran with the heir apparent and his crowd; they had often argued about the Empire, and the responsibilities that were inherent with power, the greatness and the splendor of so much, while beneath their very noses, the people often suffered appallingly. Oh, yes, she had known. She had even made a few perfunctory appearances, as she had assured Angus. She loved Justin, and they were close.

Not close enough, she realized. For she had known nothing about his growing debt, and yet, it should not be a surprise, for few men had such a reputation for debauchery as Eddy, Duke of Clarence, heir presumptive to the throne after his own father, the eldest son of Queen Victoria.

"I can't begin to imagine any venue of employment where either of you could so much as begin to make enough to clear the debts," Angus said. "I'm afraid, though, that the house must go immediately."

"We can sell the estate in the north," Maggie suggested.

Angus shot Justin a chastising glance. "It's been

gone quite some time already, dear child," he said softly.

She sank back into her chair.

Justin walked to her with purpose and determination. Down on a knee, he took her hands in his. "Don't worry, old girl. They'll lock me up, and perhaps a toothless old hag—but one with plenty of money—will come rescue me!" He tried to speak lightly.

She was angry enough for one moment to let him rot—and marry a toothless old hag. But she would never give Angus that satisfaction. Her brother was going to have a bride young enough to procreate if it killed her.

She looked past Justin. "You may arrange a meeting, Uncle, between your Viscount and myself."

"That will be satisfactory," Angus said. "Tomorrow morning. At ten. And good God, girl! Don't be dressed as a crone, in rags and darkness—and dirt!"

"I shall wear something entirely suggestive, in shocking yellow, perhaps," she returned, too angry to remember any modicum of respect. How had this man been her father's brother?

"Come to think of it, my dear," Angus said, pleasantly enough, "you are quite well and properly dressed right now—should you choose for your destination to be Newgate."

With that, he bowed and departed, calling over his shoulder, "We will call at ten. Promptly."

The parlor was still, dead still, until they heard the door slam. Angus had not needed to ask Clayton for his great overcoat—bless dear Clayton. The man had been ready with her uncle's fine wool garment, cane, and silk hat.

"There is no reason for you to marry miserably to save my skin," Justin said flatly. He no longer appeared pale and ashen, but rather resolved. "I knew better, as I incurred the debt. It is my mistake. Though the idea is not appealing, I deserve a debtor's imprisonment."

Maggie stared at him, and the anger that had boiled within her evaporated in a single breath. "No."

"Maggie, you will not pay for my sins. Seriously. This is not false bravado on my part. I don't intend to go quietly. I have made the acquaintances of a few blushing widows who would not be averse to my attentions."

"No."

"Maggie, dammit—!"

"Justin, don't be crass."

"Maggie, I've heard you say far worse."

"Justin!"

"I don't condemn you for it. I admire your ability to thumb your nose at the entire world. It gives you a dignity you cannot begin to imagine."

"Language is not the issue here."

"I fully intend to refuse your hand in marriage to the Viscount."

"Angus has, I believe, consented already."

"It is not our uncle's position. It is mine. Legally, it is my right to allow or disallow your marriage, and that is the way that it is."

She sighed softly, looking down at her hands for a moment. If her uncle had found this man, he was surely loathsome. But if he was as rich as Angus claimed, and as infatuated, he might be quite a useful companion.

"Ah, come, Maggie, dear! I cannot apologize to you enough. I will make good for this myself. If I find the right old sweetie, she might pop off quite soon enough."

"Oh, Justin, that's horrible."

"So many things that are true are horrible, as well. I mean this, Maggie, I have been a fool. I tried to be all that Angus wanted, the perfect swain, so close to the throne that I was all but perched on the edge! And so here I am. *I* am. Not you."

"Justin, do you really love me, dearly, and are you truly, truly sorry?" she demanded.

"Indeed, I am," he said gravely.

"Then, if you would do anything to make it up to me, you will give your blessing on my marriage to this man."

"Why?" he demanded in turn.

"Because, Justin, if there is anything I want in this world, it's to be aunt to a dozen little nieces—and nephews. I swear to you, Justin, there is nothing more important in this world. And we cannot count on an old dowager departing this world expediently, and if there is anything at all that would cause me untold grief, it would be Angus inheriting our father's title. Do you understand? If you love me and would make amends, find a proper young woman—rich, poor, common, or noble—and marry her. Soon."

Justin hung his head, quietly folding his hands together in prayer fashion. He looked up at her. "Maggie, for the love of God, you mustn't hate Angus more than you love yourself."

She smiled. They were grave and solemn words from him, and spoken with firm passion and resolve.

She came to him that time, taking his hands. "Justin, if this man is truly horrendous, we will talk again tomorrow. But if he . . . if he's at all decent, then perhaps he can give me things that I do want in this world. A voice among the very rich and important people. You know how I feel about the dreadful conditions in some of the orphanages. Perhaps he'll buy me a factory for a wedding present, and we can see that people are given fair wages for decent hours."

"Oh, Maggie!" Again, her very handsome and now humble brother appeared ill. She was almost annoyed. Here she was, the lamb going to slaughter, and she was trying to make him feel better about it!

"Justin, do you remember when I fell in love with Nathan? You were so strong then. You were the great baron, the head of the household, insisting that I would marry as I chose. Well, I did. You supported me when many a man wouldn't have done so. Well, I have lost Nathan. And I will never love again. So if I marry a very rich nobleman who is ridiculously in love with me—without even knowing me!—it will not really matter in the least. Hopefully, we will be friends."

He looked straight ahead. "Friends, yes. Oh, yes, because he is surely one of the most decent fellows I have ever met."

She sat back. "You know him?"

"Of course." He gave a dry laugh. "He doesn't run with the likes of Eddy. He is very close to the Queen. One of the few people she will see in private, and with whom she shares her mourning and her confidence. They console one another. His wife has been gone for years, as has Her Majesty's still so lamented dear Prince Albert. Truly, he is decent, caring, and not at all bad-looking, really. Well, you know, for such an old tar! Tall and regal. Dignified. Indeed, you might make quite a pair, turning the world upside down." He tried to smile.

She smiled. "So . . . I meet him tomorrow."

"I don't like this. I don't like this one bit."

"Yes, well, I don't think either of us would like Newgate, either," she said a little sharply. Again, for a moment, she felt the temptation to throttle him. Except that she knew that, whatever trouble he might have gotten into, Justin truly rued anything that might now hurt her. He was telling the truth. If she exhibited one bit of distress, he'd offer himself to the authorities.

"Look, Maggie, you must listen to me—"

"Justin, a few possibilities here are beginning to appeal to me. Do you know just how powerful I could become—with the right backing?"

"But there is no agreement, unless you truly wish it."

She didn't tell him that she would wish it if he produced the devil himself—as long as it kept him from marrying a dowager with one foot in the grave and not a prayer of producing an heir.

"Naturally," she murmured, and started to leave the parlor. She was shaking too hard to stay.

But at the arch to the entry, she paused, swinging back on him. "If you get into this kind of debt again, Justin, you won't need to worry about Newgate. I'll swing you from a yardarm myself, do you understand?"

She didn't want an answer. She fled.

* * *

"Nine-fifty-five," Mireau said, giving her the exact time before she could ask. She had voiced the question every few minutes for the last twenty.

Like Justin, he had tried to dissuade her. He had come up with every other possible solution, none of which was actually possible. He had wanted to wage some kind of battle himself, but they both knew, even if he suddenly managed to make himself a respected literary name, it would be eons before he actually made money in any appreciable sum.

Then they had talked about the pros and cons, because he was Mireau, and he always made her see herself and a situation clearly.

"Justin has seen the man?" Mireau asked suddenly.

"Yes."

"And his description?" Mireau asked.

"Tall and dignified."

Mireau was looking out the upstairs window above the entry. She realized that their visitors had come, and she rushed up behind him, carefully taking a position where she might be covered by the draperies.

A carriage had arrived. Far grander than her uncle's. Big, drawn by a pair of matched black stallions that were truly magnificent. A third horse was tethered to the rear. Three men stood at the open doorway to the coach, where velvet covered steps had been lowered to allow the riders to step down.

One of the arrivals looked up.

Maggie stared down at him, stunned.

He wasn't old. He was tall, and certainly, dignified. He had a head of sweeping, almost ebony dark hair. His features were hewn lean and clean, his jaw had a definite square and rugged angle to it. His eyes were

large, color indiscernible from here, but his brows
were sharply defined, and his mouth had a cynical
sensuality. In a fitted waistcoat, cravat, and sharply
tailored jacket, he appeared ruggedly well built, the
elegance of his attire almost a sham over the magnitude of his physique.

"Why . . . he's . . . gorgeous. Extraordinary!" Mireau
breathed.

"Nonsense," she murmured. But she felt a faint
shiver along her spine and something more. Something she had thought dead and buried. The slightest stirring of excitement.

Excitement . . . *desire?*

Lord, no! She quickly chastised herself for such a
wretchedly disloyal thought.

And yet . . .

"Can that be him? The Viscount?" Mireau marveled.

Then, just as she realized that she had forgotten
all about the draperies and that she was staring down
at the man just as he was staring up at her, he smiled.
And there was some kind of amusement and mockery in that smile. He made a slight bow to her, and
stepped back.

Another man appeared from behind him.

Tall, and dignified. With strong features, and intelligent eyes.

Ah, yes, he was tall. And certainly, dignified. Very
elegantly dressed, yet he wore the cut of his clothes
extremely well for his . . . maturity.

His hair was as white as snow.

But he did have a full head of it.

His face, though one time fine, was deeply lined.

Once broad shoulders were far more skeletal now. He was dignified, yes . . .

And he was also older than God himself, so it appeared.

"That must be the Viscount," she whispered hollowly.

She was marrying a man who was all but a corpse.

Chapter 2

Jamie Langdon noted every little detail about the house, his aggravation rising.

Ah, yes. Genteel poverty. Fine enough in itself. Yet someone was being sold here to rectify the situation. And he couldn't help but feel contempt.

He'd met Justin often enough, in and around the Court, at balls, teas, and social affairs. He'd seen him frequently enough at a number of other establishments, as well. He'd liked Justin; a man of a pleasant enough countenance, he was polite and courteous, usually, but quick to defend a friend by both word and deed. He had been well educated, and in the presence of Eddy, the Duke of Clarence—heir apparent, after his father's time on the throne was done, should Victoria ever depart this world—Justin had the ability to transfer his own knowledge to his royal friend, making it appear as if the man were far brighter than he was in fact. A decent chap.

Except at the gaming tables. There, he went wild.
This, then, was his home.

He'd heard there was a sister. Gossip, of course,
ran rife. She had swept the Ton by storm at her coming out, dazzling men and women alike. The former
had idolized her, while most often, the latter had
chosen to gossip about her. She had disgraced her
station in life, ignoring all the noble and genteel
young men, and falling into a wretched affair with a
commoner—a policeman, no less—and that was a
crime to many a man and woman with a title. She'd
married the fellow. And then—other than the gossip
that surfaced now and then about her strange activities—there had been little else.

He'd been on the Continent, still in Her
Majesty's service, during the days when the young
Lady Maggie had been the toast of the Ton.
Therefore, he'd never seen the alleged beauty.
Until now. And he had looked up, and seen her face
in the window.

To be fair, she was an outstanding beauty.

But that Charles should have suddenly determined, at this late stage, that he must wed again,
and a lass almost a third his own age, well, it just
seemed . . .

Well, quite frankly, it seemed revolting.

But he loved his great uncle. Title be damned. If
Charles could wed again, and produce a son of his
own, God bless him.

However . . .

Should he marry a cuckolding little twit who intended to put a bastard into the line of his own family, Jamie would happily kidnap the woman himself

and sell her off in Zanzibar, or some other foreign port. For many years, Charles had consulted him on the important decisions in his life, and on all business affairs. But when he had suddenly decided that he was going to marry, he hadn't mentioned a word of it—not until he had made preliminary arrangements to speak with the lady through Angus Graham. Charles had been set and determined. Jamie had carefully cautioned his uncle, trying not to remind him of his age, but Charles was well aware that he was seeking a very young woman. He didn't care. "Men of my age must often seek alternatives for companionship, my boy," Charles had told him. "Luckily, I am in a position of title and wealth, and therefore, free to seek my heart's desire."

So she was his heart's desire. And available, so it seemed, at a price.

Perhaps it bothered him that a man of his uncle's stature had so suddenly determined to do such a thing which lacked the dignity that had thus far ruled the Viscount's life. His uncle deserved respect and admiration. He had fought in the Queen's wars, he had been her confidant. He had helped and advised the now long-deceased Prince Consort on the advancement of technology, and he had argued in the House of Lords.

If this young lady did not show the proper respect for such a man, Jamie thought that he would find himself tempted to throttle her.

"My heart is aflutter, boy!" Charles said suddenly, catching Jamie's arm. "Wait until you meet her!"

"Uncle, do you know the lass at all yourself?" Jamie demanded.

"I saw her, nephew."

"Seeing is not knowing."

"Ah, but yes, we did speak, several years ago, and she may not remember. She was the belle of every ball, and every young swain who could come near her, did so. She was ever kind, speaking to those fellows who stuttered, who were not so graceful on the dance floor, nor so highly born, with the same courtesy. A temper has she, for I saw ice in her eyes once, when one highborn fellow would jostle out another. Ah, boy. I know her. And that she has said she will see me . . . as I said, my heart is aflutter."

"Don't let it flutter too hard, or it will shatter the walls of your chest!" Jamie advised him. His uncle grinned, not resenting the comment. "Let's enter, shall we? We are like college boys here, loitering on a lady's doorstep."

"Oh, indeed, let's enter." He was more than curious himself to meet this paragon of virtue and beauty himself. He was here, of course, to protect Charles, though in what way, he was not certain. Charles could spend his wealth as he chose. And it was hardly likely that he might have found a young *rich* woman willing to marry a man of his age, however fine a lord he might be. Marriages were often made for the sake of convenience, and for the woman involved, this marriage must definitely be convenient. Certainly, after her escapades, she'd never snare a young lord of wealth, position, or promise. She would be accepting this proposal for one purpose only, that of acquiring position and wealth. Certainly, as the wife of Charles, Viscount Langdon, there would be no house in Great Britain or the Continent where she would

not be welcome. And if her clothing were as threadbare and antiquated as her surroundings, well, she
could then afford all the silks and satins she might
desire.

"Darby," Charles told his footman, "I believe we
shall be about an hour. Perhaps you'd care to visit a
coffeehouse or newsstand."

"Ah, Lord Charles, I'll be waitin' right here for ye
and Sir Jamie, that I will. And ye take yer time. I've
me papers right here." Darby, like all the servants in
Charles's employ, adored the old man. He was gra-
cious and generous, and though born into a society
where class was a matter of total acceptance, he was
also of the belief that God's behest to man to love
one's brother as he loved himself was the greatest of
commandments. He practiced what he preached.

As Charles turned, Darby gave Jamie a frown.
Jamie gave him an imperceptible nod. *Aye, he'd protect Charles. With his last breath, if need be. Whether
against a cutthroat, an enemy in the House of the Lords—
or the wiles of a beautiful woman.*

Charles's hand fell upon Jamie's shoulder for a
moment as they walked up the steps. "Would that you
had been my son! My cousin was a blessed man," he
said softly. "First your father, dearly missed, but now
you, as well. I am rightfully proud that you are my
kin. And in the event of death if a new marriage does
not produce a son . . ."

"Sir, I will dance at your wedding with bells on,
and pray that your marriage be productive. And you
must remember, you are raising a most beautiful
young daughter."

"Ah, but we both know a daughter is not a son in

the world in which we live! Glad I am, though, boy, and never forget it, that should this marriage bear no fruit, it's to you that the title and most of my riches will fall. Arianna, though, alas!" Charles frowned, and Jamie knew that young lady had been troubling the old man lately. "I pray to see her duly wed to a good and proper man before my death! Not that she will ever want . . . But I fear for her! I might well have allowed for too much of an education for the girl! She needed a mother so badly. There was so much that I could teach . . . and so much that I could not. If the Lady Maggie only accepts me, she will see to it that Arianna learns the right and wrong of her place in this world. There is far more to wealth than play, Jamie. That you have worked and served is a pleasure to my eyes and my old heart, and yet even a lady, a wife, and a mother, must also learn the gravity of power."

"Arianna is young, and her mind runs to dreams at the moment," Jamie said. "Give her time."

Charles stopped suddenly on the top step. "Pray God that I have the time." He didn't dwell on his words, but rapped on the front door with his cane. He wasn't asking for pity, and he didn't want any. He had lived his life well, and in his mind, it was simple fact that he had only so many years left to go.

The door was opened by a butler. A living skeleton, decked out in fading, genteel elegance. Clean as a whistle, and courteous, dignified, and erect as such a servant should be. "Good day, Lord Charles, Sir James. May I take your overcoats and escort you to the parlor? Lord Angus and Baron Graham await you with the greatest pleasure and expectation. Lady Maggie . . . will be down shortly."

"Thank you, my man," Charles said, hastily shedding coat, hat, gloves, and cane, and entering the parlor on his own while Jamie was still slipping from his greatcoat. The skeletal butler was hiding a small smile. Jamie cracked a grin. "It's all right, young man, smile away," he told the butler. "Young love, eh?"

"Well, love, sir, so it appears, at any rate."

Jamie nodded, lowered his head, and followed his uncle into the Mortimer parlor.

Both Angus and Justin were there, shaking hands with Charles. Angus greeted Jamie first, and to his credit, Justin wore a look of pleasure upon seeing that Charles was accompanied by him, and it was obvious, certainly, that he had come as his uncle's champion, should there be any doubt or difficulty in the situation.

"Please, sit," Angus entreated. "My niece shall be along any moment. Women, I'm afraid, seem incapable of being on time. Especially, Lord Charles, since Maggie is, of course, in such anticipation of your first meeting."

"Ah, but we've met."

"Ah?" Angus's face held an uncomfortable flush.

"The lady must not remember, but that is hardly a surprise. She was surely overwhelmed by the number of men seeking her acquaintance," Charles said pleasantly.

Then they were all startled by a soft and feminine voice like silk.

"In all honesty, sir, I did not remember. But now that I see you, I do remember that we met, and it is delightful to see you."

Jamie swung around. Amazingly, with the width of her skirt, the lady in question had arrived in the archway from entry to parlor in absolute silence, and she stood there, definitely a vision of exquisite beauty. Light filtered in from the stained-glass sections of the slim manor mud room, seeming to set her afire in a heavenly blaze. Eyes a shade of deep and striking cobalt stared out from a face delicately crafted and defined. Her lips were full and rich, curved into a rueful smile; her cheekbones were high, eyebrows finely arched, nose straight and of a perfect size for the porcelain artistry of her features. She was dressed in blue as well, a swirl of silk, a day dress that was proper to the extreme, and which still seemed to emphasize the tiny hand span of her waist and the flare of her breasts and hips.

Jamie had to admit, he was taken aback himself.

She didn't appear to notice him. Her eyes were upon Charles, and there was a sparkle of light within them, and warmth in her smile as well as she came forward, clasping his offered hands, accepting the proper kisses he placed on either cheek.

"My dear, the years have made you an even greater delight!" he said softly.

"And they've added to your charm," she told him ruefully. "Please, everyone, do sit." She spun then, staring straight at Jamie. She offered him an elegant hand to kiss. "Sir, we've not met, I'm certain."

He could play the game, and this one meant everything to his uncle. Jamie inclined his head, taking her hand. Sparks seemed to fly, sizzling against his flesh. He bent low and brushed a kiss against fingers already being rescinded. He straightened, staring into her eyes. She appeared oblivious to any lightning he might have imagined had come between them. "Sir James Langdon, Lady Maggie. Lord Charles is my great uncle."

"Well, how very lovely that you are here with him," she said lightly. But those cobalt eyes touched his again, with a canny knowledge, he thought, and she knew that he had come as a protector for Lord Charles.

She turned her back upon him, as if he or his opinion mattered little. And in truth, he and his opinion might well mean nothing. She had apparently decided on this marriage.

He felt a wealth of irritation arising anew within him. *Money-hungry wench.*

"Please, please, do have a seat. Lord Charles, would you prefer coffee or tea?"

"Coffee. What a treat. I should love some."

She lifted a hand, and Clayton appeared. "Lord Charles would prefer coffee."

"Immediately, my lady."

Charles looked to Justin, Baron Graham. Jamie knew his uncle's initial discussions had been with Angus, but Justin was, after all, the lady's brother. And the man holding the title. Jamie realized suddenly with a certain amount of amusement that the situation galled Angus tremendously.

"Justin, certainly Angus has informed you as to the purpose of our call."

"Indeed, sir," Justin said gravely. "And though you are a fine and noble man, sir, I leave the decision entirely to my sister. She once swore never to marry again." Justin looked at his sister. With reproach, Jamie thought. There was something in his eyes. *Don't do this thing!*

She preferred not to look at her brother in turn. She stared straight at Charles.

"Naturally," Charles said. "There have been difficulties in the family, and I would intend to address every situation. My dear, you would never want for anything the rest of your life," he finished earnestly to Maggie.

Jamie gritted his teeth. Charles was like an infatuated schoolboy. And oddly, it was the young woman who appeared to have her wits about her completely.

But then, there was no question that she had not suddenly fallen head over heels in love with the man seeking her hand.

"Lord Charles, I admit to a hesitation when this matter was first brought before me." She smiled. It was a good smile. Practiced? Or was she a natural expert at seduction. "But now that we have met again, and I remember you . . . I haven't the least reservation!"

Jamie thought that Charles would leap out of his chair with joy. He prayed his uncle would commit no such indignity.

But Charles did stand. He rushed to her, remarkably agile suddenly for a man of his age, and upon a knee he took her hand.

"I will never let you regret this decision, my dear."

She stared steadily at him. "I know I never will."

Charles rose again, flustered. Jamie kept his eyes on Lady Maggie. If she shuddered, just slightly, she quickly recovered. And yet . . . her gaze slipped, just momentarily. And her eyes caught his. He must have been all but shooting venom through his own narrowed orbs, because something in her seemed to harden, and the quaking he had sensed became pure, angry conviction.

She gave him a smile that was pure fury, and pure challenge. *Yes, you think that I'm a harlot, selling out and counting my gold already. Good for you. There's not a damned thing you can do about it!*

"I'm at a loss!" Charles said.

Stuttering fool! Jamie thought, and was furious with himself, because Charles was as fine a person as a man could be, noble in truth.

"Well," Jamie drawled slowly, his eyes on the soon-to-be blushing bride. "Arrangements must be made for the nuptials to take place. I would think sooner than later, wouldn't you, Uncle? You've both been wed before . . . the banns can be cried immediately, and within a matter of weeks, you can be man and wife."

"Yes, yes . . . if that is agreeable with you, Maggie?"

He spoke her name with no title, as if he tested it, and did so with awe.

"My lord Charles, whatever you desire," she said sweetly.

Jamie felt as if he had to get out. He was going to be sick.

He rose. "Well, then, we've a busy day ahead."

"Wait, wait!" Charles said, lifting a hand. His eyes, however, never left the woman's face. "Would you prefer something more elaborate? Many weddings take time, invitations must be sent out, clothing purchased, arrangements made. And my daughter is in France, at the moment. Perhaps Lord Justin has special requests for the wedding?"

Justin looked haggard, and more than a little drained. *Hard to sit there and watch your sister prostitute herself, is it, my friend?*

"I leave it all to Maggie," Justin said quietly.

She was shaking her head. "There is no need for an elaborate ceremony." She shot Jamie a glance. "As your nephew says, sir, we have both been married before."

"Still, there is a certain propriety one must see to."

"I think the lady is anxious," Jamie said. "And why not, Charles? She seems to be a woman who knows her own mind, and her mind is set. The wedding should definitely take place with all haste!"

"Lord Charles, I am in agreement, and I accept your proposal, and leave all else to you. My brother and I are alone in our immediate family, and I'm certain that my uncle Angus will be more than happy to oblige his family to your convenience. Pray, sir, set whatever date you will, that fits in with all the propriety you wish."

She stood, bringing them all to their feet. She cast Jamie a dripping smile. "Indeed, sir, I am anxious!"

"Then, Jamie, we shall see to the legal turn of events," Charles said, still elated. "My dear!" Very tenderly, he kissed both Maggie's cheeks. Her eyes were downcast as he did so. She gave no sign that she was anything but pleased; not so much as a tremor stirred her body.

Charles strode toward the exit, then stopped, turning back. "Justin, Angus, my deepest thanks. We will meet later. And Maggie . . . I swear, lady, I will make you happy."

He was gone. Clayton, as astute as he appeared to

be, barely made it in time to open the door for his departure.

Jamie bowed his head to the two men. "Justin, Angus, I thank you as well. And Maggie, dear, dear Lady Maggie!"

Before she could snatch her hands away, he had caught them. He bowed low over them, this time keeping a grip hard on her, brushing her fingers firmly with a kiss. "It's a delight to make your acquaintance. Why, think on it. We've just met, and very nearly, we are cousins."

"A pleasure," she said, and it was obvious, in the grating sound that issued with the words, that it was anything but. Still, she was perfectly composed. He could feel the waves of angry heat washing off her, but she knew that her hands were caught, and she wasn't about to allow herself the indignity of a struggle with him. "Indeed. It's lovely to see that Lord Charles has such a staunch and loving relation to protect his interests. Tell me, do you reside with Charles?"

It was a question. It was a statement, as well. *If he resided with Charles at the moment, he certainly wouldn't be doing so after the wedding!*

"No, alas, I do not. I keep a town house for those occasions when I am in London. Uncle Charles lives at Moorhaven, an estate just beyond London. He does, however, have rooms at the club, and he is, naturally, welcome in my home at all times."

"Charming," she murmured, attempting a tug at her hands. She looked smoothly toward the doorway. "I believe your uncle will be waiting."

"Indeed. And I would not postpone your nuptials for an instant! Good day, my lady, good sirs!"

He released her hands at last. She almost managed not to snatch them back. Not quite. She loathed him. And whatever game they played before others, they both knew it. It mattered not in the least. He would be watching her. And if she betrayed her elderly husband in any way . . .

She would know that he was watching.

He didn't look back, but exited the house with long strides.

"How ghastly!" Maggie exclaimed.

"You're right. He's not just old. He's ancient," Justin agreed. "Maggie, it's off. That's it."

Maggie turned to stare at her brother. "I don't mean Charles—I mean the nephew. Sir James."

"Jamie?" Justin said, surprised. "He's quite a fine chap, really. Always off on the Queen's business, here and there. He was in the military for a few years, but whatever he does now, the work is special projects. Empire, you know," he said dryly.

By then, Mireau had made it down the stairs to join them. Clayton was surely listening from somewhere. He was the perfect servant, and as such, knew exactly what was going on in their lives at all times.

"What do you care about the nephew?" Mireau demanded. "Lord Charles is evidently quite smitten. Why, he'd give you the world."

"Yes, I realize that," Maggie murmured softly

Justin slumped down into one of the chairs. "I have just sold my sister. It's as if I have sold my very soul."

"Justin, stop it, you didn't sell me, and you haven't sold your soul. I mean it, the old fellow is quite dear. I'm certain we'll get along swimmingly."

"He's really not bad at all, for a man as old as Moses," Mireau offered cheerfully.

Justin groaned again.

"Look, there's the point," Maggie insisted. "He's far too elderly to . . . well, to expect the usual things from marriage." She flushed despite herself. This was not a topic she cared to discuss with either her brother or Mireau. But she was practical as well, and hardly a blushing innocent. She had been passionately in love with Nathan.

"Does a man ever get that old?" Mireau asked Justin.

"I rather think not," Justin said. He rose impatiently, coming to his sister. "Maggie, you must feel free to back out of this at any time. I am the one who got into the debt."

"True," Mireau reflected. "Jamie is the one who should get to marry the walking corpse."

"Jacques!" They both exclaimed.

"Do excuse me, I'm only saying what we all know!"

"Once more, I'm telling you both that it will be quite fine. Lord Charles is not a ridiculous, stinking old lecher. He is a man of dignity. I'm quite convinced that he is seeking companionship, and I will be happy to be his friend, his very good friend, until the end. And I will pray that he has a long and happy life," Maggie informed them.

Mireau and her brother exchanged looks.

She sighed deeply. "Honestly! He barely walks, barely moves."

"It looked as if he walked quite fine to me," Mireau commented.

She shook her head impatiently. Justin stared at her. "I repeat. You are free to back out of this, Maggie, until the very last moment, do you understand? I don't give a whit for what scandal we may create." He almost smiled. "Might as well go to Newgate with a reputation!"

She stared back at her brother. *No, she was not going to back out! Because she would never see her uncle with Justin's title, the family title! Never!*

"I know, Justin. I am decided. The marriage will take place."

"She has a point," Mireau said. "Imagine the woman Angus might find if he felt obliged to see that you were married off, Justin!"

"I shudder to think of it," Maggie murmured dryly.

"How much worse could it be?"

"Let's just be glad that we will not have to find out. Now, listen to me, Justin, because you will be handling the arrangements, of course. I must have my own allowance. I intend to be a good wife, and I believe that he's a charitable and good man. But if I'm going through with this, I want to pursue some of my own interests," Maggie said.

"Best not let Sir Jamie hear such sentiments," Mireau said softly.

"Sir Jamie may fall in a lake and rot," Maggie said sweetly.

"I'm aware that you merely wish to feed every wretched little street urchin in London," Mireau said. "But come, Maggie, you must look at this from the eyes of the Viscount's family!"

"I did not seek out Lord Charles; Lord Charles came here. Justin, I intend to be kind to the man, loyal, and trustworthy in every fashion. But . . ." She hesitated. "Oh, good God, let's face it. I have just sold myself—you didn't do it, Justin, I did. But the point is that, ugly as it may be, this is a financial arrangement. And I expect you to see to my part of it."

She wasn't sure what he said then. But he was very unhappy, and she knew it. He started to depart the room, but paused, slamming his hand flat against the wall.

For a moment he looked like a very old man himself.

Maggie rushed to her brother and turned him around to face her. "Justin, stop. Listen, this isn't a tragedy, and it isn't so horrible. I loved Nathan. I will never, ever love again. This will not be a bad life for me, do you understand? He can provide so much that I so desperately want. He is a decent and charming old fellow. I am well pleased with this arrangement, and it will please me greatly if you don't keep walking around as if you had signed over my eternal life to the devil." She swung around, glaring at Mireau, who looked as if he had been about to speak. "Do you both understand? There will be no more pity, no more discussion, no more guilt. It is done, and that is that. I am happy."

Justin straightened.

He made his way out of the room. This time, she heard the word he swore beneath his breath quite clearly.

"Bullshit!"

Once again, she swung on Mireau. "Not a word from you!"

His mouth had already opened. He snapped it shut. "I was just about to say . . . Congratulations!"

Maggie turned and fled up the stairs.

Three days later, Jamie reached the coast of France. Disembarking at Caan, he made short work of renting a horse, and riding the two hours inland to Arianna's school.

As any proper young lady in her position, she was being given an education in all the arts that would perfect her position as a young woman of great quality. She was taught how to walk, how to pour tea, how to converse in French without the least trace of an accent, how to sing, and how to play the piano.

Since she was definitely a free-spirited soul, and her father's beloved and much-spoiled child, she was also humored greatly, and therefore studied Latin, geometry, history, and the sciences as well. Jamie mused that her education was hardly a waste, for Arianna was a bright child, with an inquisitive mind, and a great intelligence. She also had a stubborn streak within her that stretched for acres.

He had sent ahead to say that he was coming; informing Arianna of the upcoming wedding had been his first priority after the legal machinations had been set in place. Talking Charles out of taking the taxing journey himself had not been easy, but in the end, Jamie had managed it. He was anxious to speak with his cousin himself and quickly—he didn't want her to hear about her father's intentions from another source.

Arianna met him in the drawing room of the elegant old palace where the girls were housed. She hugged him warmly as Sister Sara brought them together, her delight at seeing him childish, despite the fact that she was hardly a little girl anymore.

She was tall, with an elegant, sylph-like figure. Dark eyed, dark haired, with soft white skin so delicate in texture and appearance, she was almost ethereal. He was somewhat shocked to realize that his cousin was growing into an incredible beauty herself. *Charles had best take care in his own house,* Jamie thought.

Then he realized, he'd be the one calling men out in this lady's defense. Charles was beyond such a possibility.

When Sister Sara left them alone to talk, Arianna backed away. "You've come to tell me about my father's wedding."

He hesitated, shaking his head, then sighed. "Yes, I have. It's quite amazing how quickly gossip can travel the English Channel."

"My father could not come himself?"

"I talked him out of it."

She stared at him, her eyes widening. "Why would you do that to me, Jamie?"

"I fear for his health all the time, Arianna."

"Why? *She'll* probably just poison him and he'll die anyway."

"Arianna. What a terrible thing to say."

She was speaking so belligerently to hide her hurt, he knew.

"Terrible!" she retorted with a sniff.

"Arianna, I swear, your father wanted to be here, and I was barely able to talk him out of coming. Naturally, you'll see him before the wedding. I'll return for you myself in plenty of time. The bride has said that she wishes to keep it simple, but I imagine there will be a place for you in the ceremony."

"Don't allow it to happen, Jamie," she warned him.

"What? The wedding? I can scarcely stop your father."

"Ah . . . his bride is what? Twenty-two, twenty-three? She must have fallen madly in love with father. What a . . . a slut!"

To his amazement, he found himself defending the woman. *Only before Arianna, because this must hurt her badly.* "She is Lady Maggie, daughter of a baron, hardly a streetwalker. And where did you learn such language? Surely not from the nuns."

"Probably from you," she informed him dryly.

He groaned. "Your father would have my throat."

"Oh, Jamie! I am not so young and totally naive as you may believe. Yes, this is a convent school. And the nuns are certainly all chastity and propriety!" She giggled. "But we do slip out now and then."

"Slip out where?" he demanded, frowning.

"Don't look so fierce. We go shopping. We see the works of the new, upcoming artists. We sit in cafés and listen to the speeches of young, rebellious, handsome boys. Oh, don't worry, and don't look at me so! We go no further than that, I swear, Jamie."

"Thank God. If something were ever to happen to you . . ."

"My father will now have a witch of a wife!"

"Arianna, you haven't even met her."

"I don't need to meet her. I've heard all about her. She married a bobby, and began to spend her days in the East End. Then she thought that she was something of a detective herself, and determined to rid the world of mesmerists. Hardly an open mind there! I've seen some of these people at work. Some are quite amazing. I believe that they do have special powers to speak with the dead, to see the future, and touch the world."

"And some of them are out to fleece the rich," Jamie said. It didn't please him that he found himself defending his uncle's intended bride. "Don't judge the woman until you've met her."

Arianna shook her head. "Jamie, what is to judge? She is a very young woman, about to marry a very old man. Desperate love? I doubt it. It's prostitution, nothing less."

"Arianna, for years, such marriages have been arranged. This is not really new, or even shocking in the least. She could not marry without her brother's permission."

"He allowed her to marry the policeman as well?"

"Apparently."

"Well, then, her brother is as low a creature as she! Oh, Jamie, this is horrible. Truly horrible. At his doddering old age, my father has become infatuated with a tart! Is there nothing at all that you can do?"

"Arianna, I tell you this—I have never seen him so set on any course of action before. He is absolutely determined. Therefore, we must both accept it."

"Aha! You disapprove as well."

"My opinion on the matter is unimportant."

"It's not. Father listens to you. You're the son he never had."

"Arianna, he wants to marry this woman, and he will. I assure you."

"Men, you know," Arianna told him. "They can behave quite disgustingly."

Jamie refrained from agreeing with her. But yes, he found it all rather disgusting himself. He couldn't forget the moment when his eyes had first locked with Maggie's, when their hands had first touched. She was electric.

A witch, indeed. Tainted, society might say. Yet . . . electric. Sensual in her every movement, no matter how proper her words, dress, or manner. He thought of the feel of her flesh, and despite his devotion to his uncle, his thoughts were crass and carnal. *Such a woman needed a far younger man. Vigorous, passionate, hungry . . .*

As he was himself.

God help him! Whatever it took, he would bury such thoughts.

Yet, how to bury what burned through him at the sight of her, when he touched her?

Easy. Don't look at her, and don't touch her, he told himself dryly.

"Arianna, there are cases of deep devotion between young wives and older husbands. And vice versa, for that matter. It's not unheard of, you know, for an aging dowager to marry a much younger man," he said.

"Only if he really needs the money!" Arianna retorted.

Jamie sighed. "As I said, this will happen."

"There must be a way to stop it."

"Indeed. Should I try to convince your father that he is a doddering old fool? That he doesn't know his own mind? Or better still—should I point out the very obvious, that it is a fiscal matter, and that the bride is hardly in love with him? He is not a fool, Arianna. He wants the woman for his wife, and he can afford her, and therefore, he will have her. Nothing that I can say or do will change that. All that will happen is that he will push me away, and I will no longer be there as his confidant, friend, and champion. You must realize as well that any attempt I might make to prevent his marriage would certainly appear very badly. I am next in the line of succession to his titles and estates."

Arianna stared at him, entirely frustrated.

"Perhaps I can stop the wedding," she mused.

"Arianna," he murmured warily. Blunt, even crude speaking had not been such a good idea. But at least she seemed to understand that he would, indeed, alienate her father if he attempted to step in. "You will stay here in school and study until I return for you. And then you will attend his wedding and be pleased with whatever happiness it is that he seeks from this young bride."

"You will make sure that they make no attempt to have me be a part of that ceremony. In fact, you should inform my father that I have no intention of attending."

"Arianna, please, be reasonable. Your father expects that the two of you will be friends."

"Oh, I hardly think so!"

"I'm sure she will make every effort to make it so."

"Will she? You don't know just how fast rumor flies across the channel, Jamie. I know all about her. She was stunningly beautiful when she had her season, teased every man in the Ton, had her way, and rejected them all and eloped—with a policeman! Then he was killed. Serving the citizens of London, so they said. *She* probably planned it! Realizing that she had, indeed, married a commoner, and that there had been much more in the world for her to snare! She is able to maintain her beauty because she is so very evil. A strange magician is in her employ. He helps her make up her spells, and creates all kinds of incantations. And now, she has her eyes set on my father. She was left a penniless widow to rue her evil ways, and to rectify what she has done, she intends to milk my father dry. God knows, she'll probably kill him as well!"

"Arianna! Her husband did die in public service; he was killed by the murdering madman he was trying to arrest. I assure you, there is no witchcraft going on in the house." He hesitated. He, too, had heard about the man, Mireau. A friend of her husband, a poet, writer, in need of a patron. Was that all?

Arianna was staring at him. "She did nothing to her husband. I have done extensive research on her past. Don't you think that I would have made certain that all we had heard was truth regarding her first marriage?" he demanded indignantly.

Yes, he had done research on her. She spent too much time in districts where poverty—and crime—ran rampant. She wrote letters to the newspapers herself, indignantly exposing those who set up shop as "mediums" or "spiritualists." She had been known to dress in disguise and attend séances, then disobey the commands of the mediums, and fly from a chair to demonstrate that a ghostly spirit was nothing but a sheet on a string.

Evil? Perhaps not. Foolhardy? Extremely. And the time she spent in the East End, where every manner of pickpocket, rapist, and thief was known to ply his—or her—trade . . .

He had, without emotion, given Charles reports on everything he had learned. And every word had only endeared her to the old man more.

"You simply cannot imagine what they say!" Arianna whispered. There were tears in her eyes once again. "I will not go to the wedding!"

He sighed. "As you wish."

"Oh, Jamie!" She threw herself into his arms. "Why was I not enough for him? I love him so very dearly. I can be his companion, and his helper, there to talk about books, languages, and faraway places."

He held her tightly, not ready to explain that conversation was not what her father was seeing when he looked at Maggie.

"It will be all right, you will see," he told her gently. *It would have to be. Charles was, in all other respects, certainly of age, sane, and the master of his own fate. He'd made his decision, and his family must accept it.*

After a while, she nodded against his chest, then drew away. He held her shoulders and looked into her dark eyes. "If you really don't want to go to the wedding, I'll see to it that you don't have to go."

She returned his probing stare, then suddenly shook her head and turned away. "Oh, no. I have decided that you're right—I must go to the wedding. I don't want to be a part of it, but I will attend. You will come back for me yourself?"

"Indeed, Arianna, I swear it."

She smiled, almost brightening.

"Well, if nothing else, I shall be glad to return home for a while. You are staying the night? You cannot possibly return to the channel and make a crossing now."

He nodded. He was staying, but he wasn't pleased with the arrangement.

He was afraid to leave Charles alone with the woman.

You'll have to, soon enough, old chap, he told himself. *She would become Charles's bride, and he'd had to admit, he understood the longings set fire within the man's heart. There was something about her greater than beauty. Something of fire and tempest, scorn, and fury . . . and power. Maybe she was a witch, a puppeteer, jerking them all about by their strings. He found himself imagining the bride when the rites were completed, when the guests had gone, when the lights were low. Her hair, a halo of gold and red, freed from pins, spilling around her face. Her gown would be sheer, and every lithe limb, curve, and hollow would be exposed. . . .*

Fury within him nearly burst to the surface.

Stop the wedding?

There had to be a way to stop the pictures in his own mind.

If Charles was seeing only half the visions that came to Jamie's mind, he'd die before he let any man stand between himself and his prize.

"You must be famished. Sister Sara will see to a

meal for you, and, of course, a room for the night," Arianna was saying.

"Yes, thank you, I am quite famished."

Famished, yes, she made a man feel that way. As if he had never seen such beauty, as if he would melt if he could not touch it, taste it, dive into it . . .

He gritted his teeth.

He loved Charles. Loved him like a father.

But it was wrong. So wrong.

Why, particularly? Every word he had said to Arianna was true. Such marriages had taken place since . . . probably since marriage had begun! And yet, in this in-stance . . .

Was it because he was somewhat smitten himself?

God help him.

"Well?"

A cloud had obscured his vision. He had to shake his head to see Arianna.

"I said, which would you prefer? Fish, or pheasant? Or perhaps both. The nuns always titter so over your arrival, Jamie. They'll surely give you both."

He forced a wry smile. "Fowl," he said.

Foul. The world had gone foul.

It wasn't right that such an exquisite young woman should be wed to such a very old man! That she should love him . . .

And yet, she had best love him, and only him, Jamie determined grimly. Charles absolutely deserved no less. She had appeared to recognize that Charles was refined and cultured, that he had once been a soldier, that he had moved in the world of the highest authority of the land, and still did. Surely, she would see all things, and be a good, loyal, and *faith-ful* wife.

Or else?

She would answer to him, and she would not be pleased to do so.

Chapter 3

In the days that came to pass, Maggie truly came to terms with her decision to marry Charles.

He was an amazing man. His stories about the world, his travels, the Queen's little wars, his service to her, all were quite fascinating. He was modest when talking about himself, eloquent when talking about the Empire, and understanding when she chimed in to say that it was all well and good that they should create an Empire, but shouldn't they be looking to some of the wretched poverty and violence within their own country?

He agreed, and she was delighted to learn that he had several of her own same interests, that he supported rebuilding in the East End, and found some of the situations beneath their very own noses to be intolerable, indeed.

He took her to the Crystal Palace to see a concert, to the theater, where they saw an amazing, frightening version of the play *The Strange Case of Dr. Jekyll and Mr. Hyde.* They went to the Royal Opera House, where they had seats in the balcony next to those of the Prince of Wales and his wife, Princess Alexandra. They went on walks through St. James Park, and rides out to the country. Equally, he allowed her the private time she had always so cherished, nights with her poetry reading group at the restaurant in the Strand, social time with her small circle of friends, and more. Her "charity" time as she called it.

She had talked to him about some of her activities. Not all. There were a few events she attended that no one knew about except for Mireau. Charles might not know the actual extent of her work in the East End, but she did brush upon it.

As to the séances she attended . . .

Everyone knew about the first one she had gone to. The papers had been filled with news regarding her involvement.

Since then . . .

She didn't dare admit that she was determined as ever to stop some of the charades taking place, when she could.

But she didn't think that she'd ever tell Charles the truth about those nights.

And still, she grew to like him more and more.

He was quite a capable man, as well, having served the Crown in India, and he was equally happy to hop on public hackney cabs, and tell her how London had changed, just in his lifetime. The sewer system begun in the middle of the century had truly improved all their lives, he assured her, and the train had made distances shrink.

He shared her love of reading, and they found they could spend pleasant afternoons together just reading, from the works of William Shakespeare to Dickens, and the American, Mark Twain, and the newer works of men such as Arthur Conan Doyle. They argued Darwin's theories, and every manner of new-ism of the nineteenth century, hypnotism or mesmerism, phrenology, and spiritualism.

She learned, as well, that he had a daughter, beloved, who was in school on the Continent, coming of age that year, and headstrong and rebellious.

"Of course, she has lacked the gentler ways of a mother. I know that you will become such a dear friend to her, and guide her in all things," Charles told her confidently.

Maggie wondered if it would be quite so easy.

She learned that in his family, he had but his daughter and Sir James, who was actually his great nephew. Charles's cousin, Jamie's father, had served in India, and been knighted, and like his father, the son had gone into the Queen's Service, and helped settle many an uprising in the Empire. He'd left the military, but been knighted as well, and often carried messages of the utmost importance to various ports around the world. Sometimes, Charles admitted, he worried about Jamie. He, too, seemed to have something of a disregard for the expectations of proper society. He'd fought in one too many skirmishes abroad, woke too easily in the night at the least sound, and expected danger behind every tree. When he wasn't carrying messages or carrying out an assignment in a foreign port, Charles was pleased and relieved.

Jamie saw to the family estates, which were numerous, and Charles was sorry that he could not travel to them himself as he had done in his youth. "Young people leave the fields in droves, seeking wealth in the cities," he said sorrowfully. "But in the north country, and in Scotland, there are still vast acres and we've many tenants raising fine herds of cattle and sheep. We grow what crops we can, as well. Sad to say, I can remember the time of the great famine, striking Ireland like God's own hammer, but affecting us all. A sorrowful time it was, indeed. We must always take care that such hardship doesn't come again." And he had sighed. "Ah, but the world is changing so radically. Soon, mark you, the horse carriages will be a thing of the past, and I tell you, those machines, those automobiles will be everywhere. Technology and law have given us so much—and such unrest, as well. Radicals out in the streets, protests here and there, the poor invading even the finest neighborhoods, looting and robbing at times. Ah, well . . . there's still so much to be done in the home country, eh? But as to Jamie, he does well, seeing that the rents are fair, our own stock is properly tended, and all is well. Still, he was saying the other day that he is growing restless, anxious to be about the world again."

"He is off and about. You said he was bringing news of the wedding to Arianna."

"Ah, yes, well, that's barely a hop, skip, and a jump for Jamie. France is a ferry ride away, and the little town where Arianna goes to school is just a few miles from the coast."

Maggie gave him a smile, but heartily hoped that

Sir Jamie would be sent to the farthest reaches of darkest Africa when he returned from France.

But Charles was delightful to her brother, and enjoyed the company of Jacques Mireau, as well. He promised to help Jacques with his dreams of a writing career.

Those first days were pleasant, indeed. It was as if she had found a dear mentor. An older man, but a good friend.

All seemed to be comfortable. If not elated, she was content. Though it was coming quickly, the wedding remained in the future. This time before offered her a strange freedom.

But then, Sir James returned.

Apparently, he meant to stay awhile. Unfortunately, he was not being sent about on the Queen's business.

Maggie had never imagined just how completely the term "fly in the ointment" could describe someone.

It wasn't so much that he did anything. Or, for that matter, said anything.

He was just there. With them so frequently.

Watching her. Studying her. And forming his opinion.

And not a good one, at that.

It was the way he looked at her. As if she were a pedigreed dog—or a mutt pretending to have a pedigree!—purchased at a very high price, who would soon turn and bite the hand that fed her.

No, it wasn't in anything that he did.

He was overly polite. Courteous to the extreme. But every time their eyes touched, the contempt within his gaze, to her great distress, was chilling. In turn, she learned to accept his touch of assistance in and out of carriages, up and down stairs, and through crowded streets with an icy venom of her own. They despised one another. Naturally, for the sake of Lord Charles, they would not let on.

Nor did Maggie intend, in any way, to let the man alter her life.

Two weeks into the engagement, with the wedding but another two weeks away, she set out for the East End.

Charles was a staunch supporter of the Salvation Army, and hadn't seemed in the least shocked or horrified to find that she put her time in with the organization at St. Mary's.

It had been on a night out with members of the Ton that she had met Nathan, the husband she had so dearly loved, and lost. They had thought that "slumming" in the East End would be quite a diversion. But a gang of street thugs had set upon their carriage, and Nathan had been the one to come to her rescue when the rest of her party had disappeared.

Through his eyes, she had seen a new world.

Nathan had been the one to tell her that indeed, charitable contributions were desperately needed, but so was a personal touch.

Through him, she had learned so much. In the circles in which she had moved, she had known about the growth of the merchant class, and men who had made fortunes as entrepreneurs, doctors, politicians, writers, and even performers.

She had not seen the fate of those who were not born to family, fortune, or even simple decent income.

Few of the members of the glittering Ton of London ever ventured so far—to a place that was but a stone's throw away from their elegant homes. She'd never have gone herself—if they hadn't done so as a lark.

She had been so ignorant herself of the suffering there, and of the way that matters only became worse, year after year.

Nathan had died on the streets of the East End, trying to wrest a knife from a man gone insane with syphilis. He had killed the fellow before succumbing to his own wounds, and he managed to save the man's starving wife and eight children.

The people of the East End were like rats in a cage, Nathan often said. Too many, too close together. Unwashed, uneducated, and with no real chance of escape. Some had shops and factories, and some worked in those shops and factories. Much work was only occasional. Sometimes a woman could find work as a laundress, or sewing. Sometimes she could not. Men lined up at the crack of dawn for a chance at hard labor. Sometimes they were able to work ten to fourteen hours a day for a few shillings. Sometimes they could not. Sometimes they had an actual address, but even then, they would live with many others in a single room, and their beds would be nothing but straw or old newspapers.

So it was with the man Nathan brought down, and the family left alive.

They had lived together in a one-room tenement. In the buildings, chamber pots were emptied—into the yards—once a week. The stench was abominable. Actual bathrooms or even outhouses were completely lacking, and few of the tenements had inside running water of any kind. Even the gas lamps, prevalent on so many streets, were few and far between.

A commoner, Nathan had still been the son of a knighted soldier, raised in the St. James area. He had served in the military, the Home Guard, and been called one day to quell a riot. From then on, he'd known that he'd wanted to be a policeman. And to help those in such desperate need in the East End.

His dedication had been his demise.

Maggie had managed to arrive before he had drawn his last breath. And with his last words, he had begged her not to hate the man who had killed him. She had come from such privilege; watching him die had taught her such humility. Agony, but humility as well.

And so, in his memory, she had begun to fight for the wretched and poor.

Mireau, bless him, Nathan's friend from college, always accompanied her. He complained, but he came. After Nathan's death, he had become her champion, and constant companion. He was always writing, and managed to have a few pieces picked up by various newspapers. He dreamed, however, of being a novelist.

They set out by cab that day, as they always did, and when they arrived at the church, Maggie, as usual, haggled with the driver. Cabs always tried to double charge for excursions into the East End. Mireau sighed and waited patiently, and Maggie secured the proper price. They entered the church itself and found the young curate, Father Vickers, who worked with Maggie. He was delighted, smiling ear to ear, when he saw her.

"We've just received the most generous donation from Lord Charles, Viscount Langdon! Enough to clothe so many of the abandoned children." The brightness of his smile faded slightly, then he forced it again. "You're to marry him!"

"Yes, isn't it lovely," Maggie said.

Father Vickers looked at Mireau, who shrugged.

"Ah, yes, lovely. Well, the women are waiting out in the courtyard. It's a pleasant enough day. The air is not so foul . . ." He shook his head. "Lord, if there were but a way to really get these women off the streets! In certain areas, the police have managed to close down some of the brothels, but I don't think that it's really helped at all. Now more of the fallen are out in the alleys, and . . ." He lowered his voice to a worried whisper, "Maggie, God knows I need the gentle charity of ladies such as yourself, but I fear for you here, as well. There was another ghastly murder just a few days ago, night of the bank holiday."

She touched his shoulder. "Father Vickers, we both know that murder happens here frequently enough."

"But not like this. Ah, true, and sad! Jealousies, drunken bar fights, a wife gone mad, a husband in despair, and always, the urging of too much gin! Yes, fights are frequent, and murder, something that happens far too often. But this . . . didn't you see it in the papers?"

Maggie looked at Mireau. "It might have been in the back pages."

He sighed. "If such a thing had happened to a highborn woman, I can tell you, it would have screamed across every headline in the land!"

"What happened?" Mireau demanded.

"It's all rather indelicate," Father Vickers said uneasily, looking at Maggie.

"Please, Father, I am about to talk about birth control to women who need such a conversation since their children are seldom legitimate!" Maggie said.

"She was butchered. Not just killed, butchered. Throat slit to where her head was barely attached, and entrails removed. She was barely left as human. This was not a husband killing a woman in a rage."

"Why, I remember a report of something similar not long ago, a woman was killed by a suspected soldier. I think the reporter said police were also thinking there might be a street gang about that was harassing prostitutes."

Father Vickers shook his head. "This was not a street gang. And no one murdered this woman for what they might steal from her. It's my opinion that there's a madman on the loose, and you will begin to hear about it. So, Maggie, please, though I need your help desperately, make sure it is always by daylight, and always in good company."

"Father Vickers, I only come by daylight, and with my dear Mireau. Also, remember, the police have a special place in their hearts for me."

"That I know, and still, the police patrol—and frequently—the very places where these murders are occurring. Please, you must bear all this in mind when you are out and about."

"Father Vickers, I promise."

"The women are gathering, I see. The courtyard will be fine for you?"

"The courtyard will be fine, certainly," Maggie told him.

That day, Maggie was speaking to a group on contraception—not an idea usually condoned by the church. But Father Vickers had spent enough time in the East End to be a very practical man. He had been the one to find out about the large shipment of condoms from France.

In the past, Maggie had spoken about many details regarding the improvement of life, and at first, her audience had been small. But before she had known she was penniless, she had arranged for bread, cheese, and milk to be served to those who attended her talks, and soon after, Father Vickers had been forced to eject the men who dressed up in women's clothing and attended just for the food. She understood; the pathetic prostitutes of the East End sold themselves to more pathetic men for as little as a loaf of bread. But she couldn't feed the thousands of starving, and wanted her contributions to go to the women and children. Wives, so often abandoned, had little recourse but to resort to prostitution.

The more children they had, the more desperate, naturally, the women became.

And the more orphans who appeared, abandoned on the steps of the church.

She had learned that she had a gift for speaking, a way of making her audience laugh, and in laughing, comprehend. That day, she spoke about abstinence and timing, and condoms.

"Dearie, we can't be payin' for the condoms!" a toothless woman called to her. "Goat's bladders, did ye say? 'At's wot they make 'em from?"

"The important issue is that we prevent pregnancy."

"Why, 'alf the guvners I know are used to sheep as well, Katy!" another woman called to the first.

Maggie looked down, shaking her head. "Spend a few pennies less on gin, and you'll have what you need. Not to mention the fact that Father Vickers and I have acquired some free . . . contraceptives for you."

"Oh, m'lady!" cried a woman called Bess. "'Ow do we get our blokes to use 'em?"

"Insist," Maggie said.

" 'T'won't be easy!" Katy said. "Why, Lordy! I never heard 'ow such a thing meself until this very day!"

"Believe me, they've been around for . . . well, for a very, very long time."

Bess sniggered. "Wot if they don't know 'ow to get 'em on!"

"Between you, you'll figure it out," she said dryly. "And neither is feeding more children an easy effort. Abortions can be deadly—especially those you try to bring upon yourselves, or those performed by many a supposed physician in these quarters," she reminded them sharply. "Now, really! I'm certain most of you all are well aware of methods of prevention, and condoms—in some form or another—have been in use for more than a thousand years."

She went on to talk about emptying chamber pots more frequently, and speak about the virtue—and good health—to be found in a modicum of cleanliness, though she knew that soap, as well, was a luxury these women could not afford. But though she had secured the condoms with what had been left of her own allowance, she had gotten Charles to provide the soap to be given away that day. She realized a little uneasily that she hadn't told him a thing about her speech, and certainly hadn't discussed condoms with him. It had been a Herculean task to bring the conversation regarding "precaution" to Father Vickers, but he, at least, during his time in the area, was aware that although such a discussion was a ghastly sin in a social arena, it made the utmost sense in the East End. She wasn't sure which one of them had blushed more when they had first determined on the effort.

God told Adam to go out and be fruitful, but certainly, the "fruit" of the East End usually perished before it became anywhere near ripe.

"Thank you all for listening to me," she said, finishing her speech. Nathan had once told her that what the poor often needed more than anything was simple respect. And so, she always thanked her audience, were they toothless, penniless, or even flat-out drunk with gin, lolling on the ground before her.

The women rushed toward her, thanking her, touching her. To this day, she had to grit her teeth to endure the stench and the creeping sensation that sometimes touched her flesh. But endure she did.

And when they began to filter away, eager for their handouts given to them by employed members of the parish, she walked back toward the side door of the church, where she knew that Mireau and Father Vickers would be waiting, watching, as they always did, when she spoke. Father Vickers always saw to it that some of the local police were about as well, for her protection, if need be. They came, she knew, even when they were off duty. She had been the wife of one of their own.

Yet that day, as she walked toward her friend and the good reverend, she was startled to see that a third man was with them.

Dismay filled her.

It was none other than Sir James.

He stood with his arms crossed over his chest, a greatcoat concealing whatever manner of dress he wore beneath, a deerstalker hat adding to his impression of dominant height. His eyes—an ever-changing gray, she now knew—were narrowed. Disapproving? No, out-and-out condemning.

Her heart fluttered.

What? Had he appointed himself her watchdog? Naturally, he would report her every movement to Charles. He was spying on her!

That last gave her the impetus to brave out the situation. Yet even as she mentally squared her shoulders and lengthened the determination of her steps, she felt weak in the knees, and knew that a flush was coming to her cheeks. *Good God, the man had been listening to her talk about condoms!*

"Sir James. What a surprise to see you here," she said flatly.

He arched a brow, his mouth grim. *And not a pleasant surprise at all,* he seemed to imply in silence.

Aloud, he said, "You're quite an amazement, my lady. Your knowledge and occupations seem to be limitless."

She waved a hand in the air. "Sir Charles is very aware of the depth of the problems we face in society." She longed to bite her lip. She owed him no explanations.

"Perhaps you won't mind my seeing that you are

out of the area safely. Father Vickers has been adding to my awareness of the dangers to be found here. If simple cutthroats, rapists, and thieves were not enough, it seems there may well be a madman on the loose."

"I come here frequently. You might notice the number of policemen about."

"Yes, and despite that number, you are surely more aware than most that murder occurs here with an appalling frequency," he said.

"Seriously, Sir James," Mireau tried, "the police have a special interest in Maggie."

"Yes," he returned to Mireau, his eyes remaining hard upon Maggie's, "and still, it would comfort me greatly to see you both back to Mayfair."

"My dear lady, it cannot hurt to have another strong protector at your side," Father Vickers said nervously.

"I'm always quite willing to protect Maggie!" Mireau said, a trifle indignant. But he was aware, of course, that he was lean himself. Not quite skinny, of course, but lean. Sir Jamie was assessing him and they all knew it. And again, Maggie thought, his look was definitely one of skepticism, if not his usual gaze of contempt.

"As Father Vickers said, it doesn't hurt for a lady to have a second protector in this area. Father, it's been a delight to make your acquaintance," Jamie said, and offered an arm to Maggie. "Shall we? Unless you've further business here. I'm more than willing to wait, if need be."

"No, no, we're done for the day," Mireau said.

"Good-bye, Father. I'll see you in another two weeks," Maggie said.

"Perhaps you'll need to reschedule. You'll be on

your honeymoon," Jamie reminded her. "And I'm sure that the church and the Salvation Army will understand your eagerness to spend special time with your new husband."

She wondered how anyone could make such innocuous words sound so . . . sexual.

"I'll get word to you," she said sweetly to Father Vickers.

Jamie had a firm grip on her elbow. They moved beyond the enclosure and out to the street where Darby was waiting with a Langdon carriage. She wasn't sure if she was helped in or shoved in. Mireau quickly followed, and Jamie after him.

She faced Jamie.

"Interesting speech," he said.

"A necessary speech," she returned.

"Hardly the usual Friday afternoon for a lady," he commented.

"I'm sorry if you don't approve," she returned.

She was startled by his reply. "I didn't say that I didn't approve. I found your words to the poor creatures to be practical in the extreme."

There were shadows in the carriage. She couldn't tell if he was speaking truthfully or not.

She looked out the window.

"I'm not terribly sure that Charles would be happy if you were to introduce his daughter to this particular aspect of good works," Jamie said.

"What I do here is my choice, and my volition, though I'd not suggest it for anyone else, and certainly not Lord Charles's daughter. And is she not returning to her school in France after the wedding?" Maggie said.

"She will come of age shortly and intends to spend time in London. Lord Charles is anxious to see her wed." He glanced away. "He has certain definite intentions for her, and therefore, he wishes to see her remain in England."

Certain intentions? Maggie wondered if, despite the fact that they were second cousins once removed, Charles didn't intend to marry his daughter to his brother's grandson. She wasn't sure just what the religious and civil laws were now on such an association, but the royal family had been known to allow marriages with much closer associations.

She turned away, watching as the carriage brought them from the underbelly of London slowly back to the world of the living. As she looked out the window, Maggie marveled anew that the streets could go from such seediness and poverty to respectability and even opulence so quickly. It really wasn't far at all. And yet, there was a world of difference.

The great walls of the Tower rose before them. Soon, they'd be back.

She stared at Jamie Langdon again. "Don't worry. I wouldn't dream of bringing Arianna here."

"She never suggested that I should come with her," Mireau offered, as always, trying to keep the situation calm. "I'm happy to accompany her. Then again, I knew the area. I came often with Nathan, her husband . . . her late husband. Well, you know, Dickens loved to come down here. Naturally, you can see it in his writing. There's so much grist for the mill, you know. And actually, once the area thrived. The Flemish weavers who moved here created the finest cloth imaginable. The world has taken such a turn with industry and science! Things change ... and sometimes, they get worse. Well, maybe it seems that they often get worse. But the problem is, really, even with great writers like Dickens telling the world about the East End, no one really wants to see. Or if they see, they don't know what to do. But every little bit helps, of course."

Mireau suddenly seemed to realize that he was babbling. They were both just staring at him. "Well, you know, the little bit that Maggie can do helps tremendously. All right, so no one person could really end the poverty for the tens of thousands living in such squalor, but ... and, of course, a lot of it is because immigration is so very heavy, and jobs can be scarce, and many people don't want to employ foreigners when there are so many English out of work ... well ... you know, the thing of it is, there are families in the East End, and there are legitimate shops and many people there try desperately hard to make an income. Sadly, the English way out of a problem is often a gin bottle. And you mix alcohol with ignorance and desperation, and naturally, you have burglary, violence, rape ... murder. Of course, today, Father Vickers was speaking about something entirely different. Something truly horrible beyond conception. Surely, of course, such a madman will be apprehended. Though he was telling me more about it when you were speaking, Maggie. They're not sure if this recent murder is associated with two others that occurred not long ago. Nothing, however, has been this horrid, this ... this insane! And he's right, of course. Should anyone of wealth ever be killed with such savagery, such butchery ... "

He broke off suddenly, realizing that he wasn't helping Maggie's position at all.

"Did you do this while your husband was alive?" Jamie asked her pointedly.

"No," she admitted stiffly.

"Um," he murmured.

"And what does that mean?" she demanded.

"It means that he'd have kept you from coming here."

"Why on earth would he do so? He was a great champion of the poor!" Maggie said indignantly.

"And a policeman, one who knew that the wandering around of a lady such as yourself could well stir resentments and anger, and bring about catastrophe," Jamie said.

"I know what I'm doing," she informed him.

"It's really none of my affair," Jamie said.

"There, that's right!" Mireau burst in, well aware that both of their voices were growing more tense. "Every man and woman, noble and common, must draw their own paths, look at the world around them, choose courses and forks in the road! Maggie has chosen to take a few risks. Of course, this is just the half of it! She's really quite remarkable, you know."

"Jacques!" Maggie said quietly.

"Oh, yes, quite remarkable," Jamie agreed.

She looked out the window again. Mireau remained uncomfortably silent. "Ah!" he said at last. "The house is coming up!"

They stopped. Mireau jumped out of the cab before Darby could come around. "Thank you, old chap. The carriage was a far better ride than trying to flag down a cabbie in the East End. Why, the one earlier was quite a bad bargain, the grisly old fellow asking way more than he should have for such a ride, and the poor horse appearing as if it hadn't had a drink in quite some time."

Maggie started to move toward the door.

"I think we should take a ride alone, don't you?" Jamie said.

She froze in a rather uncomfortable position, sliding over to exit the carriage. She stared at him. "Should we?" she managed at last, straightening and looking at him. "Why on earth should we do so?"

"To clear the air?" he suggested politely.

"I don't think the air can be cleared," she told him flatly.

He reached over, swinging the carriage door closed, and the smile he gave her was grim. "Let's try."

He tapped on the carriage roof with his knuckles, but then leaned out. "Back in a bit, Mireau," he said pleasantly. Apparently, Darby had already retaken his seat; the carriage rolled into action with the smallest of jolts.

Maggie sat back irritably. "And just where are we going?"

"Not far. Let's speak honestly and quickly."

"Please, go right ahead."

"You're marrying Charles for his money."

"What an insult to a man to whom you claim such fidelity!"

He sat back. "Apparently, it's going to be a long ride."

"What in God's name do you want from me?" she demanded.

"Let's see; you were hesitant, but Charles came to your house, you took one look at him and fell madly in love, as reportedly you did with your first husband."

"Only husband thus far," she reminded him icily.

"Ah, so are you saying that you did meet Charles and suddenly fell into a passionate fit of love and desire?"

"I saw Charles, and remembered him. And remembered that he was always kind, intelligent, and dear on those occasions when I had seen him before."

He leaned forward, uncomfortably close now in the tight confines of the carriage. "You didn't think, aha! but he has aged . . . surely he cannot have many years left in him?"

"You are crass and disgusting—and all regarding a man you pretend to serve with love."

"I serve no one. I stand behind Charles because he is my kin, my elder, and an exceptional man. I'm being honest and practical. I've seen you give speeches and I can hardly imagine that I'm shocking you."

"Perhaps I don't care to accept such impropriety from *you*," she said.

That drew another of his humorless smiles. "As you wish. Still, I'm afraid you're going to have to listen to me."

She lifted her hands with dismay. "It seems I am a captive audience."

"All right, then. It's obvious that you are marrying the man for his position, and most importantly, money. A marriage of convenience. Your convenience."

She smiled as well. "Sir, many a marriage is a matter of convenience. This marriage was arranged. At the very beginning, I was not consulted. Such remains the lot of many a woman who would be a wife."

"Ah, but I do know your brother, lady. And for all his faults, he is not a fellow who would force his sister to anything against her will. And we are not living in medieval times. This is the nineteenth century."

"And you suggest that marriages are not arranged?"

"I am suggesting that had you protested the obvious incongruity of this, it would not have come about."

"You know, I believe that I will tell your uncle about this conversation," she informed him.

"Be my guest. But we've not come to the end of it."

"As far as I'm concerned, we have."

"You remain a captive audience," he reminded her. And indeed, she did. The carriage, spacious enough, seemed smaller than ever. He dominated whatever space he occupied, and that was it. He was simply dressed that day, his trousers and waistcoat pressed black, his cravat a silver gray, and his caped greatcoat equally as dark. Perhaps it was the cut and style of the coat itself; his shoulders seemed to stretch the breadth of the carriage. But were he slender, he might have seemed to consume the space as well, for his eyes seemed to be a burning silver that spoke volumes and echoed and resounded with warning. She denied the shiver that rent through her, and wished that her gaze did not fall to his hands resting on the silver-handled walking stick he carried. They were powerful hands, neatly groomed, but his fingers were long and tense, and the size of his hands, like that of his shoulders, seemed ridiculously emphasized by the space between them. She loathed the man, and yet he seemed to awake something within her. As he ridiculed and she hated, she still found herself wondering with a wicked fascination just how those hands would feel on her flesh, what it would be like to have those fingers, gentle with tenderness rather than rigid with strength, trailing down her cheek, stroking her shoulder. . . .

She jerked her head and gaze away, staring out the window, praying she didn't look desperate, or that, indeed, she hadn't given the least of her thoughts away. There had been that one fleeting moment when she had seen him, when she had felt that sizzle down her spine and thought he might be the lord to whom she would be promised.

"Yes, you're quite right. I remain a captive audience. Of course, I could shriek and scream and throw myself from the carriage, and then, when the police came and the incident was explained to Lord Charles, you might suddenly find yourself a captive audience."

"You're not going to do any such thing."

"Don't count on my being so determined on dignity!"

His smile deepened. "My dear lady, you wouldn't so much as set a finger against the door before I would be upon you, make no mistake."

"How dare you? Perhaps you misunderstand? Your uncle has asked me to be his wife, not his mistress!"

"Madam, that is precisely the point."

"Yes, please, pray, get to the point."

"You're marrying Lord Charles for his money. You seem to have a number of agendas of your own. Marry him for his money. But let me just warn you—

there will be no young lovers, no nights out on the arm of a stand-in, and he had best live many a year after the ceremony."

She gasped, stunned that he would speak so bluntly.

Her eyes narrowed, her temper flared so that it was all that she could do to keep from flying across the carriage to scratch at his face. As it was, her hand twitched, and through no real volition or thought, she leaned forward, ready to strike him.

The carriage made a sudden lurch, sending her across the short space between them, and hard against him. The fingers of his left hand were curled around her wrist; with his right, he caught and steadied her, and for a dreadful moment, she was caught against his chest, staring up into his eyes, and they were face-to-face. And in that brief span of time, she was horrified anew to realize that no matter how it seemed she truly detested him, she *liked* where she had landed, and that it was exquisite to feel his arms around her, the power of his chest, the heat that radiated from the man, the raw, carnal pull that was so simply and sensually a part of him.

Then she jerked free, straightening herself, awkward in her haste to get away from him, and all the emotions streaking through her. Her hand fell upon his thigh. Too close. She jerked her fingers away, her face flooding with crimson. She was completely rattled, and furious that he could make her so. In her scrambling to regain her seating, he tried to help her. His fingers tangled into her hair rather than catching her shoulders. Pins splayed over the carriage.

"I've got them; I've got them!" he muttered. But

they both made the effort to retrieve them, and their heads cracked in the middle. The deerstalker hat flew from his head, and for a moment, they were both nearly unseated again.

He found his balance first, straightened her, and retrieved the pins. She looked away, wishing that just the brush of her fingers against his as he handed back her hairpins did not evoke any reaction.

A sudden exhaustion had come to her. And she spoke more with that weariness than with outrage. "You may rest assured. There is no potential lover in my life. Your uncle is quite rich. You're his only male heir, so I understand. If you're worried that I shall go through your inheritance, you needn't fear. I'm sure that you've made certain there is only so much I can get in the event of his death. I've asked for an income, yes, but I believe that even you must admit that the individual allotment I've requested is less than moderate. Certainly, you've been consulted on the writing of the marriage contract."

He didn't reply for a long matter of minutes, and when he did, it was not as she expected. "My lady, I don't give a damn about the inheritance or the contract. I'm warning you only that you will not break his heart while he lives."

"I don't know what else to say to you. If there is anything I don't want in my life, it is another man."

He stared at her, and she forced her gaze back to him, and was annoyed to find herself smoothing her hair once again, resecuring pins she had already secured. As he looked back at her, he tapped the roof of the carriage again with his walking stick.

"I'm to be set free?"

"Immediately, my lady."

And he was right. She wondered if they had done m. re than drive around and around her own block of houses, for they came before hers so quickly. He was out the door himself and reaching for her hand before she could move. Stiffly, she accepted his touch and came to the ground. His eyes were now as gray and fathomless as a stormy day; he was still and composed, and she realized that her teeth were chattering strangely.

"Aren't you going to ask me not to say anything to Lord Charles about our conversation?" she demanded, swearing to herself, for her voice had a tremor.

"No. I act as I deem fit. And in truth," he added with a touch of humor, "I don't give a damn about money or inheritance. I pray you and Charles live long and happily together, and that you provide him with a dozen sons."

There was a hardness to his voice that chilled her further still. Strange, for she shivered, and yet inside, she was still feeling that strange electricity that seemed to make her movement erratic rather than fluid, cause her heart to thunder, her temper to rise and fall.

"Good day, Sir James," she said. "I would ask you in for tea, but . . . ah, yes, between us, there must be honesty! I really don't want you to come into my house. So, let's see, shall I thank you for the ride? No, I was kidnapped." She turned, and started up the walk with the late blooming fall flowers still bright on either side. She stopped and whirled around. "And do not follow me anymore, and cease spying on me!"

She did not look back.

She continued to the house, forcing the door open with a stunning burst of strength.

Mireau, who had been waiting on the other side, was apparently listening, his ear far too close to the door. As she entered, he went flying, crashing against the mud door within. He quicky regained his composure and looked at her with a weak smile. "Everything all right?"

"Oh, yes. Perfectly fine. Just—fine!" she exploded, and ignoring even Mireau, she hurried on up the stairs, seeking refuge, total and complete privacy.

"Maggie!" Mireau called to her.

She steeled herself to pause. Turning back, she forced a smile. "Everything is fine."

"He doesn't want you going to the East End."

"I'm not marrying him."

"Perhaps we'd best be very careful about your activities. Until the wedding takes place, at the very least."

"Don't be ridiculous. I will not change anything about my life because of the awful man, do you understand? Nothing!"

"But—!"

"Nothing!" she repeated. "Do you understand?"

He nodded unhappily.

She spun about again, hurrying on to the second landing.

And yet, once she had reached the sanctuary of her room, she found no peace. She threw herself down upon the softness of her bed, closed her eyes, and prayed for sleep, a slice of oblivion. But she didn't sleep. She found herself burning with memory. Not of the words that should have outraged her beyond any forgiveness or silence, but with thoughts of a single, brief moment.

And then the fact that she was marrying Lord Charles.

A dear human being.

A man old enough to be her grandfather.

To her amazement, she turned her face into her pillow and cried.

Chapter 4

"Sir!"

Jamie was at the club, playing tennis with Sir Roger Sterling, when he saw Darby at the edge of the net trying discreetly to get his attention. He lifted his racket to Roger and walked back to the right of the court, catching the toweling from the end of the net, and wiping his brow.

"Aye, Darby, what is it?"

Darby was a wonderful fellow with the face of a bloodhound and a loyalty to match.

Now, he looked very grave. "Well, sir, I've done my best, you know, keeping an eye on the Lady Maggie, with a discreet distance between us, of course. But now . . . well, I think that I've come to a situation I don't care to handle myself."

Jamie frowned. He had done everything in his power to keep his distance from Maggie while still seeing to her welfare and safety. He had to admit that his own behavior had been abominable, and that her outrage and loathing for him were certainly justified.

He wished that the damnable wedding would come about! Once he had stood up for his uncle, he could leave, and he was very anxious to leave London. It didn't matter much to him if he was sent to the Continent, Asia, or the Americas—as long as he could leave London.

"Ah, Darby, is she planning nocturnal trips now into the dark world?"

"Actually, sir, that's the gist of it. There's to be a séance tonight, hosted by a new, self-proclaimed messiah, if you'd believe all you were to read about the man!"

"Alexander. Adrian Alexander. I saw his notice in the newspaper."

"Yes, yes, he's the one. Seems a number of people have been seeing him in the short time he's been in the country. The dowager Duchess of Chesney swore to the *Observer* that he'd brought back her dear beloved Duke."

"Marian is a sweetheart, but a bit daft, I'm afraid," Jamie said.

"Ah, sir, I've seen the dowager Duchess," Darby agreed. "Well, of course you know that I am quite accustomed to looking after Sir Charles—in your absence, of course, and—"

"Darby, we both know that your skill at observation goes unequaled," Jamie said, hiding a smile.

"Yes, well, all for my lord Charles. And sir, I must tell you, servants do talk."

"Thank God. We'd never get good gossip did they not!"

"Then you'll understand that through some careful observation—and listening at the right times, and in the right places—I've learned that the Lady Maggie intends to be among the true believers sitting at the table."

"Surely, she cannot intend to go to debunk the man! There was an article with her name in it from the occasion when she attended her last séance, and found the strings beneath the table," he said impatiently.

His own opinion on the new "sciences" that had seemed to flourish so since the mid century in London— phrenology, mesmerism, and spiritualism—was that they were often silly, and usually harmless. There were those who sincerely believed in their causes; he tended to be a man who wanted more proof. But Maggie's determination to prove people as frauds might well turn dangerous. Some people were charlatans, and after the money. Generous amounts of money at that, for weeping widows were prone to pay heavily to speak with departed husbands. Grieving parents longed for a final word from a lost child. Why, it was rumored that even the Queen had been to a séance, which was not surprising, because she had remained so deeply in mourning for Albert, years and years after his death. Of course, Charles had told him that the entire country had come to mourn Albert. They had not been so impressed with the Prince Consort when the Queen had first chosen him for her husband, but his devotion to the arts, sciences, industry, and humanity had, in the end, endeared him to his adopted country. Sadly, he had died before the extent of his contributions had been fully realized.

It had only been last year, on the occasion of the

jubilee celebration for the fiftieth year of her reign, that Queen Victoria herself had even begun to emerge from decades of deep mourning.

Charles had told him that it had been true, that indeed, Victoria had delved into spiritualism, anything to speak to her dear Albert.

Other men and women of intelligence and renown played with such pseudosciences. Physicians of stature were practicing phrenology, the judging of a man's— or woman's—tendency to crime, deviant behavior, and so forth through the structure of the skull.

Maggie did not appear to be ready to make an assault on those touting the new science of phrenology. Only mesmerists and spiritualists.

He was concerned.

"She's made her appointment for the evening under an assumed name," Jamie said with a sigh. "And she'll attend in some manner of disguise, be it only a black veil."

"Well, sir, that's what I rather fear myself," Darby told him.

"Can she have no appointment with my uncle this evening?" he asked. "Shouldn't they be dining together . . . planning the wedding, their honeymoon, their life of bliss, happily-ever-after, to follow?"

Darby lifted his hands helplessly. "Sir, you are aware of all the plans your uncle has made, and that on the days when he visits her home, he leaves by eight. And when she drives out to Moorhaven . . . I drive her back to Mayfair long before eight."

Naturally. Lord Charles needed his night's sleep.

"And this séance?" he asked Darby.

"Is planned for nine."

"Where?"

"The outskirts of Whitechapel."

The address was not encouraging. It was true that crime was rampant in the area, that death by foul play was far too frequent. But now . . .

Father Vickers had reminded them the other day of a poor woman—a drunken, violent prostitute known to get into a few street fights—who had met her death, viciously assaulted with a knife—last April. Then another prostitute had died not long ago, cut up by a knife as well. She'd last been seen with a sailor or serviceman. But nothing had compared to the last horror. And that such a frenzied crime had occurred at all was horrifying.

"Ah, well, then—" Jamie murmured. "We'll need to get started. Right now. I'm assuming you've the exact address?"

"Ah, sir, you know I wouldn't come to you unprepared!"

"Um, still, you're going to rent a carriage. I don't want the crest being seen anywhere near Alexander's center of operation. Let's see, make an appointment for a Mr. Richard Riley, an Irishman of considerable wealth who just last month lost his beloved wife. Sadly, she drowned, in the pond on the family property in Cork. Be as detailed as you can, you know, gossip away as a dear and lamenting servant of the poor departed Nellie."

"Aye, Sir James, you know I love to tell a good story."

"Indeed. Get to it, then. I'll head to the town house right now."

He watched Darby as he walked away, a happy

bounce to his gait. Indeed, he'd tell good tales about Ireland, the home he'd left long ago. Thank God. He had proven himself irreplaceable and extraordinary more often than Jamie cared to remember.

"Have we finished the game?" Roger called to him.

"I'm afraid I'll have to forfeit."

"Good! I'll be able to talk about the way I beat you at the club tonight!" Roger called cheerfully back to him. "Will you be there, ready to defend yourself?" Roger joined him at the edge of the net, a slight limp in evidence. Roger had been knighted due to his service in India. The leg still bothered him when the weather was damp—a continual state in England— but Roger had no wish to ever leave his native land again.

"Ah, not this evening."

"Well, you should come. Seems Lord Ainsworth has found some spectacular new venue of entertainment."

"I'm afraid I shall have to miss it," Jamie apologized.

"Pity. Oh, well, next time!"

"Next time, yes." He wasn't sure if he was sorry to miss any of Percy Ainsworth's entertainment. The baron was known for a keen sense of showmanship— and debauchery as well. It was often said that he'd be the fall, if not the death, of many a foolish young man.

Still, he didn't particularly want to dress up and attend a séance, either.

* * *

For some reason, Lord Charles left late that evening. He had been in a terribly nostalgic mood, and though Maggie usually loved listening to his stories, she found that she was watching the clock over the mantel.

It was nearly ten after eight when he glanced up himself, let out a yawn, apologized profusely, and said that he must call Darby.

Darby, of course, had been somewhere near with Clayton, and appeared immediately.

After Charles left, Justin lingered. "You look restless. I was going to the club, but I'm happy to stay here with you." He was anxious and solicitous. As well he should be. However committed she was to their cause, however much she loved him, it remained true that he had brought about their current situation.

"Justin, please, I'm just going to read and retire myself. It would be quite silly of you to remain home."

He frowned, looking at her somewhat warily. "You haven't anything planned, have you?"

"I don't know what you mean."

"James Langdon spoke to me at the club the other day. Naturally, he was courteous. There was still the hint of the suggestion that I was lax in allowing my sister to run around the slums of the city."

She sighed, shaking her head. "It isn't his place to comment."

"His interest is on his uncle's behalf."

"Justin, we've spent our lives respecting one another's intelligence—and choices."

"And I feel that I've failed you as your brother."

"You haven't. Don't start now," she told him. "Look, Justin, in another few days' time, I'll marry Charles. And, not to be rude, or to suggest that you don't mean the world to me, what you and Sir James think is right or wrong about my behavior will not matter in the least. For the love of God, I swear to you, I have no intention of heading to the East End tonight. Go to your club."

He looked at her a moment longer, then nodded. "You're sure you're all right home alone?"

It was a little late for him to be asking. His nocturnal activities had been questionable for a very long time.

"I'm not alone. Clayton is with me. And Mireau is up in the garret, writing away."

"Of course."

"I'm going up. A good book awaits."

"Good night, then."

She hurried on up the stairs and closed her door to all but a hair's breadth. Moments later, she heard Clayton give Justin his hat, coat, and cane, and her brother departed the house.

Mireau heard as well. He was down the stairs from the attic before she had tiptoed to the second floor landing to assure herself that Justin was gone.

They both knew that Justin might have reservations about his sister attending another séance. The last time she'd been to one, she found the string beneath the table, operating the "spectral" manifestations, and Madama Zenobia had threatened her life, cursing and kicking all the way to her trial. A Belgian, she'd been deported.

Maggie had never considered herself to be in danger from the woman, her jowly husband, or even her ridiculous poodle.

"Have you the bags?"

"All set."

"Let's slip on out."

"Shall we wait a minute? Make sure that Justin has caught a cab?"

"No, he'll have gotten one. Clayton might be about if we wait too long. Let us go."

They hurried down the stairs together, slipping quickly out the door. Maggie realized that she was sneaking about her own home like a thief when Mireau pushed her back as they exited the house— Justin was just getting into a cab.

They held still for several long seconds, until the cab had disappeared down the street. Then they hurried to the sidewalk and kept going, walking briskly until they saw a number of cabs, and hailed one.

In the cab, Mireau opened the bags. He had a dark wig for each of them, and a mourning hat with a heavy veil for Maggie, a mustache, muttonchops, and a goatee for himself. Satin lined capes finished out their apparel.

The cab moved toward a questionable section of the city just opposite the Tower. She remembered that she had told her brother she wasn't going to the East End. If she wasn't in it, she was certainly close.

"He's stopping," Mireau said. He quickly opened the door, hopping out, reaching for her hand. He paid the cabby, and they both looked up at the house.

On the outskirts of a very bad area, it was a glorious old home. It was Tudor in design, and in need of repair, but it certainly offered an aura of darkness and mystery.

There was barely space between the front door

and the street, and a crumbling walk offered them but a few steps. The front door opened as they approached it.

A man, immensely tall, his pate shiny, appeared. "Lady Walsing?"

"Yes, yes, I'm Amy Walsing. Please, no titles here tonight. I believe we have none beyond the grave, and I'd not hamper any spirit who might influence my poor departed Willie."

"Ah, yes, I understand!" the man said.

"This gentleman is your . . . brother. Ben."

"Yes, of course!" she said, delighted. "How did you know?"

"Well, I'd like to say that it was intuition, my dear La—Amy. But Ben came to make the appointment this afternoon."

"Yes, of course, how silly of me!" Maggie said.

"Never silly, dear lady."

"Amy, please. Mrs. Walsing, if you must."

"Come in, come in, both of you."

They were already in. The entry extended into a very large hall with a broad stairway leading up to a second floor.

"I'm so anxious to meet Mr. Alexander," Maggie said.

"Ah, my dear Mrs. Walsing, you have met him."

"You're Adrian Alexander?"

"Yes, it pleases me greatly to say, since you are so eager for my acquaintance!"

She glanced at Mireau through the veil. He was keeping quiet, playing his part well, looking about with awe.

"The others have already arrived," he said. They had reached the second floor. Adrian Alexander extended an arm, indicating that they should enter a room to the left. Maggie inclined her head and did so, followed by Mireau, and then their host.

An elderly woman was in the room, resplendent in black. Her mourning gown was of silk and satin, trimmed in the finest lace. She didn't, however, wear a veil. A small black cap, studded with dark pearls, sat atop her graying hair.

"Her Grace, Lady Marian, Duchess of Chesney," Alexander said.

"Please!" the Duchess said. "Not so formal here!" She was whispering. They'd read that she didn't like to be properly formal at a séance. "Tonight, I am Marian."

"And I am Amy," Maggie said. Still, old ways died hard, and she took the other woman's hand with an inclination of her head. "This is my brother, Ben."

"How lovely that we shall all be on a first name basis this evening!" The Duchess applauded. "This gentleman . . ." She indicated a tall fellow standing before the fireplace, ". . . is Richard."

The man was in black from head to toe, as well. Graying muttonchops were furry upon his cheeks. His beard and mustache were not well trimmed. Indeed, they seemed to swallow his face.

The man extended a gloved hand. "Richard Riley," he said with a Dublin trill.

"Poor Richard lost his dear Nellie to a tragic drowning accident," the Duchess explained.

"So sorry, old chap," Mireau murmured.

"Indeed," Maggie echoed.

"Well, now that we have gathered . . . Ah, here comes my dear niece, Jane, who will lead me to my spirit guide," Alexander said, introducing them to an elegant, sleek-haired woman in a black tunic who came gliding into the room. She had an exotic look, as if her beauty was a derivative of a not-too-distant ancestor from the Near East.

"Good evening," the woman said softly.

"And Oscar, my control," Alexander continued.

An enormous man, bald as Alexander but with a pitch black mustache, entered. He nodded to them all, and took up a stance by the door, crossing his arms over his chest.

"Shall we gather, then?" Jane suggested softly.

"Would you have us any special way?" the Duchess asked anxiously.

"The spirits will come where they will!" Jane said, her voice ethereal.

Maggie glanced at Mireau. At least they weren't arranged in any special order. Then again, that might just be to make the appearance of anything happening all the more real.

The table was arranged for six. Jane and Adrian Alexander sat opposite from one another. There was a plain black cloth on the table with a single candle in the center. "Wherever you will, friends," he said.

Maggie sat next to Alexander. Mireau seemed pleased enough to sit next to the exotic Jane. So far, they hadn't been seated in any particular order, and they hadn't been offered anything to drink that might have been laced with an hallucinogenic. Adrian Alexander was good at appearing entirely legitimate.

Across the table, the Duchess was seated on Alexander's other side. The Irishman, Riley, was between her and Jane.

"Now . . . Oscar, the lights, please."

Oscar turned off the gas lamps overhead. The

room was pitched into darkness. A faint glow gave an orange cast to the area of the hearth; the single candle burned on the table, affording just a whisper of light.

"We will all hold hands atop the table, please," Adrian Alexander said. He had a booming voice, and yet it seemed filled with gentle authority.

They all obeyed.

"Are you ready, Adrian?" Jane asked.

"Yes."

"Adrian, you must clear your mind. Sit back. Let all that troubles your mind slip away; let all that brings tension to your limbs be eased. Watch the flame as it brings its light to the darkness, watch it, focus on it, feel it. Feel the warmth bring to you the comfort and ease that are present when the mind is freed. Sit back and feel the warmth, see the light, know the comfort. Watch the flame and rest, rest . . . let go of this world, and open yourself to the next."

Jane's voice was certainly one of the best Maggie had ever heard. Soft and fluid, like flowing water. There was power in that voice, definitely. Mireau's eyes were half closed as he stared at the flames. Marian, Duchess of Chesney, seemed nearly in a trance herself.

Adrian Alexander had been staring into the flames. He slumped forward suddenly, his eyes closed.

"Adrian, can you hear me?" Jane asked softly.

"Yes."

He straightened. It seemed that his eyes had rolled back into his head, that they were white now. Maggie felt a chill herself, and was stunned.

"Are you alone, Adrian?"

"No."

"Who is with you?"

"Many . . . I am in the tunnel, the hall . . . the light is ahead of me. Others move with me."

"Where are you moving to?" Jane's voice was clear, and yet it never rose above a whisper.

"The light . . . we all seek the light."

"Who are the people with you?"

"The recently . . . dead."

The chill shot right into Maggie's heart. She was amazed at how eerie and frightening the room had become.

"It's cold. So cold . . . and that is why we seek the light."

Cold wind suddenly seemed to blow in. The windows were closed.

"There are those here seeking loved ones. Can you help them tonight?"

"Speak. Those who would talk, must speak."

"May I?" the Duchess whispered fervently.

Jane looked around the table. No one protested.

But as Marian started to form a word, Adrian spoke again. "Someone passes me now . . . catching my arm. Ah, she is lovely, blond hair free and flowing . . . her clothing is damp . . . she is anxious . . . she knows I am with them, but not of them. Her name is . . . Nell . . ."

"Nell?" Jane murmured, looking around the table.

The Irishman across from Mireau made a choking sound. "Nell? My Nell?"

"Adrian . . .?" Jane prompted gently.

"Nell . . . yes, she longs to touch her sweet Richard. She is so worried about him, afraid that he will think that he wasn't home when he should have been, that he might have saved her. She tripped, and it was no one's fault . . . and she is anxious for the light. One day she will meet her Richard on this side, and she will be there, welcoming him into the light."

The Irishman let out something that sounded like a soft sob.

"Is there anyone else?" the Duchess asked anxiously. "Oh, please . . . please, please tell me that my dear husband is still there?"

"Touch!" Adrian Alexander's voice deepened to a rumble.

"Touch?" the Duchess whispered.

"The Duke . . . he longs to touch you . . . longs to say good-bye."

"Oh, dear God!" the Duchess mouthed.

And there, in the air before them, a white mist began to appear. Then slowly, so it seemed, it began to become substance.

The Duchess gasped.

"Oh, please, yes, please, yes!" she said.

"Don't break the circle, don't let the contact slip away!" Jane warned, when it seemed that the Duchess would break free to reach out. "Wait, wait . . . don't frighten the spirits!" Jane warned.

Don't break the circle; don't let the contact slip away.

The mist floating in the air appeared to become a hand. Detailed, down to the ducal ring on the finger.

Marian's mouth was now formed into one huge O.

That was it; this had gone far enough.

Maggie slipped her hand free from Mireau's subtly, making sure not to lose her hold on the hand of Adrian Alexander.

In a swift movement, she reached upward, grabbing the floating prosthetic that hovered above the candle.

"Frauds!" she cried angrily. "Duchess, these people are frauds, just like the others."

"What, oh, no! Oh, no, oh, no!" the Duchess cried, her hand to her heart as she stared around her.

"The old bitch is about to have a heart attack!" Jane exclaimed.

"And the other is about to die!" Alexander growled in a furious voice.

"Eh! Now, now, there's a bit of trickery here, but no need to go calling the very fine ladies here such names!" the Irishman said, rising slowly. "Sure and there's some good way to make all here happy."

He rose. Maggie realized with sudden horror that Alexander's giant "control" was rushing toward the Irishman's back.

"Sir!" she cried with alarm.

But apparently, the Irishman had heard. He was already swinging around and ducking the tackle that had been intended to take him down. His ducking turn continued in a smooth sweep, and he rose on the return, his fist connecting with the big fellow's jaw. The man crashed to the table.

The Duchess was on her feet, screaming.

"This is really quite enough!" Maggie said furiously. She picked up the candle and stick, ready to break a window and scream for the police to come quickly. She meant to disappear herself—before the officers could arrive, but she was quite determined that they should come, and come quickly.

The Duchess would bear witness to what had occurred there tonight.

But she never reached the window.

Fingers latched onto her arm. She was dragged back.

"Oh, no! There'll be four new corpses here tonight, heading for that light."

"Are you mad?" Maggie demanded.

She saw that though the woman might be partially insane, she was serious. She had a small dagger in her right hand, and she was preparing to use it.

Self-preservation and instinct certainly saved her life at that moment. Without thought, she swung the candlestick, catching Jane on the right temple. The woman slumped to the floor with a whimpering exhalation.

"Oh, dear, oh, dear, oh, dear!" the Duchess was chanting.

And suddenly, they heard the deafening sound of a bullet thundering into a wall.

The room went still.

"Now, the noise will stop!" Alexander roared.

He smiled. Where he'd kept the pistol he held, Maggie didn't know. That it was solid and real was certainly a fact.

The Irishman had the giant Oscar down on the table, but the man was groaning. Jane remained on the floor. But Alexander appeared to have the power.

"You intend to kill us all, don't you, Alexander?" the Irishman said. "What else can you do? If one of us leaves this room, you're ruined."

"Alas, I am so sorry. But perhaps one of you will come back in truth to haunt me!" He took aim with the pistol. "You first, Irishman. Though it should be the bitch in black. She just had to reach out!"

He started to swing the gun toward Maggie. She gasped with amazement, the shock of the situation setting in.

Knives, and guns. They were more than shysters. They were prepared to be murderers.

And she was going to die. She'd been warned, and she had underestimated the danger she might face.

She stared at Alexander, too stunned to do anything but wait to die, her thoughts racing. *Why hadn't she left some clue, some warning, so that the police might be there already, in case this occurred? Why was she so determined on her own way that she never let Justin know what she was doing, that she had kept the truth from Charles?*

Now . . . she would pay for her determination and pride!

But the Irishman shouted, and suddenly, Alexander was falling back. The gun exploded, but the shot went wild. The Irishman had hefted up the giant Oscar and gone hurtling into Alexander.

For a moment, the room was still.

Then, the Duchess started screaming again.

But Oscar, Jane, and Alexander were down. Completely down. The Irishman was rising from the tangle of Oscar and Alexander.

Maggie grabbed Mireau's hand. "We've got to get out!" she whispered. "The police might well have heard this kind of commotion."

"The Duchess is louder than a siren!" Mireau agreed.

She tugged him toward the door. They burst into the hall and ran for the stairs that led to the second floor.

A bullet rang out. Another man, clean shaven like

Alexander and Oscar, was coming up the stairs—firing at them.

Maggie stood dead still, amazed once again.

Frozen.

Staring straight ahead, once again seeing her life fly before her eyes.

Another shot exploded. Maggie screamed.

The bald man in front of her fell to the floor.

She spun around. The Irishman was at the top of the stairs, behind her and Mireau, a smoking gun in his hand. "This way!" he told them, as they heard the police whistles. "This way, quickly!"

She rushed back up the stairs, dragging Mireau in her wake.

"Back stairs!" the Irishman said.

She realized only then that he had lost his accent, and yet, it didn't seem to register in her mind that it meant . . . something. Between them all, they had managed to draw the police.

And now, it was really time to disappear.

"Come on! Now!"

They ran. As they flew down the back steps, they heard the thunder of boots from the front. They followed the bearded Richard Riley down the back stairs, bursting out into a fetid alley. A single black horse was tethered there.

"Let's go!" Riley commanded.

"Three of us on one horse? We won't get far!" Maggie said.

"Get up!"

He didn't wait to be obeyed. Maggie was thrown up on the animal with very little ceremony and grace; her skirts went wide, and her linens were clearly visible.

No time to worry about such things.

"Now you, quickly," the Irishman said to Mireau.

Her friend was all but tossed up behind her, while the Irishman continued giving commands.

"Get to Aldgate, the station. I'll meet you there!"

He slapped the horse on the rump, and the animal burst into action.

They galloped down the street, into the darkness and mist, into what seemed to be the very bowels of hell itself.

Chapter 5

"What on earth?" Lord Justin Graham cried as he and his party were nearly run down by a massive stallion being ridden by what appeared to be one giant blob of black.

"Egad!" swore Percy Ainsworth, nearly thrown from his feet.

But then, they had been staggering along the street already.

Their party of rather ribald nobility and gentry was rather the worse for wear.

They had begun drinking at a less than noble establishment, one hovering on the edges between notoriety and total abandonment. The pub keeper, a Luther Green, had learned in his less than illustrious career that often, the more straitlaced and proper a man appeared to be—or felt that he must be—the more in need of real entertainment.

And so Luther had learned the one element most important to any business—supply and demand.

The demand was out there, and he knew how to find the right supply.

It had only taken the acquaintance of one really important fellow, and he had managed that through Lord Percy Ainsworth.

Justin had come into play with the various forms of entertainment provided by Luther Green through Ainsworth—just as Prince Eddy, Duke of Clarence, eldest son of the Prince of Wales, heir apparent to the Crown of Great Britain.

Eddy had a fascination with the East End. He was very young, and sadly, not very bright. Justin actually liked him, and felt sorry for him. He was good to those around him through a natural generosity. Most of those around him, however, made jokes about him when he was not among them. He hadn't been educated for any particular goal in life. That he would one day be king had seemed enough.

And still, Eddy was like every young man of his age. A few years older than Justin, he was fascinated by play, and was known in certain circles as "Prince Collar and Cuffs." He loved being a dandy, gambling, and he loved women and, a few very close to him knew, men as well. He was wary of many of the women who swirled around him in his grandmother's world at court—as well he should be. Despite an outward appearance of adhering to the strict morality and devotion to legal spouse and family brought in by Prince Albert, many of those hanging about were vultures.

Eddy was aware he was a vulnerable target.

He especially loved the East End. He came without a title, even if his entourage was often with him. He met women, and Luther Green saw to it that a

steady supply was available. The East End was filled
with the worst kind of prostitutes—aging women, often
close to death through cirrhosis of the liver from too
much gin, and frequently pockmarked, filthy, missing teeth, and certainly, simply ugly. For the prices
they charged, a loaf of bread, doss money for a single
night, they sometimes managed to get by. Their ugli-
ness didn't matter, for such business was usually carried out quickly, from behind, and a woman's ravaged
face need not be seen.

But these "fallen angels"—as they were sometimes,
ridiculously, romantically called—had all begun somewhere. Of course, there were those who began their
careers late in life, deserted by a husband, or, sometimes, consumed by alcohol addiction.

But there were those who came fresh off the boats
from foreign lands, young and innocent, not even
aware of the profession that was about to engulf them,
ruin them, and make old women of them far before
their time. There were poor-paying jobs to be had in
factories, and many started out there with dreamy
eyes, praying for a better future. For them, a night
with a "gentleman" paid more than a week of hard
labor.

It was these fair maidens who men like Luther
Green found for his "special" customers.

That night, with Percy, he had planned a rather
spectacular event in one of his private rooms. Belly
dancers and harem masters, scantily clad, engaging
in theatrical sex, moving on to afford whatever entertainment a man might require. The room had a secret stairway that led to small private rooms upstairs,
and in the midst of pageantry play and raucous be-

havior, a man might choose among the entertainers for a private assignation.

The belly dancers weren't real at all. Nor did they really know how to belly dance. But both the men and women brought in for the play had been ordered that cleanliness was demanded for the roles they would play, and the scanty apparel provided had indeed been provocative. Justin himself seldom engaged in such base play; he had a mistress, Louisa, who served the Crown Princess Alexandra, was widowed, and perfect for his needs. Their affair was quiet and unremarkable; neither expected marriage or everlasting fidelity, and it suited them both well. But tonight . . .

One of the young women had been quite alluring. Truly fresh, with huge green eyes, a wicked free length of ink-dark hair, and breasts the size of melons, rouged and exposed. She had lured him up the stairs, and he had discovered that her innocence was but play. Her lips were sensual and well-formed and she knew how to use them, along with various other body parts. It helped that he had imbibed far too much cheap whiskey, and, of course, by that time, it seemed that anything at all might be amusing, so when the first young beauty was joined by another, he just lay back and enjoyed. They expected payment, though, and somewhere, in the dull recesses of his mind, he realized that he was able to afford his entertainment because he was allowing his sister to take on his debts. That had left him feeling ill, filled with self-loathing. As it happened, he owed no one anything for the evening, since Percy Ainsworth had paid for it all beforehand. Still, Justin had to wonder if that absolved him of guilt or not, and then, later, as they staggered into the streets, Eddy among them, and the horse nearly ran them down, he found himself not angry, but wondering just what a loss there might have been if he had died there in the streets.

"Sweet Jesu!" Eddy exclaimed suddenly, and Justin realized that the Prince was staring at him. He had dark deep-set eyes in an almost handsome face. "You saved my life, Graham!"

"What?"

"You pushed me out of the way!"

Justin shook his head. "Eddy, the horse would have shied away; that was a well-bred animal. Trust me—we were all startled, but I don't think that I pushed you out of the way, I think that the horse managed to sidestep us. Lord knows, my head is reeling. I might well have knocked us all into the animal."

"Well, all's well that ends well, eh?" Among their party that night was Walter Sickert, the artist. Justin personally thought many of his paintings were a bit too base and bizarre, but Walter was gaining a following. Like Eddy's mother, he was Danish, and therefore, the Princess thought he was a good person to teach Eddy about life.

Justin wondered if Princess Alexandra knew just what Sickert was capable of teaching Eddy about street life, but then again, with the friends Eddy already kept, he couldn't think of anything much more base or degrading the Prince could learn. He had it on good report that there was a certain house on Cleveland Street where the Prince played. It was a brothel which offered male prostitutes.

Roger, who had somehow remained the most sober of them, was still staring in the direction the horse had run.

"Rather fine animal for a place like this," he commented.

Percy burst into laughter and clapped a hand on Roger's back. "And so are you, Sir Roger!" he proclaimed. "And me, of course, I'm really far too fine an animal for this place, but then again, I am an animal."

"Listen!" Roger said. "Hear those whistles? The coppers are all about!"

Roger was right; somewhere near, whistles were sounding. Pretty soon, he thought, the streets might well be filled with bobbies, hurrying about, after some criminal—petty or other. In these streets, they often enough stepped over bodies. Most of them still warm and breathing, but so far under the influence of drink that they were dead to the world—for the present.

Upon occasion, there was that body of one gone forever. Men knifed men in these parts for whatever pennies might be found in their pockets. They killed out of jealousy or rage, or because of a barroom brawl—when glass was broken, then driven into the jugular of one poor fellow or another. Little notice was taken.

Paupers died without fanfare.

Not that the police didn't try. Justin knew that they tried very hard.

But the roots of evil here were deep. They were in the filth and grime of the streets, the tenements with their shattered windows stuffed with rags to keep out the worst of the cold and the stench and the wind. They were in the desperation caused by starvation, and a life so severe that all the civility earned in thousands of years of existence was reduced to simple survival.

"We've got to get back to my coach," Percy said, and even he sounded somewhat disturbed; none of them wanted to be caught.

Many things went on in truth. But they were all hidden from the Queen. They might be living in the nineteenth century, but her virtuous disapproval could be known.

"There! Percy, there's your coach now!" Roger said.

And indeed, the massive carriage with the Ainsworth coat of arms displayed on the doors was thundering down the street, heading their way. It pulled to a stop.

To Justin's amazement, the head that popped from the doorway belonged to none other than Sir James Langdon.

"Get in, fellows, get in. There's some commotion going on down the street."

They all leapt in, quickly. As the coach jerked and set off, Justin looked back. They'd barely made it. The streets were indeed beginning to fill with police officers. More whistles were blowing, and men were running down the dank, misty, gas-lit streets.

He leaned back in the coach, staring across at Jamie Langdon. The man was staring back at him.

But Eddy was the first to speak. "Bless you, Langdon! How on earth did you manage to get hold of Percy's carriage and bring it so swiftly?"

"I was about on some of my uncle's business," Jamie replied. "And, of course, I knew you boys were out and about tonight—Roger had told me earlier. I got quick wind of a bit of trouble due to some new mesmerist and thought to check on you fellows. But then again, séances aren't really part of Percy's usual scheme of things; still, I knew the house was near Luther Green's, and took a chance you might need a quick getaway. Good thing your coachman knows me, Percy."

"Indeed. That was a wonderously timed arrival!" Eddy applauded.

"Glad to serve, Your Grace," Jamie said dryly.

"Where's your conveyance?" Walter Sickert demanded, his voice strangely suspicious.

"Up ahead," Jamie said. He grinned across at Percy. "If all failed, I didn't intend to be caught in my own coach. So . . . was the night's entertainment worth the excitement?"

"I have memories that will allow incredible creation," Sickert said.

Justin felt uncomfortable. He didn't like Sickert. He might be an acclaimed artist, and his friendship might appear popularly Bohemian, but there was an undercurrent about him that seemed to hint of something beyond simple bawdy play or pleasure. Percy had told him once that Sickert had a fine wife, but preferred the basest of mistresses. He was fond of delivering a certain amount of pain from which to derive pleasure. Sick-ert. The name fit the man.

And yet Justin felt that sense of nausea again. He was out with this group. And they all had their little oddities. Maybe not Roger, but the others . . .

He had sold his sister . . .

For this.

He wondered if that was what Jamie Langdon was thinking as he stared across the carriage at him.

He'd never know. "Here, stop here," Jamie said suddenly, sticking his head out the window to shout to the coachman. Sitting back, he told them, "Darby is waiting for me, just ahead, on the corner."

He exited the carriage to another round of thanks. The evening had been an adventure rather than a disaster.

Indeed, Justin thought.

They definitely owed the man their thanks.

Still, he found himself wondering if James Langdon would mention Justin's presence at the pub cum whorehouse to his uncle, and if, in turn, Charles would mention it to Maggie.

He found himself remembering her words. She was determined on Charles because she desperately wanted him to find a wife and continue their line— and keep the title from Angus. They had loved their father, and, admittedly, neither of them cared much for their uncle.

So, he should marry. A noble or a commoner, Maggie didn't care.

But he wasn't sure that Maggie understood why he hadn't done so.

He had seen what she had felt for Nathan, the commoner, the policeman. He had seen her eyes when they rested on the man, and the way she came to life, just because he was near. And that was what he wanted. Silly as it might be in the great scheme of things, he wanted what his sister had once had. He wanted to be in love, and he didn't want to vow the rest of his life to a woman if he did not feel that he could love her, live only for her, forever and ever.

It took Jamie longer to arrive at the Aldgate station than he had planned, but the appearance of the men in the street had been just too good, especially after he had noted Percy's carriage just a block away.

He wondered if he would find Maggie and Mireau, and indeed, his horse for that matter.

Maggie and Mireau he could find.

He just prayed that they didn't abandon Newton anywhere. His horse was exceptional, a gift from the Prince of Wales, bred from the finest English stock and an American mare, product of a sire who had won the Kentucky Derby. The Queen, it seemed, didn't trust her eldest son with much, and yet, from what Jamie had seen, the Prince of Wales was an excellent statesman, and a fine judge of horses. He was a gambler and a rake as well, but kept his affairs discreet— for the most part, at least. The Princess Alexandra tolerated his behavior lovingly, and yet, they all seemed dismayed with Eddy. The Queen gave her son no trust; he, in turn, despaired of his own heir.

Jamie reflected that he could hardly solve the problems of the Monarchy; he was having difficulty dealing with his own small fraction of life.

But, at last, turning a corner toward the station, he saw Newton. Both Maggie and Mireau were standing awkwardly by the horse, looking to be quite anxious that he had taken so long.

"Ah, there you are, Newton, my boy!"

As he walked up, patting the nose of his huge black

stallion, the two stared at him. He realized with a twinge of humor that, through it all, neither had recognized him. And now, of course, he had shed his own disguise.

Mireau was losing his mustache and muttonchops. Maggie was still hidden behind the darkness of the black veil.

"Sir James . . . ?" Mireau said carefully.

Maggie elbowed him fiercely in the ribs. "We must be going—Ben."

"Oh, please, Maggie. Must you insult my intelligence so?" Jamie demanded.

She swept the veil back, defiant. "Are you going to send Mireau on home and give me another lecture?" she asked impatiently.

"Actually, yes. In fact, there's a carriage."

"Mireau, don't you move!" Maggie said.

"Mireau, the cab is just there . . . it won't hover forever."

Mireau groaned softly.

"Oh, good heavens, go, then!" Maggie said.

"He saved our lives tonight!" Mireau reminded her softly.

She had the very good grace to flush furiously. She looked down. "Yes, yes, you did," she admitted. "Thank you."

There was even a touch of humility to her voice.

"I think I'll employ that cab," Mireau said, walking away.

Maggie's eyes rose, and locked on Jamie's. They both seemed to wait. Though neither really watched Mireau leave, they didn't speak until he was in the cab.

Now and then, a conveyance passed them by. A straggling walker skirted them once or twice.

At last she said ruefully, "Yours was a rather good disguise."

"Thank you."

"Do you use it frequently?"

"No."

"You just happened to be there tonight?" she queried.

He shook his head.

She looked away. "So, you are spying on me all the time, and you did know that I was going."

"Yes, I knew you were going."

She looked away. "Well, naturally, on this occasion, I have to be grateful."

"What you have to be is . . ."

"Proper?" she inquired, looking at him again. "I'm afraid it's a little late."

"Whatever makes you do such things?" he asked.

Her eyes widened. Their blue was as deep as the night. "Such things as tonight? They have to be stopped! There are far too many people thinking to make their fortunes off the tragedy in the lives of others. What they do is cruel, terrible!"

"Maggie, many people purport themselves to be spiritualists. They sit in dark houses and imagine that they commune with ghosts. Most of them are harmless. And at worst—usually—they do a little fleecing. The problem is, of course, that you can come across those who are intending to acquire real riches from the wealthy, such as tonight. People who wouldn't wink at murder in the pursuit of their own gain. Tonight could have turned into an absolute tragedy, with poor Lady Marian being a victim as well."

Maggie gasped. "You do think she's all right?"

"She'll be more than all right. She'll delight in all the attention that she'll get. She'll tell wonderful tales about the mysterious men and woman who saved her, and she'll be in all the papers, even in America. She'll love it. But you, my lady. You apparently weren't at all aware that you were risking your life."

"I admit, I've not come across frauds with guns before," she said stiffly.

"Would you consider swearing that you wouldn't entertain such a venture again?" he asked.

He was startled when a touch of tears created a glitter in her eyes, making them crystalline. "You don't understand. What they do to people is . . . horrible."

He sighed deeply. "Maggie, I can only assume from what you're not saying that one of these people managed to draw you in after your husband died. That you were in such a state of grief that you were desperate, and willing to believe anything, and that you then discovered you were being taken."

"Does that make me truly pathetic?" she asked him.

He shook his head, barely aware that he had reached out to move some of the veil from her face, moving it back over the length of her hair. "It just makes you human," he told her. "And still, you can't go around risking bullets or knives or other danger all the time. And . . . you shouldn't risk your life in the East End. The danger there is not just a desperate cutthroat, but the disease that can run so rampant in those horribly crowded and squalid conditions. And what is happening now goes beyond all that we have heard before. Maggie, did you listen—really listen—to Father Vickers? A woman was not just murdered, but disemboweled."

"I heard Father Vickers. My husband was killed there, Sir James. I am very aware of the dangers to be found. You'll note, however, that it is a particularly sad kind of woman who is being killed. I hardly fit the description. Though my brother might have accrued some debts, my type of female is not the one being slain."

"Your 'type of female,' as you label yourself, is not usually to be found walking the streets of the East End. The point is, your carelessness can make you a victim."

"I can't turn into a hothouse flower," she said.

"Perhaps for just a while. Besides the obvious, as I said, typhoid and other fevers plague the area as well. Think of it this way. You could return to the house with a wretched flu that might not do too much to you, but would kill Charles."

Her lashes fell. He realized that she had not considered such a possibility.

"I must hail a cab," she said. Her chin rose and she met his gaze again. "I am grateful that you were there. You did save our lives."

"That was certainly my pleasure. We don't need a cab. We've Newton."

She glanced at the horse, flushing. "Riding astride in a dress is hardly very proper."

"A little late to think of that now, eh? Look, I can't leave the horse, and I don't wish to leave you until I see you safely home. I've already had quite a fantastic view of petticoats and ruffles."

She swallowed silently, not looking away.

"Turn about."

She did so. He spanned his hands around her waist once again, wincing as he felt the temptation to hold tight, and just remain as he was. He lifted her, and her skirts swung once again. He leapt up behind her. His chest to her back. The warmth . . . the vibrance . . .

The veil in his nose.

"This has to go!" he said, and pulling the hat and wig from her head, he tossed both to the breeze.

"Wait!" she cried. "I need—"

"In light of this evening, I think you owe me at least the pretense that you'll not be about such business again!" he said.

The veil was gone. Now all that teased his face was a whisper of her own glimmering hair, the scent of it, sweet and clean. And once again, his arms around her, he felt it the most natural thing in the world, and it would be more natural still to pull her back into his embrace, run his hands down the length of her arms . . .

"Time to move on, Newton!" he said, nudging the horse.

The ride took perhaps ten minutes. He kept to the back roads as they headed for Mayfair. He was anxious that they should get there quickly, yet everything in him wanted the ride to go on forever. She angered him, infuriated him, and played at being a fool. Dangerously so. But he was aware now as to just why he so often felt such wrath rising in her direction. He had wanted her, yes. Few living, breathing men could not look at such a stunning woman and not feel a rise of desire. But there was more—that fire he had known from the beginning, and now, the fierce pride in her heart, the passion for what she believed in, the conviction of purpose that would make her so determined on a marriage with a man three times her age.

At her house, he dismounted quickly. "You should go in. Your brother will be home soon." He reached up for her, glad to span her waist with his hands once again, and certainly not so pure of heart and mind that he didn't relish the moment when she slid against his body to reach the ground.

She gripped his upper arms for a moment, gathering her balance to stand on her own.

Their eyes met. "Have you . . . been spying on Justin, too?" she asked.

He thought she sounded a bit breathless.

He shook his head. "I happened to run into him."

She nodded, stepping back. "Thank you, again. You are quite resourceful, actually."

He swept her a deep bow. "I do my best. And yet, I fear, with you, I may not always be resourceful enough." His tone became serious. "Quite seriously, you might well give my uncle heart failure, you know."

She seemed to stiffen. "The wedding is but days away, now."

"You really must consider your position as the wife of such a man."

She sighed deeply. "I swear to you, I have found him to be an exceptional man, noble in his words, thoughts, actions, as well as title and appearance. I mean to be absolutely loyal, and do everything in my power at all times to insure his happiness and good health."

He nodded. "Good night, my lady."

"Good night, Sir James."

And yet neither moved, and the distance between them might not have been, for he felt her heat and the burning energy and passion that were so much a part of her. Wild imaginings flooded through him; he pictured a world in which his uncle did not exist, in which they were just two people who had met, who had felt that burst of electricity in just a moment when their eyes had first met. He saw a mist of silver in which he was free to draw her into his arms, ravage and explore with the passion of his kiss, send clothing scattering to the winds of time, and sink into clouds of floating wonder where naked flesh burst into a glory of sensuality, touch and taste. . . .

"Good night," she said again, and there was a strange and desperate sound to it.

Silver clouds evaporated.

She turned and started up the walk.

They would pay!

Crouched in an alley, his shoulder bleeding, the man who called himself Adrian Alexander kept himself from passing out again by concentrating with a fervor on the extent of his wrath.

The three of them—the fake Irishman, the so-called lady with her brother. He had considered himself such an astute judge of human character! And they had taken him down in one night, despite all his precautions, his simple resolution that he would prevail, even if it meant murder.

All dead, his own people, dead—or in the custody of the

police. Jane! His beloved Jane. They'd have her in Newgate, awaiting trial, and he'd have no way to reach her.

But he would. Oh, yes, he would. He'd find a way. But first . . .

"Gar-dez the loo!" someone cried from a window high above him in the darkened alley.

And then, a pile of foul-smelling slop fell atop his head.

Urine and fecal matter crept down his forehead to his face, and he nearly screamed aloud with a terrible rage.

They were dead! They were all dead! The two men, and the woman.

The woman . . .

He'd have a few surprises for that wretched beauty, indeed. She'd wish she were dead, long before he delivered the coup de grace!

"Maggie!"

Maggie had nearly reached the steps, nearly reached what was becoming in her mind a simple place of salvation. Her house. Just her house. And still, then when the door had closed between them, with walls around her, she would be all right.

Go, go! she urged herself. She had never know a fear like the one suddenly seizing her, not even tonight, when a bullet might have burned through her flesh at any instant.

Go, go . . . run. Run into the house, as fast as you can!

"Maggie!"

A curious tone in his voice brought her to a halt. She turned. He hadn't moved. He remained where he was, a slight breeze lifting the shoulder capes of his coat, his stance still and strong, the great horse at his side.

"Yes?"

She hated herself. The word sounded like a whisper, almost a plea.

A plea for what?

She was walking back to him. She hadn't in the least suggested to her feet that they carry her back, and yet . . .

She walked. She almost *felt* him as she did so. Almost felt . . .

Lord help her. She couldn't begin to understand all the emotions seething through her as she stood there. Anger, regret, longing, admiration, perhaps grudgingly given, a strange kinship, more, *longing*.

More.

Desire. As strong as any she had known in her life, as strong as she had felt for . . . a man long buried. Dearly loved, but long buried. While this one . . .

Was alive. Very much alive. Vibrant. Vital. A wealth of heat and seduction, even as he stood, not moving, just his eyes touching her, and that look . . .

Dear God, the visions that look brought to her mind's eye.

She came to a halt before him and fought the images of what might be with such a man.

Still, he hadn't moved, and he didn't speak.

Despite the fantasies sweeping through her mind at the wicked pace of a blustering wind, she was startled when he touched her. His forefinger first, touching slightly against her chin, lifting it, then his hand, stretching out, cradling her jaw. His thumb ran down the length of her cheek, then brushed over her lower lip. Then suddenly she was closer still, not at all certain if his touch manipulated the angle of her head, or if she had stepped forward herself. His mouth formed over hers, and it was no subtle, hesitant, brushing kiss, but a consuming invasion. Rockets exploded within her mind as she felt the reckless, passionate sear of his tongue, the thrust and sweep, a molten, liquid fire, heating her blood to pure lava. Her heart thundered, she heard and felt the cacophony. His arms seemed a shelter of iron, the pressure of his body a torment that teased down into the very essence of her, stirring within her breast, a shattering reawakening of sensuality that stroked and teased from her breasts to her thighs, and her very center. His hand, so large and capable, fell at the base of her spine, pressing her closer, and she didn't realize till long after that she hadn't taken a single breath in all the long seconds that he held her so.

God help her! How she wanted this! How wonderful to be in his arms. She was so ridiculously familiar with his eyes, voice, scent.

She could have stayed forever, feeling the sensual sweep of his tongue. It evoked so very much, led her to imagine what could be. She had really believed herself immune to such feelings ever arising again, and yet this was as if they were born entirely anew. It wasn't nostalgia, loss, the memory of something gone before. It was James, this man, this touch, this feeling, and she was stunned to feel that the wanting inside her was shatteringly deep and desperate, that there was longing, physical, and in her heart, and . . .

Physical.

A burning, a desire that was more than just hot and urgent and . . .

Then, quite suddenly, he stepped away, and staring at her, swore. She didn't stumble, nor did her knees buckle, yet she stood there, just staring at him, stunned, feeling the dampness remaining upon her lips, the swell of them from his touch, and as if she would blow away like a leaf were the slightest breeze to arise.

"You are a witch!" he said softly. And he wiped his mouth suddenly with the back of his hand, as if he had indeed tasted something evil.

Silver clouds evaporated.

She turned at last and headed up the walk, and into the town house.

Chapter 6

Jamie stayed by Newton several long seconds, gathering his equilibrium. His muscles hardened, stiffened, and chilled, and his jaw locked. Good God, what was the matter with him? He loved Charles, owed him so much.

If he believed in it, he'd say that he was indeed bewitched!

But he didn't believe in such things. And it hadn't been all the raw hungers she evoked simply by looking the way she did that had seemed to mesmerize him that night. It had been in those few moments when he had seen the pain and the passion within her, the hurt that had led her to the type of reckless action she had carried out tonight. It had been something in her voice, something in the glimpse of honesty.

He swore aloud.

Did he blame her? Not with any sense of right or

dignity. She'd taken her leave. He had called her back.

Ah, but she'd fallen quite easily into his arms! No protest there. And she was the one getting married. He had rather just proved that she was far too young for Charles, that she would eventually hurt him, taking on a lover.

Or was it just him? Had she found something so incredibly unique and special in him?

"Nice conceit, eh, Newton?" he said to the horse. "Bit of ego on my part, there, eh?

"Well, let's head home, shall we, Newton? It seems there's little else to do tonight."

He mounted his horse, and turned the animal from the house and the woman who would haunt him forever.

His mind was set. He had intended to keep her from danger, and yet, it seemed, he was the greatest danger she might encounter at the moment. Darby would have to look after her on his own until the wedding.

The wedding.

A taste of acid nearly choked him.

Hopefully, she would lie low and keep her peace for a week, at the very least! Because, if he could help it, he didn't intend to see her again until after she was duly wed to Charles.

"Here we are at last. Moorhaven," Jamie said, looking at Arianna, trying to smile. The carriage they had taken from the rail station drew to a halt at the end of the estate's long drive.

Arianna didn't respond. She'd been dour the entire trip—except when they had first approached London. Then she had started quizzing him relentlessly on news regarding current events in the city, and she'd had a morbid curiosity when he'd talked about some of the private individuals trying to improve conditions for the poor in their own country.

Then, entering the countryside, she'd fallen silent again.

As the cabbie came around for their baggage, he caught Arianna's hand. "I've never seen your father so happy, or look so well. Try to be pleased, for his sake."

She stared at Jamie. "I will never let him know how I feel."

"Maybe you'll feel differently. You've not met Lady Maggie yet."

She gave him a frighteningly icy smile. "You're so right."

Jamie sighed, shaking his head. Mrs. Whitley was rushing out to greet them. Darby followed her, ready to get Arianna's bags.

"Welcome home, welcome home!" Mrs. Whitley almost hugged the girl. Not quite. She stopped short. She was a no-nonsense woman, but kind enough, even if she appeared remote.

"Thank you, Mrs. Whitley," Arianna said. Then, looking around Mrs. Whitley, she smiled with honest warmth. "Darby!"

"Little Miss!" Darby said, and he didn't seem to have a problem in the least accepting Arianna's enthusiasm as she threw herself into his arms.

Uncomfortable himself, Jamie watched the proceedings.

"Sir James, will you come in for tea? Your uncle will surely expect you to do so."

"No, I've much to keep me busy today, I'm afraid, Mrs. Whitley. Please tell Uncle Charles that I will be here bright and early tomorrow."

"Indeed, Sir James, I'll tell him," Mrs. Whitley assured him.

He nodded, and turned back to the cab.

Arianna let Darby loose, turning back to him. "Jamie!"

"Yes?"

She flew the distance between them, hugging him suddenly as she had Darby. "Thank you . . . I wouldn't have been able to do this if you hadn't come to France for me yourself."

He nodded. "Until tomorrow."

Then, still feeling the urgent need to leave Charles's house, he hurriedly climbed back into the cab. He'd been restless the entire trip to France, and uncomfortable with Arianna, whom he'd known since she'd been a wee babe in his arms. He'd always been the older cousin, like a tolerant, amused, brother.

But this time he'd been as anxious to be rid of her as he was anxious simply to be done with the whole of it!

A drink might be in order.

Hell, a slew of them might be in order.

"This, my dear, is Arianna!"

The day before the wedding, Arianna had come home at last.

They stood in the grand salon at Moorhaven,

Charles's estate on the Thames. Tomorrow, the salon would host the wedding reception, and already, it was festooned with candles and flowers.

Maggie had just arrived, driven there in the new coach that her marriage portion, paid to Justin, furnished.

Clayton had loved driving it.

Mrs. Whitley, Charles's elegant head housekeeper, had seen her in, bringing her here, straight to the salon, where, at one of the tables not yet set for the reception, Charles and his daughter were having tea, awaiting her arrival.

And here, at last, was her stepdaughter-to-be. She hoped that she could win the young girl over, but she herself was not in the best of moods.

First, there was the matter of the strange moment of intimacy she had exchanged with Jamie. She had thought that she loathed him.

She didn't dare think of the man. She didn't know what she felt, or perhaps she did. Horror, sadness. A terrible sense of *if only*.

She had disliked him so intensely. Because of his feelings for her. And surely, those hadn't changed, they had only intensified. Now, he must think so much worse of her, that she had allowed such a kiss.

A kiss only.

No, a kiss that hinted at so much more. A kiss that had made her feel more than any simple touch of the lips should do.

She had to clear her mind. When she thought of that moment, she started to shake. There were other matters, very serious, to be worried about as well.

In the last few days, she had anxiously read the papers, praying that there was no speculation at all that she had been "the woman in black" who had been present at the séance where one man had been seriously injured, with a gunshot wound to his shoulder, a young woman had been found with a serious bruise to her forehead, and another big fellow had been discovered unconscious. The three were under arrest—Lady Marian, Duchess of Chesney, had given the police detailed information as to the proceedings that night, but she was entirely unaware as to the identities of the others who had attended the séance.

Adrian Alexander himself had not been found. It was his cohorts who sat at Newgate, awaiting trial on serious charges, including those of attempted murder.

Maggie should have been relieved. She remained nervous. And she was still so when she stood in the grand salon at Moorhaven and greeted the girl. She forced herself to focus on the situation at hand. The young lady had to be skeptical of her, and she hoped to change her doubt.

"Arianna, how do you do?"

Maggie's initial greeting to the girl was honestly warm.

And then she saw the way that the girl was looking at her. Much as Jamie had done, when they had first met.

In her father's presence, she didn't intend to be overtly rude. She accepted Maggie's hand, her own as limp as a wet noodle.

"Charmed, I'm sure," the girl drawled, surely using her most autocratic and bored tone.

"I've been so anxious to meet," Maggie said. Charles

stood with an arm draped around the girl's shoulder, beaming with pride.

"Isn't she beautiful?" he asked Maggie.

"Indeed, outstandingly beautiful," Maggie said, and whatever her thoughts, her words were not a lie. The girl was exquisite. Hair as dark as India ink—like Jamie's. Her eyes were brown, however, a true, deep, dark brown, whereas Jamie's were gray, that ever-changing gray. Her skin was flawless, ivory, without a hint of imperfection.

"Well, shall we sit down, enjoy our tea?" Charles suggested, and so they did. Arianna had seen to it that she retained her chair—between Maggie and her father.

"So, you've been studying in France," Maggie said to the girl.

Dark eyes lit upon her with annoyance and contempt. "Yes."

"How lovely. I spent a year in Paris when I was seventeen. My Uncle Angus had suggested it was the best place to go to finishing school, before being introduced to society."

"And did you enjoy being finished there?" Arianna asked.

"I enjoyed Paris very much," Maggie said.

Charles frowned, his hand upon the teapot. "The water has grown cold. I'll just call Mrs. Whitley."

"I'll do it, Father," Arianna offered.

"Nonsense, child. You and Maggie are just getting to know one another."

He walked toward the door leading to the grand foyer and from there, to the kitchens.

Arianna leaned toward Maggie suddenly. "And

what did you study in Paris, Lady Margaret? *Witch-craft?*"

"What?" Maggie said, astonished.

"A wonderful woman, Mrs. Whitley!" Charles boomed, returning to the table. "She's seeing to it already. Fresh tea and scones! So, how are my two beauties getting along?" He took his chair again, his smile proud at the sight of them.

"I was just asking Lady Margaret if she studied the sciences in Paris," Arianna said sweetly.

Maggie allowed her the lie, her eyes narrowing as she smiled. "And I was just informing your lovely daughter that no, I had actually studied the sciences right here, in London. I did, however, enjoy a few seasons in Italy, during the winter, while my father was still alive."

"Italy!" Lord Charles reached across the table, capturing Maggie's fingers, squeezing them. "We must make a trip to Italy. And if Arianna doesn't instantly fall in love with some rake come the spring, she'll most certainly have to accompany us." He winked at his daughter. "Of course, my dear, I am anxious that you meet a certain young man. A proper one. Very handsome, of course."

"I'm young, Father. And young men can wait. To travel with you—and Lady Maggie, of course—why, I can think of nothing that I would rather do, dear Father!" Arianna said.

"I'm so sorry your brother couldn't be here," Charles told Maggie.

"I am, too, but he had his last fitting for tomorrow."

"You have a brother, Lady Margaret. How nice for you," Arianna said.

"Yes, he is very dear to me."

"And he must think, as I do, that this wedding is a blessing and wondrous event," Arianna said with such scathing sarcasm that Maggie was amazed Charles could miss it.

"Oh, yes," she replied.

"Lord Charles!" Mrs. Whitley came hurrying in, her manner conveying great distress. "Father Gaines has come and needs a word with you."

"Well, bring him in for tea!" Charles said.

"He begs your forgiveness but has a very busy afternoon. Can you spare him a few minutes in your office?"

"Certainly. Ladies, my very special ladies! Please enjoy your tea, and don't wait for me. Naturally, there are last minute problems to be straightened out!" He rose again, planted a kiss on his daughter's head, winked at Maggie, and headed out.

Maggie leaned forward. "Your father's gone. So, please, feel free to speak plainly. I will do so right now. I don't intend to pretend to be your mother in any way; you're a breath away from being of age, so I'd be a little late."

"My mother! You're scarcely four or five years my senior!"

"That's true. Except that I'm afraid those years have been long and hard."

"You're quite busy, so I hear."

Maggie frowned. What did the girl know about her?

"I'm not at all sure what you mean, but I've lost a husband, I saw him murdered, and I tried, for his sake, to understand why."

"Tell me, Lady Margaret," Arianna demanded, both hands on the table as she faced Maggie down. "Did you fall in love with my father?"

"I intend to be a very good wife to your father."

"Until you kill him, too?"

She came so close to slapping Arianna that she had to leap to her feet. "You are hateful!" she told Arianna. "I don't know what on earth has made you so bitter and nasty, and you're quite welcome to hate me until your own venom chokes you, but don't speak about my past in such a way."

"What will you do? Beat me? Poison me?" Arianna suggested. "Let's see; kill my father, kill me! Alas, you'll have to go after Jamie, then, though, if you want all the money. Of course, even if you get rid of Jamie, you won't get the estate. They'll have to find some long-lost male relative for the title and estates. I guess, however, that you will have your marriage portion. I'm sure that this particular marriage of convenience was arranged with your legal interests well tended to."

Maggie held very still. "Please inform your father I suddenly realized that I had to leave. I will see him tomorrow, at the ceremony."

Maggie turned and exited the salon and the foyer. She marched out to the new family carriage and was chagrined to discover that, of course, Clayton wasn't there. He would hardly expect her to be ready to return home so quickly.

But then, just as she stood by the carriage door, stiff and furious, Clayton arrived. He opened the carriage door quickly, and as he helped her in, he said, "Ah, lady, try to understand the lass. She feels as if she's failed as a daughter."

"Oh?" Maggie looked at Clayton, who flushed.

"Begging your pardon, m'lady. Servants talk, you know."

Maggie nodded, then whispered, "But Clayton. She's . . . *vicious!*"

"Just a scared child, trying to be much, much more," he told her sadly.

"I'll try very hard to take that into consideration," Maggie told him. But once she was seated in the carriage, she felt a chill. She had expected that Lord Charles's daughter might not greet her with open arms. But she'd never expected the girl to be this passionately vile!

The carriage lurched forward. Justin had actually haggled for it, and it wasn't new, only the coat of arms on the door. Their debts were paid, but apparently, her brother had set what wasn't direly needed aside, should she discover that she needed it.

Rather than take a chance that he fall into gambling again, Maggie had quietly agreed.

So, here it was, the day before the wedding and she had been well and duly bought and paid for.

She began to shake. It was true that she had come to care deeply for Lord Charles. It was true as well that she couldn't help but note the liver spots on his hands, the gauntness of his cheeks, the snow white color of his brows. Which would be just fine, if only she, too, had snow white hair, wrinkling flesh, and perhaps even a token liver spot somewhere.

True, too, that she couldn't stop thinking about a younger man, one whose lightest touch evoked a very uncomfortable fire that seemed to burn and consume every part of her flesh, and take special heat into the very core of her.

She gritted her teeth, grasped her hands tightly in her lap.

Yes, she'd been bought, and paid for.

No wonder the girl hated her with such a violent fervor. She had a right. *Had she suddenly fallen madly in love with Lord Charles? No, of course not. Did she intend to be a good wife? Yes, Lord Charles had made her world right again.*

Would she dream about Sir James Langdon late at night?

No, no, no, she would not allow herself to do so!

Forget James, forget him, forget the feelings of hunger. Forget how you're discovering just how much you admire the man, how you feel when his eyes touch you, when his hands are upon you, when his lips . . .

Forget!

Charles, Charles, Lord Charles.

Yes, Lord Charles. And she would be a good wife. Perhaps he would try to stop her visits to the East End, but if he continued with his more than charitable contributions to the church and the Salvation Army because of her, wouldn't it be worth it? He'd never, never approve of her determination to expose mediums and mesmerists, but then, she'd decided herself that she was going to have to rethink that situation, after she had realized that some of them might commit murder to maintain their practices.

It didn't matter that she hadn't suddenly fallen in love with Charles. Lots of people were still married by arrangement. And most people didn't just suddenly fall in love.

They might fall into lust, though. And discover that the object of their lust was decent and intelligent, worthy in thought and deed, and body.

Body . . .

She stuck her head out of the carriage, calling to Clayton, "Please, stop! I think I'd like to walk around a bit, Clayton, have a sip of tea at a coffeehouse."

Tea, hell, a nice sip of sherry would be lovely. Maybe several sips.

From the driver's seat, Clayton gave a nod. A moment later, he drew the carriage to a halt, out of the way of traffic. They were not far from Buckingham Palace, and there was a row of shops and coffeehouses along the very hectic and busy thoroughfare.

Still, Clayton looked at her worriedly as he helped her from the carriage. "M'lady . . . shall I wait? I can find a good place to draw up, read me papers, while some time."

She shook her head. "I really need some time, Clayton." She touched his dear old cheek. "I will so miss you every morning, Clayton."

"You'll be fine. You'll have the good Mrs. Whitley."

Maggie made a face. "She's very stern. And proper."

"As a good housekeeper should be."

Maggie shook her head. "I prefer a dear family butler with whom one can enjoy chocolate and gossip in the kitchen. Even if the gossip is all about one's self! Get on, now. I shall be quite fine by myself."

"I can wait, Maggie."

"We've done just fine with hired carriage for several years now, Clayton. I know my way home."

Sighing, he left her.

"Maggie! My, my! Dear Lady Maggie Graham!"

Maggie had found a darling little place on the corner with an outside garden area, and there, she'd ordered tea and scones, had been sipping the first and playing with the latter, when she heard her name called. Looking up, she saw Cecilia, now Countess de Burgh, since her marriage to Count Eustace de Burgh of Cornwall.

They had come out together, attending their first season of balls and teas and the social whirl of the Ton together. Maggie had liked Cecilia, despite her friend's absolute determination to marry Eustace, who hadn't seemed very interested in marriage, other than that his family had determined that he would find a wife, and quickly. He was more than a bit of a fop, a total ne'er do well, but he also owned several castles, manor houses, a dozen racehorses, and all manner of property.

Cecilia looked as charming as ever, brown curls artfully arrayed, her lavender day dress only a shade too risqué, and the parasol she carried a pretty little piece that added nicely to her outfit. Her bonnet was small, emphasizing the richness of her curls.

"Cecilia, how are you?" Maggie rose with an honest pleasure at seeing Cecilia, who was ever cheerful, and, customarily, far too honest. She had always enjoyed a sense of adventure and fun, and hadn't been appalled when Maggie had determined on marrying Nathan. She had thought Maggie entirely foolish, but hadn't excluded her from any social events. However, in the last few years, they had grown apart.

"Delightful, absolutely delightful," Cecilia said. "Preparing the town house for the autumn season, you know, and then we'll stay through Christmas and head to the Continent. We've decided to winter in Spain."

"Lovely." Cecilia had found the spare chair across from Maggie. She beamed. "And you—about to become the wife of none other than Charles, Viscount Langdon! I'm quite thrilled for you."

"Are you?"

"Well, of course. Aren't you thrilled for yourself?"

"He's a very dear man."

Cecilia laughed delightedly. "Oh, Maggie! Leave it to you. 'He's a dear man!' He's one of the most important peers in the realm. Marriage is a contract, a convenience, something for the perpetuation of heirs, and society. Good heavens, do you think that people believe you're required to be madly in love with the man? Ah, yes, well you did marry that poor fellow. Nathan. He was gorgeous, but . . . Maggie, Maggie, Maggie! Gorgeous men are one thing, and marriage is quite another. You should have had an affair with your glorious young Nathan, and married such a man as Charles from the very beginning."

"Cecilia!" Maggie protested. "I loved Nathan."

"Yes, yes, all well, good, and fine. And our dear Queen Victoria adored her Albert, and so now we're all supposed to be so moral. Well, she is deceiving herself, of course. Her son is a tremendous rake, and his son, I assure you, no better. We all pretend that such things aren't going on, but underneath, well . . ."

"Underneath," Maggie said, "a lot is rumor." Her smile deepened. "It is good to see you. You and Eustace are doing well?"

"Indeed, it's nearly a marriage made in heaven."

"There! You love your husband."

Cecilia hesitated just a moment, then shook her

head. "Maggie, Maggie! Of course I love the fellow. He's provided magnificently for me."

"Congratulations. I'm very happy for you."

"We've two sons now, you know. A three-year-old and a two-year-old. One to inherit, and a backup."

"Cecilia, what a way to talk about your children."

"Oh, I adore the little urchins. But you've always been such a practical girl, Maggie. Surely, you still are."

Maggie must have stared at her a little blankly because she leaned forward then, a strange smile curling her lips. "Maggie, please! Eustace prefers different company."

"He has mistresses?"

Cecilia giggled. "No, silly. He prefers . . . the company of men. I always knew, of course. Ours was very much so an arranged marriage. We've done the proper thing and produced two legitimate heirs. Now, he enjoys himself as he prefers . . . and I do the same. And we're very dear friends. Actually, ours is a far better marriage than most. We never fight. And!" She lowered her voice, speaking excitedly, "I tell you, I know many a rumor about young Prince Eddy is true, because Eustace has assured me that it is so!"

Maggie gasped. "My brother is friends with Prince Eddy."

Cecilia laughed, shaking her head. "Your brother and many other a man with more customary preferences is friends with the Prince. There are friends, and there are friends."

"I'm relieved."

"Are you judging?" Cecilia asked.

"Never. I'm just hoping my brother will find the

woman of his dreams soon, marry, and produce an heir."

"Well, my Lord, he should be able to do so easily enough. He's as handsome as a fairy-tale prince!"

"Thank you."

"So! You'll be the wife of Viscount Langdon. It will be fine. The old fellow has a child, doesn't he? Oh, that's right, how could I forget? A daughter. He'll be trying for a son. Give him that heir as quickly as you can, and you'll be on your own." Her eyes twinkled. "Have you considered any prospective lovers?"

"Good Lord, no!"

"Oh, come, Maggie! You might be a widow as we sit, but you're young and, sad to say, you were the most stunning among us the year we hit society. I've no lack of confidence, myself, mind you! Maggie! This wedding is tomorrow. I have an idea. Come out with me tonight. I know places where we can go. I can see already that you're thinking about being all moral and dedicated and loyal once you've wed, but . . . well, you're not wed until tomorrow. Let's play tonight!"

"Cecilia," Maggie began, but her words caught in her throat. Looking just a few feet beyond her friend's parasol, she froze. There was a man at a nearby table, now peering at the two of them over the top of his newspaper.

He hadn't been there when she had first chosen the table.

It was Jamie.

He lowered the newspaper. She wasn't certain whether he was just realizing that she was there as well or not. He stood. "Why, Lady Graham. How lovely to see you. And your friend, of course."

"How lovely to see *you!*" Cecilia exclaimed, looking him up and down a bit too boldly. "Sir James
Langdon! Indeed, what a pleasure." She extended
an elegantly gloved hand. "We have met."

"Forgive me, then, my memory is sadly faulty."

"Cecilia, Lady de Burgh. You knew me as Sir Cava-
naugh's daughter."

"Ah, yes. Forgive me. What a pleasure to see you
again."

"Well!" Cecilia said, "How amazing that the two of
you should just happen to meet at a coffee shop, just
the day before the wedding! You must be delighted
for your uncle, Sir James."

"Indeed. Delighted," Jamie said.

"Are you standing up for him?"

"Quite so."

Cecilia smiled wickedly. "Are you having some form
of a wonderful party for Lord Charles this evening? I
was just trying to convince Maggie that she should
allow me to take her out for a last evening as a single
lady. Well, she's widowed, but the point is really, before she's married again."

"Don't tell me Lady Maggie is hesitating?" Jamie
said, staring at her.

"She's being no fun at all," Cecilia pouted.

"Ah, well, neither is my uncle. He is heading off to
bed at an early hour, anxious for the morning to
come, the day of his wedding."

"Is he really?" Cecilia said, her eyes sparkling. "Well,
then, Sir James, perhaps we could convince you to
join the two of us!"

"Cecilia, I haven't agreed that I'm going anywhere,"
Maggie said uncomfortably. She was also tremendously

uncomfortable with the way that Cecilia was looking at Jamie. A bolt of something shot through her, and she was disturbed to realize that it was jealousy.

"What did you have in mind?" Jamie asked Cecilia.

"I would never dream of being rude to Sir James, but if he accompanies us, it would hardly be a night out for the ladies," Maggie said.

"Alas, true," Cecilia said. She stared at Jamie with a smile that was so blatant that, even given the conversation they'd just had, Maggie was shocked. "But, of course, with my dear friend Maggie marrying into the family, I'm sure we can meet again, Sir James."

"Yes, definitely," Jamie said, bemused. "I am acquainted with your husband, my lady, which makes it all the more pleasant to make your reacquaintance."

Cecilia's smile deepened. Maggie wanted to hit someone.

She stood. "Cecilia, if we're to be out and about this evening, I believe I'll head home so that I might be properly dressed for the occasion."

"Fine." Cecilia didn't even look at her. She was still staring at Jamie. "My coachman will call for you at . . . eight, say?"

"Perhaps you shouldn't go out this evening."

She was startled by Jamie's words.

"Harmless play," Cecilia said.

"Ah, but tomorrow will be such an event in Lady Maggie's life," Jamie pointed out.

"All the more reason I should go out tonight," Maggie said. She really would have preferred to spend her last evening at home instead of an evening out with Cecilia, but the very fact that he suggested that she not go, made her determined that she would.

And all the more because of the way he and Cecilia were staring at one another. The conversation going on between their eyes was almost audible. Cecilia, so blatantly saying that she was married to a man who cheerfully gave her total freedom, Jamie musing that entertainment was all he really sought at the moment, the two of them thinking that together they both made prime candidates for a night of simple sex and pleasure.

"Well, I shall see you both at a later time, then," Maggie said.

As she departed, the two were still staring at one another.

Arianna paced her room.

She adored her father so much. How could he be doing this thing? It was all so silly, almost embarrassing. And it was deplorable that even her father could be such a fool—whatever was he thinking?

She couldn't do it. She couldn't go to the wedding, and she certainly couldn't live with that woman!

Definitely, she was evil. One look at her had assured Arianna that she was evil. And she hadn't been in the least placating! She was too tall, too regal in her bearing, far too assured, and far too willing for this wedding for there not to be something terribly wrong.

That was it, certainly. Her family was down on its luck. No great surprise. And still . . . there had to be something. Something about the woman, something in her past. Arianna hadn't met her friend Mireau yet—a man her father talked about with amusement and pride—but there was something not quite right about him, either. He was probably Lady Maggie's lover, and her father was simply too besotted or too naive to see such a thing.

She sat at her dressing table and stared at her own reflection. They said that she looked like her mother. She barely remembered her own mother, and therefore, it was hard to know if people were right. She loved to imagine her mother, though—she had been the daughter of a Welshman knighted in India. Then, too, it was said, her father had thrown caution to the wind and married almost immediately upon meeting her. She had died of consumption, many years ago. But Arianna had seen paintings, and they had been beautiful.

She touched her cheek. Was she beautiful, as well? Could she win the heart of a man so completely that nothing else mattered except for her—not the world around him, money, society, position?

She pushed away from the dressing table, suddenly determining that she wouldn't actually attend her father's wedding.

Rather, it would be a far more intriguing time to note the guests, and perhaps venture out from Moorhaven when those concerned with her welfare might be occupied elsewhere.

Maggie had nearly decided to tell Cecilia that she was sorry, she simply wasn't going out, when Clayton came into the parlor to tell her that Lady de Burgh had arrived.

It wasn't much of a surprise to discover that the

coachman approaching her was a strapping young fellow, very tall, and with massive shoulders. He informed her with the greatest courtesy that Lady de Burgh awaited her in the coach.

When she reached the coach, she found herself helped in and embraced by Cecilia. But once sitting at Cecilia's side, she informed her friend, "Cecilia, I'm sorry, I'm afraid I'm rather exhausted, all the preparations, you know." She hadn't actually done anything; Charles had seen to it all.

"Oh, dear! Please, you mustn't disappoint me now!" Cecilia begged.

"Perhaps a quiet supper," Maggie said, giving in.

"Oh, yes, a quiet supper!" Cecilia agreed. The coach was already moving. Cecilia produced a small valise. "Now . . . for the fun of this supper, let's dress up, shall we?"

"Cecilia, I was thinking of a lovely restaurant not far from here—"

"Oh, but we've reservations at a very exclusive place. Trust me, knowing you, you'll never have this opportunity again. Now, here."

Cecilia dug into the bag. She handed Maggie a deep red wig and a cocky little hat with a tremendous amount of rich plumage.

"Where on earth are we going?"

"There's a great cape, and a mask for you, too."

"A mask?"

"It's a Venetian supper club," Cecilia said with a laugh. "Lovely, exotic food."

"Cecilia, we dress up in masks for supper? I'm not sure—"

"Oh, come on. Live on the wild side for just one

night! My dear friend, you are about to marry a man old enough to be your grandfather. You've not the least problem getting out and about on your causes. Have one night for yourself."

Before she could protest again, Cecilia had grabbed Maggie's small bonnet and was replacing it with the wig and mask. Maggie had forgotten the extent of her friend's acquired wealth. The mask was jeweled and gorgeous.

"Sit still, will you?" Cecilia begged. "Let me get this on straight!"

Cecilia was determined. Finishing her task, she sat back, surveying her handiwork. "Beautiful. You make a stunning redhead. So exotic." She leaned toward the window. "Here! Here we are!"

They hadn't come terribly far from Mayfair, but Maggie hadn't been watching their direction. The coach came to a stop. Cecilia dug into the bag again, coming out with a dark wig for herself, and a mask with dangling gems.

"Capes!" she muttered, and reached across the coach. "Now, you must wear this! Trust me, no one will recognize you. No one will ever know that you were here!"

They stepped from the coach. Maggie looked around quickly, but knew that she had never been on this street. The building they were approaching was Georgian in style, and only slightly seedy, she noted, as they hurried up the steps.

She could hear music. As they entered the doorway, they were met by a woman in gray satin and lace. Her dress was quite proper; her hair was almost orange, and her cheeks were highly rouged. From the entry, a door led to a theater. A woman was singing, and Maggie could hear the laughter of men and women alike.

"It's a dance hall?" Maggie whispered to Cecilia.

"Yes, and no!" Cecilia told her.

"Ah, Mrs. Peabody?" the woman with the orange hair said to Cecilia.

"Yes, indeed, and I've a companion with me. Mrs. Bird."

What ridiculous names Cecilia was using! Maggie began to feel a twinge of real unease.

"Branson will escort you to your table."

"Cecilia . . ." Maggie murmured.

She felt a touch on her shoulder and turned. Her jaw nearly fell. Branson was a huge man, ebony black, dressed in nothing but what appeared to be native African garb—a concoction of grasses that fell from his waist to his mid thigh.

"Live a little! You're entering the realm of eternity and death tomorrow!" Cecilia whispered. Later, those words would come back to haunt Maggie.

She might have left at that moment, except that Branson was blocking the doorway by then, and Maggie decided it would be easier to reach their table—and escape.

"We're going *downstairs!*" Cecilia told her with pleasure.

Maggie found herself between Cecilia and Branson. They passed around the center theater, and along a hallway. One door was slightly ajar. Maggie took a peek in as they passed. She was shocked. A girl dressed up in harem garb was lying on a pillow with a massive fellow, sharing a pipe with him.

"This is an opium den!" Maggie said, shocked as they reached a bookcase.

"Only if you choose," Cecilia assured her. "Have you tried smoking?" she asked Maggie.

"No!"

Branson pushed at the bookcase, which proved to be a well-disguised door. There were steps that led downward.

"Really, Cecilia—"

"Maggie, we'll only stay a few minutes if you're too uncomfortable. But, please! Give yourself a chance to have fun. You can't be that much of a prig!"

It shouldn't have mattered what Cecilia suggested. She should have fled right then. But for some silly reason, perhaps because she was marrying a man three times her age, she allowed herself to be led down the stairs.

There was a stage. There were a few tables. Other diners were masked, in capes, and probably wearing wigs as well.

Branson led them to a table. As she was seated, Cecilia allowed her fingers to cruise down the ebony musculature of Branson's chest. He smiled, perfect white teeth flashing in a proud face.

Then he was gone. "What kind of entertainment is it onstage?" Maggie asked."Music? Drama?" She doubted the latter.

"There's music, of course," Cecilia said. She smiled wickedly.

Another man appeared at the table. He was white— but dressed like Branson. He poured champagne into the glasses at their table. Maggie turned away as he did so, and felt her heart thunder against her chest as she saw the server at the next table, where two men were seated. Their server was a woman. Her long dark hair was free-flowing down her back. She, too, wore a grass skirt, and nothing else. Her breasts were bared. Very large, and it appeared her nipples had been rouged.

She gasped aloud.

"Maggie, please!" Cecilia gasped. "You're not behaving in the least Bohemian!"

Maggie clamped her jaw shut and turned back to Cecilia. "I'm not Bohemian!" Maggie informed her.

"May I suggest that you gaze upon young male flesh tonight? As of tomorrow, you may never have the opportunity again."

"I don't think I want the opportunity!" Maggie said.

"Drink your champagne, and I swear, the food will be delicious."

She took a long swallow of champagne. It seemed the thing to do. The champagne was excellent. She swallowed down the glass of it, attempting to steel her nerves.

Cecilia, looking at her, giggled. "Oh, Maggie, you're so deliciously shocked! Come now, men have always taken such pleasures, and absolutely nothing is thought of it. Men will be men, or so they say. And women are given the lot to look away, and pretend that the world is all morality, and sex is in the dark . . . and, well, for your sake, I hope it's in the dark as of tomorrow!"

"Cecilia, that's terrible."

"Maggie, it's true."

"I'm certain this place is illegal!" Maggie hissed.

Cecilia leaned closer. "That's a perfectly legitimate dance hall upstairs! Maybe not the Royal Opera, but . . . legal! Besides, relax, I can promise you, there will be no police raids tonight."

"And how can you guarantee that?" Maggie hadn't even thought of a raid, but the concept was just dreadful. She could see the headlines: "TAINTED BRIDE OF THE ILLUSTRIOUS LORD CHARLES, VISCOUNT LANGDON, ARRESTED IN BAWDY-HOUSE RAID!"

"There," Cecilia said.

"There what?"

Cecilia lowered her voice still further. "At the far table. That's the Prince of Wales."

Maggie gasped. "No!"

"Maggie, quit staring!"

"But—!"

"Please, everyone is quite discreet here."

Discreet. She couldn't help looking at the man in question. He was almost ridiculously dressed in a wig reminiscent of the age of Charles II. His mask was dark leather with a huge nose.

"Maggie, don't stare!"

She turned back around. She wasn't sure when the half-naked man had returned to refill her glass, but it was full again. She swallowed it down, wincing slightly, and asked Cecilia, "How do you know that it's the Prince of Wales?"

"Trust me, I know."

Maggie stared at her and gasped. "You've had an affair with him!"

Cecilia smiled. "Eustace prefers the son. I like the father."

A plate of oysters was set before them. "Food for

lovers!" Cecilia teased, delicately slipping the meat of one down her throat. "I'll bet that Lord Charles will see to it that they're served tomorrow."

"Cecilia, please, the intimate moments between a couple do not constitute the entire meaning of life!"

"Shh! The show is beginning!"

And indeed, it was. The curtain on the small stage was slowly being drawn. A giant shell was present stage center. The gaslights in the room drew very low.

The shell opened. Slowly, to the music of a sitar, a woman began to emerge. Strawberry hair curled over her naked shoulders and down to her thighs as she elegantly rose to stand within the shell. A drumbeat slowly began to throb. Two young men suddenly leapt onto the stage, dancers, yes, their movement that of the very well trained, but they were not the customary figures Maggie had seen at the ballet. They were clad in skintight leggings and nothing more.

A story began to evolve, the first dancer, the darker of the two, attempting to seduce the young woman— *Venus rising,* Maggie thought dryly. The second then vied for her attentions. Harder and harder the two tried.

Then the first abducted the girl, sweeping her away into his arms. As the second man pretended to search for the lost beauty, the first began his seduction.

It was absolutely, totally indecent. Maggie thought she should look away.

But she didn't.

The female dancer was flat on the floor, while the male moved above her, touching her, not really touching her, evoking thoughts of all manner of things. His body began to gyrate, and Maggie realized that her mouth was open again as she watched—she had never imagined that someone could so completely simulate the act of intercourse without having it. It was decadent. Total debauchery.

She had to get up and leave immediately.

She was terrified to move. Horrified that anyone would see her witnessing such an act.

She remained in her chair, all but frozen there.

Suddenly, the second man was there, tearing the first from the beauty, his actions showing his fury, and his hunger. And the girl was up, her body rubbing against his, her elegant long legs curling around him in a manner which was surely not natural for the human body.

Then both would-be lovers were with the girl. She was pressed between them, and again came a simulation of movement. From the edges of the stage, more young dancers began to crawl on. One of the men was drawn away, and a beauty with a length of blond hair crawled behind the girl with the red, and they writhed to the floor together.

It was all quite disgusting!

And absurdly . . . evocative.

Maggie heard the scrape of a chair and turned her head. The diners themselves were beginning to rise; they were disappearing into little curtained alcoves in the shadows on the sides of the room. She turned once more to see that the man in the Charles II wig and mask was approaching their table, offering his hand to Cecilia.

To Maggie's horror, Cecilia giggled, and accepted the hand.

She was about to shout a protest, then realized
that she shouldn't shout her friend's name, but then,
neither should Cecilia even think about deserting
her in this room!

Something brushed her body and she turned.
One of the nearly naked dancers was now at her side,
gyrating his way down to his knees before her.

"No, no, thank you . . . no," she murmured. He was
persistent. She rose, trying to wedge the chair between them. He seemed to think that she wanted to
play. She started to back around the table. "Young
man, quite seriously, no!"

She backed into something.

Someone.

Another of the dancers.

"No, and I mean no!" she cried, panic setting in.
She turned and shoved hard at the chest in front of
her. "No!"

The man started to drag her against him, against
his oiled and formidable chest. She realized that
she might well find herself the victim of rape, because it seemed evident that they assumed she had
come for the fantasy of the chase and the ravage-
ment.

She wanted to skin Cecilia alive. But her friend
wasn't there—she was behind one of the curtains
with the bewigged fellow, whether he truly was or
wasn't the Crown Prince.

She started to scream. The man behind her clamped
his hand over her mouth. The one in front began to
lift her.

Then, another man in a Charles II wig and a huge-
nosed mask stepped up from behind.

"Whoa, there, my friends. The lady has been waiting for me."

The dancers were still. The new arrival passed a number of coins into one of their hands. "Share, my good chaps, but the lady comes with me."

"Wait! The lady doesn't belong with anyone; she wishes to leave!" Maggie exploded.

She was instantly released into the arms of the stranger. She stared up at him, wondering if her own mask hid the sheer panic, which must now be more than obvious in her eyes. "Let me go this instant! This lady isn't with anyone!" she cried, and catching his shoulders, did her best to fiercely wound him with her knee.

"Stop it, Maggie, stop it!"

The voice was familiar. And so were the eyes. Steel gray now, glaring at her from behind the mask. His teeth were clenched.

Jamie, she thought.

But she was in a fever to get away. Out of this place.

And he had either thought she would recognize him instantly—or not fight. She had struck gold. He was in pain, and for a moment, his hold had eased. Instinctively, she jerked free. For an instant, she was free. She tore back the way they had come to the table, discovering that now the staircase was dark. Still, she stumbled up, and in her wake, came . . . someone.

She came to a landing and sought the door out. Darkness surrounded her. She slammed against the wall before her, but it was solidly closed, and she stumbled back.

Into a body.

The body of someone large and powerful. Fingers gripped her shoulders.

She was pulled back.

"No!" she cried, and threw herself against the darkness where the door should have been, and this time, when the hands came upon her, they plucked her up physically, and she started to scream in sheer terror, certain that she was about to be dragged back down into a true den of iniquity.

Chapter 7

"Damn you, shut up, they're coming!"

Jamie. It was Jamie there with her, surely intent on helping her out.

She heard footsteps pounding up the stairs. Others were definitely in pursuit. Instinct caused her to inhale to scream again, but his groping hand found her mouth, and a whisper shocked her to a further state of ice-cold panic.

"Maggie! For the moment, may I suggest you pretend to be with me, and most happily so? Don't you understand? They think that pursuit and force is part of what you want!"

She managed to nod, her mind racing.

How had he come to be here? Had he agreed with Cecilia's invitation after all?

She was shaking, aware that other footfalls were hitting the stairs, coming closer and closer.

He set her down and his arms came around her.

In the darkness she could see nothing, but felt him searching the obstruction they had hit for a secret catch. A moment later, the door sprang open.

Maggie burst out, with Jamie in her wake. The place was a blur as she streaked through the hallway to the entrance. From the dance hall, she could hear raucous laughter and applause. The woman remained at the door.

Ignoring her, Maggie caught the handle and ripped it open. She flew out onto the pathway to the house, racing for the street.

"Stop! Damn you, Maggie, stop now, before you become the victim of a common thief or footpad!"

She came to a dead standstill, chilled, and miserable.

"My carriage is around the corner," Jamie said, reaching her, turning her to face him.

She nodded. Her own misery, the way that she was shaking, made her behave very badly. "So . . . you must come here often, sir."

"Just come and get in the carriage, Maggie."

Stiffly, she accepted his arm. She stumbled as he led her around a corner and down a gas-lit street to where his carriage waited. His coachman stood by the door, a tall, well-proportioned fellow with an easy smile and pleasant hazel eyes.

With his assistance, she nearly tripped trying to enter the conveyance. Jamie, thanking Randolph, came up behind and caught her by the hips, keeping her from falling. He crawled in to take the seat opposite from her.

"Ready, Randolph!" He tapped the roof of the carriage, and it began to move. Once it did so, he dragged the mask from his face, and the heavy wig from his head. She hadn't stirred. He reached across the carriage, far too close, as he performed the same service for her.

He sat back then. She knew that her own hair was tumbling down her face in a riot of dishevelment. The bodice of her evening dress was askew.

"Well, it was good to see that you weren't intent on enjoying all the entertainments of Madame Bridey's salon," he said dryly. "What was this tonight? Another of your causes? Your life does seem to be full of secrets. Have you done this before?"

"Don't be ridiculous! Never!"

"You did seem anxious to leave."

"She . . . Cecilia . . . she said it was a supper club."

"It is, of a variety. Surely, you understood that variety?" he asked, his tone harsh, as if she definitely had.

"No, I didn't."

"Oh, come! From that conversation you were having with her this afternoon?"

Maggie felt the blood rush to her face. "Evidently, you're familiar enough with the place!"

"I've been there before, yes."

"Do you know what?" she demanded icily. "Cecilia is actually quite right. Men are all really wretched creatures, thinking that their indecencies are acceptable—just because they're men! You're all horrid!"

"Sorry, didn't mean to rescue you. Shall I bring you back?"

"Yes, perhaps you should."

He arched a brow and made as if he were about to

tap on the roof of the carriage. It was a bluff, but it worked, because she wasn't quite certain. "No!"

"You know what would have happened if I hadn't been there?" he inquired.

"Yes, I'd have broken the nose of one of those fools."

"A fool to the very end, no matter what, Maggie?" he asked softly.

And to her true and absolute horror, she felt the sting of tears bite into her eyes. The champagne. She had swallowed too much too quickly. "Really, what difference does it make? It isn't as if your uncle believes he's marrying a chaste and naive innocent. I've been married before."

"So, it wouldn't have made any difference—if the dancers hadn't been stopped?"

This was a lesson to her, of course. Another lesson about her willful life. She wondered if he would believe that she had never even dreamed of doing something like this in all her life.

She stared at him, frowning, her temper suddenly flaring again. "You followed the two of us there, knowing we were going?"

"That's rather evident, isn't it?"

"So you were there all along. You were at the table with the Prince of Wales!"

"I was there all along," he said.

She flew across the carriage suddenly, in such a whirl and rage that she managed to catch him with a firm slap against the cheek. He swore, catching her flailing arms so that she wound up sitting on him, captured on one side of the carriage.

"What in God's name . . . ?" he demanded, somewhat breathless in his attempt to keep her struggling arms from freedom.

"You let me go into that panic! You let those men come up to me, trap me, terrify me . . . and you were there all along! You—rat, cad, bastard!"

"You shouldn't have been there! I remember you swearing what a good and loyal wife you intend to be."

"I'm no one's wife at this minute!"

"That's not the point. You act rashly all the time. It's amazing that you've managed to live so long. Down into the East End. Into the very homes of villains who are not at all averse to murder when the purpose warrants. Into every pesthole in the city!"

"I'd have never agreed to go anywhere with Cecilia tonight—if it hadn't been for you!"

"Oh?"

"You dared me, you oaf!"

"I didn't dare you to do anything."

"Wait! I left the two of you together. Were you supposed to meet Cecilia there? Slide behind one of those curtains with her? Were you waylaid in your purpose by royalty? Am I saved tonight simply because you were outranked?"

"What?" he all but shouted incredulously. She remained on his lap. Her wrists were painfully vised by his fingers.

"It's none of my concern, but you two were practically making arrangements when I left. But don't you dare engage in such affairs and then behave as if I'm the one at fault!"

He was silent for a second. The whole of his body seemed to be clenched so tightly that it was dangerously explosive. "Your friend Cecilia interests me not in the least, my lady. I was afraid of something like this, when I saw you with her today. She is usually cautious, but despite that, she has quite a reputation. Apparently, you are aware of all kinds of social evil, yet blind to many things taking place in your own circles. And I am really growing weary of rescuing such a nasty, ungrateful trollop!"

"Trollop! How dare you!"

"Easily—damned easily. Considering we have just left an erotic sex show!"

"Oh!" she cried furiously, yet finding no quick comeback.

The carriage jolted to a halt.

"You're home," he told her.

He wasn't confining her anymore, she realized. She jumped back to her own side of the carriage, staring at him.

She could see that Randolph had come down from the driver's seat and awaited Jamie's motion to open the door.

Maggie stared at Jamie, disturbed.

A glance out the window had assured her that Justin indeed was home; the carriage was in the drive, and the horse had been stabled for the night.

A light burned in the parlor. It wasn't late; whatever had made her brother choose to stay home tonight?

She was a disaster. A complete disaster. Hair completely mussed, clothing all untidy. Her nerves were quite shattered.

Staring at her, Jamie arched a brow. "Alas, this doesn't look good, does it?" He leaned out the window. "Randolph, the lady had a rather bad night. I think we should take her home for a brandy before she tries to sleep."

"Ah, sir! Home, then."

Randolph returned to the driver's seat. They heard his command to the horse and his flick of the reins. The horse jolted back into motion. "Does this suit you, m'lady? At my town house, you can take all the time you need to get yourself together. Don't worry. This is my coach, and Randolph is my personal servant. He can pull around to the back. You'll not be seen coming, or going."

She suddenly buried her face in her hands. "All right."

His "town house" was not a row house, but a single large dwelling, old, dating back to Tudor times, she was certain, and elegantly designed, as if it had been planned, perhaps, for the mistress of a king. A sweeping drive brought the carriage around to the rear, which was surrounded by lush vegetation. In fact, the house sat in its own private park, not far from Buckingham Palace, in the St. James area of the city. They exited in the carriage house, a generous structure with a passageway through to the manor itself. They came into an empty kitchen where lights had been left burning low.

"Come along. There's a guest room up the stairs; you'll find all you might need," Jamie told her.

The whole of the house was darkened. She was certain he had live-in servants to keep such a large place so immaculate, but if so, they had long retired. She saw little of his home, but found herself curious, and tried, as they hastily moved along, to see all that she could. The parlor was elegant with oak furniture and damask coverings, and was warmed by a hearth that ran almost the length of a wall. A door stood ajar that led to a library with a large mahogany desk occupying much of the far center of the room and endless rows of books covering the walls. A staircase, curving handsomely against a back wall, was not terribly broad, but the old oak banisters were richly carved.

Up the stairs, Jamie pointed down the hall to a door. "The guest room." He turned. "My door," he said, indicating the one at the end of the hallway. "Whenever you're ready, I'll see you home."

She nodded stiffly and forced a "Thank you."

He didn't respond, but walked the distance down the hall to his door.

She hesitated, then hurried into the room he'd indicated to her. Quite nice, for guests, she determined. But then, he lived alone. Or, at least, she thought that he did. And certainly, if he was in the Queen's service, in whatever capacity, he was making a fine income. And, of course, he was Charles's nephew. Great nephew. But she didn't think that he derived much income from his uncle's estates. Then again, what did she really know at all?

The bed was pleasantly large and had a canopy hung with fine white Belgian lace. There was a light wood wardrobe in the room, a small secretary against a wall, and a dressing room. There was also a very modern bathroom, the size of which indicated that it had recently been remodeled, perhaps from another small room that might have extended off the guest room.

A sink offered running water, hot and cold, and she washed her face, then looked into the mirror above the basin, and saw her reflection with horror. Pins were escaping everywhere; she needed a brush badly.

There was one out on a dressing table. She returned to the room and began plucking the pins from her hair. In a few minutes, she found that she couldn't quite reach the tangle of hair and pins that had knotted in the back. She hesitated, gritted her teeth, winced, and then stepped into the hallway and hesitantly walked to the door he had indicated as his own.

At her rap, she heard "Come in?"

He had shed his greatcoat and made himself a brandy. His own quarters were both masculine and comfortable. The canopy on his bed was broad and in a deep crimson velvet. The bedroom itself was in an alcove, and beyond the minor arches was a sitting area, where he now sat casually on a small sofa, sipping the brandy, staring into the hearth, where a fire burned warmly.

He turned as she entered.

"Sorry." She indicated the back of her hair. "If you would be so kind . . . ?"

"Come here, then."

He set the brandy down on the small occasional table before him. She moved to the little sofa and gingerly took a seat before him, turning her back to him. She felt his fingers move expertly into her hair.

"A fine mess you've made," he murmured.

"Of many things," she agreed softly.

"If you were going to be my wife, I'd probably see to it that you were locked in on a daily basis."

"Thank God I'm not going to be your wife."

"Thank God."

Pins were plucked from her hair and cast upon the table near the brandy glass. With his fingers, he began to work through the snarls, seeking more stray pins. She felt the brush of his fingers against her nape. She closed her eyes, but when she did, she envisioned the very graphic display she had witnessed that night.

"Where do they get people willing to perform so?" she whispered.

"Are you deceiving yourself, my lady? Haven't you seen the poverty that afflicts so many? The young and poor consider themselves privileged to find work in such establishments. Surely you're aware of what women sell themselves for on the streets? Nothing. The smart pocket their earnings, do their best to acquire very rich patrons. Those who are frivolous too often join their brothers and sisters in the brothels, and then, the streets and lowest gin houses. I need a brush." He stood for a moment, striding across to his dresser, finding what he required, and returning. He remained standing, physically turning her to get to the tangles and working with what she thought was a rare patience for him. He set the last long, smoothed lock against her shoulder, and his hands tarried there for a moment. "My God, you're still shaking. Can this be the woman who gave whores a lecture on condoms in the dankest slum of the city?"

He came around her, sitting so that he faced her

then, looking into her eyes. She lowered her head and the mass of her freshly tended hair fell about her face like a waterfall. He smoothed back a side, tucking it behind her ear. "You need a brandy."

Did she? She'd already imbibed far too much champagne. But he was up, striding to the decanter on a table by a floor-length window that must have overlooked the rear gardens. He brought her a snifter of the rich amber liquor, handed it to her, picked up his own, clicked it to hers, and said simply, "Cheers."

She tried a weak smile and swallowed down a sip. Hot and fiery, it burned her throat. He shook his head. "I'm still at a loss. Surely, one couldn't have been more blatant about their activities than Cecilia was today!"

"You were eavesdropping."

"Yes, of course."

"Maybe, I don't know. Maybe I did crave something more, before, before stating vows before God," she murmured. She looked up at him defiantly. "As I said, I'm not married yet!"

"No, you're not, are you?" he said, very, very softly, almost as if he hadn't spoken at all. Then he reached down, catching her hands, drawing her up to him, and taking her into his arms.

"Ah, lady, if there is something you feel you must have, then I am here."

It was incredible, it was bizarre, or perhaps it was merely the end of a night that had begun with such wicked suggestion. The minute he touched her, then drew her against him, she suddenly knew that Cecilia had, oddly enough, been right in a way. She had wanted something, needed something, as a last fling. But it hadn't been the practiced display or manipulation of strangers. It had been this one and only sensation, coming into his arms, and feeling the uniqueness of this man's scent and vibrance, stroke and taste. His fingers curled into the hair he had carefully tended, drawing her eyes to his, and though he didn't speak, he waited several seconds, and then his lips touched hers, and he was oddly gentle at first, then that streak of pure fire and hunger that had gripped them once before took flight, and the way his tongue moved within her mouth was far more evocative than any act she had witnessed that night, far more intimate.

Clothes were so complicated; they might have been awkward, and yet, when his lips left hers, he turned her deftly, fingers amazingly nimble on tiny hooks and eyes, on draws, strings, and stays. Perhaps it was the champagne, the brandy, both, but it seemed that she simply stepped from a sea of clothing, like an old skin left behind, and turned back into his arms. Then memory was awakened in a surge of sensation as she felt the touch of his hands against her naked flesh, and it seemed that each finger branded a new wave of heat against her skin, and each around a tiny streak of lightning to rip through the length of her, grounding in the center, the apex of her thighs. His mouth ravaged and pillaged her once again, met the heady fever that had taken hold of her, a complete abandonment of right and wrong, and what was to come tomorrow.

She was not so adept. Her fingers trembled. Subtly, rather than be choked, he slipped the knot from his cravat, shed waistcoat and shirt, and enveloped her in his embrace once again. Her breasts crushed against the wall of his chest, muscle that was taut and honed, sleek and hot and welcoming. His palm cradled her cheek, and she looked in his eyes, her own captured there as his fingers teased down her throat, brushed her collarbone, and curled around her breast. Her breath caught, and she nearly cast back her head to shriek, for so simple a touch seemed to rouse so much, and again, the streaks of fire and light, radiant as the sun, seemed to tear through the length of her. Then she discovered that all that occurred so far had been a tease, for his lips fell upon her shoulder, then trailed down the valley between her breasts. His tongue created strokes of lava across her chest, teased the peak of her nipple before the caress of his mouth fastened around it. She had shivered, now she quaked. And as he moved lower, she realized that there had been times tonight that she had not been able to draw her eyes from the stage because this was what she had been imagining. She had watched the players and thought, *yes, that is where I want his hand to stray, where his touch should probe. God, yes, that is where I would have his kiss fall upon me . . .*

He far exceeded all visions. Fingers drew a trail, followed the liquid paintbrush of his tongue, tending to ribs, brushing against her navel, laving a hip. And then . . . lower. A touch of fire, stroke of silk, searing damp wetness, giving, demanding. She thought, then, that she would surely fall, knew she could not. His hands drew a pattern over her hips, gripped and held her buttocks, pulled her ever more tightly against the wanton erotism of raw seduction and carnal pleasure, and in the end, she cried out, falling despite herself, yet falling only into his embrace, dazed, in a state of intoxication no sweet amber liquor could bring. She looked up into his face as he carried her to the bed, the awe she felt at that moment staving off embarrassment, and her hand moved to caress his jaw, and she felt wonder again, just at the proportions of it, and then the feel, slightly rough, of his shaven chin, and again at the strength of it, and the sleek bronze of it, the tautness of the skin . . .

He came down beside her, every movement supple and controlled, and shed shoes and hose and trousers, and she lay and watched him, mesmerized by each movement, ripple of muscle, stretch of flesh. She had been like someone stunned, silent and unmoving, but when he turned back to her then, she found a strange new life. A small sound escaped her lips and she rose, eager to meet him again, almost throwing herself against him, and burying her face against the wall of his chest, savoring the richness of him before pressing him back, fevered to respond to every touch, caress. To know him, breathe him, feel him, seemed imperative, an urgent drowning in a swell of sensation. There was a second in which she thought that she was insane, this was insane, against every grain of moral fiber that she had once thought that she possessed. And yet, to be with him seemed the most ethical tenet in the world—it was right, it was incredible, it was everything she desired in life.

And would never have again.

And so she teased and savored, admiring the curve of his calf, the line of his thigh, tautness of buttocks, length of back. His spinal column was fascinating, and she explored it with her fingers and kisses, and she adored his shoulders, abdomen, and below with the same preoccupation, until she was caught against him with the unyielding strength of his arms, brought beneath him, captured in the gray mist of his eyes. In seconds he had thrust within her, sunk into her being, and she felt as if she were a delicate shell, cracked and shattered by that intrusion, crystalized then, and made into something new. His body arched and moved, so subtly at first that the rub against the most intimate of her flesh was like the sweetest taunting, and then it was as if the whole of the earth shook with the fervor and passion of his rhythm. She heard the clamor of the wind, and it was her breath, the thunder of a summer storm, and it was the cadence of her heart. Sleek, damp with perspiration, earthy and real, she felt the scratch of his ebony chest hair against her breasts, and it, too, was arousing, and she felt the pounding reality of desire and instinct, and the wonder of something that, to her, seemed so much more. Anchored to the bed, in the most natural of human needs, she felt, too, as if she were still encapsulated in silver, something shimmering, something better, and panting, still seeking the utmost oblivion.

It burst upon her with such a wave of force that she clawed at his shoulders, crying out despite herself, heedless of who might or might not hear. Raw pleasure gripped her like a vise, allowing her to come down only slowly, creating tremors in her like aftershocks. She was excruciatingly aware of the moment when he climaxed for it seemed that a flood of liquid

fire washed throughout the length of her, as if it
spread to her every limb, indeed, her mind and soul.
And then, again, she heard her breath, felt the slightly
rough embroidered pattern of damask spread beneath her nakedness, never torn from the bed in
their sudden state of urgency. Her cheek was slightly
chafed, she knew, her lips swollen, thighs sore, and
yet . . .

The drumbeat of her heart was low, very low, and
he slipped to her side, not turning away from her,
but staring up at the ceiling in the gas-lit room. She
realized somewhere at that point that she should be
feeling an agonizing shame, that she should be sorry,
that she needed confession in the worst way, and that
she was a horrible human being. By right, she knew
these things, and still, all that she could think was
that he was magnificent; she had thought that she
could never want anyone again, really never care
about anyone again.

If she cared about him, she wasn't just horrible,
she was stupid to the extreme.

She closed her eyes, realizing that he had turned
to her. And she felt the coolness of the air strike the
damp nudity of her skin, and she suddenly wanted to
draw a cover around herself, but there was none, for
their weight and bodies kept it firmly affixed to the
bed. She couldn't bring herself to open her eyes, yet
when he touched her again, her lashes flew open,
and she fixed her eyes upon his face. He was not staring at her face however, but watching his hand as it
trailed softly over her breasts and abdomen, belly,
mound, and thighs. He studied her, gazed at her
with a dark fascination that seemed to bring a rush of

crimson to every limb and particle of her flesh. She was flushed to feel that so slight a contact could rouse sensation once again, that she could have turned into his arms, eagerly known it all again.

"Now, it's getting late," he murmured.

"Yes." She could think of nothing to say.

"Hell," he murmured and drew her against him again. "There should be time. But then, there isn't any, is there?"

And so it began again. And it shouldn't have been so staggeringly cataclysmic, so volatile, so base, and so beautiful. She'd always heard that if you wanted something desperately, simply having it would take the urgency away. Like a hunger for a particular fruit, or food. And yet, she had wanted him desperately.

The hunger was not eased.

Only increased.

And so it was that the time slipped away, and the things that should have been said were not. There was room for nothing but savoring each taste of the fruit, relishing feel and taste and sight and touch . . . dying a little, as written by poets she had not believed before this night, not even when she had loved before.

And somewhere, the wonder turned into exhaustion and dreams, for the next thing she knew, he was urgently waking her.

"My God, it's nearly dawn. I've got to get you home."

He was up, and it was over. Naked, supple, sleek, he drew his fingers through the darkness of his hair as he headed for his bath.

She didn't want him coming back to find her still

upon the bed. She rose, gathered the pieces of her clothing strewn about, and ran desperately for the door. As she threw it open, she prayed suddenly that she would not come so, stark naked, upon a member of his household.

God was with her. She did not.

She burst into the guest room, washed and dressed quickly. Her fingers shook as she tried to make neat work of a head of hair more tangled now than ever. Everything, she did with the most tremendous haste.

She burst back out into the hallway. His door remained as she had left it; closed. She stared at it a moment, tension and indecision ripping through her.

Then she turned and fled down the stairs, praying she would find Randolph in the kitchen.

She did.

He glanced up, and if he saw the tempest in her eyes or form, he gave no indication.

"Would you mind . . . I need to go home now."

"As you wish, my lady. Certainly, as you wish."

"You don't have to go through with it. You do not have to marry Charles. He will be terribly sad, but he's a fine man all the way through, and he will understand."

Jamie returned to the bedroom saying the words.

But she was no longer on the bed.

She had gone to the other room, he thought. Swearing, he reached for his readily available clothing, but there seemed to be pieces everywhere.

He dug his smoking jacket from the wardrobe, threw it around himself, and headed into the hall.

Mrs. Angsley, his housekeeper, was up and moving down the hall.

"Morning, sir!" she told him cheerfully.

"Morning. I had a lady in the guest room, Mrs. Angsley. Could you check on her for me, please?"

She was a broad, kindly woman with cherry red cheeks and stone gray hair. "Why, sir, I'd be happy to do so—but she's gone, I'm afraid."

"Gone?" he said, startled.

"Yes, Sir James; I believe so, for I heard Randolph pulling the carriage out, just as I came up the stairs."

"I see. Thank you."

He stepped back into his room, shut his door, and leaned against it.

So that it was it. Lies and pretense. Not all lies. She had wanted him as badly as he had wanted her.

But that hadn't been enough.

For the woman who had once married a commoner, he wasn't enough. She'd been offered nobility, and real riches, and she meant to have them.

At whatever cost.

She had betrayed Charles. Yes, she had not wed the man yet. He had betrayed his own uncle, a man he admired and loved. And yet, it had been with the same justification. Charles was not married to the lady as yet.

Well, fine. He'd dance at her wedding, then.

He glanced at the bed, where it seemed that he'd finally found just what he'd looked for, all of his life.

A mirage.

His mouth tightened, and with it, his heart hardened.

Indeed, he would dance at her wedding. Somehow,

he would step back. He would forget the night. He had known from the beginning that she was dangerous. Very dangerous to his uncle. He had known that she could twist men around her fingers, just with the strength of those blue eyes. He would have never thought that he might have found a strange vulnerability in her. Never imagined that he could be so taken himself. So entrapped. Halfway in love . . .

Never in love, he told himself harshly.

She was a lie, and that was it.

And if he ever saw her look at him again, as she had that night, endless blue eyes naked with sheer honesty and need, he'd call her a liar, a harlot, the worst kind of whore, right to her face.

To hell with her.

And still . . .

Images haunted him.

No.

Pain seemed to tear at his muscles, his limbs . . . his heart.

No.

He'd been a fool. He'd betrayed a man he loved.

Never again.

Never.

Chapter 8

Between Darby and Clayton, they had organized everything Maggie might need and it had been brought to Moorhaven the day before. Justin's clothing, too, for the ceremony, had been brought to the house. All they had to do was ride out to the estate.

Maggie had had no sleep and suffered with a pounding headache. She felt as if she moved about in fog, but when Justin knocked on her door, she smoothed her hair, and opened it with a pretense of well-being.

"Good morning."

"You don't have to do this."

She sighed softly. "Justin, we've gone through this so many times. Charles is a really good man. He's embraced the projects that mean so very much to me. He doesn't spend his life moving from his club to the nearest cigar bar. I'm going to be a countess; not a

bad lot in life. I'm resigned, now you must be resigned as well."

He looked away. "Well, you would break his heart
if you were to back out now, but, still, Maggie, Lord
knows you don't deserve to pay for the things I've
done. You know, I've been talking to some American
businessmen at my club, and do you know what we
could do? Emigrate! Start all over in a new country.
Get jobs!" He gave her a pretend shudder. "Seriously,
it's a possibility, don't you think?"

She smiled. "And forfeit the title and what little
land we have left to Angus?"

"We can go there and get rich, and I'll still be
Lord Graham. Then we can come back."

"Or I can just marry Charles, and make a good
man very happy. Go away—let me get ready."

With a sigh, he turned and left her.

She was quiet most of the trip to Moorhaven. And
when she arrived, she asked Darby if he would get
Lord Charles so that she could speak with him.

Darby returned. Charles was distressed. It was bad
luck to see his bride before the wedding. Maggie sent
back the message that she didn't believe in luck; she
wanted to talk to him in the chapel where they would
be married, and it was important.

Charles came, his concern apparent in the frown
that wrinkled his forehead.

She was standing in the aisle, feet from the altar,
when he came to her. She turned and he took her
hands. "My dear, have you decided that you cannot
marry such an old buzzard? If so, I will understand."

She shook her head. "I want to make sure that you

want me, that you know the woman you're marrying."

"From the first time I saw you, years ago, you were
a dream. And when it came to me that such a dream
might be realized, I knew all that I needed to know,"
he told her.

She shook her head. "But you don't really know
me. Not even after this time we've spent together."

He arched a white brow. "I know, Maggie, that
after your husband's death, you spent months in the
deepest grief. I know that you heard of a medium
who could speak with the dead, and that you attended a séance, and found out that the man was a
charlatan, who looked into the history of those he
would entertain, and found out little facts and the
like to make himself look credible. I know that your
brother was worried, and managed to feed the man
false information, and that you were hurt and horrified when you discovered the treachery. I knew a
year ago when you debunked a Madam Sara; please,
dear, it was in the papers, and I believe that you realized then that you'd been foolish to allow your name
into the news, because it would hinder your efforts if
you tried again to find the truth. I know, and I understand. I know about your forays into Whitechapel,
of course—I knew that financial charity was not
enough for you, that you had to see how the money
was being spent. I know these things, and I admire
them. I was not looking for a meek little maid to do
as I said, my dear."

She smiled, touching his face. His very dear face.

"And I know how you have fought for social reform, and that you have always believed that privi-

lege comes with responsibility. I know that you did service in India, that you have lived your years in the most incredibly admirable fashion."

"Then what is it?"

"Charles, I loved my husband with all my heart."

"I know."

"But . . . what if I weren't exactly a pillar of virtue? What if . . . what if there had been someone else . . . since my marriage."

He lowered his head, then he looked at her, a very small smile on his lips. "Is it over?"

"It never really began."

"We're not married until we come into this chapel today, and say our vows. Your life before that moment means nothing to me. Naturally, what comes after . . . and there is nothing that you have done that could keep me from wanting to bind my life to yours. Unless you feel that you cannot bear to live with me. I do freely give you the opportunity to escape."

She shook her head. "I'm trying to give *you* the opportunity to escape."

"I am hopelessly wrapped in the chains of my own heart, my dear. I could only turn away if you were to say that you couldn't bear the sight of me." He brought her hands to his lips and kissed them tenderly. Something inside her heart shuddered, but there was another place within her where she knew just how truly fine a human being she would wed. She knew, too, from his eyes, from the passion in his voice, that he truly loved her.

And she could not hurt him. Nor, by any sense of right and wrong, could she renege when such arrangements for the welfare of her family had already been made.

She stroked back his rich white hair. "Charles, thank you. If you don't mind, I'd like to make a little peace with God."

"I will leave you. And when we meet again, rest assured, it will be the fulfillment of my dreams, and I don't care in the least how many men there were before in your life, for we'll begin life anew together."

He didn't kiss her. He smiled, dropped her hands, turned and left.

When he was gone, Maggie fell to her knees, asking for forgiveness.

And she hated herself because the most vile thoughts still came to mind to haunt her. *Was this right? How could it be? Jamie would still be in her life, he was Charles's great nephew, his heir—unless this marriage brought forth a son, and God help her, but that idea made her shudder. Memories of the night gone by were too vivid in her mind, and she knew that she could never go back, that she would always wonder. . . .*

And yet, Jamie didn't share his great uncle's belief that her worldly pursuits were in the least intelligent. He was quick to her rescue, but because of Charles. And he had felt that same desperate pull she had known herself, and they had spent a night together, but what did that mean? A moment's pleasure, and nothing more.

The Christ figure from the crucifix above the altar, carved hundreds of years ago, stared down at her with reproach.

"I will be a good wife to Charles, I swear it. I will be all that he wants!" she said, and she knew that she was pleading, seeking redemption for her sins. She suddenly felt that they had been many.

At last, she crossed herself, rose, and left the chapel. It was time to dress for her wedding.

As she left the chapel, she reflected that she might have told Charles that his daughter despised her, as well.

To hell with both Arianna and Jamie. She would be a good wife.

Despite the fact that the chapel was a small distance from the house, Justin could hear the music as he adjusted his cravat. He was late; his fingers kept tangling with themselves. He was to give his sister away.

He shook his head, annoyed with himself, afraid that even now, in the midst of the ceremony, he would suddenly rise and scream. He would protest. It would be horrible. He'd shout out that Sir Charles was an old, old man and his sister was young and good and beautiful and it was simply disgusting and wrong.

No, no. Lord Charles would have apoplexy from the horror. Maggie would probably drop dead on the spot with shame. She had sworn again and again that she wasn't just resigned to her marriage, she wanted it. And maybe it was true that the youth and desire once in her heart had died along with Nathan, and that her passions in life, with which Lord Charles could help her, were now of utmost importance to her.

Swearing, he started out to the hall, still trying to tie the cravat.

"Hell's fire and dog's balls!" he swore, quite certain that he was alone.

But a soft giggle alerted him to the fact that someone was near.

"Here! Let me help you, sir!"

A girl stepped out from the archway. She was dressed in a poor woolen cap, a servant's bonnet on her head. She must have been watching the pageantry below from the safety of the archway at the top of the landing.

"Can you help me?" he said. "And forgive my slip of the tongue."

"If only that were the only thing to forgive today!" she muttered.

"Pardon?"

"Oh, nothing!" she murmured.

"Will you help me?"

She stepped closer, leaving the shadows of the archway behind. His breath seemed to catch in his throat. He'd never seen skin so delicate, so pure, an ivory, almost as fine and white as snow. Her eyes were the darkest he'd ever seen. Her hair . . . a pure symphony in black velvet.

She paused, looking up at him. Her eyes widened as she surveyed him. She moistened her lips suddenly.

"I . . . I . . ." she stammered.

"I'm so sorry to ask your assistance," Justin said. He couldn't draw his eyes from hers. It seemed that he breathed her now. And what he inhaled was youth and beauty and purity. It was intoxicating.

He heard the damnable music again.

"I'm desperate!" he whispered.

"Yes, yes, let me help you."

She came closer to tie the cravat. Their faces, oh, God, just a whisper of a breath, and he'd be kissing her. A servant girl. Ah, imagine the scandal! The sister, marrying a man old enough to be her grandfather. The brother, taking up with a serving wench.

What the hell did he care? What had Maggie told him? Marry anyone, noblewoman or commoner, just so long as she was young and . . .

This incredible sweet beauty was young.

He felt the expulsion of her breath against his lower jaw, his lips. And he couldn't help himself. "You're . . . incredible," he whispered.

She shook her head. "It's not tied quite properly."

He smiled very slowly. She hadn't really moved away. He saw her eyes widen again, and the way that she looked at him, and he suddenly understood what all the poets meant when they said that their hearts sang. *Yes,* she felt it too, this wonder, amazement, sensation, incredulous belief that the entire world would be right, if only they were together.

He took hold of her shoulders suddenly, telling her, "Wait for me, please? Wait for me, until after the ceremony. I have to know you. And no, please, nothing, nothing . . . there is nothing not perfectly right in this, really. I'll . . . I'll explain."

The music rose high with a thudding urgency.

"I'll be back!"

Justin raced on down the stairs. Maggie was waiting for him in a little antechamber. The wedding itself was down a few steps from the grand salon, in the family chapel.

"Justin!" She was anxious and nervous, near to tears.

"Maggie!"

He stepped back, breathless again, amazed at the sight of his own sister.

She hadn't worn white. She was marrying for a second time. Neither had she chosen a beige or off-white. She had gone for a soft, aqua-toned blue.

And she was a vision, shattering, awe-inspiring. Her hair was free, her veil was attached to a small, pearled crown, one proper for the wife of a viscount. The veil was sheer, floating behind her. With her reddish-gold hair falling in waves behind her, she looked like a fairy queen, an ice queen perhaps, perfect in her face and form.

He took her hand.

"Please, Justin, we've kept them waiting."

They started across the salon.

He balked suddenly, almost weeping. "I can't do it, Maggie. I can't."

"Justin! I'm going with or without you!" she warned, and her voice threatened tears as well. "Please, please, please, don't do this to me now!"

"Maggie!"

He hugged her tightly.

"Go!" she whispered.

He nodded miserably and took a deep breath.

Then, with tremendous dignity, they started for the chapel.

The bride was late. Standing at Charles's side, Jamie wondered if that meant she was having difficulty going through with the wedding. For several moments, his sense of bitterness was tempered with hope.

Except that he shouldn't feel that way. One look at Charles, and he knew that the man was living for this dream. *And why not? He would have a lifetime of magic.*

Charles had confided in Jamie that he'd met Maggie earlier, here, in the chapel, that she had been near tears, that she had tried to make all kinds of confessions.

Jamie wondered then if he should make a confession of his own. Then, he thought, no. He could not. Because if the bride had decided to go through with it, he didn't have the right.

Bitterness filled him again. *She had been nothing less than fantasy and magic, as sensual as the earth, and something far above. Thinking of last night made his blood pound against his veins, and his cravat seem far too tight at his throat.*

She must have felt, surely, she had felt something of the same!

She would not come. She would not go through with this.

But there she was, on Justin's arm, coming into the chapel. And she was a vision. God, yes, her hair was loose, brushed to a high gloss, shining like a halo around her. Her eyes were as deep a blue as the ocean at its depths, her stature, her walk, her every movement, supple, graceful . . .

He almost groaned aloud. Almost spoke.

And then he saw his uncle's face.

His hands balled fiercely into fists at his side. He wouldn't speak, God help him, he wouldn't speak.

She had made her choice.

* * *

Maggie had chosen to keep the wedding as quiet as possible, and Charles had tried to accede to her wishes. But though the Queen had decided not to come, Her Royal Majesty had sent gifts and envoys, since Charles was one of her favorites. Maggie had attended some social functions in the last years, but admittedly, after her marriage to Nathan, she had not been on many guest lists.

So, she only knew half the names Justin murmured to her as they walked down the aisle and there were at least fifty people present. A few were her own friends from the limited circle she had maintained. Andrew and Missy Kelton, from her reading group. Sir Arnold Brighton and his daughter, Lindsey, from the Salvation Army. Father Vickers. She would have smiled at them as she passed, except that she couldn't seem to do anything other than keep one expression glued to her face.

There, naturally, was her Uncle Angus, her cousins, and their wives. Strange, she never seemed to visit her family. Today, they might have been as close as a band of thieves. She was marrying an important man, so naturally, they were in attendance. Frankly, she should be grateful that Angus had found the husband for her—and not an aging bride for Justin. Angus stood to gain a great deal, if Justin were to perish without a male heir. Before the demise of Angus's wife a good twenty-something years ago, she had given Angus three sons, Sean, Stuart, and Tristan. In turn, her cousins had married well, and their offspring included half a dozen boys. They were darling children, however, they weren't at the wedding. She enjoyed the boys, and many times, had tried to tell herself that it wouldn't be so terrible should one of them inherit the title.

It was only Angus himself who galled her so.

Angus, who watched her come down the aisle, an ever-calculating smile on his face.

She looked away.

Justin gave her a nudge in the ribs.

She realized that her brother was pointing out Her Grace, the Duchess, Lady Marian. Both the Prince of Wales and his son, Eddy, were in attendance, along with Princess Alexandra. That meant, certainly, that a number of the fashionably dressed fellows in attendance were guards for the royal family.

The royalty might have given her a start, except that her attention was diverted elsewhere.

Jamie stood beside Charles, somber and elegant in a black waistcoat, jacket, and trousers, and perfectly starched white shirt. His hair appeared as dark as pitch, an absolute opposite to the snow white cap of hair upon the groom.

He stared at her, straight at her. And she felt a shudder within, for he looked at her with such loathing, and such contempt!

How had he ever been so passionate, so vital, and so tender?

That had been last night . . .

And this was now. And now . . .

She had been engaged to Charles, and still, she had fallen into his arms so easily! Did he hate her just for that . . .

Or because he hated himself, just a little, too?

She missed a step, and nearly tripped. Her brother's strong arm kept her from falling. She quickly recov-

ered, and knew that she would be all right, as long as
she didn't look at Jamie.

When she refocused her gaze, she saw Mireau.
Very handsome in his formal attire, he was near the
front, and he smiled encouragingly to her.

You are beautiful, like an angel! he mouthed to her.

She managed a smile.

Then all the names and faces became a blur as her
brother handed her over to Charles. She was afraid,
at first, that she was going to have to tug away from
her brother. He didn't seem to want to let her go.
What a scandal that would make. Brother and sister
busy at fisticuffs in the midst of such a noble and
solemn rite!

But Justin released her at last and kept quiet
when the Very Reverend Father Ethan Miller asked
if there was anyone present who might object. Then
the ceremony went on, and Maggie felt as if she had
entered a netherworld, as if she were there, but not
there. She watched as if from afar, as if she had
somehow brought her soul to rest high above the
altar, as if the proceedings involved someone else
entirely, a shell of herself. She heard all the words
she had heard before, and she felt in her heart that
she was the greatest liar ever to live. Love, honor,
and obey? She did love Charles, but as a good
friend. Honor? Certainly, he was a man worthy of incredible honor. Obey?

Sadly, it wasn't in her chemistry to obey anyone,
and for one absurd moment, she considered stopping the Anglican priest to argue the point. Why
did such a promise have to be in a wedding ceremony? They were not living in the Dark Ages.

Women were doing incredible things, laws were changing, and . . .

"You may now kiss the bride!"

And Charles turned to her. She saw his smile, and felt him draw her close, and then he kissed her.

Dry parchment against her lips. She felt nothing, and even as that kiss ceremonially sealed her vows, she found herself remembering a touch that was liquid fire, glorious in the extreme, awakening every fiber of her being.

And then it was over. Charles's eyes were on her with sheer delight, and they had turned. A hail of rice fell upon them, and she was blinded as they walked back down the aisle.

Charles had hired a photographer, and the man waited for them just outside, determined to take advantage of the last rays of sunlight. He was every inch the Viscount then, noble and kind but authoritative, directing his guests as to where and when to pose. First, naturally, the royals were asked to join with the bride and groom, and they were charming. She had heard that the threesome had been at an opera house lately—the booming industry of the last decades had brought about many changes, and there were those who were heartily against what they considered the excesses of the Royal House. Perhaps with good reason, for though Maggie knew that the Queen was distressed by many conditions within the city of London and its surroundings, she was blind to many of the activities practiced within her own family.

She now knew, with certainty, that the Prince of Wales was a flagrant philanderer, and that Prince Eddy . . . had many different tastes.

There was a moment when she felt a small seizure of panic, as she wondered if the Prince of Wales himself might recognize her as being the woman at the table so near his own the night before. But he gave no sign, and Princess Alexandra was as sweet and courteous as one could hope.

The royals moved on to the house, where the reception would take place, and then, Charles wanted photographs with just himself and Maggie; then the wedding party, Justin and Jamie, then her family, including Angus, the sons, and the wives. Then his family, Jamie and his daughter.

Except that Arianna was not to be found.

He threatened no violence, and yet Maggie realized that she would not want to be his daughter, facing his displeasure.

"Jamie, then, if you will, with my new lady wife!" Charles said, beaming.

And so, she was stood beside Jamie, and in those terrible moments, he looked at her, and she felt as if she wanted to crawl beneath the earth and die. And though he was far too well-mannered and schooled in the mores of their society to make any outward show of his displeasure, she felt the way that he touched her as they stood for the camera. As if he had been forced to pick up dung in the streets, as if he could barely stand it until he could release her. It was as if he had touched something filthy beyond comprehension.

"My turn!" Mireau called happily.

She felt almost giddy with relief as her dear friend came to stand beside her, his warmth real, his friendship and loyalty always unconditional.

At last, the photo sessions came to an end. They

moved on to the house where an orchestra played, and a grand march began for their entry. Then, the first wedding dance, a waltz, and she was pleased to discover that she could fall into step with her new husband beautifully, and despite the tremors that had taken hold of her somewhere during it all, she could move about the floor without being an incredible embarrassment to Charles.

A magnificent dinner had been planned, and she had to marvel at the elegance and grace with which everything moved. Champagne was served, and she drank liberally, knowing she would need the fortitude for the hours to come. She met friends of Charles, and others she knew through her brother. She was walked around on her uncle's arm to speak with various people, all members of the elite, friends from his club, those he would consider to be the *right* people for her to nurture in her new life.

Each of her cousins and their wives greeted her warmly, watching her with a new esteem. Seriously, the boys were not so bad. Tristan told her that he had been studying some of the latest reports on work regarding investigations in France, and though he hadn't told his father yet, he was seriously considering police work himself. She encouraged him, and he admitted sheepishly that he hadn't yet admitted it to his wife.

"There is nothing wrong with honest work, Tristan," she told him.

"Easy for you to say."

"I'll support you, whatever you choose. So will Justin—and Charles!"

Tristan nodded, grinning slowly. "I may well need

your support, and you just might find that I'm forced to seek a bed within your walls."

"Tristan, the world has changed, and I believe that the rest of our family will have to figure that out soon."

He moved closer to her, speaking softly. "Indeed! It's actually getting quite frightening. There are so many people who feel that royalty and nobility alike take such advantage of their situation—the insurrectionists are often in the streets. The royals are often booed on the streets. Not Her Majesty, the Queen, of course . . . but there are others . . ."

She knew that he referred to the Prince of Wales, and his son, Eddy.

She looked to the group and noted that they were in deep conversation with her uncle, Charles, her brother, and a few other guests.

A few moments later, the threesome, followed by their "escorts," came to her side, wishing her well, saying their good-byes. The Prince of Wales assessed her rather openly, as if amused by the night ahead for Lord Charles. Eddy, whom she had met often enough in social circles, was simply pleasant. Princess Alexandra was lovely, and exceptionally sweet, apparently pleased in the company of her husband and son, and Maggie found herself wondering how the woman put up with her husband's behavior, and all that was constantly whispered.

But then, perhaps it was worth it all to her, for one day, she would be queen of the greatest empire in the world.

A trade-off . . .

Just as she had made her own trade-off, Maggie thought, and it was not a pleasant image in her mind.

When the royals departed, the discussion turned openly to the Crown, the state of the country, the shortcomings of the home secretary and the prime minister, and how it seemed that they were moving ever closer to disaster because way too many immigrants from other European countries found their way to English shores.

She stood with Charles, listening to Lady Marian give a tirade on how they wouldn't need to worry about the dreadful conditions in the East End if they could just keep the riff-raff from spilling across the channel. "Why, most of them just believe that they can come here and live off the charity of the land—or worse! Stealing their incomes from those who have been born to class or even those gentlemen who had created such fine businesses!"

"Oh, come, Marian!" Charles said. "We've come a long way from the days of the Regency. Remember, we've our modern police forces now, and those fellows do extraordinary work. Imagine life before the Police Act of 1829."

"Pish-posh!" Marian said. "Now we've police! And we've decided that horrible criminals deserve the decency of private executions, and we've turned prisons into places of solitude and comfort."

"We're trying to truly reach an age of enlightenment," Mireau said quietly. "Sadly, despite our incredible technological achievements, there are still those who don't mind making a living off the suffering of others. Those who charge massive rents for slum living conditions are criminals, as sure as petty thieves are."

"It's only the charity of the rich that keeps those

poor devils in the slums alive!" Lady Marian said. "The wealthy are the ones seeing to the very livelihoods of the poor! And if punishments were sterner, we'd find there would be more law and order!"

"Oh, come, Marian!" Sir Roger argued, slipping into the group. He winked at Mireau, who looked quite taken aback. The Duchess had looked at him as she might her old bath water. Roger was attempting to lighten the moment. "What? Would you bring back the chopping block and axe?"

"We need stronger deterrents. Quick action. Why, just the other week, I might well have been shot and killed because of a wretched charlatan pretending to be a great medium! And what did the police do? Let the head fellow escape! One was killed outright; the woman involved was a pretty thing and the police were kind to her, though she might well have committed murder herself! I tell you, if it weren't for the ordinary citizens there . . . I shudder to think of what might have happened to me."

Maggie felt herself growing increasingly uncomfortable.

"And, I tell you, it is coming to a truly wretched state!" Marian continued. "Have you kept up with the papers? There is a real monster afoot in the East End. Surely a foreigner, for no Englishman would ever be such an insane animal! There will be more, mark my words. Now, I grant you that this madman is killing women who can hardly be granted such a term in themselves, drunkards they are, the worst kinds of street harlots. But still, cattle are surely put down with less frenzy! We should rid the country of all of these people!"

Maggie turned away, as if seeking another glass of champagne, and she turned directly into Jamie.

His eyes were dark, like the stormiest day in the midst of winter. She trembled the instant she saw him, for he was stark, imposing, and incredibly attractive in the black dress attire he'd chosen for the occasion.

"Well . . . Auntie Maggie," he said dryly. "Will you dance with me?"

She floundered, lifting the empty glass in her hand. "Ah, more champagne," he continued. "Well, you do seem to gain incredible . . . energy . . . on champagne."

He took the glass from her, setting it down on a silver tray carried by a passing waiter. Then she was in his arms, and they were swirling across the floor.

"You left rather abruptly," he said.

She couldn't find her voice at first. "It seemed the proper thing to do."

"Proper, yes, of course. And here we are; you're duly wed."

"What should I have done?" she whispered miserably.

"Called it off."

She lowered her head, shaking it. "You don't understand. It wouldn't have been right."

"Um. That's right. You'd already been paid for services to be rendered."

"Do you have to be so vulgar and hateful?"

"Well, I rather think I'm being honest. Let's see . . . it wouldn't be right to call off the wedding. But it wasn't wrong that you didn't call it off—after last night."

"Last night was—"

"A terrible mistake, of course."

She felt as if she had been slapped. What had she expected?

"A terrible mistake," she agreed.

"Never to happen again."

"Of course not!"

"Still, it should have shown you that you should never have married Charles."

"Last night I was not married."

"And now you are. And look at you! Not in the least the worse for . . . wear."

Her cheeks colored. "I am quite miserable enough, thank you," she said.

He didn't skip a beat in leading the dance, but his lashes lowered and his eyes seemed to pin her where she stood, tight in his embrace. "Well, as the saying goes, you have made your bed, and now you must lie in it. God help my uncle."

"If you felt so, sir, you had your chance to protest."

"It wasn't my place to protest. It was yours."

"I had to go through with this!" she whispered. "That's why I left as I did. Don't you understand? I had never imagined . . . I mean, I would never again . . . Now I am his wife, then I was not. You are his nephew, his trusted confidant!"

"I am neither a husband, nor engaged to be one, and men, naturally, are prone to seek entertainment where it is offered."

She gasped, longing to strike him. But there was an awful truth to his cold brutality. Men were forgiven for their escapades; they were expected to have them. Yet it hurt beyond definition to force herself to realize that she was nothing more to him.

"I admit, I have seldom been so . . . mesmerized.

But, of course, now you are my uncle's wife. And, Auntie, I shall never, never, forget that you did indeed go through with the ceremony, that you married my Uncle Charles. As arranged."

As duly paid! he might have said.

"I had to wed your uncle!"

"Actually, no, you didn't. You chose to," he said. And he whirled around the floor, returning her to the place where Charles stood, continuing the debate on law and order. "Duchess!" Jamie said, "You've not granted me a dance!"

And so, he went off with her, and minutes later, when Maggie looked at the floor again, he was with Lady Marian's niece, a gorgeous young girl with a perfect complexion, slim figure, and glorious smile for her partner.

The jealousy that swept through Maggie was agonizing. She turned away. She had made her choices. And she would never, ever, allow Sir James Langdon to believe that he had been anything more than a last fling to her.

A mistake. The culmination of a very strange evening, indeed.

She danced with her brother, who now seemed to be in a cloud, as if his thoughts were elsewhere. And she danced with Percy and Roger, and others of his friends. Charles became distracted as well, and she realized that still he hadn't seen his daughter.

Later, the guests began to leave.

Jamie must have left quietly; Maggie never saw him go.

Just as well. She couldn't bear the thought of meeting his eyes again. With him, she felt ashamed, and she felt a fever. She dreaded the night to come more deeply with every passing second.

Mireau and Justin stayed until almost the very end.

Mireau embraced her, again, offering as always, his support, his unfailing friendship.

Then Maggie hugged her brother fiercely, and he swore that he'd see her the next day; she and Charles would remain at Moorhaven a few days, then they would honeymoon, beginning at Bath, perhaps moving on to the Continent. They would go, Charles had said, where the slightest whim led them.

A few of the guests still lingered. Charles whispered to Maggie that she looked exhausted; she should escape up the stairs, and he would be with her as soon as possible. She dreaded the moment when they would be alone, but it was coming, and she couldn't stop it. Best to hurry ahead and gather what resources she could in the time she had left.

As she escaped up the stairs, she heard Charles's voice boom out below, "Arianna! Where have you been?"

"Father! I am so sorry. I witnessed the ceremony, but departed quickly for a ride."

"You went riding? On my wedding day?"

"I felt terribly ill and thought that fresh air might help me feel better. I didn't want to ruin your happiness by moping around, feeling so terribly ill."

The girl was a liar. A wretched liar, Maggie thought.

She crept back to look down the stairs. Charles had taken his daughter in his arms. He kissed the top of her head. "Are you better?" he asked anxiously.

"Oh, yes, much."

"I shall put off the honeymoon. Maggie will understand."

"Father! Don't you even think such a thing. You and your young bride must go and enjoy yourselves—be wild, be young, be wicked!" she teased. "Get every little thing out of your new wedded bliss that you can!"

"My sweet, sweet, child. Always thinking of my happiness!" Charles said.

Shiite! Maggie thought.

"I shall run up for some sleep, Father. Since you're not leaving, we'll have precious time together in the next few days—that is, if I can draw you away from your beautiful wife!"

"But you've got to get to know Maggie as well, my dear."

"Of course. I can hardly wait. Good night, Father."

The girl was coming up the stairs. Maggie quickly retreated down the hall, slipping into the master's chamber.

She closed the door and leaned against it, and nearly jumped a mile when she saw that Mrs. Whitley was in the room.

"I thought you might need some help with the gown, Lady Maggie," she said.

Maggie stared at her blankly for a minute. Her eyes flew to the massive oak master bed. It was dressed in elegant sheets, with a multitude of pillows. And there, lying atop the lowered spread, was an elegant see-through nightgown in the sheerest white gossamer silk. Suddenly, the rich food, the champagne, welled to her throat.

No! Good God, no! She couldn't marry such a

good man as Charles and vomit the minute he took off his clothing.

"I think I can manage," Maggie said. She pushed away from the door, resolved. "I'm sorry . . . I'm rather accustomed to taking care of myself. If you wouldn't mind helping with the hooks and then the tie on the corset . . ."

"Indeed, madam."

The very dour housekeeper was still marvelously adept. In seconds, Maggie was freed from all manner of restraint. She was uncomfortable in such a state of undress, but apparently, Mrs. Whitley had served many a young woman and before Maggie knew it, she was bereft of everything, and clad in the white gown.

Which was rather still like being bereft of everything. Mrs. Whitley, ever the perfect servant, seemed not to notice. She directed Maggie to the dressing table, where she removed all the pins from her hair, and began to brush it.

Maggie thought that she'd crawl from her skin. The last time she'd had someone tend to her hair so, it had been Jamie.

"Thank you! Thank you, Mrs. Whitley," she said, jumping up. "I think . . . I think I'm quite fine now."

"Aye, my lady. There's champagne in the bucket at the foot of the bed, and a tray of fruit, cheese, and sweets, there on the marble table near the door. Naturally, if you need anything . . ."

"I'll ring," Maggie assured her.

At last, the woman was gone.

Maggie made a beeline for the champagne and guzzled down two glasses. She briefly considered the headache she'd have the following morning, then determined that the pain would be worth it, if she could just survive the night.

She was on her fourth glass of champagne when the door opened. Lord Charles had arrived.

He had evidently prepared for his wedding night elsewhere, for he entered the room in nothing but a rich cranberry smoking jacket.

Maggie met his eyes, then found that her gaze traveled downward to the legs, bare beneath the hem of the jacket.

Thin. Very thin. He wore matching maroon slippers.

She brought her gaze up to his knobby knees. The gaslights were down, but too many candles burned through the room.

She swallowed her fourth glass of champagne. Forced a smile to her lips.

"Well, here we are. At last," she breathed.

"My dear . . . my dear, dear, dearest!"

He walked into the room. Maggie nervously grabbed another glass from the tray at the foot of the bed, poured him one, and a fifth for herself. She handed it to him. "Charles."

"My dear, dear, dear . . ."

He took the glass of champagne, but set it immediately down. He took Maggie's from her hand, despite her protest. His hands came around her waist. He lifted her, setting her standing on the bed, the white gossamer trailing around her. He was far stronger than she had expected.

"Charles . . . I think we should share a glass of champagne!" she whispered.

He came closer, ignoring her words. And suddenly, it seemed that everything about him changed. His eyes were flatly . . . lascivious.

"No more champagne. I think I've had quite enough."

He buried his head against her abdomen, his hands coming around her ankles, sliding up around her calves to her kneecaps and her thighs. She gritted her teeth in misery, remembering that she had chosen this path, that he was a good man, that she had known exactly what being a wife meant.

"I'm not sure I've had enough," she whispered.

"You're nervous, my dear? When you know that I adore you beyond life itself?"

She nodded. His hands against her flesh felt as dry as his lips.

"One more glass!" she whispered.

Again, he lifted her. This time, his hands against her bare waist. The sheer gown rose, then fell as her feet touched the ground and she scampered across the floor. She was tempted to grab the champagne bottle and drink straight from it.

She retrieved her glass instead. Charles had kept his distance. He was still just staring at her. She realized, with the light of the fire behind her, she might as well be wearing nothing.

A swallow finished off the glass of champagne.

"Come here, my love," Charles said.

"The lights! The gaslights, the candles . . . I'll put them out."

"No," he told her. "No . . . come here."

She walked back across the floor to him. She hated herself. She felt as if she were walking to her own execution.

He put up a hand, and she stopped, puzzled.

"Slip from the gown," he said.

"Pardon?"

"Slip it from your shoulders. Untie the little white ribbon at the nape, and let it fall to the floor."

Maggie inhaled. "I'd actually be far more comfortable if . . ."

"Please, Maggie. I am besotted with your exquisite beauty. Allow me my enjoyment of it." Then his voice changed, ever so slightly. "Come, Maggie. We both know that you are a woman of some experience. And now, you are my wife."

Yes, she was his wife, and the reminder was a very firm one.

"Maggie . . . the gown."

A simple enough request. She had married him. And yet, she suddenly felt more deeply shamed than she had in the whole of her life.

More like a . . .

Whore.

She wasn't sure that she could have felt worse if she'd been working the filthy, trash-lined streets in the East End.

"Maggie . . . slowly, please. Very slowly. And turn about for me as you do it."

She swallowed hard and pulled the ribbon, turning about.

"Let it come off your shoulders as you turn back to me. Now . . . let it fall to the ground."

Mortified, she let the gown fall to the floor. She blinked then, as he gave her another command. Walk . . . across the room, back again. Crawl onto the bed, turn, position herself, do it all slowly . . . slowly, rise again, come to him.

The sound of his voice was suddenly horrible to

her. Despite herself, she was nearly in tears. She had been convinced that he would be the kindest man in the world. She was beginning to feel that he was . . . sick! Lecherous as they came . . .

He jerked off his smoking jacket. She looked away from his withered flesh, and the sadly pathetic rise of his excitement. He strode to the bed, hopping upon it, lying back.

"Now, Maggie, come to me . . . walk . . . walk, and do what I tell you as you walk. . . ."

In two seconds, she would scream and say no, and he could divorce her, annul the marriage—shoot her!—for all she cared. She couldn't bear this. If only . . . if only he had allowed her to douse the lights, crawled in beside her . . .

God, dear God! She was suddenly desperate to . . . just die! Sink into the floor. Whatever she had done, surely she hadn't deserved this. God, sweet Jesu, sweet Mary! She prayed for deliverance, for salvation, to drop into a dead faint, and never awaken.

"Maggie!"

She reached the bed.

He reached up for her.

Then . . .

She heard a choking sound. And he was frozen there, an arm reaching out to her, his eyes bugging in his head.

"Charles!" she gasped.

The choking continued. But he didn't move. His one hand remained outstretched. His face was growing . . . mottled.

"Charles!" she cried.

He fell back.

"Charles?"

His eyes were closed. He was still. Completely still. Dead still.

"Charles?"

She touched his face, his throat, and began seeking a pulse. There was none.

Her heart thundered. Naked, pale, ashen, withered . . . he lay on the bed. Dead still.

Dead?

No, he couldn't be!

Hysteria bubbled within her.

Maggie began to scream.

She had prayed for deliverance, salvation.

And in the most ironic way, it seemed that God had answered her prayers.

Chapter 9

Jamie would not have been at his great uncle's house at all, if it hadn't been for Arianna.

He'd been stunned to find his young cousin returning discreetly to the house from some sojourn, exiting a cab at the end of the long drive rather than allowing it to come all way to the house.

And the young lady, usually attired in a most attractive and fashionable manner, was decked out in the very simple manner of a serving maid or common lass, a plain gray bonnet covering her rich dark hair, a drab, matching shawl her only protection from the cold.

He'd been on his way out when he'd seen the cab stop, and naturally, had discreetly asked his coachman to stop so that he could watch his young cousin.

Telling Randolph to let him out and settle in for the time being, Jamie left the coach, and waited, his presence hidden by the thick cluster of trees and bushes that lined the drive. When Arianna walked past him, he stepped out to confront her.

She let out a bloodcurdling scream, her hand flying to her throat.

"It's me, Jamie," he told her quickly.

"Jamie! You very nearly gave me heart failure!" she told him.

"As well you might have deserved," Jamie said sternly. "You disappointed your father deeply by not attending the wedding. And now I find you . . . God alone knows what I've found you doing."

"Nothing!" she protested.

"Ah, yes, this would be your usual attire."

She flushed. "I did nothing. Except set out to explore a bit of London. I've been away a long time, you know."

"Not so long that you're not aware that the streets can be dangerous."

She waved a hand in the air. "Don't be ridiculous. I didn't go anywhere I shouldn't have been. I took in some air. I wandered a few shops. Many are open quite late, you know."

"Your father would be furious."

"If he knew," she said sharply, staring at him. "Jamie! There are so many people out and about, I was in no danger. I wandered the streets around Covent Gardens, and that is all. I stopped by a silversmith's, a bakery . . . I sat and had tea. And that is all. Oh, come, Jamie, many young women of great respectability shop alone!"

"Not at night."

"I had a right to be out, and that's that. I don't care what you want to say to me, what my father did was disgusting."

"I'm not going to discuss that with you right now. Go on in, before he discovers that you're still out somewhere."

"Jamie—"

"We'll talk tomorrow."

And so, Arianna had gone in, and though Moorhaven had been the last place on earth he'd wanted to be at that time, he'd followed her slowly back. Randolph had been with Darby in the kitchen, playing gin, the last of the reception debris had been cleared away, and the house was very quiet.

He'd decided to have a last brandy and cigar in the now empty grand salon. Staring into the low burning embers, he'd let his mind wander to his uncle's master room atop the stairs, and despite himself, there had been tremendous bitterness in his heart. He was worried about Arianna, and equally anxious that he get away—really away—himself. But how to do so when the girl was in such a rebellious mood she might well do some serious harm to herself?

That was when he heard the scream.

First, he thought that it was Arianna again, startled by a servant, perhaps—or just determined on causing mischief. But still, he moved to the stairs, and when the sound came again, he sped up to the landing and realized that the sound was coming from his uncle's chambers.

He burst into the room.

It was Maggie doing the screaming, and she seemed to be in shock. Naked, hair a sea of gold around her face and shoulders, she stood, just feet from the bed, staring at it, screaming.

Charles was flat out, looking pale and pathetic, nude, wrinkled, and flaccid.

Jamie heard footsteps coming along the hall as others of the household hurried to find the source of the chilling alarm. He quickly caught up his uncle's smoking jacket, slipping it around Maggie's shoulders, and drew the sheets over his uncle's prone body.

Maggie was still screaming. He slapped her. Wide-eyed, she stared at him with no recognition, her hand slowly moving to her cheek. She nearly lost the smoking jacket.

"Maggie!" He caught her shoulders, shaking her.

"Get your arms into that!" he commanded her, but it didn't seem she was capable of moving. "Maggie!"

At last, and by rote, she began to slip into the garment. He hurried to the bed, checking for a pulse at Charles's throat.

Faint . . . but there.

Darby, Randolph behind him, came flying into the room. "What happened, sir?" Darby cried in distress.

"Maggie?" Jamie said, looking at her. She was shaking so violently now that it was amazing she was still standing.

She shook her head. Giant tears welled in her eyes. "He . . . he . . . he just . . . he just . . . one minute . . . then the next . . . ."

"His heart," Randolph suggested sharply.

Mrs. Whitley, in a robe, her gray hair hanging down her back in a long braid, made the next appearance, just as Jamie was saying, "Randolph, ride for his doctor, quickly, please."

"Sir William Gull! The Queen's own physician will see him," Mrs. Whitley said.

"Randolph, go for Dr. Mayer," Jamie said.

"The Queen's physician will see him! Sir William Gull saved the life of the Prince once; he is excellent—"

"He is seventy and has had a stroke himself!" Jamie said irritably, then swore and added, "Randolph, go for Dr. Mayer. Darby, ride for Sir William Gull."

The two coachmen left. Mrs. Whitley quickly came to Charles's bedside, straightening the sheets, checking for a pulse, as well. From the corner of her eyes, she covertly stared at her employer's new lady bride. There was venom in that look.

"We'll see that you're tended, dear Lord Charles!" Mrs. Whitley said. "Protected, aye, we'll see to it!" she murmured.

That, apparently, sank through to Maggie's mind. And it was as if a sudden fury awakened her, as if something actually snapped in her mind. She strode to the bed. "Mrs. Whitley, just exactly what are you insinuating?"

"Nothing, madam, nothing," Mrs. Whitley said, her eyes falling. "I'll get his daughter, Sir James."

"No," Jamie said. "Let the doctors come. There is no reason to disturb Arianna right now. Perhaps you could get some cool cloths, and we'll soothe his forehead. And Mrs. Whitley, a brandy, please."

"Do you think he can drink a brandy?" Mrs. Whitley asked skeptically.

"The brandy is for Lady Langdon," he said.

Mrs. Whitley stiffened and pursed her lips, and appeared loathe to leave the room.

"Mrs. Whitley, if you will?" Jamie persisted.

The woman left the room. Maggie didn't look at

Jamie, but lowered herself to the bed by Charles. "He was fine," she whispered. "More than fine," and that sounded a little bitter. "Frisky, one might say. And then . . ."

"I believe it's his heart," Jamie said.

"Can't you do anything?" she whispered.

"I'm not a physician. I can tie a tourniquet, remove a bullet, and manage a few stitches on a battlefield, but as to matters such as this . . ."

"What can we do?"

"Wait."

She swallowed hard. He had never seen her in such a state of agitation and distress, so . . . lost.

But then again, he'd never seen her in a circumstance such as this. And still, she was customarily such a determined young woman, composed—hardened by the world, somewhat, one might have said.

Tonight . . . she looked young. Young and lost and . . . frightened. The smoking jacket left a deep V upon the ivory expanse of her flesh, nestling deeply between her breasts. The red-gold mass of her hair, streaming down her back in a wild cascade, was all too familiar. So were those eyes, cobalt blue and wide as they met his.

He wanted so badly to hate her. His beloved kinsman was at death's door. And it was quite possible that she had, inadvertently, brought this about. Charles might well be lost to them. And yet . . . *if so, it had been Charles's hunger that had brought him to this state.*

That thought was disloyal.

Yet true.

And try as he might, no matter what emotion

brewed in his heart regarding Charles, he knew that she had done nothing to purposely bring this on.

She started to tremble again. "She thinks . . . Mrs. Whitley . . . thinks that I did something to him!" She was both outraged, and like a child, scared.

"It's his heart, Maggie. The doctors will tell them that."

She buried her face in her hands. "Maybe I did do this . . . but . . . but . . . he . . . oh, God! I might have done it, but he . . . oh, God!"

Jamie loved Charles. He had done so all his life, and with all of his being. But he understood exactly what had happened.

Charles had gotten what he wanted. And it had been too much.

Mrs. Whitley returned with two snifters of brandy. She was too good a housekeeper to blatantly state her disapproval of the new Lady Langdon, but it was evident. Jamie ignored her, steered Maggie to a wing-backed chair by the hearth, and forced a snifter into her hands. "Drink it."

Mrs. Whitley was back at the bedside. A tremendous sob shook her frame.

"Mrs. Whitley, the doctors are coming. Cold cloths might well soothe his forehead."

"Aye, yes, yes, yes!"

And she was gone again, returning shortly.

Maggie looked like a statue, a wax figurine, holding the snifter in her hands, staring at Charles, not moving. Mrs. Whitley returned with the cold cloths. He began to administer them to his uncle's forehead.

At last, Randolph returned with Dr. Mayer. Approximately thirty-five, Mayer had studied at the best schools in London, and in the United States. He was not the Queen's Royal Physician; he was far superior, Jamie thought.

Mayer entered the room with his black bag in hand, gazing at Maggie in the chair, and surely, despite himself and his total professionalism, pausing for a moment. Jamie was up, walking across the room to greet him quickly.

"Can you tell me the circumstances, please?" Mayer asked, striding to the bedside, searching out a pulse, then opening his patient's closed lids to study the eyes beneath.

"He was married today," Jamie said.

"Yes, of course . . . I've heard," Mayer murmured, then glanced at Jamie. "Sorry . . . there has been talk around the city."

Jamie gazed at Maggie again. "Forgive my manners. Dr. Mayer, the new Lady Langdon."

"Lady Langdon," Mayer said politely. He sighed, looking from his patient to Jamie, and then Maggie. "I don't mean to be indelicate here, but . . ."

Maggie swallowed hard, closing her eyes for a moment, then looking at Mayer. "We had retired for the evening. He was fine, talking . . ." Her cheeks colored a bloodred shade of crimson. "Preparing for . . . bed. And then . . . he just . . . went out."

Mayer nodded, and turned back to his patient, administering all that he could. He produced a syringe of something, and gave Charles a shot, then waited.

A moment later, another man entered the room. Sir William Gull.

He was adored by the Queen because, once, years

before, in 1871, he was credited with saving the Prince of Wales when he was stricken with typhoid fever. But many years had passed since then. Gull was old. And he was slow on the one side, and a certain contortion now marred his features. He, like Maggie, lived in London's very exclusive Mayfair section, and it was reported that he was worth a small fortune through his association with the Queen. To his credit, he was loyal to Victoria to a fault, and surely, would have died on her behalf, if ever so required.

Right now, he appeared totally indignant that another physician was already in the room.

"What is happening here?" he demanded, and sounded entirely autocratic.

"Heart attack, I'm afraid," Dr. Mayer said.

Gull glared at the man, who stepped back as he came forward. Mayer informed Gull of his findings, of his treatment.

Gull listened, irritated, the one side of his face seeming to take on a sinister sneer.

"You could not await my arrival?" Gull said to Jamie.

"My uncle's condition seems dire, sir. I sent both men out for the sake of expediency."

Now Gull turned and glared at Maggie. "Precisely what was happening when this occurred?"

She glared back at Gull. Jamie was pleased to see the temper and spirit that seemed to see her through most events leap to the fore. "We were just married this afternoon, Sir William."

"You are saying that . . . ?"

"Good God!" Jamie found himself exploding. "Yes, he was in a state of sexual excitement!"

Once again, Maggie reddened. She didn't dispute his words, nor did she elaborate on them.

"All of you, out!" Sir William said. "I will now see to the patient alone!"

Jamie was not about to be pushed about by the man. He approached Dr. Mayer, though. "Perhaps you could see to Lady Langdon. I believe she might require a sedative. I intend to stay with my uncle."

Sir William glared at him.

"Are you suggesting, sir, that I need assistance?" Gull was outraged.

"Never, Sir William," Jamie assured him. "It's just that this man is very near to being a father to me, and I would not leave him now."

"I'm . . . I'm his wife," Maggie said, her voice one of quiet steel.

All three men looked at her.

Dr. Mayer was the only one with the sense to talk to her in a manner to improve the situation. He came to her, kneeling before her. "My lady, you are looking gravely ill yourself. Should he need your tender care in the days to come, you must see to your own health. Please, come with me."

At his gentle behest, Maggie rose at last, and allowed him to lead her out.

Sir William Gull made a sniffing noise in Jamie's direction, but then went on to examine Charles.

And when he was done, he turned to Jamie. "His heart."

That was quite obvious. Jamie didn't say so.

"He is in a coma. I don't know whether he will survive the night or not. If he does . . . there is a chance that he will pull through. A slim chance. I will stay for the evening. However, if he dies . . . I shall autopsy the body."

"For what reason?"

"I will see if he has been poisoned."

"Why should you suspect such a thing?"

"That answer is quite obvious. The lady stands to make quite an inheritance, doesn't she?"

"The title will be mine, Sir William."

Sir William waved a hand in the air. To him, the answer was quite obvious. Jamie might have said that he would refuse to have an autopsy for his uncle.

But to do so would be foolish. And an autopsy would show the truth.

"I will stay here as well," Jamie said softly, and took the chair by the hearth himself.

Maggie awoke in a state of misery. The world was foggy—Dr. Mayer had gotten her to take a dose of laudanum, and so she felt groggy, and her head pounded, but the events of the last evening were far too clear.

She had been sleeping in a guest room and some of her belongings had been hastily brought there the night before. She needed to rise, quickly dress, and prepare herself for the day, sure to be a long one. But she couldn't quite bring herself to rise, her feeling of dread was so great.

As she lay there, trying to force herself to get up, her door suddenly burst open.

Arianna stood there.

"You . . . witch!" she cried. "You've killed him. Murderess!"

And then the girl came flying across the room, throwing herself on top of the bed, flailing away at Maggie.

Arianna wasn't a weakling, and neither was Maggie. She was entangled in the sheets, and unprepared for the assault, but she caught Arianna's flailing arms. "Stop it! Stop it! I did nothing to your father, I swear it!"

"Arianna!"

Jamie was at the door, dark hair in disarray on his forehead, his immaculate wedding attire now wrinkled and the worse for the night he had apparently spent up. The girl didn't seem to hear him. Maggie was left to maintain her desperate fight to keep her stepdaughter from gouging out her eyes.

"Arianna!"

Jamie strode into the room, grappling to draw his cousin from her determined attack.

"She killed him! She killed him. She murdered him for his money!" Arianna cried.

"No!" Maggie protested.

Jamie caught Arianna by her shoulders, dragging her away at last, and into his arms where she burst into a flood of tears. Against Jamie's chest, she sobbed out her accusation again. "She killed him, she killed him, she only married him for his money."

Jamie's eyes touched Maggie's above Arianna's head. Maggie felt ill, wondering if Jamie believed that was what had happened.

Her heart sank. She leapt from the bed, realized her state of undress, for she had fallen asleep in the smoking jacket, and turned and fled into the dressing room and bath.

There, she started to shake. It occurred to her that she might really be accused of murder. Surely, no one would believe such a thing.

She saw her reflection above the marble sink. She looked ghastly, gaunt and white, and totally disheveled. She lowered her head, realizing that Charles had died. She wasn't sure if she felt pain, or if she was still in such a realm of shock that it was natural she should feel nothing but a crippling numbness.

She had to gather herself together, she knew. And yet, it was almost impossible to do so. Either minutes or hours passed in which she just stood there. She dimly heard a knock at the door. Not Arianna this time, since the girl had no intention of knocking. And still, she couldn't bring herself to call out.

"My lady?" the door opened. Maggie still couldn't move.

She realized that a young woman in a maid's attire had gingerly entered the room, and now waited just outside the bath, looking in. "Ah, my poor lady!" the woman murmured. She had an accent, that much registered in Maggie's mind. Irish. She had dark hair, a smattering of freckles, warm brown eyes, and a fresh face. "Come out, please. Lie down. I'll draw you a bath, get your clothing together . . . I'm so sorry. So, so, sorry!"

The kindness suddenly shown her brought tears to Maggie's eyes. "Thank you!" she managed.

"I'm Fiona, upstairs maid," she told Maggie. "Come along, now, please, let me help you."

Maggie looked down, gritted her teeth, and straightened. "Thank you," she said again, some dignity back in her voice. "Perhaps that would indeed help."

She left the bathroom and allowed Fiona to prepare her a bath with good, hot water. Maggie sank
into it, praying for the steam to ease the wracking
pain in her head. At length, she was ready to rise.
And thankfully, due to the periods of mourning
Maggie had already observed, there was a black satin
dress among her belongings in the room. She allowed Fiona to help her dress, and then, she was
grateful when the girl made quick and efficient work
with the wild tangles of her hair. At length, Maggie
appeared presentable.

"Sir James . . . Lord James, I believe it is now, is in
the grand salon, my lady," Fiona told her when she
had finished. Stepping back, she surveyed her handiwork. "And Dr. Mayer has left laudanum, should you
need it, in the days to come."

Maggie nodded. She had to face what was happening. She rose. "Thank you, Fiona."

"Aye, my lady. I'll report back to Mrs. Whitley now."

"No," Maggie said, suddenly determined that she
wasn't going to allow herself to be bullied by a housekeeper—not unless the police hauled her away for
murder. "Fiona, I would you like your position
changed in the house. You'll be my personal maid
from now on."

Fiona looked distressed. "I'm afraid Mrs. Whitley—"

"Mrs. Whitley is not the mistress of the house,"
Maggie said. "I will see that she is informed."

"Would you like your things moved back to . . . to
the master chamber?"

"No, I would like the rest of my things brought
here. I don't believe I'll be staying that long," she
said, and quickly exited the room.

The great manor house was quiet, terribly so after the excitement of the day gone by. Maggie walked down the stairs, and from the landing at the entry to the massive grand salon. Jamie was there, standing before the fire, looking thoughtful and solemn.

"Ah, there you are," he said. "Charles, as you must know, did not make the night."

She sat down, shaking.

"The Queen," Jamie continued, "has sent word that he should be interred at Westminster. He was very fond of it, always telling her that he preferred the truly ancient stones, despite the artistic talents of Sir Christopher Wren, and the beauty of St. Paul's. Naturally, this must also be in accordance with your wishes. You were his legal wife."

Maggie lifted a hand. She tried to speak, couldn't, tried again. "I'm sure that the Queen was more privy to certain of his thoughts; whatever you and Her Majesty agree upon is certainly fine with me."

"Arrangements will be made for a proper wake . . . tomorrow night."

Maggie nodded again. It all seemed surreal.

"Arianna is now under sedation. Dr. Mayer has kindly agreed to remain here as a guest for the next few days."

"Very kind of him."

His voice seemed to harden. "Next week, you will have an opportunity to spend time with the solicitors for the estate. Naturally, I'm assuming you'll want your brother to be present."

She waved a hand in the air. "There is no part of the estate that I want; certainly, there were no such agreements made."

"Ah, but you do receive a third of the inheritance. Certain assets go to Arianna, and—unless there is the chance of a male heir being born posthumously— the title and properties come to me."

She lowered her head. "There is no chance of a posthumous heir."

"Well, it might not do to speak so candidly at any other time," he said flatly. "Arianna is convinced that you . . . did something to her father. She might attempt to go to the courts and see that the marriage is annulled."

"What does it matter?"

"Your family estates could be confiscated, in lieu of goods illegally obtained by false promise," Jamie said.

"What?" she gasped.

"The law can be complex and detailed. Excuse me, due to the circumstances, there are many affairs that I must attend to," he told her. "Unless, of course, there are certain matters you feel must have your personal touch?"

He was deferring to her as the wife of the deceased. Laughable, of course. She had been engaged for a month, long enough for legal banns to be cried, and no more. She had no right to the life of a man so important, for so many years, to others.

"I have no right to infringe upon your handling of affairs," she said simply.

"Good. I have sent for your brother. He will be with you soon."

"Thank you."

They were stiff, so terribly stiff and formal! Impossible to believe that just two nights ago . . . and yet, impossible to believe that the world had changed entirely, so quickly. Charles was dead. She had determined that she would be a martyr to marriage, albeit he had been a dear one . . . until last night. And now he was dead. And his daughter was screaming accusations of murder against her!

Still, Jamie hesitated. "There is going to be an autopsy," he told her.

Frowning, she stared at him.

"Why?"

"Sir William wants to make sure that it was his heart, and there were no other factors that brought on his death."

"Such as . . . ?"

"Poison."

A chill enveloped her. She stared at him. "Surely, you don't believe that I . . . ?"

"It doesn't matter what I believe. Sir William is beloved of the Queen, as was Charles. There will be an autopsy."

Jamie walked out. She heard the sounds of his footsteps receding.

She rose and fled back to her room. A few moments later, Fiona arrived with a tray of tea and toast. She thanked her, certain she couldn't begin to eat a bite.

But the tea she wanted.

She realized how badly her hands were still shaking when she poured. Fiona had arranged her tray very attractively, with flowers and the morning newspaper.

She glanced at the headlines and started shaking all over again.

"Another Murder in Whitechapel!" glared the front page of the paper.

Of course, the murder in the daily paper had nothing to do with the death of the dearly beloved and esteemed Lord Charles. And still . . .

Maggie stared at the word and started to laugh, and then she started to cry, and it seemed that hours passed in which she endured her own private hell of denial and . . .

Guilt.

After a while, she cried herself out and sat numbly once again. She paced, thoughts racing through her mind at a terrifying speed, then leaving it empty and cold.

At last, ready to tear her hair out, she picked up the newspaper.

Horrible murder of a woman, another Whitechapel mystery.

Maggie found herself reading the appalling description of the murder.

. . . lying in a pool of blood . . . throat cut from ear to ear . . . the lower part of the abdomen was completely ripped open and the bowels were protruding . . .

She set the paper down, feeling a sense of terrible despair. The woman's name, she noted, had been Annie Chapman. She had been discovered in the early morning hours of the previous day, in the backyard of number 29, Hanbury Street. A poor prostitute, her death was of note because of the ghastly mutilations done to her body—similar to those of the woman named Mary Ann, known as Polly Nichols just nine days earlier on the night of August thirty-first.

The article went on to describe the mutilations

done to the body in gory detail, and then to talk about the life of the woman slain. She was among the worst of the "unfortunates" working London's East End. Aged forty-two, missing teeth, she had been turned away from a doss house the night before, lacking the money for a bed. She had been "in a state of deep drink," and had told friends and whoever would listen that she had earned her doss money three times that day, but had spent it, yet she would make it again.

Poor Annie. The woman had taken pride in one of her garments, a new straw bonnet, trimmed with black velvet. She'd been the mother of five, but hadn't seen the children in years, nor her husband, William Nichols, who had ceased to pay her six shillings allowance because she had begun to live the life of a prostitute.

So much for the victim.

The article went on to lambast the police, society, and even the Queen. It declared that there was a madman loose on the streets, and that he had now struck twice, if he hadn't also perpetuated previous killings. Because a leather apron had been found near the body, the killer was now being referred to as Leather Apron.

Once again, the article went on to talk about the deceased. She had held a domestic position in Wandsworth but had absconded with several pounds sterling worth of clothing, which she had probably pawned.

The article, though condemning of both London itself and the woman, brought nothing but a terrible sadness to Maggie's heart. She already knew far more than any article could bring to light about the East End.

Murder in the East End. Never really noted—until now. Now that the bodies of the victims were being so brutally torn assunder.

Maggie stood, thinking that by tomorrow morning, news of the death of Lord Charles, Viscount Langdon, would be in every paper around the country. And what would those articles say? *Tragically, he was murdered by the woman he adored, a young thing, desperate for money, marrying him thus, just the same as any East End prostitute, just demanding much more in the way of payment!*

God, no!

She hoped the articles would state that he had died from heart failure, and not give details.

No, the details would await the autopsy.

She had done nothing to him, and she knew it. The autopsy would prove it.

A shiver of ice crept down her spine.

Dead was dead. The prostitute was dead, and Charles was dead. She had done nothing to him, and yet she felt the heavy burden of guilt.

And yet . . . for all her guilt, Charles had died happily, contemplating the fulfillment of a dream, and he had died in his own bed. While the poor woman in Whitechapel . . .

How she must have suffered. What terror had she endured, before death had given her peace? And what kind of a horrible animal could perpetuate such a crime?

Staring at the paper, stunned by the brutality of the murder and the grisly details so carefully chronicled in the paper, Maggie found herself wondering if she should ask Charles if they could perhaps make a donation so that the family of the poor woman might see her properly buried. Then, she felt hysteria rising again. Charles was dead. Sometime, between last night and this morning, he had passed away. He couldn't agree to help her with anything anymore. But . . .

Unless she was arrested for murder herself . . .

There had been agreements in the marriage contracts. She could help on her own, if she so chose. She swallowed hard. And she began to cry. And she was sorry, so sorry, Charles had been a good man.

Lecherous.

No worse than any other of the male of the species!

A good man, and she was sorry, sorry, sorry, and . . .

God help her, as honest as her sense of loss and sorrow were, so was another feeling that she tried desperately to bury. One that made her realize a sensation of guilt that ascended all the rest. And what she couldn't help to feel in a tiny place in her soul—that place which had felt so mortified the night before—was a sensation of . . .

Relief.

Justin and Mireau arrived a few hours later, along with a messenger from the Queen, sending her deepest condolences.

"Do you want to come home now?" Justin asked her rather awkwardly. "Moorhaven reverts to James, you know. Of course, as long as you live—and don't remarry—you have the right to live here. Charles, of course, made that provision. I just didn't think . . . Well, I guess it can't be terribly comfortable for you."

"Justin, I can't wait to escape and come home," she told her brother. "But . . . I think it only proper that I wait until after the funeral. And the autopsy," she added bitterly.

"Yes, yes, you're right, of course . . . it's just . . . well, if he'd died a day earlier . . . well, of course, we'd all be grieving, still, but . . . ."

Mireau made a strange noise in his throat. Maggie realized he was staring at her. "What?" she demanded.

"Nothing, nothing."

"Say what's on your mind, Jacques! Why should you cease to do so now?" Maggie demanded.

"No."

"Mireau!"

He let out a sigh. "All right, Maggie! If you insist. Did he have the heart attack before, during, or after?"

"Jacques!" she and Justin exclaimed together.

Justin put up a hand. "Please, let's not have this conversation!" He lowered his hand and looked perplexed. "I wonder if . . . ."

"No, both of you—just stop wondering, please!" Maggie said.

"Well, it may have legal implications," Justin said. He was studying his sister.

"I have no intention of discussing my private life with either of you—or anyone else! The debts are paid, Justin, right? No one can take back what was offered to the family as a marriage portion. So . . . whatever happens now, happens."

"Maggie, there may well be an inquest," Justin told her uneasily.

"He died a natural death," she said.

"I'm merely saying that you may be called upon to explain exactly what happened," Justin told her.

She stared at her brother and Mireau, who looked at her with a wry grimace. "Maggie, I've heard you talk about many subjects usually considered taboo," he reminded her.

"I'm your brother," Justin reminded her.

She couldn't find the words to explain why that made the whole conversation all the more uncomfortable. Instead, she sighed with impatience. "I don't understand what's so difficult for anyone to understand! We were alone. We were getting ready. And he was anxious. There. Period. That's it. He suddenly constricted, froze, I guess . . . and lapsed into unconsciousness."

"I'm sure it will be all right," Justin said.

"Of course," Mireau agreed.

Neither of them eased the tempest in her mind a bit.

"Arianna! Let me in."

The door flew open and Jamie gazed at the young girl's tear-stained face. "I thought you might be *her*," she said.

"Arianna, Maggie didn't kill your father," Jamie said.

"Even Mrs. Whitley believes that she killed him!"

Arianna insisted. "That woman married my father, and murdered him, all for money!"

"Arianna, you know that I inherit the estate."

"Ah, but she inherits a fair amount, nonetheless!"

"You inherit a personal fortune as well. That doesn't mean that you killed him."

"Jamie, what a wretched thing to say!"

"The point is, people don't murder people they care about for money. There are people who wouldn't commit murder under any circumstance."

"I am my father's daughter. I truly loved him, and he was generous to a fault. She didn't love him."

"I believe that she did."

"What an absurd lie, Jamie!"

"Not as she did her first husband, not passionately . . . perhaps not even as a wife should love a husband. But since they first met, they were together frequently. They talked endlessly and shared many views."

Jamie entirely understood how Arianna felt, because as the hours had gone on, he had found himself going through many stages of grief. He remembered how Charles had been there for his father when his mother had died, and how he had come for Jamie himself when his father had passed away as well. Walking through his uncle's library, he had thought of the way that Charles had loved books and learning, and enjoyed contemporary fiction as well as old classics. The shelves were lined with texts that were hundreds of years old, priceless, antiquarian tomes by the likes of da Vinci, Dante, and Dafoe, works on astronomy, geography . . . a half dozen tomes by or about Charles Darwin; poetry by Shelley,

Keats, stories by Robert Louis Stevenson, Lord Byron, and even romances by the Brontes and Jane Austen.

The newspapers he had kept regarding world events were neatly filed in one corner. He kept dozens of journals. He'd read about medical breakthroughs, faraway cultures, military achievements, and even breakthroughs in the pursuit of police work and investigation. He'd been an amazing and well-educated man.

And like so many others before him, he had been determined on a young and beautiful wife when he had felt the pall of age creeping upon him. Jamie believed he knew, as most would suspect, that the actual realization of nearly possessing his bride had brought on the seizure of his uncle's heart. There would be scandal, and certainly mockery, to come.

But that didn't make the beautiful, too-young bride a murderess.

"Arianna, I'm so sorry, but please!" he said to her softly. "Your father's death is a tragic loss, but he was an old man. Arianna, he might well have been a grandfather the year you were born. He was well into his seventies."

"She knew it! Knew he was old, with a poor heart, when she married him."

"No one ever suggested he had a poor heart, Arianna."

"She knew it! Somehow."

"Arianna, please. Harboring these thoughts will not help you with your loss and grief."

"But hating her does help me, Jamie. Hating her, and . . ."

"And what?" he asked sharply.

She shook her head, but he was afraid he knew what she might have intended to say. *Hating her and . . . planning revenge!*

"Arianna, I wish so badly that you would believe me, trust in me."

She stepped back, away from him. Her face remained tear-stained and stricken, but she suddenly seemed to have gained a certain strength. "She's bewitched you as well."

"I don't know what you're talking about," he said harshly.

Arianna couldn't know what had been between himself and the young widow, but his own sense of guilt and wrong stirred hard within him. Bewitched, yes, it would be easy to believe that she had special powers, and therefore, had seduced him into sin. But he had simply wanted her, and resented Charles. He hadn't wanted his uncle to die, and he was equally certain, in truth, that she had certainly not anticipated the death of Lord Charles, either.

"Look at you! Your beloved uncle and mentor has perished at her hands, and you are defending her!" Arianna accused.

He sighed. "Arianna, you are far too young and naive—"

"No, don't even make such a suggestion, Jamie. I'm neither that young, nor naive. She gave my father something, probably slipped it into his champagne. Some substance that would—along with her oh so subtle charms— would cause his heart to fail. She knows exactly what she is doing. You are the one who is naive, Jamie!"

Right or wrong, anger swept through him like

lava. He stared at her very coolly. "Arianna, please don't suggest that I'm an idiot. You will only make fools of both of us. And perhaps you should look to finding a way to get along with the woman."

Arianna frowned. "Why?"

"I'm not certain, but your father was extremely anxious for you to have some guidance as you reached your majority and made your debut among the Ton. If I'm not mistaken, she will have been appointed your guardian for the next several months."

Arianna stared at him, stricken. She shook her head. "Oh, no! I was his daughter. I'm certain my father saw to my inheritance."

"So he did. You are a very rich young lady. Unfortunately, you've not quite reached your birthday. And I believe you will discover that your stepmother is legally your guardian."

She gasped out loud. "No, Jamie, you inherit the title and the estate. You must be my guardian, certainly."

"I don't believe that your father's will is known to anyone in exact terms—other than his solicitors. Yet, how very sad. He has not been dead a day, and already his heirs are arguing over the bounty he has left behind."

That, at last, brought the anger and resentment slipping from her eyes . . . and tears filling them once again.

Jamie didn't know whether it was better for her to be miserable, or filled with such fury and a blind sense of justice that she was . . .

Dangerous.

"Arianna?" He took a step toward her, trying to offer a caring shoulder to cry on once again.

She accepted a hug, but stepped back quickly. "I'm all right, Jamie."

"Really?"

"I just need . . . to be alone."

"You're certain?"

"Absolutely. Please, Jamie, I've lost him! I was gone, at school, I so seldom saw him . . . and now, he's gone. I need to mourn for him in my own way now."

"I'm here if you need me."

She sniffed and nodded.

He studied her carefully. "Arianna, please, throwing about accusations that she killed your father will just create greater pain for all of us."

"Why? Are you afraid that they will discover I'm right?" she demanded.

He sighed. "No, not in the least. And there is going to be an autopsy."

"Ah!" she cried with pleasure. "So—the doctors even believe she might have murdered him."

He couldn't contradict that. "The point is, you running about and screaming will only draw scandal upon the family."

"The wedding was scandal enough," she said icily.

Jamie sighed. "Arianna, I'm not particularly one to care much what is said myself. But you're young now. And it may prove wise that you care, because, in the future, there might be a young man. And though he will surely love you with all his heart for you and you alone, he may be a man of note, a nobleman, perhaps, with a family determined that he marry a young woman of good reputation."

"As I've just said, the wedding was scandal enough."

"Your father's choice, not yours. But if you run about saying these things, your name could become tainted with every manner of evil thing said."

"If there is to be an autopsy, I'll not say another word. But what will you do, Jamie, if it's proved that she did do something?"

He stared at Arianna and answered flatly, "I'll see that she is prosecuted."

"Hanged!" Arianna said.

"I disagreed with your father's decision to marry, Arianna, but I don't believe that she's guilty of any wrongdoing in his death. If it proves to be true, then I will see that she's prosecuted."

"Hanged."

"We'll not go in circles here, Arianna. I am not judge and jury."

She nodded, then, at last. And huge tears of loss came to her eyes again.

"Arianna—"

"I'm fine, Jamie. Honestly. As I said, I just need to be alone."

At last, not at all comfortable, Jamie decided that maybe he had best leave her be.

When he was gone, Arianna closed her door. And locked it.

Tears streamed down her face, and she walked about the room, swearing. Swearing in English, and then in French.

Jamie would be appalled if he heard her!

But Jamie continued to think of her as a child. A

child! No, not at all. But he'd never understand such things. Neither he nor her father would have ever suspected the way the highborn young ladies had managed to slip beneath the noses of their guardian nuns.

But now . . .

School days were over. The point was that she was really far more mature and world-wary than Jamie would ever suspect.

And her father was dead.

And that wicked witch might be her guardian until her birthday.

No . . . never. Never!

Her birthday was just a matter of months. And what did that matter? The wicked witch might very well have murdered her father, no matter what Jamie had to say. A single day with that hateful woman having any kind of say over her whatsoever was too much!

She wouldn't allow it, she simply wouldn't allow it!

But that was not the worst of it. One way or another, with assistance or pure cunning, the woman had murdered her father. And she had to pay for it. Except that not even Jamie would accept the fact that murder had taken place. There was going to be an autopsy. That might prove that some foul play had befallen her father. But what if the autopsy showed nothing? Then, Jamie would never prosecute, never insist that she answer before a court of law, or even bring up such a matter to the Queen.

Arianna felt a new stream of tears well from her eyes.

She had to pay. The witch had to pay!

But she had said that she wouldn't run about casting out wild accusations. The family could not take anymore scandal. Because, Jamie had said, one day, it might matter to her. But it wouldn't. Nothing could matter anymore. She wouldn't fall in love with any gentleman or nobleman of esteem, because her father was gone, and . . .

She hesitated. And once again, found herself wondering just who that man had been. Handsome, charming . . .

A guest at her father's wedding. He had assumed she was a servant, and still, he had looked at her with such regard. She might, one day, fall in love with such a man . . .

No! How could she even be thinking about such a thing when her father was dead?

Sitting on the foot of her bed, she wiped the tears from her cheeks. Her father! She must think only about her father right now, and the fact that he had died at that woman's hands. What if there was no justice to be had for her father, legally, in a court of law?

Somehow, such a malicious and horrible creature must be punished.

She was going to have to do something about it, and the sooner she moved, the better.

She needed help, though, that was certain.

For a moment, she paused. Then she swung her door open and went in search of Mrs. Whitley.

Chapter 10

For Maggie, the days began to pass in a blur.

She had not intended to take any of the laudanum—she had known far too many women who had come to depend on it to deal with headaches, backaches, female aches, and even the simple ache of ennui.

But by the afternoon of the first day following her wedding, she discovered that she could survive what had happened, the arrangements, her horrible sense of remorse and guilt, and even the way she felt about knowing that she would never live through such a night again—with laudanum.

And so, the first two days following Charles's death became manageable. She simply spent them in her room, and she asked Fiona to see that her meals were brought and that she wasn't disturbed.

She awaited the results of the autopsy.

And at last, they came.

There was no hint of poison to be found in his body. His heart had simply failed him.

When the information was brought to her by her brother, she barely acknowledged what he said. That Justin was concerned was evident.

"You should be jubilant," he said. "You might even run around screaming and proclaiming your innocence. Of course, that wouldn't be in the best of taste, but . . ."

She felt no real pleasure at being vindicated. Those who condemned her as a murderess would continue to do so. Of course, she might be grateful that there hadn't been poison in his system administered by someone else—*she* would still have been arrested for the deed!

And yet, thanks to the laudanum, she felt very little.

"Now it's time for the wake, and funeral," Justin told her. "Maggie, whatever is wrong with you? Proprieties must now be met."

"I know."

"You'll have to be present, and present this evening. Charles will have his wake in the grand salon, in the house."

"Of course."

"Maggie—"

"Justin, please. Let me be. I will follow every propriety exactly, I swear."

And so she did. And despite the autopsy findings, several things were just as she had expected.

She was aware that when she was in a room, Arianna was not.

Her stepdaughter never spoke, and she appeared

only when it was absolutely necessary, and then, in the most comprehensive mourning attire Maggie had ever seen. She was swathed from head to toe in a black dress with a sweeping skirt and heavy brocaded bodice, and a veil so dark, Maggie wondered how she didn't trip.

When her father was waked in the grand salon, Arianna appeared, then managed to slip away, feeling ill. She refused to speak with Jamie, or anyone at all. Maggie kept her vigil, not retiring until the last of those who came to pay their respects had left.

Then came the solemn day of the funeral.

Once again, Arianna avoided a conversation with anyone, lifting a gloved black hand to stave off sympathy from any well-wisher. She was, in fact, so completely immersed in black that, if Maggie didn't know her stepdaughter was the one joining her and Jamie, she wouldn't have recognized the girl.

She expected the ice and silence she received from Charles's daughter. Thanks to the laudanum, she didn't care. Arianna was welcome to be as headstrong and wretched as she chose. For her part, Maggie determined not to fight the girl. It was all difficult enough.

Jamie, however, seemed irritated. But even he seemed to feel he had to give Arianna time to accept the situation in her own way.

There were other factors that might have upset Maggie more at the time.

There were whispers that stopped when she passed, and began again as soon as she was assumed to be beyond earshot. There were those who found it all amusing—the poor dear old fellow had gotten far too excited over such a young bride and . . . well, such things happened. There were others who mused that it was quite amazing that she'd managed to wed the old boy, and then have him drop dead so conveniently. Perhaps she hadn't poisoned him but still . . .

The Queen herself, surrounded by royals, nobles, and servants, attended the actual funeral service at Westminster; she arrived to a moment's high fanfare at the stroke of twelve, when the archbishop was to begin the service, and naturally, time was arranged for her to depart. There was a tear in her eye as she listened, and Maggie was heartened to realize that the Queen really had considered Charles a very dear friend. It was said that since her very good friend, Mr. Brown—rumored at times to be more than a friend—had died in '83, she had depended heavily at times on her friendship with Charles.

The Queen didn't, however, stop to speak with Maggie or the family; she gave Maggie a very royal nod before she departed, and Maggie assumed that was her way of expressing sympathy. Later, when the rites were long over and Charles's coffin was taken away to join others in the catacombs for his eternal rest, Justin told his sister softly that she should be very grateful for the Queen's appearance, and her acknowledgment. Victoria, by her appearance, had not just shown her grief for an old and dear friend; she had shown her support for Maggie, and that would influence the society throughout London, indeed, through all of the country and beyond. Maggie was vaguely grateful, but still in her blessed, drugged fog.

She was correct in every way; she painstakingly

made certain of that fact, and that she kept a cool distance from Charles's family.

She spent no intimate moments with Jamie, but did stand with him and Arianna at the reception following the funeral, and thanked all those who attended, many of whom had just been there for the wedding. Eventually, it was all over.

Except that it was not.

That night, both her brother and Mireau planned to return to the house in Mayfair. She was eager to leave, herself, eager to leave Jamie and Arianna to one another, and yet, the attorneys were coming sometime soon, and, according to Jamie, she had to meet with them.

That night, however, she asked Fiona to see that she was brought her supper in the room, along with a pot of strong tea—and a bottle of stronger whiskey.

Fiona faithfully followed her every wish, as she always did.

Except that she must have been worried about Maggie and the laudanum and the liquor, because Maggie had barely chewed a few mouthfuls of some meat concoction and enjoyed two cups of whiskey-laced tea before there was a knock on the door.

"Please, I don't wish to be disturbed!" she called out.

And was ignored.

Jamie entered the room.

"Good God, what on earth are you doing?" he demanded.

"Dining?"

"You barely touched the plate. And it smells like a distillery in here."

She arched a brow. "Drowning my sorrows?" she suggested.

He walked over to her tray, picked up the bottle of fine, single malt Scots whiskey, and threw it angrily into the fire. She leapt up from the winged-back chair at the hearth in protest.

"What on earth are you doing?" she demanded.

"Growing impatient."

"With what?"

"You!"

"I'm not really your concern. You said that I had to stay to see the solicitor. After that, I'll be out of your hair."

"What? Are you trying to prove Arianna right?"

"In what way?"

"That of being a worthless . . . witch."

"You're simply too kind, Lord James!"

She stared at him furiously, wishing with all her heart that she had not come to know him so well, and that she were back in her encompassing widow's weeds, and not dressed in the thin fabric of a cotton nightdress and only slightly thicker robe.

"Actually, under these circumstances, I am. I don't remember you being a blazing coward above all else."

She was about to respond angrily, but suddenly found herself deflated. She stared at the fire. "Perhaps I am a coward—because I am a worthless witch."

"A self-pitying one, so it seems."

She shrugged, watching the flames, then stared at him. And to her horror, tears, which surely, she should have been out of, sprang to her eyes.

"What if she is right?" she whispered.

"You are a worthless witch?" he queried.

"Perhaps I killed him," she said.

"Did you poison him?" Jamie asked pointedly.

"No! You know that—there was an autopsy!"

"Shoot him, stab him?"

"Good God, you know that I did no such thing, whatsoever!"

"Then how did you kill him?"

She paced before the fire, exhausted, nervous. "I . . . I . . . oh, God!" There was too much laudanum in her. That should have made her half asleep, apathetic, calm, and silent. The opposite seemed to be occurring. She clenched and unclenched her hands, staring at him, groping for words. "I hadn't imagined that . . . he wanted . . . oh! God, I felt mortified. Miserable. And I tried to do what he wanted."

"Um," Jamie murmured, eyeing her, "Charles was a dear man, especially so to me, but if you did what he asked after your wedding, you are hardly responsible."

"But I was responsible."

"Um . . . but you were manipulated. You'd married the man. He expected intimacy. You can hardly be blamed for trying to avail him. You shouldn't have married him, perhaps, but that's my opinion, not what he wanted."

She shook her head, swallowing hard. It was none of his affair, really, her determination that she had to go through with the wedding. Of course, if she had known then what she knew now . . . would she have changed anything?

Oh, God, yes! Being in frightful debt and at the heart of a simple scandal would surely have been far better than being in this position.

"You really don't understand."

"Then, keep trying."

"If you would just go away . . . !"

"Sorry."

"Jamie, don't make me be rude. Just get out."

"Not until we finish this conversation. What else is it that's making you feel so atrociously guilty?"

"I am not guilty!"

"Then . . . ?"

"Oh, Lord! Yes, I am guilty!" She backed into the chair.

She was startled to look up and find that he was standing before her. She was more startled when he hunkered down in front of the chair, closer still. "Explain," he said, and his tone was gentle, but had an edge.

"I think I prayed him dead!" she whispered.

"Prayed him dead?" His brows shot up.

She shook her head, face coloring as she turned to the flames once again. "I had thought . . . I don't know what I had thought. I'd wanted . . . darkness. I knew what marriage was, but I had thought . . . and he wanted light. And he wanted . . . a show. And I was miserable and mortified, and I was praying that I didn't have to go through with it, and then . . ."

He was just staring at her. She'd expected total condemnation. She was stunned to see a slight curl to his lips.

"Maggie, I don't believe that you prayed him dead."

"But I did."

"You said, 'Oh, God! Please strike this man dead!'"

"No, but, you see, I prayed that I wouldn't have to go through with it . . . and then Charles fell back."

Jamie's smile deepened. "I wouldn't divulge this line of thought to anyone else."

"I didn't intend to divulge it to *you*. You were simply too rude to leave, and so boorish as to demand an answer."

"Yes, well, do excuse me, he was my uncle, and I loved him very much."

"I did love him, too. I really did. I recognized him for a truly honest, considerate human being, one who cared about the world, people, social reform . . . I love the man he was. I just . . . I didn't actually want to be his wife, though."

"Maggie, I don't believe that God just decided to strike Charles dead because you wanted to avoid your wifely duties," he said.

"He wouldn't, would He?" she said, hopefully.

"I quite honestly don't believe so," Jamie assured her. "Actually, it's a little presumptuous of you to be so worried."

"Presumptuous?"

"Charles was a good man. God wouldn't have taken him unless it was his time—I mean, certainly not just on your say-so."

She flushed again. "Yes, you're right, that was horribly presumptuous of me. But still . . . I was so awful. In what I was thinking. I mean, after all, I did marry him."

"Yes, you did," Jamie said abruptly. He seemed very angry again, and stood, moving away from her. "The solicitors will be here at ten. Please be ready to see them. And stop with the laudanum, now. It was something you perhaps needed at first. No more."

He strode across the room, reaching impatiently for the door. The he paused, looking back at her. "The thing is, you see, there is no going back. And you're now Charles's widow, and there are responsibilities." He stared at her curiously another minute. Then, impatiently, he turned and nearly took the door off its hinges in his haste to leave.

Justin awaited Mireau in the grand salon. It seemed incredible that Lord Charles, Viscount Langdon, had been dead nearly a week. As he stared at the flames, he was grateful that his sister had been cleared of wrongdoing. Officially, of course, she had never been charged with anything. Unofficially, of course, there were those who still remained highly suspect of her.

He wondered at the wisdom of all that he had done. Perhaps Angus had been the one to make the contacts and inform them that it was really their only choice, but he was Lord Justin, Baron Graham, and he had set his signature to the consent forms. He reflected that, most men of sense and business would still consider that the right moves had been made. Lord Charles had been elderly—it wasn't as if the marriage might have gone on for a spectacular number of years. He was a good man, and his death was sad.

And in the marriage, he had become free from debt, free from the threat of debtor's prison, and he was even in position again to take charge of his own finances—and make something of his life. Perhaps that was it.

He had gone through the proper training to acquire a military position, and he had served for a few years. But the greatest action he had seen had been that of controlling a riot in Trafalgar Square when the insurgents had protested factory conditions. He had served a requisite time, and left the military. And since then . . .

He'd gambled away the estates his father had left him.

Lord Charles's death had left him feeling that his own life was quite a waste. His sister had come this far in his behalf, and asked only that he find the right girl, marry—and keep the family title from Angus and their cousins. Fine. He had simply not found the right girl. Never, in all the whirl of teas and hunts and balls had he found that one person who . . .

But actually, he had. Glaring at the flames, he remembered how he had come across the girl of his dreams in this very house. Hair like India ink. Skin as fair as snow. Eyes dark, lips so sweetly, and yet lusciously, red. The servant girl who had helped him adjust his cravat . . .

He'd not seen her since.

He heard the front door open and close. He turned, striding toward the entry. "Mireau?"

But no one had left the house; someone had arrived. It was Lord Charles's daughter, dressed—as had become her constant apparel—in a barrage of black attire that would shame the eternally mourning Queen. From head to toe, she was swathed, veil so thick it was a wonder that she hadn't tripped over her feet a dozen times, crashed into furniture, or, at the least, her fellow mourners.

"Good evening, Lady Arianna," he said gravely.

She lifted a black gloved hand. Justin realized that he blocked the stairway.

"You've been out and about alone? That's dangerous, these days. The bloke is attacking women of the poorest stature, but, still . . . my Gods, the murders going on these days! The papers are full of it all, you know. But then, I'm sure you'd never venture into the East End?"

The woman shook her head.

She didn't speak.

Suddenly, Justin wondered if he hadn't been tricked the day of his sister's wedding. He had heard Maggie complain about Arianna often enough. The girl loathed her, despised her, and accused her of murder still, no matter what the autopsy report showed.

Had he perhaps encountered the young lady of the house on the day of the wedding? Was this then the beauty he had met?

He walked toward her, suddenly determined that he would find out.

"Ah, my poor lady! It's quite understandable that your mourning is so deep. What a truly fine man your father was. We all miss him gravely."

Still, standing before him, she did not reply.

But Justin was determined. He blocked the stairway so that she couldn't run around him. He shook his head with sympathy, and then, with a flash of smooth speed, he reached out, lifting the veil that covered her face.

Disappointment filled him in the brief second before she rescued her cover.

She was not hideous by any means.

Neither was she the incredible stunning beauty who had so seared his sense upon the fateful day of the wedding.

Her hair was a simple brown. Flesh far from perfect. Lips narrow, and colorless. Indeed, she had a pleasant enough look about her, but she wasn't the little breath of perfection who had spoken with him on the day of the wedding, and she did not in the least resemble Lord Charles.

"Forgive me," he said, and stepped back awkwardly. "I shouldn't have intruded.

She didn't chastise him, or really, respond in any way at all. Veil back in place, she sped on up the stairs, nearly crashing into Mireau, who was then coming down.

"Your pardon, my lady!" Mireau said.

And received no reply.

As he reached Justin, he shook his head sadly. "Women!"

"Yes, it seems there will be quite some difficulty getting Lady Arianna to accept her father's death."

"Then there's your sister," Mireau said.

"Now? What has Maggie done now?"

"I'm heartily worried about her. She just isn't acting like Maggie."

"She won't speak with you, either, eh?"

"Told me to go on with you. If she could but leave herself, she'd be happy to do so. Shouldn't you be here for that meeting with the solicitors?"

"I've kept mum about it," Justin said. "I'm meeting

Angus at the club for breakfast tomorrow, and therefore, I'll be keeping him away."

"It's not his place. It's yours."

"Yes, I'm aware of that." He sighed. "Ah, Mireau. What a strange turn of events. Here, I worry about my sister. And I worry about myself. And time seems to stretch ahead with no great purpose."

"Perhaps you should make your first purpose in life a firm stand against Angus."

"You're right, my friend, you're right," Justin agreed. "For now . . . I'm ready to depart this place of death. When Maggie decides that it is time she can leave, we will come back for her."

They started to exit the manor house. At the door, Justin turned back. The disappointment he felt was monumental.

Where was the girl? Who was she?

And he wondered if he would ever find her again.

Arianna paced nervously back and forth in her room, waiting.

A moment later, the door burst open. "Well, what have you found out?" she demanded.

The girl in the black veil pulled it from her head, staring at Arianna in a tempest. "What have I found out! I was nearly caught. The man in the hallway . . . your stepmother's brother! He lifted the veil on me, and he saw my face!"

Arianna shook her head. "My stepmother's brother . . ."

"We can't keep doing this. I will wind up in the streets. Without references! In fact, if your stepmother were to pass along awful things regarding me—that I was a sneak and a cheat, say!—I might never find work!" her stand-in cried worriedly.

Arianna waved a hand in the air. "I've never met my stepmother's brother, so you're completely in the clear. What do you care what my stepmother says? When I get my story to the right people, she will be an absolute pariah if some honest man out there doesn't discover a way to get her in jail. You'll work for me, and you'll be fine."

Fiona stared angrily at Arianna. "Arianna, you are a dear lady, and a good friend to me, but you are not the head of the household."

"I inherit a third of my father's estate," Arianna reminded her.

"You haven't yet reached your majority. We've a few months to go—if you recall. And speaking of jail, I could wind up in jail for the things you have me doing."

"No . . . don't be ridiculous. Even if we are caught, I will say that I was in such a state that I couldn't attend the services for my father. I was prone with grief. There is no way that you will suffer for any of this."

"Hmmf! So far, Lady Maggie has obliged my urging to take laudanum, and thus she has not noticed that I'm not there to serve her when I should be. But what if she decides that it's time to be fully awake and aware, no matter how painful."

"I'll be out of the house completely soon, and you'll not have to worry," Arianna assured her. "Now, please, tell me what you've found out!"

Fiona sighed, taking a seat at the foot of Maggie's

bed as she undid the hooks on the encompassing black cape she wore. "Very little. Yes, Maggie is known at St. Mary's, and even at other parish churches. And she's loved, Arianna. Loved. She's contributed to the people with not just money, but her time, as well. She's rolled up her sleeves, as they say, and doled out food. And do you know, if you gave yourself a moment to get to know her—"

"Get to know her? Are you daft? She plotted this all out, and it's so obvious that I can't believe the world isn't screaming for her head! She married my father. The prenuptial contracts gave her brother a tidy sum to clear up his finances. The Graham solicitors were clever, or my father was entirely besotted, because none of that was due back, *even if she opted out of the marriage!* Now she stands to inherit a fortune as her widow's portion of my father's estate. And yet! How bizarrely convenient for her! He up and dies on their wedding night."

Fiona was silent for a minute, looking at Arianna in a way she didn't like. "Arianna, has it occurred to you that your father simply had a heart attack?"

"She planned it! I am not a fool, a child, nor so protected from the world as my father would have liked to believe. Maggie is a widow. Widow. Married to a young man she loved. She is surely very worldly. She knew what to do to my father to excite him to such an extreme that he . . . She did it on purpose, I tell you, and that is murder."

Fiona shook her head. "Arianna, I love you dearly, and I want to help you, but I can't help thinking that you are wrong, very wrong. I have seen her in the greatest distress!"

"Of course she's distressed! She may yet be caught—and hanged!"

Fiona sighed. "I must change and get to her."

She started to rise, but Arianna caught her arm. "You must have heard more, out in the streets."

"Yes, I did. The East End is in a terrible panic. Women have been horribly butchered. There's a maniac loose. They're calling him Leather Apron, and the entire city of London and the outskirts are all in a dither. Naturally! Imagine that! People are concerned about a *known* murderer who mutilates those he kills."

"He is killing common prostitutes," Arianna said.

"How kind of you to notice!" Fiona said.

Arianna flushed, and shook her head. "I'm sorry, I was making no dispersion on commoners. I'm merely suggesting that there would be no reason for you to be afraid. I sent you out for information, not to walk the streets for business. Of course, I'm concerned. It's terrible, what's happening. But perhaps, if these women didn't drink themselves silly and solicit men for more money to drink themselves sillier, this wouldn't be happening to them."

Fiona sat stiffly. "And perhaps, if money weren't spent on massive jubilees and extravagant luxuries, more of it could find its way to areas where people have no hope—leaving them no choice but to drink and seek prostitution as a means to eat."

"Most of them drink!" Arianna reminded her.

"Arianna! What would you do if you had nothing, nothing but the clothes on your back, not a room, not even a bed . . . unless you came up with the few pennies you needed!"

Arianna buried her face in her hands. "I'm sorry. So sorry. But I loved my father, so much. And he was such a good man, always sharing his wealth with the poor."

Fiona relented. "Of course, your pain is very deep. But honestly, I went to St. Mary's, where you suggested I might learn about her. And I met Father Vickers, and he glowed when he spoke about your stepmother. He had but one area of concern."

"And that was?" Arianna demanded, quickly jumping at Fiona's slip.

"She has a hatred for mesmerists."

"Mesmerists?"

"You know . . . hypnotists. And spiritualists. Those people who think that they can bring back the dead. Or pretend they can bring back the dead. If you had just come to the wake and the funeral, instead of sending me, you'd have heard Lady Marian talking about her 'dreadful' experiences. Apparently, there are all manner of people out there who believe that they have special powers. The Lord knows, maybe they do. But some of them are out to find silly old rich fools like the Duchess—and take them for all that they are worth. Anyway, the Duchess is always trying to talk to the late Duke. She went to a séance and in the middle of it, a woman reached out, breaking the 'circle.' If I have the story right, the man—the medium—had said that her husband wanted to touch her one last time, and a hand had appeared. But this other woman at the table leapt up and grabbed the hand—and it was fake! The fellow and his cohorts tried to kill them, then, but there were others at the séance, and they fought back. Apparently, one man was killed, a man and a woman are to stand trial for attempted murder among other things, and one man escaped. Lady Marian talks about little else. She had me cornered for a half hour at the funeral, and I couldn't escape, of course, because she knows you, so I didn't dare talk and excuse myself!"

"There were others in the room?" Arianna said curiously.

"Not the Lady Maggie—surely the Duchess would have said so."

Arianna studied Fiona. "Why? The Duchess didn't recognize that you weren't me! So far, no one has."

"That will change, I tell you! I was terrified when Lord Graham lifted my veil this evening."

"Lord Graham! Why should we care about him in the least? He won't be around anymore. I believe that there is a meeting with my father's solicitors tomorrow morning, and then Lady Maggie will be out of the house, and her brother won't be around anymore. And I don't even know him, so there's nothing for you to worry about!"

"Arianna, I tell you that this game of yours is dangerous."

Arianna shook her head miserably, and despite herself, she felt tears flood to her eyes once again. "Fiona, I loved him. I'm not playing a game, I'm desperate that there should be justice for him."

Fiona sighed. "Well, I'm sorry. I haven't found out anything at all that Lady Maggie has done that was illegal or immoral or even bad. She married for love, and so became a disgrace to her family. I'm afraid that I find that to be rather romantic. And surely, no matter how wealthy she is—and perhaps even overly impressed with her place in society—you must believe as well that she shouldn't be fleeced out of her riches!"

"Fiona, you've done very well. Perhaps I need to get farther out into the streets myself," Arianna mused.

"You know the shops in Coventry Gardens, and about the city, Arianna. You know nothing about the truly mean streets!" Fiona cautioned her.

"Perhaps I should find out more about them—firsthand."

Fiona sighed. "Arianna, you're scaring me."

"Don't be silly. There's nothing to be scared about."

Fiona rose, nervously casting off the cape, the black satin skirt, and the brocaded black bodice she had been wearing. "Where are my work clothes?" she asked Arianna. "Mrs. Whitley will be looking for me soon enough."

Arianna waved a hand in the air. "Oh, don't worry. My stepmother roused herself enough to tell Mrs. Whitley that you had to answer to her, and only to her."

"Did she really?" Fiona mused.

"Don't you dare start liking that woman, or feeling the least sorry for her!" Arianna protested.

"Arianna, I am not an heiress, just a working girl from Dublin."

"You know that I'll see to it that you're well paid for everything you do for me."

Fiona sighed. "I will not do anything illegal or immoral, Arianna. And I beg you to think about the way that you feel. There was an autopsy. Your father died of a heart attack."

"Good night, Fiona," Arianna said.

"Oh, please! Don't be angry with me. I am your friend, and I want to help you, and make you feel better."

"Of course. Good night; I really must get some sleep."

Adjusting her maid's cap, Fiona nodded. "Good night, Arianna."

When Fiona had left, Arianna stoked her fire, set her hands out before the warmth, and shivered still.

Mesmerists . . .

Spiritualists . . .

Hm. It was natural that she might seek out a few. She had just lost her dear father.

Chapter 11

The solicitors were Mr. Green and Mr. Green, father and son. Maggie was disturbed to find that she was meeting with them alone—Jamie had spent a half hour with them before the appointed time, and it seemed that he was impatient to be off, leaving her to herself.

Thankfully, he had gotten through to her the night before. She had done nothing but marry a man who had fervently wanted to marry her, and she was not going to spend any more time moping about, feeling guilty. A strenuous argument with herself had finally convinced her that she wasn't evil—it had been natural to feel discomfort with such an aging man, and she would have done her best to be a good wife.

Charles had died. All men died. Age had taken him. She had not.

And so she had sworn off laudanum, and was completely in her right senses when she sat with the men in her late husband's library.

The elder Mr. Green was a severe man with stern gray muttonchops and a balding pate. The son was his exact copy, except that he had a head full of rich brown hair. One day, of course, he would resemble his father completely.

She was gratified when they first read a letter in Charles's own hand, speaking of his happiness when he was with her. She sat in silence when they went on to read and then explain the circumstances of his estate. Naturally, James Landgon inherited the title, the lands belonging to the title, Moorhaven and grounds among them. She, however, had a right to consider the property as her address throughout her natural life, lest she should remarry, and then, of course, she must vacate the premises. She was informed as to the accounts set up in her name, the amount of funds she'd have available, and the limitations of what she might use at any given time, since Charles had wanted her inheritance to sustain her through life should she choose not to marry again. Still, each month, she had a generous allowance.

She listened in appreciation.

But then they came to the point of her stepdaughter. She was the girl's legal guardian. Charles had been quite concerned about his girl, bereft of a mother for so very long. He had every intent for the girl to marry, and his nephew, James, was well aware of the particulars. However, she was to reach her eighteenth birthday first, have a season out for balls and teas and solid friendships to be made. Until that time, he asked that Maggie do her best to see that

Charles's beloved Arianna was given advice, love, and guidance.

She sat stunned. There was no condition in the will; she could walk away and refuse to have anything to do with the girl—other than to dole out allowance and guard her accounts. But in his own hand, Charles had left the plea that she do her best to understand and love the young woman, in his stead.

When the younger Mr. Green finished speaking, he cleared his throat, looking at her, then his father.

"Do you understand all the terms, my lady?" the elder Mr. Green inquired.

"Yes."

"You're not obliged to anything, but..." the younger Mr. Green said.

"But in his own hand, my husband asked that I care for her," she said.

"Yes. Of course, you are in complete control of her inheritance, until such time as she reaches her majority."

"I understand, yes."

She hesitated, barely knowing the men. Then she asked, "Is Arianna aware of the terms of this will?"

The younger Mr. Green cleared his throat again, looking at his father.

"We speak with her next," he said.

She wondered how to delicately broach the subject of her stepdaughter's complete and total loathing of her. Then she decided that plain speaking was best.

"She hates me, and believes that I killed her father. I'm not sure that I would be a proper guardian for her. James is her cousin ... or second cousin twice removed, and far closer to her affections."

"Lord James is aware of the terms of the will."

"And?"

"Charles specifically asked that you be there to guide his daughter."

She sighed. Charles had never known that Arianna so despised her.

"But . . ."

"Are you refusing, my lady?" the elder Green asked, looking at her sternly.

"I'm not refusing, I'm explaining that the child detests me."

The elder Mr. Green wore a look of total impatience. "She is a child, just that. The child of your late husband. With power comes responsibility, Lady Maggie."

Maggie rose, lifting her hands. "I can do my best, gentlemen. But, perhaps, after you've spoken with her . . . you'll see my position. I sincerely thank you for your time."

"We're available, whenever you need us, my lady," the elder said. Of course they were available, she thought wearily. They might consider her to be a murderess themselves, but they derived a handsome income from handling the affairs of this household. She didn't begrudge them that, and Charles had trusted them.

"Thank you. I may well need you soon enough. I'll see that Arianna is sent to you, if she isn't awaiting her time as well."

With that, Maggie swept from the library.

Arianna wasn't outside waiting, but the maid, Fiona, was.

"Fiona, can you tell Arianna that her father's solic-

itors wish to see her? And then, please, consider
yourself free for the rest of the day. I have . . . business
elsewhere."

She left Fiona to deal with Arianna, and Arianna
to deal with the solicitors. Right now, if she didn't escape the house for a time at the very least, she
thought that she would die.

As she started up the stairs to her room, she nearly
collided with Jamie. He had a bag in his hands.

"Ah, Maggie. Clear-eyed at last!" he said dryly.

She frowned, looking at his valise. "You're leaving?"

"I have my own home."

"You've just inherited this one."

"Yes, well I'm afraid that I have some very pressing
business affairs that must be attended to as well. This
house remains your home, as you well know. Until
such time as you find another husband."

"I'm scarcely seeking another husband, Lord
James."

"Um. Well, I suppose, as matters stand, you certainly don't need one."

"Marriage, Lord James, should scarcely be a matter of need."

"Oh?" he said, his tone polite enough, his skepticism more than obvious anyway, considering recent
events.

She flushed, and was annoyed that she did so, and
yet, refused to be cowed.

"I believe that Arianna will need you."

"Charles specifically believed that she would need
you, Maggie. Therefore, I think that, perhaps, you
and Arianna need some time together."

"You, too? This is ridiculous, and dangerous. She loathes me."

He didn't reply at first. She gripped the banister, feeling a strange new sense of agony. There was a distance between them, naturally. Charles had died. She knew that she had suffered a terrible sense of guilt and betrayal. He must have known it all the worse. And yet . . .

That night . . . all magic and seduction to her . . . had just been . . . a moment of undeniable urge for him.

And now, he wasn't just the illustrious adventurer who had so nobly and loyally served the Queen. He was Viscount Langdon. Titled, and rich. Every mother in the Ton would be pushing her young and beautiful daughter in his direction. She had been a moment's fancy, and worse. She was the tainted woman who had married a commoner, been caught in an indecent club, married his great uncle, and possibly contributed to his early demise.

Not only that, the solicitors had said that Jamie had been well aware of Charles's intent for his daughter. Did that mean that she was supposed to marry Jamie? Was that why he was so determined that he must not live at the house now?

"Arianna is young, and at the moment, in a great deal of pain. Somehow, you both must reconcile."

"I'm seriously doubtful that we shall ever reconcile."

"But you must."

"I should leave the house, and you should stay," she said coolly.

"Really?" he inquired. "You should take the money—and run?" he added politely.

"I am saying no such thing!" she told him angrily. "I'm not at all sure that my handling the girl will be good. How can I guide her in any direction when she can't abide being in the same room with me?"

"You'll have to figure it out, won't you?" he said. "Good day, my lady."

He started to move past her on the stairs.

And for a moment, they were close. So close that she could remember being in his arms, remember his eyes when they were gentle, and suddenly, the agony of it seemed more real than even her long cherished grief for Nathan, and the horror of the days gone by. And she knew that he had come to mean far more to her than even that night of intimacy that had seemed greater than the world itself. She had liked him, what she knew about him, the way that he saw the world, the way that he had seemed, beneath it all, to understand certain things about her.

And yet he did not, and what she remembered was an illusion, nothing more. For though it seemed that he hesitated for a minute, that he might even look at her and smile with a touch of gentle longing and understanding, he did not.

He stiffened and continued down the stairs, calling back, "If you need me, send Darby to me. I'll be at my town house, or within the city at least, for a few months to come."

She didn't wait for him to exit. She suddenly felt that she had to reach the top of the stairs before she burst into wretched tears.

She had sworn that she would cry no more.

For the moment, it seemed imperative that she get

out of the house herself. She didn't look back as Jamie left the house, but hurried to her room to collect her cape and reticule.

It seemed amazing to Jamie that so fragile and ordinary a woman should be the queen of such a vast empire.

And yet, Victoria, for all her simplicity in dress and manner in her own home, looked at him with eyes that were intelligent and wise, even for all her years. Her hair was gray and smoothed sternly back. She was in black, as she was always. Albert was gone so many years now, and still, Queen Victoria lived for her memories of a better time. Her memories of love.

He had been surprised that she had summoned him, yet glad to come. She met with him in the little sitting room beyond her bedchamber, and with no ceremony or preamble. The tea service set before them was elegant, but the Queen herself was quite down to earth.

"I apologize for summoning you when the loss of your dear uncle is so recent," she told him, waving a hand that indicated he must take a seat.

"Your Majesty, you know that you may summon me at any time, and I am grateful for the love that you gave my uncle. Indeed, his loss is a great one," Jamie said.

"To me, as well."

"Thank you."

"The country has never needed the likes of him more!" Victoria said. Her hand shook slightly with indignation as she moved to pour.

"Your Majesty, the insurrectionists are opposed by many loyal Englishmen and women—of all classes—who admire you tremendously, and are totally loyal to the Crown," Jamie assured her.

Her eyes flashed. "Ah, but surely you are aware that there are those who would happily destroy all that has been forged throughout the years. We are not just a country, Lord James! We are an empire, and all the glory has been gained by those men who have gone out and fought for our glory. So many of whom gave their lives . . . and yet, yet here, we struggle!"

Since she had taken the throne of England, Victoria had faced her detractors. There had been attacks on her very life. They were living in a new world, and they both new it. The prime minister and the parliament were the true law of the country, and many believed that indeed, the monarchy itself was an anachronism. But it was equally true that, despite the lives of many of the royal household, Victoria herself was loved and esteemed; she was a great figurehead, a grandmother, a woman who, despite her years of mourning and the many times she had shut herself away, remained beloved.

"Is there something in particular to which you're referring, Your Majesty?" he asked.

She waved an elegant little hand at a stack of newspapers on the table by the tea service. "What is happening now is deplorable! There is a maniac at large in the East End. And what is being written . . . well, I understand. You have passed sad days. But there is a madman on the loose who is busy at work in our country . . . chopping up his victims. And there are those who are using the situation to . . . to topple the Crown."

"Your Majesty, surely it's not quite so serious as that?"

"Read!" she said, and it was a command.

Jamie looked at her, and then at the stack of papers. He picked them up. The first was a story on the inquest regarding the death of a certain Annie Chapman. Horrid details regarding the mutilation of the body were written out clearly. At the end of the article was a paragraph suggesting that the tragic circumstances of life in the East End were to blame, and then, the article went on to suggest that debauchery in the highest places might also be to blame. He glanced at the Queen who waited patiently and picked up the next article.

It was much the same.

There were several of them, and they suggested that the nation itself was responsible.

He set the papers down. "Your Majesty, there will always be those who seek not news, but sensationalism, and to turn anything written into a treatise on their own beliefs."

"The police really have no clues; they arrested a man named Pizer—there's an article in there about it—and they had to protect the man from being butchered by the mob! At the inquest—if you'll look at that article—he was called as a witness, really so that he could give his alibi, and clear himself. If you keep reading, you will find that some people believe he is an immigrant, and Lord knows, they can create havoc in an area where so many of the residents do come from other countries. They are crying that the man is surely a Jew, and God help us, but we are responsible for the lives and welfare of all our subjects! There will be mob violence if something isn't done. Descriptions of the fellow have him as a butcher, a short man, a tall man, a rich man, a poor man. And, if you keep reading, you will discover that the police are receiving all kinds of letters, confessions by dozens of disturbed individuals, missives from mystics, clerics, hypnotists, dreamers, and so forth. There are those who suggest that an eyewitness account states the fellow was exceptionally well dressed, a gentleman, nobleman . . . or—well, so far, they have not stated royalty!"

"I'm sure the police are desperately working as hard as they can," he said.

She lifted her royal nose. "Yes. Some of the officers on the force are most exceptional men, doing all that they can. Some are . . . perhaps some of them have gained their appointments through political associations. There are even those out there who believe that these heinous crimes are not being com- mitted by a butcher, but by a Communist! I've received copies of a few of the letters the police have received as well!" These she drew from a pocket in her elegantly laced black skirt, along with the monocle she used to read. "Listen. 'I was in Hyde Park the other day when once again a number of the Communist fellows were raising up their red flag. One said to the other, You jolly well wait. Once there's a few murders happening here in the West End, and they'll be screaming like stuck pigs!' " The Queen paused to stare at him, making certain that she had his full attention, and that he understood the gravity of the situation. "Here, then, Lord James, another. 'Someone out there is saying, with these horrors happening, that the police might be brought quite low, and then the government might fall. Lord Salisbury would be forced to resign, Gladstone would come in, and voila—there you have it. The ruin of the greatest Empire on earth certain, and a secular object obtained, again, voila—a republic!'"

Again, the Queen paused, looking at him. And, indeed, he understood the gravity of the situation. Political balance was always a tightrope walk.

"I understand the concern being caused. However, I have read the details regarding the murders, and I don't think that they are being perpetuated by anyone with a political design. For most men and women alike, killing is not that natural a business, and certainly, carving up another human being is not something most people are willing to do."

"I, too, believe that only a madman, a true lunatic, could do such a thing. But I must get to the bottom of this situation. While he—they, she, though before God, I cannot believe that a woman could do this thing—is out there, these horrible affairs might well continue."

"I'm afraid so," he said quietly. One thing he had learned was that though it was wise to watch one's language with the Queen, there was nothing she liked more than honesty.

"I'd like you, Lord James, to quietly step in, make a few discreet inquiries, and do all that you can to find out just what is going on!"

"Your Majesty, of course, I am ready to do your bidding. But every policeman in the area is surely combing the streets—"

"I'm not asking you to find this crazed killer for me, Lord James. I am asking you to slip in, watch the police, the people, and keep an ear to the ground for the political climate, and God help us, save the monarchy—and perhaps even the Empire."

It was a hefty assignment. Jamie just looked at her for a moment.

"Be my eyes and my ears!" she said softly.

She waved a hand in the air, and he knew that he was dismissed.

And that the Queen might have given him an impossible task. And yet . . .

He was quite suddenly grateful to her. With such work before him, he could perhaps, at last, tear his mind from his thoughts of what had been, and what was . . .

And the terrible hunger that remained inside him. When he should have been filled with nothing but pain . . .

All that he felt was need. And when his dreams should have been those of memory and loss, they turned to vivid recall instead, and now, more than ever, she seemed to whisper in his sleep, and haunt his days and nights.

"I will gladly do all that I can, Your Majesty," he assured her.

Departing Buckingham Palace, he found Randolph awaiting him in the carriage in the vast drive.

"Where to, Lord James?" Randolph asked him.

"The East End," Jamie said.

"Is your uncle's widow already busy and about again?" Randolph asked him.

Jamie shook his head and scowled. "She'd best not be!" he replied. Then he paused, reflecting on his vague but impassioned orders. "Home, first, Randolph. Perhaps it's time for a change."

Chapter 12

"Have ye heard, have ye heard?"

Maggie was amazed by the number of women in the churchyard. She couldn't be overly flattered that they had come to hear her speak—or even that they had come for a handout. She hadn't announced that she was coming, and had decided on finding Mireau and bringing him here simply because she'd so desperately felt the need to do something. Making some kind of arrangements with Father Vickers for future work had seemed her only straw.

But even as they left the cab they had taken down—she had sent Darby on home after she'd reached her own house in Mayfair—the women had begun running out to her.

"Oh, m'lady!" moaned a tall, slender woman. "Have ye heard what he did ta the poor souls?"

"The murders?" Maggie said. "I'm so sorry, yes. I've read about them."

"Blimey!" Another of the women elbowed the tall one a bit roughly. "Lizzie, ain't you 'eard? The poor lady's married, and lost another 'usband already!"

A sound of sympathy arose from the crowd. "Thank you," Maggie said.

"Are you all right, ducky?" said the tall thin one.

"Ye can't be callin' the likes of 'er 'ducky,' Lizzie!" came a voice from the crowd. "She's more of a lady now, she is! Married 'erself a Viscount, she did!"

An "Ooooh!" went up then. Maggie waved a hand in the air. "My dear friends, it doesn't matter what you call me, what does matter is that you've got to start taking care of yourselves. You must watch out."

" 'Cause 'e'll stike again, 'e will." It was the one who had called out from the middle of the crowd. She inched her way forward. Short and round, she might have been forty, looked eighty, and like most of them, was missing several teeth. " 'E'll strike again, 'cause the coppers can't catch 'im!"

"I still say it was that Pizer fellow, Leather Apron!" Lizzie volunteered.

" 'E 'ad himself an alibi, that one, 'e did!" said the rounder woman.

"Did you know the victims?" Maggie asked.

"Aye, and sad they were!" said a younger woman, coming forward and drawing her shawl more tightly around her shoulders as she shivered. "I was at one of the workhouses with Polly," she said. She shook her head. "She could have a mean way with her when she drank, but no one deserved such a fate!" The woman standing before Maggie then was almost still pretty. She had huge brown eyes, and her hair was a sable color.

"Did you 'ear what the coroner said after the inquest?" Lizzie demanded. "Said that Annie Chapman 'ad 'er uterus taken! What a bloody mess it all was. The coroner, 'e gave the police a piece o' his mind, I daresay!"

The younger woman told her, "It's all brought back whispers of Burke and Hare, and what they were up to with their body snatchin'! Seems an American was offering upwards of twenty pounds sterling for certain body parts."

Someone giggled. "Ah, with both Polly and Annie, eh, the body parts 'ould be preserved in plenty o' gin, eh?"

The others giggled, then fell uncomfortably silent. They stared at Maggie as if she had an answer for them. She shook her head. "There's really no answer for such a fiend," she said. "But until the police do catch him, you need—well, frankly, you need to find other work!"

"What other work?" Lizzie said. "There really ain't no other work for the likes o' us, and that's the sad truth of it."

Maggie shook her head firmly. "Some of you have been laundresses. There's casual work out there, you have to look for it." They all stared at her blankly. What they knew was prostitution, and that was that. Most of the time, they were looking for enough money for a bit of gin, and then a doss for the night. If they could only keep down their gin consumption, that meant perhaps one man, and a few quick minutes standing in an alley somewhere and tolerating the few moments it might take. There wasn't much that went with the actual sex act.

"It's your lives at stake!" Mireau called out impatiently.

Again, the women appeared uncomfortable. "Did ye bring us anything, m'lady?" someone called out hopefully.

"No," Maggie said, truly sorrowful. "But we've a bit of money, don't we, Mireau?"

He stared at her as if she had gone completely mad. Then she understood why. The women began to press forward.

"Me doss, just me doss!" the pretty younger woman said.

"Now, back off a bit!" Mireau insisted. Maggie had her reticule out, and Mireau took it from her, fierce as a bulldog. "One at a time, one at a time!"

In seconds flat, her purse was emptied, and despite the camaraderie the women could have at times, there was jostling, shoving, and swearing as it happened. Once the money was meted out, they began to move off, calling back their thank-yous.

Mireau looked at her, shaking his head. "You know where they're all headed, don't you?" he demanded. "The nearest pub for their gin!"

"Some," she admitted. "But not all."

He shook his head, still, staring at her. "Maggie, this fellow is going to strike again. And no matter how you try to help, you can't keep these women off the streets. Ask Father Vickers."

"Mireau, if we've helped one—"

"Yes, yes, we've changed humanity! Did you want to see Father Vickers? Let's pray that I have cab fare home, since, God forbid, you chose not to let a coachman take us—even now, when you've got a man such as Darby at your beck and call!"

"If we have to, we can borrow from the poor box," Maggie said.

"Right. Like there's anything in the poor box here!"

"Shall we see Father Vickers?"

"Yes, yes, let's go on in."

They walked into the church. Father Vickers was lighting candles with a young altar boy.

"Maggie, Jacques!" he said, surprised. He left off at his task and came hurrying down the aisle to meet them. He looked at Maggie with concern. "My lady! What on earth are you doing down here? Your poor husband, hardly buried! My dear, bless you, but God will understand that you need your time."

"What I don't need is time, Father," Maggie said wearily. "It's down to where I stare at the walls in misery. I need to be busy again, Father."

"Surely, there are friends you need to see."

"I think not," Maggie murmured, uncomfortably remembering her night out with Cecilia.

"This is not a good time to be risking this neighborhood," he told her.

"We've heard. It's all simply ghastly," Mireau said.

"You don't know just how ghastly," Father Vickers told them. "Two poor souls—or more—gone on to God in a most horrid manner! The police can't rightly figure just how many this one lunatic has done in. But it's only the last two who have been so horribly butchered. Yet it's the letters to the police . . . the articles written, that are nearly as frightening. Anarchy could well be at hand." He looked very nervous, actually craning his head to see over their shoulders, as if someone might have followed to hear their conversation.

"Whatever is the matter?" Maggie said.

He shook his head.

"Father Vickers! I would never betray a confidence, and you know that!"

"Come, come, then, let's go on to my little room, shall we?"

Father Vickers had a small, private place in the vicarage, adjoining the church. He had a bed, a table, a few chairs, and a stove and kettle. He set water on for tea and as he worked, he told them, "The rumors down here are running rife! At these inquests, the witnesses have given different descriptions of the men they last saw with the dead woman. Most of them point out a nondescript fellow in shabby clothing. Some say that he was well dressed. There are those who seem to believe that this murderer rides here in a grand carriage, then rides away, and that's why the blood is not seen on the fellow. Then again, there are slaughterhouses near, and someone might not be noticed walking about covered in blood!"

"But a rich carriage would surely be noted on the streets," Maggie said.

"Maybe. And maybe it moves out so quickly that it's on streets where others might be. We all know that the rich sometimes like to play among the poor." He poured water over the tea leaves.

"You're still not saying everything," Maggie told him gravely.

He hesitated, looked around again, and when he spoke, it was in a whisper. "Prince Eddy himself has played in these parts."

"I have no difficulty believing that Prince Eddy

might hire a prostitute, but surely . . . I think she'd be a bit more comely and younger than the girls hereabouts!" Mireau said.

"The one he was with . . . wasn't a prostitute. She worked in a shop."

Maggie shook her head. "Father Vickers, I'm lost. Prostitutes are being killed, not shop girls."

He brought the tea to the table then, discarding even the offer of milk or sugar. "No, listen. He met a shop girl. A young, *Catholic* shop girl. There's rumor that there was a marriage, and that the girl had a child."

"But I don't understand. What would that have to do with anything?"

"What if someone were furious. Did you hear me? *Catholic* shop girl! And there was a child!"

Maggie sipped her tea, shaking her head. "Father Vickers," she said gently. "If this had happened, it wouldn't matter. If there was a marriage, it would not be legal. Eddy cannot marry without the Queen's permission, and an heir to the throne cannot marry a Catholic. And you said that she was a shop girl. What has that to do with prostitutes?"

Father Vickers sighed. "The shop girl hovered on the verge of prostitution. She might well have been friends with these women. And perhaps . . . they're being silenced."

"The theory is ridiculous," Maggie said flatly. "If someone were to be silenced—they'd be killed. Simply killed. I mean, if someone were trying to cover something up—and none of it really seems to go together—why make such a huge production of it? We all know that it's sad but true—simple murder here goes unnoted. People have only cared, the newspapers have only gone wild, because of the beastly details."

Nodding at her, Father Vickers continued to look glum.

"Why are you so worried, still?" she asked him.

"Because there's truth, and perception of the truth. I'm very afraid of what people will say, and what they will believe, whether true or not, if these murders continue," Father Vickers said.

"We have to pray that this man is caught," Mireau said. "And by the way, Father, Maggie didn't come with any handouts. No food. So she gave away our money."

Father Vickers stared at her.

"What do you think they'll do with that money, so early in the evening?" Mireau asked Father Vickers.

"Buy gin," he said.

She let out a long sigh. "Let's arrange for some food, then, Father, shall we?"

As it happened, Mireau did have the money on him for the cab ride home. Father Vickers walked them out. After Maggie was seated, before closing the door, Father Vickers gripped her hands in his own. "Bless you, child. And don't you worry. God above knows that you're innocent."

A creeping feeling settled over her.

"Innocent?" she said.

"You haven't been keeping up with the papers, have you?" he asked.

"No."

He drew a clipping from his pocket and handed it to her. She noted the paper, and then that the item was unsigned. "Dead is Dead," the caption read. She scanned it quickly. "While the police are insane seeking a murderer who relishes his task with grotesque mutilation, it seems the authorities have forgotten that whether brutally slain or killed quickly and in silence, dead is dead. Perhaps the authorities should be looking in higher places, for murder which does scream out in blood. They look to madmen, and not the fairer sex. A beautiful face can hide an evil heart. Be warned."

She looked at Father Vickers, and didn't flush, nor betray her anger. "Thank you for showing me this."

"Most readers will have no idea what it means—or to whom they're referring."

"But enough will," she said softly. "It's all right. I have been the subject of scandal before."

"For your marriage to Nathan, not murder," Father Vickers said worriedly.

"There was an autopsy. And the Queen attended my husband's funeral."

"The wrong person could point out that the rich can be protected because of the Queen—if that were the case, the anarchist would be justified in tearing down the Crown," Father Vickers reminded her.

"I'm forewarned, Father. And I believe I know where this came from," she said. "Thank you again. And we'll return—with bread next time. No more coins to be spent on gin."

He grinned. "God go with you."

"And you, Father," she said.

Their cab jostled onto the street. Mireau was staring at her. "So—where did the article come from?"

"I'm not certain, of course."

"But you suspect . . . ?"

"Who else?"

"The incredibly sweet, young, beautiful Arianna?"

"Young and beautiful, yes. Sweet? Like acid!"

"Do you think she'll keep it up?" Mireau asked worriedly.

"I think we'll have a mother-daughter talk," Maggie said. "And then I shall go to the paper and threaten a suit for slander."

Mireau grinned. "There's my girl! Back in form." He frowned suddenly as he looked out the window.

"What is it?"

"I don't know. Strange . . . I've never been down here looking for a prosti—" He paused, looking at Maggie and flushing. "I'm not saying I've never . . . just never here."

"What are you babbling about?" Maggie demanded.

"I don't know. There was a woman on the street, and her face was mostly hidden by her scarf and shawl. And yet . . . I saw her eyes. And she looked at me as if she knew me."

Maggie shrugged. "Maybe she does know you."

"Maggie! I told you, I would never come here to . . . to. I simply wouldn't!"

She smiled. "Mireau, she might have seen you with me when we come down here to help the poor wretches."

"Oh. Oh! Of course," he said, and sat back.

"This is all very scary," Maggie said.

"Of course. There's a madman loose."

She shook her head. "Yes, of course, but that's not

what I meant. I mean, it's very scary, the way people come up with rumors and talk. Suggest that women might be killed because they knew about an illicit affair."

"There's always talk!"

"Father Vickers is right, though. Talk can hurt."

"Maggie, we should go away. On a holiday."

"One doesn't go on a holiday when newly widowed," she said.

"Ah, but one can retreat from daily life," he reminded her. "Winter is coming. We can go to the south of Italy."

She shook her head slowly. "I have a child to raise, remember? And I intend to do a bit of raising when I return home."

"He saw me!" Fiona said in despair.

"Hush up!" Arianna told her. "He has no idea of who you are. You are just being silly. Now, come along. This looks like an intriguing pub."

"You'll never get away with this," Fiona said. "I might, but you won't!"

"I always said that if I weren't my father's daughter, I would have loved to go on stage," Arianna said. "You watch me. I can do this."

She slipped into the pub, Fiona sighing and following in behind her. They had certainly managed to get fitting clothing. And she had to admit, Arianna, when determined, had her means and ways. They had come to Aldgate, then started walking. They had come in servants' garb, and made themselves appear as shabby as possible.

They'd found a woman from whom to rent a room.

The room was quite terrifying. It smelled like a sty and the floor was thick with rat excrement. But it was a base. And from there, they had easily found peddlers selling the lowest grade of cloth and clothing, and it had been even better that their newly purchased skirts, petticoats, and bodices fit so poorly. A little soot on Fiona's face, and she had really appeared the part.

"You," she'd informed Arianna, "are simply too pretty."

"A lovely thing to say," Arianna had acknowledged. "But not true. So . . . here we go."

And they moved out on the streets, and now, into a pub.

"I'll never be able to drink this wretched gin!" Fiona said, as they ordered, and took their glasses to a crowded table.

"So don't drink it!" Arianna hissed in return.

"Well, 'e don't strike in daytime, do 'e, luv?" a woman next to Arianna said loudly. "We makes our money in the day, then!"

"And drinks it by night!" her companion said, causing her to roar. Then the first woman turned, studying Arianna, and scowling.

"Eh! 'Ere's a pretty one fer ye, Maeve. Will ye looky 'ere? Where'd ye come from, luv? I've not seen the likes of ye on the streets in a fair while, I can tell ye!"

The woman had frizzy red hair and a gaunt face. She was long past her prime, and further past whatever looks she might have once had herself.

To Fiona's amazement, Arianna was ready with a reply. She scowled fiercely as well. "I had a job in the city, I did. A fair enough one. Only the old buzzard wot hired me thought that I was for the likes o' him!"

"Couldn't 'a been worse than wot ye'll find on the streets 'ere, deary!" Maeve cackled.

Arianna made a face. "Didn't say I wasn't willing to take his shillings, did I? 'Twas his wife wot threw me out!"

"Ah!" Both women clucked in sympathy with her.

"Still, ye are a pretty thing," the first woman said. "And 'tis dangerous in these parts, now, 'adn't ye 'eard?" She shivered.

"I know . . . have you heard of any other work?"

Maeve made a noise. "Ye'd be seein' one o' us two scared enough to be doin' it off the streets were we to know about it, luv."

"You know, I've thought about goin' straight to the police. Sometimes, I've kind of a special sight," Arianna said.

"Special sight? Wot's that?" Maeve asked.

"She's one of those medium people, you know, wot talk to the dead!" the first woman said. Then her eyes widened and she smiled. "Suppose I find ye a job, one that pays well? I get a cut on it, right?"

"Certainly!"

The woman produced a raw, work-worn hand. "I'm known as Red Hannah. My 'air, you know. My friend 'ere is Maeve. Maeve the Slave, some of the boys calls 'er."

" 'Ush it, 'Annah!" Maeve growled, and Hannah grinned. "Don't know about yer friend 'ere, the silent one," she said, indicating Fiona, "but there's word out that there's a fellow putting together a business. 'E's one of those spiritualists. 'E's been around, looking for a girl, and 'e hasn't liked a one of us, but 'e'd like you, I think. You make sure I take a cut, and I'll set you up a meetin'."

"I swear, you'll get your cut," Arianna told her solemnly. "I'm Annie."

"Another Annie!" Maeve moaned.

" 'Ere, then, this time, say . . . four days from now," Hannah said, sizing up Arianna again. "Be 'ere, now!"

"I'll be here," Arianna said, then she rose. "It's gettin' dark. We'd best be looking for a bed, Janie."

Arianna had to jab Fiona, she was looking at her so strangely.

"Yes, yes! We'd best find a bed."

They waved to the two they had just met and hurried out to the streets.

"This is daft!" Fiona protested.

"This is perfect!" Arianna countered.

"And how do we get home?"

"In a cab, same way we came."

"Now we're filthy, in rags, and it's very late."

"We'll sneak in through the tree."

"I'm not climbing that tree!"

"You'll have to," Arianna told her. "Why, *Janie,* dear, this is almost fun!"

Fiona rolled her eyes. It wasn't fun.

It was frightening. Terribly, terribly, frightening.

Maggie walked purposely to her stepdaughter's room. She was tempted to merely slam the door open. She refrained, and knocked. There was no answer.

She walked down the stairs, sliding her black mourning cap from her head. "Mrs. Whitley!" she called, and the woman came in from the direction of the kitchen.

"Yes, my lady?"

"Has Lady Arianna gone out?"

"I believe she took a sedative, and is resting."

"Ah, fine. Well, I shall let her rest. However, in an hour, wake her."

"For supper? Then I shall have to quickly get the cook moving. We assumed, my lady, that you were dining out, when you left no orders and didn't return. I'm afraid a decent meal will take a bit more than an hour."

"I don't want a meal, Mrs. Whitley. I just want Arianna awakened. In an hour. Thank you so very much."

She turned and started up the stairs. She wondered how it would look if she fired Mrs. Whitley.

In her room, she thought about calling for Fiona, but she'd always done for herself, at least, in the last many years she had, and so she discarded the clothing she had worn to Whitechapel, washed, and dressed anew. She went to her desk, pulled the newspaper clipping from her reticule, and read it again, her temper growing.

Then she smiled and settled in to wait.

She thought that she would have to go after Arianna, that Mrs. Whitley would arrive—distressed, of course—to say that the young lady simply refused to come.

But at the appointed hour, Arianna knocked at her door. Maggie bid her to enter, and she came in, looking somewhat flushed and hurried.

"Good evening," Maggie said quietly. "Thank you for arriving so promptly."

"I wouldn't dream of being disobedient to—my guardian," Arianna said, making the last word sound like *ogre*.

"How thoughtful of you," Maggie replied sweetly. "I can see that we are going to get along fabulously well."

"Um. I need my allowance."

Maggie nodded. "I'll see that Darby has it for you tomorrow. But really, how could you possibly need money? Didn't the newspaper pay you?"

"Of cou—what newspaper?" Arianna said, quickly changing her tune.

"Arianna, there has been an autopsy. I did nothing to your father. And the article you wrote was inflammatory, to say the least. The paper is barely within the limits of the law. But . . . well, I have friends who wish to write as well. Still, it wouldn't do for you to have too much spending money on you. Terrible crimes are taking place in the city, but there are still simple thieves out there as well! If you're going to continue to dabble in the art of writing, I'm afraid I'll feel entirely obliged to hold back your allowance. Yes, let me think, I believe that would be among the duties the Misters Green outlined to me this morning. Does that agree with what they told you?"

Arianna stood very still for a long moment, staring at her.

Maggie smiled, then let her smile fade. "I'm sorry.

I can't tell you how truly sorry I am that your father died. I'm even sorry that he left you saddled with me as your guardian, when I know how difficult it must be for you. I wish that there was something I could say that would make you believe that I was innocent of any wrongdoing."

"You married him," Arianna reminded her sharply.

"And are you aware that he had plans for your marriage?"

Arianna's frown showed her that she was not.

"He wanted you to be a good wife, I believe."

"He intended to force me to marry?"

"I fully intend to leave that matter to Jamie."

Arianna smiled. "Interesting."

"What?"

"The way you refer to my cousin. As Jamie."

Something in the way she spoke gave Maggie the chills. Was her feeling for the man evident in her voice when she simply spoke his name?

It wouldn't be. She vowed that it would not be.

"Jamie is his name."

"Lord James, or Lord Langdon, or Viscount Langdon."

"Your father called him Jamie, and thus, so do I. At any rate, I believe it was he your father intended for you. But I don't wish to press that matter—it will be between the two of you when you reach your majority. Since your father has passed, I'm not sure if it will be the proper season for you to come out, even if the time won't be until next spring. We can see on that matter. But until that time . . . well, I think there are lessons you might want to take. And your father suggested it might be an excellent thing if you were to learn that we are among the privileged few, and there are those out there who suffer terribly. I do think it's time that you quit maligning me, and that we learn to work together, no matter what our feelings for one another."

Arianna stood tall and still and tried very hard to contain her fury. "There will be no more newspaper items, madam. I am well warned. I will ask Darby about my allowance. I need a bit more time to mourn my father's passing. How quickly you seem to have gotten over it. If there's nothing else, I most respectfully crave leave to return to my room."

"Please, feel free, return to your room," Maggie said.

Arianna left the room. The door slammed in her wake.

"Ah, that went very well!" Maggie murmured sardonically to herself.

But she was certain that there would be no more newspaper articles.

At length, she decided to retire, herself.

The bottle of laudanum seemed to be watching her, tempting her.

She ignored it and prepared for bed.

And lay awake, staring at the darkened ceiling. She would sleep, she told herself. And she would not resort to drugs.

She tossed and turned, and found that she was more wretched than ever. Thoughts churned in her mind, Fathers Vickers's words, the fright the women had betrayed that day, and the way that they had run, so quickly, to find solace in gin.

Jamie.

Leaving.

And again, the way that he had looked at her.

She winced, wondering what on earth was the matter with her. He had never claimed any affection for her. He'd not wanted her to marry Charles. Perhaps, the night before . . . perhaps that had been his way to prove that she shouldn't marry, and not even the great longing for her that she had imagined.

Strange, in the days before, he had been in the house, and she had not thought of him so much, other than that he was there. But then, she had been taking the laudanum.

And she really needed to take it now, if she was ever going to sleep.

She rose, and walked for the bottle. With it in her hand, she hesitated, and winced, remembering the poor women of the East End. There was a monster loose. And still, they had gone running for their gin.

She set the bottle down and went back to bed. She swore at herself, for when she wasn't thinking about the horror that was occurring, her thoughts turned to those of the man. And she remembered, and burned, and was haunted by the memory. She had married, and her husband had just died, and already, it was true, her memories of Charles were receding, while the memory of one night with Jamie was vivid beyond reason. . . .

At last, she slept. And in the middle of the night, she woke with a scream. She was sweaty and shaky. In her dreams, there had been a figure stalking in the dark. And she had followed, seen when he had attacked, tried to scream, tried to stop him . . .

And when she had reached the struggling victim at last, she had looked down. In her dream she had been terrified that she would see herself.

But she did not.

It was Arianna, Arianna prone on the ground, blood oozing from the bright red gash that slashed across her throat.

Chapter 13

The first night, Jamie walked the streets.

And it was amazing how many others were about as well, no matter what the hour.

Many women worked late. It wasn't much of a surprise that at midnight men and women both were crowding the pubs. In a number of places, the gaslights were out. The area was filled with gates, walks, and alleyways.

In the pubs, they talked about the Whitechapel murderer, and did so with whispers and fear, and he heard the women talking about the fact that they were afraid, and still, what were they to do?

He heard talk of the many letters sent to the police, so many, already, that they said the coppers were inundated with them.

And then, as he listened, everyone had a theory. One prostitute wedged by his side at a pub, and suggested, "Why, he might even be a bloke like you, mister!"

She gave him a smile. Toothless. "Were ye in the mind for a bit o' fun, eh?"

And so he had adjusted his collar around his throat and lifted his hands. "I'm out. Just bought my last gin."

"Why, there's time a woman might be thinkin' that it's not only the money wots important, my fine fellow. Haven't seen the likes of you around here, not lately, and that's a fact!"

He'd slipped away from the bar, the fear, and the stench.

At two A.M., the streets were quieter, and still, men and women moved disparately about in the darkness. Mute light continued to burn from some of the houses. Peddlers returned to their homes, their carts banging with their wares.

By three A.M., laborers were beginning to rise. Men who worked in the slaughterhouses, women who had found jobs in the factories. By five, before the darkness had lifted, the streets began to fill again.

He could find no fault with the police. He had seen them about constantly, walking their beats. No matter what streets he traveled, there was never a period of more than ten or fifteen minutes that passed in which a constable didn't follow his tracks.

He was stopped himself several times, but proved to them that he carried no weapons, and was allowed to pass by.

Randolph awaited him, doing his part, nursing a gin through the night at the pub, and listening.

They spoke after they returned to the town house.

"If this monster were an anarchist," Randolph told Jamie, "he'd be getting where he wanted to go. The mood in the streets is ugly, indeed, I cannot tell you how ugly."

"I've seen."

"In the pubs, they call for the head of Sir Charles Warren, swearing that he don't care enough, that if it were a finer class of woman being murdered, they'd have the bloke by now. And the theories! It's an American, out to sell body parts—after the inquest, you know, the coroner stated that there were clues aplenty, that the police should be looking for this fellow who wanted to buy the body parts. Then, of course, there are the other rumors."

"That somehow, even the Royal House is involved?" Jamie asked.

"Well, they whisper about Eddy, you know. He'd been known to play in some areas of town not reputed to be of his ilk. Have you heard about this girl, this Annie Crook?"

"Yes, he's said to have married her. But she was a shop girl," Jamie reminded Randolph.

"Shop girls have been known to supplement their incomes, you know," Randolph said sagely.

And that was true.

"And what did you discover?" Randolph asked.

"That, most probably, if the fellow isn't discovered, someone else will die," Jamie said. "I'm going to get some sleep, and you need to do the same. Then, we'll pay a visit to a few of the fellows walking the beat."

Jamie retired to his room, and opted for a very long bath, and a glass of his best port. He soaked in the water and reflected that none of his tension seemed to be easing.

He closed his eyes. For several seconds, the street scenes filled them. And then drifted away. Not the tension. He could think of nothing but cobalt blue eyes, and how the world itself had disappeared in an awesome feeling of being alive, when she had been at his side. He winced, reminding himself that if Charles were alive, they'd be having deep and lengthy conversations regarding the situation at hand, and that Charles would have something brilliant to say, perhaps an idea that would lead in the right direction. In his steadfast loyalty to the Queen, he would be out himself, no matter what his age or health.

But Charles was dead.

And no matter how he tried to mourn, Jamie kept losing his grasp on those memories, for here he was, in the room where she had been with him.

He jerked up in the tub. *She* had her wretched sense of passion for the East End!

There had to be a way to stop her from going there.

"Up!"

Mireau rubbed his eyes, wondering what rudeness had invaded his sleep. He blinked, and there she was. Maggie, smiling, looking absurdly like a mischievous angel, far too vibrant above him.

"Up?"

"We're going back to the church."

He groaned. "Maggie, don't you think that you added to the drunkeness of the city enough yesterday?"

"I've arranged a large handout of food. Come along."

He groaned again and asked, "Does Justin know what you're doing?"

"Justin isn't here. It seems my brother has taken up an interest in politics. He does have a seat in the House of Lords, you know."

"And they're in session?"

"He has a meeting, that's all I know. Clayton told me. Now, get up!"

And so he did. Maggie allowed no other recourse. He grumbled as they took another cab.

When they arrived at the churchyard, Father Vickers was waiting for them. And several pony carts had come. Maggie had not just bought bread for her wayward masses, but bacon as well. The police were poised around the yard, determined on keeping order.

They watched as the people came, men and women, and at one point, Maggie slipped away to rest a spell in Father Vickers's room.

Curious, Mireau followed.

When he neared the room, he heard a woman talking. It was the younger, pretty creature he had seen in the yard the day before. "I'm trusting you, because there is no other hope," the woman was saying. "I'm desperate! So desperate. There are already rumors about, and sooner or later, I will be recognized. It's not Eddy, you must understand. Ah, he tired of my sister, yes. But he was kind; and he would send funds, I think . . . if he remembered. The thing of it is, what if any of what is being said is true? Eddy would hurt no one, but surely there are those, blindly loyal to the Crown, who would seek to hurt the baby. God above us! No one, no one must ever know. She must disappear, and I will do so as well."

"But you're speaking of giving up the child," Maggie said.

"And that would be a loss to the poor babe?" the woman said. "And the child was not mine, she was actually Annie's, but Annie has now escaped to the North, and she hasn't even sent word to me, she's so terrified. So that is it, you see; we must all part, and pray for one another. But the babe, if she is kept here . . . she will die."

Mireau stood outside the door, rigid with shock. So it was true. Prince Eddy had gotten involved with a Catholic shop girl. He had gone through some kind of a sham wedding with her. She had apparently escaped the city, fearing repercussions not so much from the Crown itself, but from those who might not realize that a scandalous truth might be better than a supposition of evil. And now, Maggie was going to become involved.

A second later, the pretty young prostitute came through the door. Mireau flattened himself against the wall and waited until she was gone.

He burst in on Maggie. "And what, pray tell, are we going to do with a baby?"

"Save it," she said simply.

Jamie met frustration at every turn. Mrs. Whitley told him that the lady Maggie never chose to disclose her whereabouts to her, and suggested that he talk to her ladyship's personal maid, Fiona. However, Fiona wasn't to be found, and neither was Arianna. He didn't know whether or not to be glad that Arianna was no longer moping in her room, or to worry about her equally.

Darby said that he had taken the lady to her home in Mayfair, and then been dismissed.

No one was at Mayfair but Clayton, who said that neither Lord Justin nor the lady Maggie was about. Justin had headed to the government buildings quite early, and Maggie and Mireau had talked about a poetry reading.

From there, he had Randolph take him to the church, where Father Vickers said that indeed, Maggie had been there, but was no longer. Unable to outguess her, he forced himself to swallow his fear, and look for an old friend on the force, Constable Harry Bartley.

He found Bartley at the Bow Street station, and since the man had been working around the clock, he was exceptionally pleased to see Jamie, and eager to have a coffee with him. He was equally eager to leave the area, and so they went into a little place in the square mile that actually constituted the City of London. And there, Bartley reminded him of some of the problems facing their desperate search. "Politics!" Bartley told him, and lowered his voice, leaning over his coffee cup. "There's the City of London, and then there are the Metropolitan Police. The murders have taken place outside the city, and so they fall in the district of the Met fellows. Sir Charles Warren is commissioner, and a fine man, but always wanting to be independent. He fights with Henry Matthews, the home secretary, constantly, and both want to be in control! Now, to complicate it all further, Warren also quarrels with James Monro, head of the CID, or Criminal Investigation Division. Then, there's the ages-old rivalry with the City Police. There's another can of worms. The commissioner of the City Police, you know, is Sir James Fraser, but he's almost retired, always out of town, and so in the city, it's Lieutenant Colonel Sir Henry Smith in charge, and he's the assistant commissioner. Now, you see, the City Police don't have to answer to the home secretary, just the Corporation of the City of London. Sir Henry is determined on catching the bloke, though the murders have not occurred in his territory. Now, actually in charge of the investigation is Detective Inspector Frederick Aberline. You know him?"

"He's a good fellow," Jamie said. "The area of Whitechapel and Bethnal Green was his ground for many years, then he was transferred to Scotland Yard—but sent back to head up this investigation because of his experience with the area."

"Aberline is a good fellow, and I can think of no one better for the job. He's just got so very much red tape to get through. The politics of it all, like I said. There's a storm brewing on the streets, and I've not seen anything like it in all my days. But do you think that they'd all put their differences aside in such a desperate situation? Bah, and they do not, and there you have it!"

"Anger is growing against Sir Charles Warren," Jamie commented.

"Aye, and that's a fact. Anger is growing against us all, and likely, it will come far worse. There's a letter that's come in—well, there're thousands of letters that have come in—but this one has got the boys at the top squeamish. The fellow wrote to 'Dear Boss.' Said that he was 'down on whores' and wouldn't quit 'ripping' them till he was caught. He'd wanted to write his letter in blood from his last victim, but it dried up. He says that the next job, he's going to clip

off the lady's ears and send them to the police officers—just for 'jollies.' And he signed it 'Jack the
Ripper.' "

"A name to send a chill down the spine, indeed,"
Jamie said. "Do you think that the letter is a hoax?
There have been so many others."

Bartley grimaced. "Um. There was one recently,
must 'ave come from a big fan of Edgar Allan Poe,
reading about the *Murders in the Rue Morgue.* He sug-
gests that there's a giant ape out there, committing
the murders! Trust me, everyone has a theory, and a
suggestion. We are dressing some fellows up as prostitutes, sending them out on the streets. Some think
all the prostitutes should be fitted with mechanisms
in which some kind of trap would spring shut once
they were grabbed! Others claim it's an American
killer, a Chinese killer, a Buddhist, an Indian Thuggee
out for revenge, a Jew, a Polack—and, of course, a
rich man who might have gotten a disease from his
play with a prostitute of low class. Then, you know,
there were the ritualistic aspects of it. When Annie
Chapman was found in the yard, she wasn't just mutilated. She was . . . *arranged.* A few cheap rings, some
pennies, and two new farthings were neatly laid at
her feet. A wee bit of muslin, a paper case, and a
comb were aligned by the body as well. So . . . is this
madman a religious freak? A Satanist? A totally sane
man, with a particular agenda in mind, playing with
us all? God knows. I just walk the streets now, trying
to keep the ladies of the night from getting their
throats slit, even those filled with gin and ready to
spit in my face, calling me a big cock and all other
names!"

"If there's anything you think I should know, you'll get in touch with me?" Jamie said.

Bartley nodded. "Eh! I hear we're nearly related, in a fashion, now."

"Oh?"

"Nathan Lane was my cousin. Married to Lady Maggie Graham, who recently was wed to and widowed by your uncle, Charles. Pardon me! I'd forgotten you're not just a 'sir' anymore! You're Lord James Langdon."

"And not a hair on me has changed a bit, Bartley. So, then, you're acquainted with Lady Maggie?"

"A true angel!" Bartley said, his smile wistful. "Heard she almost caused a riot the other day."

"I'm not surprised."

"She came to the church without food, and decided to give out money. She and her friend were nearly trampled."

So Maggie was an angel. She'd be living in heaven all right, if she didn't change her ways.

"Ah, but the people here love her!" Bartley said.

"The problem as I see it is that individuals do give, while the government itself has not determined on a way to deal with the overcrowding and starvation," Jamie pointed out.

"Oh, people give money. But Maggie comes here, you see. No matter what her title, her station in life, she walks among the people. She ignores the stench. She risks disease. She talks with them, and can be seen, and touched. That makes her an angel."

Bartley's awe was irritating, and Jamie, to his shame, knew why. His uncle was barely cold. And all he could do was dream about being with his beloved kinsman's widow himself. Being with her, alone. In shadow or light, alone together, tangled in the sheets.

He rose abruptly. "Have you seen her—about, being seen and touched today?"

"No, that I haven't." Bartley gave a deep sigh. "Lord James, thank you for the respite. And rest assured, whatever I hear on the streets that you might not, I will bring to your attention with haste."

"This is insane!" Mireau said.

"Isn't she beautiful?" Maggie countered. And the baby was beautiful. Dark curls crowned her head, marble-like eyes stared out at them. She was dressed in rags, and was a year old, perhaps a little less, or a little more. She had a single dimple. Her smile was captivating.

"She's beautiful, and this is insane."

Maggie shook her head, smiling at him. They were clipping their way rather slowly through the streets of Whitechapel. People were everywhere, at the sides of the roads, in the middle, all nervous, all talking— and few paying much heed to the traffic.

"I have this strange feeling, Mireau, that saving her is rather part of my destiny."

"Maggie, waiting a proper period of mourning, falling in love, marrying a man who is not standing with one foot in the grave already, bearing a child of your own. That would be destiny."

"She's simply beautiful!" Maggie said again.

"You've a stepdaughter who is simply beautiful. Even more beautiful than you are, perhaps. And she is nothing but trouble. Mark my words—this little beauty is already trouble."

Maggie glared at him and hugged the baby. The baby giggled, reaching for one of Maggie's golden locks. Maggie was in rapture, and started when the cab suddenly came to a halt.

"What . . . ?" she demanded.

Mireau looked out. And paled to ash.

"Jamie," he said quickly.

"Jamie?"

"Lord James Langdon! Your *great nephew*, remember? Viscount Langdon—the new version?"

"The baby, take the baby!"

Maggie stuffed the child into his arms, thinking quickly to jump out of the cab and forestall Lord Langdon. For a moment, the wee girl looked up at Mireau as if she were about to let out a horrendous scream.

"No, no, please!" he whispered. And he started to hum, trying to think of some song from his youth, desperate to keep her quiet. "Please, baby, please, please, please!" he crooned, and amazingly, she looked up at him, almost as if she understood.

"Lord James!" he heard Maggie saying, and not with pleasure. *Oh, brilliant!* he thought. *Start right off being hostile, Maggie!*

"What are you doing down here?" Jamie asked her, voice deep, resonating, and truly aggravated.

"Taking in the air?" Maggie suggested. "It's none of your business what I'm doing!"

"Oh, isn't it? Amazing, because I'm trying to protect your wretched life!"

"It's my life to do with what I please. Charles is gone; you have no rights over me."

"I am head of the Langdon family."

"I was born a Graham."

"Whatever your intentions down here, Maggie, if you don't cease these visits, and immediately, I'll begin to make a few suggestions of my own. Such as that I believe you may well be responsible for the death of Lord Charles. You'll find that you're cooling your heels once I make such an accusation."

"You wouldn't!" Maggie gasped, and yet, it seemed that she believed he well might, for there was a touch of fear along with indignation in her voice.

"Try me, my lady."

Mireau couldn't see her, but he could well imagine Maggie. She must have been standing there, straight as a ramrod, furious, and yet, at a loss. Then she spoke again, quickly. "All right, Lord James, Viscount Langdon. I will get back in my cab, and return to the house, and stay there."

"No. You'll come with me. I'll see that you're out of here."

Apparently, she chose not to mention that Mireau remained in the cab. From his place deep against the seat, Mireau saw as she turned and stared at him, and now there was naked pleading in the depths of her cobalt eyes. *Get her safely away. Let no one know. For the love of God, help me in this, Mireau!*

"Maggie, I mean it!" Jamie continued harshly. "I want you out of here, with me, now!"

"As you command, my lord!" she responded. "Go on, cabbie!" she cried to the hackney driver, and he saw that she was stepping forward, paying him.

She gazed in at Mireau, pleadingly, one last time.

Then she was gone.

"What in God's name do I do now?" Mireau said,

staring at the baby as the carriage jolted back into action.

She waved a tiny hand below his nose, eyes staring gravely into his. And he sighed, because he would do something, rack his brain, come up with an idea . . . he had to. He had fallen a little bit in love.

Jamie was evidently furious with her, and she couldn't quite understand why. He knew that she came down here.

Maybe she wasn't properly mourning.

Or maybe he did blame her for Charles's death, despite his words to her to get over her self-pity.

He "helped" her into his carriage with such a firm hand she nearly collided with the door on the opposite side. When he crawled in, he didn't look at her, but out the windows. His jaw was set in such a lock she was surprised that it didn't snap. His hands, so large, capable . . . were knotted into fists in his lap.

"What the hell is the matter with you?" he demanded suddenly and harshly, staring at her, fire in the gray smoke of his gaze.

"What the hell is the matter with *you*? You know that I come down here!"

"Not now! There is a murderer on the loose."

She sat back, staring out the window. "There's often a murderer on the loose in Whitechapel. People have just noticed for a change."

"All right, Maggie, let me rephrase. There's an exceptionally heinous madman on the loose down here, and if a recent letter is to be accepted as from the real fellow, he's calling himself Jack the Ripper.

And he claims that he's ready to strike again, eager to strike again!"

"I'm not a prostitute," Maggie said, and winced inwardly, thinking that, like these women, in actuality, she had been sold. Her price had simply been much higher.

"And do you think that if you wind up in this madman's path, it will be any different?"

She sighed. "Jamie, I'm not your concern."

"But you are."

"How is that?"

"You were charged with looking after Arianna. I was charged with looking after you."

"Charles is gone. Sadly, we are left with the truth of our lives. I will probably never have any influence over Arianna. And you have none with me."

"Then you'll listen to me because I'm threatening you."

She felt her fingers curl into fists. *He was taking her back to Moorhaven, she was certain. And he would remain, trying to make sure that she didn't leave the house. Well and fine. She could play that game—he couldn't stay forever.*

But Mireau had the baby!

"I stand duly threatened," she said. Then she leaned forward, ready to plead. "Listen, Jamie, I'll stay out of Whitechapel for a while, I promise. But I can't abide being at Moorhaven."

"You have to abide it. You're there to watch over Arianna."

She sat back, her jaw twisting into a rigid lock.

The carriage moved on.

The ride seemed interminable. And still, at last,

they came to Moorhaven. She tried to jump out of the carriage before he could assist her. He was faster. They crashed into one another, trying to vacate the conveyance. She forced herself to allow him to go first, to reach for her, help her out.

"Thank you, Randolph!" she called cheerily to the coachman. "Good day, Viscount," she said coldly to Jamie.

She marched into the house and raced up the stairs, swearing to herself as she realized that he was following her.

The ever annoying Mrs. Whitley must have arrived in the foyer after she had headed up the stairs. She could hear the woman talking to Jamie.

"Lord Langdon! What a pleasure. Will you be having supper? The house is in such a state of . . . confusion, these days!"

She didn't know what Jamie replied. She reached her room, entered, slammed the door, and began to pace. Where was Mireau? How on earth would he hide the baby? What would he do with her?

She was so deeply entrenched in her worry and thoughts that she was stunned when her door burst open. Jamie had followed her up.

He stared at her, his fury evident.

"What?" she cried. "I'm in the house! In my room, going nowhere!"

"Why are you so astonished that I don't care to see you killed—and ripped to pieces?"

"I will not be killed and ripped to pieces!" she protested.

He strode across the room, tension evident in the set of his shoulders, the length of his stride. And she found that she didn't move, that she longed for him to accost her, couldn't wait to fight back, pound her fists against his chest.

He stopped before her. She expected some violence. She was ready to return it with a vengeance.

He reached out. His fingers settled upon her shoulder with such a power that she nearly cried out. But then she was crushed against him. And when his thumb lifted her chin and his lips settled upon hers, she gave up the concept of a fight in less than a second.

Longing swept through her with lightning speed, with shameful fervor. She parted her lips to the deep wet depths of his assault, and returned the volatile force of the kiss. She felt his hands, molding her against him, touching her. Beneath his trousers she felt the force of his arousal, and it only caused her to feel a weakening in her knees, a drastic need to shed any of the barriers between them. It was ungodly to want someone so badly. To not care in the least about propriety, to not even realize the manner of the sin to be committed. And yet . . .

She felt the length of his fingers against her. Amazingly quick, and adept. She was breathless, gasping, reaching for his cravat, his waistcoat . . . scarcely aware that her clothing was being strewn as well, bit by bit, falling in a trail across the floor as they broke to discard some other piece of cloth, met and dueled with lips and teeth and tongue again, moved . . . discarded, and at a last, hit the bed with all flesh bared to one another, lips locked once again in a kiss that held both fury and need, defiance and argument, and sheer wild sensuality.

What happened then was quick.

And desperate.

And still . . . so complete.

She felt him all over her. His hands . . . those long fingers . . . trailing, sweeping, brushing the length of her. Cradling her breasts, teasing the nipples, until she felt the very hardness of them herself, taut, craving ever more attention. The caress of his tongue obliged, until passing farther—and always, against flesh that seemed to scream and screech, so sensitized that the slightest breath was an erotic seduction—against the terrain of her body, savoring for seconds the terrain of her belly and hips. His touch, a step ahead, a brush . . . an intimate probe, sensation that nearly tore cries from her lips, stopped only by the renewed assault of his mouth against hers, until it departed down the length of her flesh again, inundating her with a liquid blaze, centering upon the very center of her arousal, drawing, evoking . . .

She nearly screamed again, but he was above her, and within her, and again, it was the fever of his mouth that swallowed her cries, while the volatile power of his length moved within her, and then it seemed that there was nothing, nothing on the earth except for him, and the intoxicating realm in which they reached and surged, swathed in the swirling rise of sensation, seeking, needing . . .

And skyrocketing.

The world became ablaze with light; sweetness saturated the length of her, touching every finger, toe, soaking through to her mind. Her hair was a tangled damp mess, curled between them. His body was hard and vibrant still, even as he remained within her, the aftermath creating little tremors within them both as passion and their climax took due course. Body against body, the force and weight of him remained. And for long moments, she wavered between reality and dream, wishing that she could curl against him, rest her head, rest her *soul*, and let sleep creep over her now, there, where she was sheltered, in his arms.

But he withdrew. She closed her eyes, not wanting to meet his. But she sensed that he wasn't seeking her out, but rather, that he had thrown his legs over the side of the bed, and was running his fingers through his hair.

"Sorry," he said briefly, as if he had bumped into her on a stairwell.

She winced, but turned away, said nothing. Surely, there would be more. There had to be more between them.

But there wasn't. He rose. She heard him dressing.

And then. "Truly, forgive me, my lady. I had no right. My temper was unduly provoked by the fear and horror in the streets. I'll take care not to invade your privacy again."

Then he was gone.

Mireau was truly at a loss.

He had the cab take him to Moorhaven first, but when he saw that Lord Jamie's coachman was there, he quickly changed his mind. The child was going to get hungry.

All right. He had to get her out of the City of London.

He needed some things for her, and definitely, more money. And so he instructed the cabbie to take him to Mayfair.

With relief, he saw that Justin had not returned. He hesitated. Hold the cab and leave the child in it?

He couldn't.

Swearing, he hurried from the cab with the baby, praying no neighbor would notice. In the house, he ran straight into Clayton.

The slender, ever perfect butler-valet stared at him, and then, to his amazement, broke into a smile. "A babe, Monsieur Mireau?"

"Clayton . . ." Mireau thought fast. "Oh, God, Clayton, may the Lord forgive me! The wee babe is . . . mine. Her mother has recently departed, and God forgive me my sins! I can't have them fall upon her."

Clayton arched a brow high in his gaunt face. He looked at Mireau as if he were a total reprobate. But then he sighed softly. "The sins of the father should never be visited upon a poor wee babe!"

"God help me, man! What can I do? I'd never have anyone know. Ah, look at her, Clayton! She's a sweet innocent."

"I might have an answer, Mireau."

"Yes?" Mireau was hopeful.

And Clayton sighed. "I've three sisters. They live north of the city, far north, in a bit of a cottage in the woods."

"Would they . . . care for her? I'd earn the money for her upkeep. I'd . . . I'd give up dreams of writing. I'd get a . . . egad, I'd get a real job!"

Clayton reached for the baby. "Pack some things,

Mireau. I'll get this wee precious thing a bite to eat, appropriate for her size, and write you a note."

"Bless you, my good man!" Mireau hadn't really intended to go on his knees to the butler—they just gave.

"Up, up, my fellow!" Clayton protested.

"No one must ever know," Mireau said.

"The note will not identify you as her father," Clayton assured him. "I'll say that she was an orphan. But hurry. You'll have to take your cabbie . . . it will be a very expensive ride."

"Whatever the price."

"Hurry, then!"

Mireau raced up the stairs, quickly gathered money and a few goods that might be pawned, and hurried back down the stairs.

Clayton had bathed the girl, cleaned her wee clothing as best he might. She was happy, smiling, saying a few words, laughing as Clayton helped her down a glass of milk. She carried a crust of bread in her tiny hand.

Clayton looked a bit like a jester, playing with the child. But his smile evaporated to a look of sheer sternness and censure as he greeted Mireau again. "They're lonely up there. Never married, and make their way with a fine garden and a few good animals. They brew a few medicinal teas and the like. 'Tis very small; the wee lass will do well, and be dearly loved, I daresay. But you! You will mend your ways!"

"By God above us, I swear I will!" Mireau vowed.

"No more sinning!"

"Ever!" Mireau vowed.

"And you will support her!"

Mireau crossed himself. "As the Lord God is my witness!"

"Take her, then, hurry. Lord Justin may return at any minute."

With his precious little bundle, Mireau fled.

Maggie lay in misery for the longest time without moving.

Then, at last, memory of the child surpassed the tempest she was feeling, and she bolted out of bed.

She washed and dressed in a frenzy. When she burst back out into the hall, she was dismayed, for once, to see that Arianna was there.

"Good evening, Stepmother," she said sweetly.

"Arianna."

"Will you be coming down to dinner?"

"I . . . no. Not tonight. I'm afraid I need to speak with my brother. At the Mayfair house."

"Ah, yes. Your brother."

"Arianna," she said with a sigh, "please, don't despise Justin on my account."

"I don't even know him."

"Of course you do! He was at the funeral . . . at the wedding, at the wake!"

"Of course, you're right; how silly of me." She smiled. "I had thought that we might talk tonight."

"I would love to sit down and actually talk!" Maggie said, dismayed. Here she was, the stepdaughter she was supposed to love and guide, actually wanting to talk to her! And she couldn't take advantage of the situation. "I have to go to Mayfair House . . . but I'll be back. Perhaps we can have a long conversation later?"

Arianna nodded. "Indeed. I believe there's much I really need to learn about you."

Maggie smiled. Then, anxious, she turned and fled down the stairway.

"Madam, shall I assume there's to be no normal seating for dinner this evening?"

At the bottom of the stairs, Maggie turned. Mrs. Whitley again. She forced a level tone to her lips. "Please, speak with Arianna and find out what she would like to do. I'm going to my brother's house. Don't concern yourself with me."

Ignoring Mrs. Whitley, she headed to the kitchen. Darby was there, the good man. "Darby, I must get to my brother's house, quickly, please."

"Certainly, my lady. Right away!"

He folded his paper. Maggie saw the headlines. "Jack the Ripper Stalks the East End!"

Another read, "War on Warren!" A smaller caption went on. "The bungling police commissioner must do what's right and resign!"

"A bad time, my lady. A sad time," Darby said, shaking his head.

"I know, Darby."

"I know your heart, my lady, but it would be a wise time for you to stay as far away from the East End as you can!"

"Of course, Darby," she said absently.

They went out; Darby brought the family carriage around.

Maggie was so nervous that she chewed her thumbnail as they drove. When they came to the house at Mayfair, she ran out of the carriage before Darby could help her. Bursting into the house, she cried, "Clayton!"

"My lady!"

He appeared from the area of the kitchen and stared at her expectantly.

"Clayton, is my brother here?"

"No, my lady, he's still down by the Parliament."

"Mireau?"

"He did come by."

"And?"

"He's gone off . . . a bit of a holiday, perhaps."

"Gone off?" she gasped.

Clayton narrowed his eyes, studying hers. He took a step toward her. "I would know . . . it would be quite impossible . . . my lady!" His voice was but a whisper. "The wee babe, she isn't yours, is she?"

"No!" Maggie gasped. "No, no, but I've . . . sworn to protect her. She is mine now, my responsibility."

Clayton shook his head sadly. "Monsieur Mireau does not deserve your love and patronage!"

"What?"

"He dallies, and you are willing to pay the price."

"Clayton . . . you really don't understand."

"It's not my place."

"Clayton, please! Do you know where Mireau took her?"

"Come into the kitchen, my lady. I believe I can enlighten you . . . but I believe I'm entitled to some enlightenment as well!"

"Is the baby . . . is she all right?"

"Right as rain, and soon to be swaddled and loved by the sweetest of women."

"Who?"

He smiled. "My sisters!" he said proudly. "But now you! You may be a countess now, m'lady. Tonight, however, I think you owe your dear old butler a few words!"

There was nothing else to do.

She followed him into the kitchen, and soon forgot that she had ever promised Arianna that she would return to Moorhaven and talk with her that evening.

Chapter 14

The man who sat across from Arianna called himself Heath. Jeremiah Heath. He was tall, broad shouldered, with strange dark hair that seemed to stand straight up, but then, it was very short, and certainly had no customary cut which she was familiar with. But what he had was dark, and after he removed his cap, she studied his face as they spoke, playing it all as she went along.

"I have no family. I lost my mother years and years ago. My father died recently. He was a tailor in Birmingham. Well, at least, he worked for a tailor in Birmingham. He kept us alive. Friends suggested that I might find work in London, so . . . here I am. I've looked on the West Side for a domestic position, but . . . the grand ladies don't seem to be inclined to hire me."

He assessed her with his very strange dark eyes.

"Look, I've come to you because in the short time

that I've been here, I've seen what happens to young women. I'm not looking for a place with any . . . I'm not looking to work in a brothel. I have some talent as a mesmerist, I believe."

"You have some talent, all right," he muttered. "And I'm not looking for a whore. They're a ha'penny a piece around this place. Granted, not many so young and so fresh. And I don't give a whit about your so-called talent as a mesmerist. I do need that you keep your mouth shut, that you can play a part, and that you turn a blind eye if you don't like what you see."

Arianna smiled to herself. "Are we going to take some of those rich old buggers?" she demanded.

"Exactly."

She inched closer, leaning toward him across the table. "What if . . . what if someone comes who expects to be taken? I mean, don't the bobbies get in on it, now and then—plainclothesmen?"

"Um. And would-be outraged, honest, upright citizens. As it happens, I'm rather hoping to see one I know again. A few, in fact."

"Really? What if one were a . . . woman?"

His eyes gave her chills. "Why, there are places where such ladies can be taken down a peg."

"So, is there a . . . place, a house, where we work?"

He shook his head. "We go to places. And avoid being found when it's over."

"I'm to be a thief?"

"You've a problem with that?"

"Not in the least. I'm quite excited, but . . . quite seriously, I read a newspaper article once about a night when a man was killed, when a woman exposed a fraud, and there was a huge upset. I believe a few are still rotting in Newgate now!"

"I think that I've put together quite a fair team," Jeremiah told her. Smiling, he hiked a brow, suggesting that she look around.

The pub was crowded with men and women alike. It reeked. Men from the slaughterhouses were there, those from factories, and all about. Women drank gin and moaned about the problems of working the street.

And still, Jeremiah's men were evident. They lolled against walls, sat at the rickety tables, or leaned against the bar. She noted them all for particular reasons. One, they were wary, watching the others around them. Two, as soon as Jeremiah had indicated them, they were all looking at her. Three—they had a certain look about them. Young, strong, sharp, and with a certain glint to their eyes that assured her they would stop at nothing.

A little tremor trilled through her. She was making a mistake. In this crowd, someone could get killed. But in time, Lady Maggie would hear about Jeremiah Heath. And she would come to a séance. And when she tried to show that he was a fraud . . .

He might kill her.

Again, her heart fluttered. Did she really want the woman dead? Last night, she'd run out on her, and never even returned to talk. Of course, it was true that Arianna had merely wanted to probe her for some personal information. But . . . it might have been a chance for the lady to try to redeem herself in her stepdaughter's eyes.

Apparently, she hadn't wanted that chance very

badly. Her own world had been far too important to her.

What could possibly be so important, now that Charles was dead?

Arianna very purposely hardened her heart. This was the course she had chosen. And nothing could change the fact that her father had married, and died that night.

If it came to it . . .

Lady Maggie had killed her father, as surely as if she had brought a gun to his head, and pulled the trigger.

And still, she wasn't the type of woman such a business usually killed. There was a market for such fine specimens as her stepmother.

"One more thing."

"Yes?" Arianna said.

"You ever betray me, and you'll wish you were dead, long before you reach the peace of that state, do you understand?"

"Of course!" she said irritably. "You can trust me—as long as you don't cheat me!"

He sat back. "I don't think I have a mind to cheat you." He lifted his hand. The ruffians who had lazed around the pub straightened themselves and stood, and came to stand by the table. "Here you have Matthew, Luke, and John. Seriously, those are their names. Sebastian, Raoul, and Garrett."

"Hello," Arianna said.

They lifted their caps and gave her strange grins.

"This here, fellows, is Annie."

"Annie," they said in unison.

"She's going to be helping us out. I'll train her to be the guide." He offered Arianna a grim smile.

"Hannah told me that you had a friend. What's she know about this?"

"Nothing, except that I was looking for work."

"Hannah said you had a working girl's accent. I don't hear it."

"I was actually able to take some really good lessons with the tailor's daughter. When I first came here, naturally, I wanted to blend in. I was afraid to do anything but."

Jeremiah Heath seemed to accept everything she had to say. "Well, then, if your friend was staying with you, she's not now."

"I can't leave her on the streets, not when . . . not when there's a madman on the streets!"

"You keep your peace about others or you don't work with me."

"Let's hope you make me a decent income, then. And don't be asking me to come walking out on the streets in the middle of the night, not with a murderer on the loose."

"You'll be safe—the boys will see to it."

The boys . . . She looked at them all again. Matthew, Luke, John, Sebastian, Raoul, and Garrett. And, of course, Jeremiah Heath. They were like a pack of sharks, watching, seeming to drift, ready to strike. Sharks . . .

But sharks who would protect her in the murky waters of this evil underworld.

"When do we start?" she asked.

"We've an appointment tonight," Jeremiah said.

"Tonight," she murmured. She had to stop herself from looking across the room. Fiona was there, of course, swaddled in a black cape, scarf, and hat.

Well, she wouldn't be able to speak with her; she'd

have to understand that it was all going just as it should.

"One more thing," she said.

"What?" Jeremiah asked her.

"Red Hannah. I owe her. She set up this meeting."

Jeremiah nodded to one of the boys. The one named Matthew, she thought.

"He'll see to Red Hannah," he told her.

"Fine."

"For now, Sebastian and John will go with you to your place. Get your things, bring them to mine."

A flutter of nervousness seized her. "I thought that we went to our . . . clients' houses?"

"Oh, we do. But the group resides together. A lodging house near the old pump. I like to keep a firm eye on my brood."

Again, a certain sense of nervousness seized her. Recklessly, she wondered if it really mattered what happened to her. Her father was dead. Maggie had suggested that he'd left a wish stating she should marry Jamie! Jamie, like a brother to her, but not . . .

The man she'd seen but once. Who had seemed to be so very entranced with her, when he hadn't even known her name.

She'd probably never see him again, never know his name.

So what was there in life, really?

Revenge.

Something to take away the dull ache in her heart.

"Fine. Come along, then. Let's get my things." Yet even as she walked, she felt the surge of fear again. *Seven of them. Surrounding her. Cutthroats and thieves. As long as they thought that she was truly on their side, she was fine.*

But if they ever discovered where she had really come from . . .

She wouldn't stay around that long, she assured herself.

As she went out the door, she turned, and caught Fiona's eye. She winked, trying to assure her friend that everything was all right.

And then . . .

She walked out of the pub, and into her new life.

For two days, Maggie lay low, waiting. She didn't hear from Jamie, and when she had remembered that she needed to talk to Arianna, she had gone to the girl's room, only to be given a muffled excuse. Arianna was feeling ill.

On the third day, Mireau returned. She was upstairs when she heard his carriage, and ran down faster than the wind. When he came in, she realized that she must have been staring at him with such anticipation that the most casual of observers would be very curious as to what had happened.

Mrs. Whitley was not just a casual observer. She was a spy. For whom, Maggie wasn't quite certain, but the woman never tired of getting into her business.

"Mireau!" she said, and forced her voice to be casual. "How are you? Clayton told me that you headed out on a bit of a holiday! Come into the library. We'll have tea brought in here. You will see to it for me, won't you, Mrs. Whitley?"

Naturally, Mrs. Whitley nodded and left them.

Maggie caught hold of Mireau's arm and quickly dragged him into the library. "Well?" she demanded, shutting the door.

He smiled broadly. "I don't think I have ever felt so proud or happy to be part of something."

"So . . . the baby is fine? Clayton's sisters are really so kind and wonderful?" As she asked the question, she was somewhat ashamed to realize that Clayton had been an accepted part of her life for so long and she hadn't known a thing about *his* family until the night she'd rushed over to find Mireau.

"They're lovely. Truly lovely. She's in a small village, out in beautiful woods, and they have a charming cottage, and you would have thought that I brought them a basket of gold. They were delightfully arguing all that each was going to do for her when I left. There's Violet, the eldest, Merry, and Edith. Edith is a schoolteacher, and there's a wealth of books in the place! Violet is the leader, so it seems, and it's the most amazing thing! All three of them are spinsters. They are wonderful. The cottage is delightful. She'll have her own little room, and she'll be raised in just the right way."

"Oh, Mireau! It is wonderful to think that we were able to be in the right place at the right time, fall in the love with the little urchin ourselves, and then find such a wonderful place for her to grow up!"

He nodded. Mireau was just as suspicious of the household at Moorhaven as she was, and slipped the door open slightly to look out. "You know, the story we were given might well be a lie. Little Ally might be the child of a whore and a dockhand."

"Does it really matter?" Maggie asked him. "She's a beautiful babe."

"It only matters if someone believes she is the illegitimate daughter of Prince Eddy, and if that someone wants to see she's never in line for the Crown."

"She can't be in line! There are dozens of legitimate heirs."

"Still . . ."

"No one knows that we have her. And if she's ever traced to us, then . . . then you're a father," Maggie told him, grinning. "It worked with Clayton. Until I told him the truth."

"And he'll keep the secret?" Mireau said worriedly.

"Mireau! You've lived in that house long enough. He'll keep the secret to his dying day."

He cleared his throat. "Naturally, they do well enough, they wouldn't starve, and they adored the baby and are delighted to raise her, but . . . I'm broke. You know it."

"Thanks to Charles, I have plenty," Maggie said. "Of course, I'll see to it that the sisters get plenty of money. And, of course, we can visit her. She's part of Clayton's family now."

He nodded. "Funny, I thought that I'd perish on the spot when you stuffed her into my arms, and then . . . I just fell in love with that funny little face!" He sobered suddenly. "But you—were you all right? He didn't see the baby, did he? Lord James, I mean. I take it he was rather harsh. And threatened you."

"It didn't matter," Maggie said, waving a hand in the air. She hoped that her flush didn't give anything away. "He brought me here, stayed a bit . . . and I haven't seen him since. As soon as I could, of course, I went rushing home to Mayfair, talked to Clayton, and since . . . well, I've bided my time here, waiting."

Waiting . . . with her own company. She'd had time alone. Way too much of it. Time to realize that when other things were really far more important, all she did was think about Jamie. And there had been time, of course, to realize that she had been falling in love with him, no matter what her temper, since he had first looked up, since she had seen his face from her window, when she had tricked herself, for only a second's silly luxury, that he was the man she was to marry.

She'd had plenty of time as well to berate herself for the stupidity of her feeling. She was definitely not a foolish and dreaming young schoolgirl. His opinion of her was surely of the lowest. She had betrayed Charles—with him, of course, but sadly, it was a man's world. He might have been angry with himself, but still . . . as he had said, he hadn't been engaged to be married.

Then, of course, there was the very simple fact that he and Arianna were destined to be married. It was something Jamie would surely bring up to Arianna, when she'd had time to come to terms with her grief. When she reached her majority. And Arianna clearly adored her cousin. What could be more natural? Jamie, with all his knowledge of the property and estates—the male who had inherited the title—taking on the old lord's daughter as his wife.

Arianna, whom he knew so well, an absolutely stunning beauty—as even Mireau had been quick to point out.

She was a fool, putting herself into position for greater pain and humiliation. And yet . . .

When he touched her, it was as if he did so because he had to, as if he had no other choice in the world, as if she were the greatest, most alluring treasure in existence . . .

"So! He forced you to be the well-behaved widow, eh?" Mireau demanded, slightly amused. "I must say, at least you were safe in my absence."

"Safe, yes," she murmured. Well behaved? Certainly not in the visions and memories that had so haunted her every moment since Jamie had walked out that night—apologizing.

"I—um, I guess I'll have to stay out of Whitechapel for a while, I imagine. Until they catch that monster."

"They may not catch him," Mireau said unhappily. "And, quite frankly, Maggie, it's never been safe. There's so often something terrible happening there. Just not usually quite this awful."

There was a tap at the door.

"Your tea, mum!" Mrs. Whitley called.

Maggie walked to the door and opened it. "Thank you so much, Mrs. Whitley. Oh! Mrs. Whitley, would you be so good as to go ask Arianna if she'd care to join us?"

The girl wouldn't come down, Maggie knew it. But she wanted to make sure that her invitations were constant.

"As you wish, madam."

Maggie closed the door on her. She walked to the tea service, preparing cups for the two of them. "My brother, so it seems, has taken an interest in politics."

Mireau grinned. "So he has. He's been listening in to many of the arguments going on. He is a baron, of course, and has a place, should he choose to take it."

"I hope he does. How wonderful it would be to see Justin . . . happy."

"I think he's in love," Mireau said.

"Oh?" Maggie was definitely surprised.

"Oh, don't go getting too happy—he saw the girl once, so he told me. But she had the most beautiful face in the world, and he plans to make himself worthy, and then find her—whatever it takes."

"Wonderful. My brother is finally in love—with a mystery woman." She sighed, then looked at him. "Mireau, I'm going to go mad here, always afraid and . . . I can't bear it. I'm supposed to be a guardian to a girl who despises me. I'm good at the work I do with the poor, but now, I'm banned from going where I'm needed."

"Surely, once some time has passed and you're not expected to be in deep mourning, you'll be receiving all kinds of invitations."

"I don't want a bunch of social invitations, Mireau."

"Then you can join me at more of the writers' tables."

"I haven't the patience."

"But you have the opinions!" he reminded her. He studied her. "My dear! You are restless. You have the strangest look about you."

"I don't. There's nothing strange about me at all," she assured him.

"Yes, you're different. There's the most amazing blush flooding to your cheeks now and then."

"Don't be ridiculous."

"But you are different. From just those few days ago. From the time . . . when Lord James caught us in that cab!"

"It's the baby, of course. I've been worried about her. And you!"

He shook his head, studying her. Then he suddenly grinned. "'Methinks thou doth protest too much!'" he quoted.

She was saved by a knock at the door. It was Mrs. Whitley. "Yes?"

"The Lady Arianna says that she is still feeling poorly."

"Really?" Maggie said, as she glanced back at Mireau, who was getting far too close to the truth of her agitation. "I think I shall run up and ask if Arianna doesn't wish to see a doctor," she told him.

"By all means," Mireau told her.

Maggie started out, past Mrs. Whitley.

"My lady! I'm sure it's nothing that serious!" Mrs. Whitley cried to her.

"I'll just see."

Maggie marched up the stairs, aware that Mrs. Whitley was following her, and determined to ignore the woman. She knocked on Arianna's door. There was no answer.

"She was just there, really," Mrs. Whitley said.

Maggie frowned, then a feeling of dread rushed through her. What if the girl really was ill? She pushed open the door and entered the room. Arianna was not in it, and her maid, Fiona, was just picking up clothing from the flloor.

"Fiona, where is Arianna?" Maggie asked.

"I . . . believe she just left."

"But she just answered to me!" Mrs. Whitley protested.

"She must have just . . . run out, then," Fiona said. Maggie, however, didn't move. She'd gotten to know

Fiona a bit in the days since she'd come to Moor-haven. And Fiona looked scared. Very scared.

"I'm sorry, m'lady, really," Fiona said.

"But she was ill," Maggie told her.

"Perhaps she needed fresh air," Fiona said.

Maggie stood very still, listening to the girl. She realized that, sometimes, especially when she was unnerved, as she was now, she had a really pretty lilting sound of old Eire in her voice. Sometimes, when she was careful with her speech, she did not.

"Strange," Maggie said.

"What, my lady?" Fiona asked.

"Well, no one came down the steps . . . and I didn't hear the door open or close." She walked toward Fiona, who looked very uncomfortable. "Do you know what I think?" Maggie asked her very softly.

Wide-eyed, Fiona shook her head. "What—my lady?"

"I don't think that Arianna was here at all just now. I think that you have been in this room—and that you answered for her."

Fiona was not at all good at lying. Her face flooded with color. "No!"

"Oh, yes, Fiona."

"Fiona! You're fired. You must leave instantly!" Mrs. Whitley cried.

"No, you're not fired," Maggie said, casting a stern glance in the woman's direction. She might have been Charles's housekeeper for many a year, but Maggie did not intend to have her place usurped. And she was angry, as well, because Mrs. Whitley either knew something, or was an idiot. Fiona seemed to be their connection to Arianna.

"Where is she?" Maggie demanded sharply.

Fiona seemed frozen.

"Fiona, listen to me, and listen well. In her mood, she could easily place herself in harm's way. Tell me, where is she?"

"I don't know, m'lady, honestly, I swear, I don't know!"

Maggie sat calmly at the foot of the bed. "Mrs. Whitley, will you please tell Mr. Mireau for me that he must make himself at home? I'll be speaking with Fiona for a few minutes."

"But, my lady! You may need me," Mrs. Whitley protested. "I am the head housekeeper! If there has been something going on—"

"Beneath your very nose?" Maggie said. "You needn't worry. I will deal with this."

"But my poor Lady Arianna!"

"My stepdaughter. Yes, the poor innocent. Mrs. Whitley, please convey my message to Mr. Mireau. This is my household, like it or not, and I will deal with matters my way. If you can't accept that . . . well, I will give you excellent references."

Mrs. Whitley pursed her mouth, but then snapped her lips as tightly shut as if she were a clam. She turned abruptly and left.

"Now, Fiona," Maggie said firmly.

Fiona stared at her. Then words seemed to rush from her lips. "I was never spying on you, really! I was supposed to have been . . . I told Arianna that you were really nice and decent, and I didn't think that you'd ever do any harm to Lord Charles!"

"Fiona," she said dryly, aware that the girl had seen her at her worst, "thank you for that vote of confidence. But it doesn't matter."

"You're firing me, aren't you? I guess you have to."

"I'm not firing you! I need your help. Where is Arianna?"

Fiona shook her head, tears welling into her eyes. "I don't know. I really don't know."

"But you know something."

"I know that she . . . she wanted to get even with you."

Maggie felt a chill. She said, "I'm more worried about her right now than myself. Talk to me, help me, please. When did she leave?"

"She's been gone . . . a few days now."

Maggie gasped. "You've been answering as her— *for several days?*"

"I'm so sorry. You've a right to be angry."

"I am angry—but angrier with myself than I am with you. And I need you. Please. Fiona, you must tell me what you know."

"I . . . I know that she met with a man. In Whitechapel."

"In Whitechapel?" Maggie repeated, truly alarmed.

Fiona nodded miserably. "Where?"

"I can show you the pub."

Maggie shook her head, trying to maintain a sense of calm. "Fiona, with her looks, with the finery she wears, she would have been a victim of some thief . . . or worse. Almost instantly."

Fiona shook her head strenuously. "No . . . she had clothing, poor clothing. We rented a room, a rat trap! And we went and traded even the servants' things we brought."

Maggie stood. "We're going to that room right now. And if we don't find her there, we'll go to the pub." She rose, truly alarmed. Then she spun back. "Fiona, what was she trying to do in Whitechapel?"

Fiona hesitated. "She wanted to work for a mesmerist."

"A mesmerist?"

"You know . . . a mesmerist, or a spiritualist."

"Why?" Maggie said, frowning. "Was she trying . . . to contact her father?"

Once again, Fiona shook her head miserably. "She wanted . . . she wanted to lure you to this person, and . . . I'm not sure what then," Fiona said.

Maggie stiffened. She could well imagine what Arianna would envision for her.

And still . . .

"Dress as poorly as you can. And hurry. We've got to find her." Maggie went running out of the room. As she suspected, the housekeeper, Mrs. Whitley, was back up the stairs—hovering very close to Arianna's door. Eavesdropping.

"Mrs. Whitley, please—just get out of my way!" Maggie told her.

She literally moved the woman, managing not to shove her, and raced on down the stairs, bursting into the library.

"Mireau!"

"Yes?"

"We've got to get back to Whitechapel. Now!"

"But Maggie—"

"Find Darby. Have him help you get into some shabby clothing, and be quick!"

"But Maggie! Jamie will have your throat—"

"He will have to hang me, then. Wait, we need more than just the right clothing."

"Oh, God, Maggie . . . we can't do this. What, have you lost your mind?"

"Mireau, Arianna is there, somewhere."

"What?"

"Fiona has been confessing to me, Mireau. She's been out there several days; she met with a mesmerist, a spiritualist, knowing that I would be tempted to come, once I heard about the operations."

"Maggie, you can't just go running around the streets of Whitechapel."

"You're right, we must go in more than poor clothing. We're going to have to be seriously disguised."

"Maggie, we're all going to get into serious trouble. This is a matter for the police."

"Mireau! First, we've got to try to find her. If we go barging in somewhere with the police, I'm afraid we could put her life in danger. Fiona knows where they took a room—"

"They took a room? In the East End?" he said incredulously.

"Mireau, please, just move!"

"I'll have to head back to the Mayfair house, find the wigs and disguises—"

"Yes, yes . . . wait! No."

"Why not?"

"What if—what if Adrian Alexander is still out there, in disguise himself, starting over? What if he's the spiritualist that she found?"

"There are hundreds of thousands of people out there, Maggie. If you're in such a hurry, what do you suggest?"

She thought for a moment, then exclaimed. "Cecilia!"

"Who?"

"Cecilia, Lady de Burgh. Mireau, she's at her town house. Go to her now, and tell her that we need something very different. And please, please, hurry. Get back here, for me, as soon as possible."

Once upon a time, Arianna had thought that she knew misery. Her father's death had been the greatest pain she had imagined possible.

Now, she knew that there could be worse things than hurting for the loss of a loved one. There could be living as she was now, and it had been just a matter of days, and already she had learned a bitter and sad lesson.

It went beyond the filth and the squalor of her living conditions. The lack of privacy. The fear that touched her heart constantly. It was in all that she was forced to see, and the realization that she had become a prisoner, and that if she ever lost her cover and bravado, even for an instant, she would know greater pain and humiliation, and then she would die.

It was true that Jeremiah Heath intended to go for the really large scams to be had; he used the poor people, easily pleased with some small trinket, to convince them that he had communicated with someone lost. The first few hours after her meager "poor" possessions had been taken from the room, she had been moved into a partitioned space in a small set of two rooms. She had protested her nearness to the seven men, and been ignored. Worse. She had seen the leers of the fellows in Jeremiah's employ, and she knew that if she didn't please

Jeremiah at all times, she would be fair game for the
fellows.

He warned her flatly that it would be so, and not
so tragic, for if she didn't perform as he required her
to, she might as well learn the trade of obliging such
blokes. She was to learn to be silent and regal, to talk
to him, to "lead" him on a path to the dead. She did
as he asked, and he seemed pleased, and informed
her that their first séance was to be that night; they
had been invited to the home of a factory owner
whose wife was grieving; she had just lost a child. The
"boys" were sent out to find out everything they
could about the child, and they were also ordered to
bring home some "handy cash" needed for the
event.

They returned with wallets and reticules. One was
covered in blood. And it was the sight of that blood
that first made her realize just what kind of a situation she had gotten herself into. "Trouble?" Jeremiah
asked simply.

And Matthew—it was Matthew, she believed—
shrugged off-handedly. "He squealed a bit. Don't
worry, none, though. He was drunker than a swine . . .
looks as if he fell off the stairs coming down from the
pub."

Jeremiah had nodded. And Arianna had felt
sick.

"Dead?" Jeremiah asked.

"Stone cold," Matthew assured him.

It was all she could do to keep from gagging, from
passing out, and yet she knew that she could not. If
she showed the slightest sign of weakness, she knew
now, she would be killed, and somehow, her remains

disposed of in a way that would make her demise appear accidental.

"Maybe we should be acquiring our cash from women only these days," Matthew said. "If there's an obvious sign on the body, we could just cut it up, make it appear that Jack the Ripper fellow has found himself another victim."

"There's thinking, my boy, but still, I'd prefer our petty needs not be obvious in any way. I keep telling you—we're going for much bigger hauls. We're starting small, I'll warrant, but . . . we'll bring in riches."

They came back with cash, and information. Arianna discovered that she was to be dressed in simple black, but part of the cash went to buying her a strange red ring, which Jeremiah said she would use as part of her powers. "Now, bear in mind, hands are never to be released around the table. One or two of the boys will always be part of the "séance" goers, ready to strike down any troublemaker among the guests. But, my dear, you bear in mind, you must never let go of the hands!"

They had traveled on foot, in a pack, until they had neared the humble but respectable house. Then four of the fellows had broken off, and Arianna realized that they were to guard the entrances and watch for interference.

In the home, she met the grief-stricken mother, and two other women, both of whom had lost loved ones recently. It wasn't necessary to reach all the loved ones, Jeremiah taught her. Just one convincing performance would bring others back, and spread the rumors of their true ability.

That first night, she conducted Jeremiah into his

"trance." The man was a true actor. Matthew acted as his control, standing alone in the darkened room, creating the smoke that appeared. But Jeremiah had eschewed the use of any real props for the event, speaking in a child's voice, and, apparently, saying the right things.

He was rewarded with an exceptionally fine pocket watch, and they left with a few pocketsful of silver, as well.

That first night, it seemed, Jeremiah was well pleased with her. When Luke made a few comments that she could actually be useful in many ways, Jeremiah sharply told him that she was to be left alone—she was proving herself a fine addition to their group.

The next night, a sailor, a friend of one of the guests, had imbibed in a fair amount of his host's wine before the affair. He mocked Jeremiah before the company, but Jeremiah never lost his pretense of being in a trance. With a deadpan expression, eyes rolled back, he warned the sailor that he was doomed to meet with an accident.

Which he did, as soon as he left the house, and was met by a number of the group's thugs.

Arianna would never forget the sound as his head was struck, his skull crushed. He was deposited in the Thames. When his body was found, it would appear that he had taken a tumble from the bridge, and certainly, if there was an autopsy, it would be discovered that he had been drinking.

She was never left alone.

By the third day, she began to fear what she had longed for—that Maggie would come. Because Maggie would die instantly. Once, it had been what she thought she had wanted. Now, she had learned the truth about such a horrible death. She knew what a pathetic, wretched little fool she had been, certain that she knew so much, that she could handle herself, that she could wile any man into letting her have her way. She had thought it would be a lark, as well as a simple revenge. Now, all she knew was fear.

The moment the woman began to scream, Jamie was ready. He crossed the darkened alley at a swift pace, swinging her attacker around by the shoulder, and catching him with a right jab to the jaw. The fellow let out a howl of pain, and crashed against the stone wall that bordered the narrow throughway.

"What'd ye do that fer, ducky?" the woman cried out, rewarding him with a swift slap of her shabby reticule against the side of his head.

"You were screaming, I was trying to save your life!" Jamie informed her.

"I didn't mean to 'urt 'er!" the man cried. He was a lean fellow, light-haired and mustached. Like the prostitute, he was missing several teeth. He carried a small valise.

"What's in the bag?" Jamie demanded.

"Me carpenter's tools!" the fellow said. Both he and the woman stared at Jamie as if he had gone daft. Jamie looked into the bag. Not a knife in it, or even a sharp-bladed instrument of any kind.

He passed the bag back to the man. "Why were you screaming?" he asked the woman.

" 'E cheapened out on me, 'e did! Trying to cheat me out o' a few d's!"

Jamie looked to the man.

"Got to have me doss money!" the woman said.

"Pay her," Jamie told the man.

"She weren't worth what she wanted!" he complained.

"Pay her," Jamie insisted.

The fellow looked disgruntled, but dug more deeply into his pocket. "You a copper, or something like that?" the man asked, irritated.

"No," Jamie told her.

"I didn't need to pay 'eh, then!" the fellow whined.

"You needed to pay her," Jamie told him sternly.

"If ye're not a copper, wot are y' then?" the fellow demanded belligerently.

"Call me a simple member of a citizens vigilance committee, and quit griping. What can you be thinking, cheating her out of a few pennies when you know she should be inside? There's a killer on the loose."

"Aw . . . needs me own doss money," the man said. "Lost me room today, I did."

"So far, this fellow isn't after men," Jamie reminded him. He looked at the woman. "Get to your doss, then. There're dozens of lamps out tonight, so it seems."

"Thank you, sir!" the woman said, and she sped on across the alley. As Jamie watched, she disappeared into darkness again.

"Not a copper, eh? I'll be on me way, then!" the man said. Frustrated, Jamie leaned against the wall, watching as he, too, started to disappear into the darkness.

Then he called back to Jamie, "Don't matter much wot I paid that one, sir! She'll be spending it on 'er gin, long before she looks for a bed for the night!"

Chapter 15

Maggie was quite convinced that she'd never had a better disguise. Cecilia loved to play at her masquerades, and she was equipped with all manner of wigs and makeup.

The thing that worried Maggie somewhat was that they had wound up with Cecilia as an accomplice in their endeavor.

She would never have agreed, but Mireau returned not only with disguises, but with her adventuresome friend, as well.

"Now, explain to me just what we're up to?" Cecilia demanded. They had enlisted Clayton for the evening, afraid that Darby would feel that he was obliged to go for Jamie, or some other authority. Maggie wanted only to find her stepdaughter, and get her out of harm's way as quickly as possible.

"We're going into Whitechapel, and possibly to a séance," Maggie explained, "and it could be very dangerous. Cecilia, you've two young sons, and you shouldn't be with us."

"Oh, but I shouldn't be half the places that I am!" Cecilia said, smiling. She had out a box of makeups, and cursed now and then as the carriage went over a few ruts. She sat back, surveying her handiwork. "Oh, but I'm very good, actually. Mireau, take a look! Why, Maggie. You're nearly an old hag! Can you imagine that—I've made her look quite ugly."

Maggie had no idea what Cecilia had done with her theatrical paints. But Mireau was staring at her now as well, shaking his head. "Like an old crone," he agreed. "Maggie, no one will recognize you now!"

"Here, I've a mirror!" Cecilia said, and offered it up.

Maggie looked at herself in the dim light, and nearly jumped. The wig Cecilia had given her was drab and gray. With the makeup, she had added lines and an aged, haggard appearance. She had gone so far as to give her an ugly mole.

"Perfect," she marveled, looking at Cecilia.

"See, aren't you glad I'm here? I'm amazingly handy."

"Yes, but if things go badly, I shall never forgive myself," Maggie said.

"I owe you," Cecilia murmured.

Mireau frowned. "I took Maggie out for a last fling, having no real idea that she didn't wish to have one."

He stared at Maggie sternly. "It was fine. I was able to leave."

"A gentleman helped her out," Cecilia explained.

"Maggie!" Mireau said.

"It's over, and we've tonight to concentrate upon!" She stared at Fiona, silent and wide-eyed in her corner of the carriage.

"Ah, yes, tonight!" Cecilia said.

The carriage came to a halt. Clayton came around, decidedly unhappy about their course.

"We're at Mile's End," he said.

"Fiona, where was this room you rented?" Maggie asked.

Fiona came out of the carriage and stood at her side. "I don't know!" she moaned.

"Fiona, you must think!"

"It's dark," the girl murmured.

Clayton became helpful, pointing out streets and landmarks, and at last, Fiona said, "There, down that alley, and around the corner. I think."

Clayton remained with the carriage while the four hurried down the street. Maggie noted that it was well into the evening, but early for the East End where pubs stayed open all hours and the homeless drifted the streets endlessly.

As she walked, she tripped over something. A body. She looked down, terror filling her heart.

"'Eh! Watch where ye're goin', luv!" a man cried out angrily.

She breathed again. Down the street, they came to a stop before a door. Maggie stepped forward, banging on it.

No answer, and it was dark within.

"We rented it from a woman down the hall," Fiona told her, pointing as Maggie lifted a brow.

Again, Maggie marched forward, and knocked on a door. It was answered by a portly woman with a heavy chin. She peered at them in the dim light that filtered out from her own quarters. "What ye want?" she asked suspiciously.

"I'm looking for the young woman who had taken the room down the hall," Maggie said.

"Ah, she moved out! Barely moved in, and she moved out! The room's vacant—there! You were with the girl!" she declared, pointing at Fiona. "I'm owed on that room. In fact, if ye're kin to the girl, ye can give me wot's due!"

"How amazing. Most people ask for their rents in advance!" Mireau said.

"She did ask for her rent in advance," Fiona said, staring back at the woman.

"Where did she go?" Maggie demanded impatiently.

"Am I goin' ta git me money?"

"Give her some money, Mireau," Maggie said. "And missus, you tell me where the girl went."

"The usual," she said, taking the coin from Mireau, and studying it. Apparently, she decided that she had received a satisfactory bribe. "With a group of men."

"A group of men!" Fiona said.

"Aye, a group of young cutthroats, I daresay. Where they went, I don't know."

"All right, then," Maggie said. "Perhaps you can help us in another way. Have you heard about any mesmerists or spiritualists working in the area?"

"Ah . . . I've heard about a new fellow. Called Jeremiah. But if you want to know more about the bloke . . ."

"Mireau, give her more money," Maggie said.

The woman grinned, pleased, and was happy to accept another coin.

"Sorry," she said. "Seems the bloke don't work out of one place, though he is gaining something of a reputation! Goes to diff'rent places, he does."

"We should take the money back!" Mireau muttered.

Maybe the woman thought it was a real threat. She stepped back. "I can tell ye this—head for a pub just around the corner, called the Blarney Stone. His fellows are known to occupy the place. The gin is very cheap."

She slammed the door in their faces then.

"The Blarney Stone, I take it?" Mireau said, rolling his eyes.

"The Blarney Stone," Maggie agreed.

Midnight.

Now having moved on to a second pub, Jamie leaned against a wall, watching as the evening's customers came and went. There was a killer loose on the streets, and it seemed that men and women alike were quick to whisper in hushed words about the goings on, but it didn't appear to stop them from frequenting their favorite gin houses—and the streets.

The police were out and about, making their presence known. But that night, more than ever, Jamie became aware that they could not protect every woman on the street—many hundreds of thousands of people were crowded into London's East End.

As he watched the doorway of the pub, he was startled to see a fine carriage drive by. For a moment, his blood quickened, as he feared that Maggie had ignored his threat, and had come to Whitechapel on another of her missions. But thus far, he'd never seen her in the foggy, misty, gas-lit streets at night.

He kept to the shadows, watching the carriage, and noted that there was no coat-of-arms upon the door. A block past the pub, in a field of haze, the carriage came to a halt. Someone in a black cape and tall hat stepped from the carriage. As a woman walked by, the fellow stopped her.

Frowning, Jamie walked along the row of cottages, remaining in the shadows, until he reached the carriage. He strode out, then, but paused at the rear of the carriage, surprised to see that the man was Baron Justin Graham.

Jamie couldn't hear the words being exchanged, and he started to come around, and identify himself. But apparently, he had a made a noise, and Justin jerked his head around, then stepped back into the carriage. The woman stepped away, staring after the carriage, her eyes aglow.

"Missus!" Jamie said. The woman looked at him, and backed away, deciding whether to offer him her services, or scream bloody murder.

He lifted his hands. "Don't be afraid. I won't come any closer. I . . . I'll pay you for information."

"Information?" she said cautiously.

He produced a silver coin from his pocket and tossed it to her. "What did that gentleman want from you?"

She started to laugh, and slumped against the brick wall that gated a factory on that side of the road. She was drunk, and the sound of her cackle actually made him want to snatch his coin back, but he reminded himself quickly that one look at the surroundings made it easily possible to understand why gin seemed the best remedy for life.

"Please," he said evenly, "I need to know what that gentleman wanted."

"Why, just like you, sir! He wanted information."

"About what?"

"Had I seen anyone suspicious! Everyone in the streets is suspicious these days, dearie! Then, did I know anything about a fellow claiming quietly to be a great spiritualist, or did I know about any particular house of . . . ill repute."

What in God's name was Justin up to now? He'd heard the fellow was trying to turn a new leaf—to have more purpose in life. Still, these were mean streets. Justin had served his time in the Queen's army, Jamie reminded himself, and still . . . it was somewhat uncomfortable to think about him trying to clean up the streets of Whitechapel—on his own.

"Thank you," Jamie said. "Where were you off to?" he asked her.

"You've something in mind, ducky?" she said, suddenly coy.

He shook his head. "It's getting late. I'd hoped you were heading home."

"Well, wot a sweet one ye be, and handsome at that! You've given me quite a pretty coin here, sir!"

"Take it, and go home," he said, and turned, and started walking down the street again.

Watching the pubs would avail him little. The murderer would not strike so close to so much activity, where there was so much light.

As he moved down the street, the mist-shrouded night was suddenly rent asunder by a scream, a man crying out, "Murder! Oh, my God! It's another murder!"

Jamie started to run in the direction of the shout.

At the Blarney Stone, Mireau went to the bar and ordered a round of drinks, then joined Maggie, Cecilia, and Fiona at a table.

"What's going on at the bar?" Maggie asked him.

Mireau shrugged. "They're talking about the murders. And about their jobs, the casual work some of them get now and then, how the police should be doing more . . . how there's not enough work, and not enough gin. The woman with the paisley shawl is trying to get the short fellow in the tan cap to take a stroll into an alley with her. And don't stare now, but there's a young fellow, tan trousers, black jacket, shaggy brown hair, and a half a day's beard whose been watching us since we came in here."

"Oh?" Cecilia said, craning her neck to see over the head of others.

"I said, don't look now!" Mireau reminded her.

"All right, all right!" Cecilia said. She had worn ragged, fingerless gloves, and as she picked up her gin, Mireau made a *tsking* sound.

"What?" Cecilia said.

"A perfect manicure. Ah, they'll think you're a working girl, all right!"

Maggie had covertly taken notice of the fellow. And he was watching them.

She suddenly let out a loud moan, and let her head slump to the table.

"What is it?" Mireau cried, with real alarm.

Cecilia was quicker. She let her voice rise. "What is it, what is it? Are you daft man? How can you ask her such a thing when you know how she's suffering, poor lass! Ever since her dear Frank died of that awful fever . . . there, there, lass!"

Maggie raised her head just slightly, sniffling. "You don't understand, you can't understand . . . we'd argued that day! He died, and I was never able to say that I was sorry . . . never able to tell him just how much I did love him!"

Cecilia pulled her into her arms, rocking with her. "Don't sit there like a useless bum!" she charged Mireau. "Can't you see, the poor dear needs another gin?"

"Right. Righto," Mireau said, rising, and heading for the bar.

"Have you ever seen that fellow before?" Maggie asked Fiona, her head resting against Cecilia's shoulder so she could continue to rock and moan while getting a good look at the man.

"No," Fiona said. "Wait! Yes . . . maybe. Yes, I think that he *was* in here the day that Arianna met with that Jeremiah man."

Maggie nodded imperceptibly and let out another moan. Her heart jumped as the fellow approached Mireau as he stood, asking the bartender for another gin.

Mireau turned to him, and he either was startled at first, or was joining in on the act. He took the gin, listened to the fellow, nodded gravely, and then set a hand on his shoulder and indicated the table where they sat. The fellow came along with Mireau.

"This fellow says his name is John," Mireau said.

Maggie sniffed, giving him a curt nod and no more.

"Hello, John," Cecilia said. She gave the words an appreciative sound. "Sorry, me old auntie is not up to herself this evening."

Old auntie? Maggie thought that Cecilia was enjoying herself.

"She's not usually so rude. There's Flossy there," she said, indicating Fiona, who blinked once and nodded, extending a hand.

"Pleasure," Fiona said.

"Don't mean to be intrudin' on yer grief, mum," John said. "But I couldn't help but hear."

Maggie waved a hand in the air.

John lowered his voice and leaned low to the table. "Frankly, you don't look much like you belong in these parts."

"We'll belong here soon enough. Uncle Frank kept us all eating," Cecilia said with a sigh. "Still, we've a few pretty little things left to pawn—not on us, of course!" she added sternly. She looked at him furtively, as if realizing she should be suspicious.

"Y'needn't be afraid o' me!" John told her. "I didn't think ta meet ya for evil gain. I heard the moan, and the sorrow from the poor woman and thought as I knew how maybe you could make it all a bit better."

"It was the argument, you see!" Cecilia whispered to John. "If they hadn't argued . . . but they were quite a couple. After so many years, still in love like young folk!"

"Has she ever thought about reachin' her lost man, eh?" John suggested.

"Reaching him? Why he's cold in his grave!"

Cecilia said, lowering her voice to a whisper once again.

"No, you don't ken wot I'm sayin'!" John told her, giving her a sad and rueful smile. "There's those out there can sometimes break through the barriers . . . of life and death."

"Posh!" Cecilia waved a hand in the air.

"Spiritualists, ye've not heard o' them? Ye must be living in a dark cave, mum!" John said.

"I know about them," Mireau volunteered. And he sniffed. "Fakes!"

"No, no, not the real ones."

"Where do you find a real one?" Mireau asked skeptically.

"Not in the fine manors!" John said. "Not silly rich folk, thinking they can light a candle and talk to ghosts! But there is a man . . . and his daughter. Beautiful lass. He goes to folks' homes, when he hears about such a distress."

"We have no home where we can invite such a man," Cecilia said. "No more. And like as not, he's a fake as well."

John lowered his voice. "Ye've not heard the name, *Jeremiah Heath*?"

"Why, I have heard the name. Flossy, you were with me . . . there was a woman buying a bit of gin earlier . . . remember? She was telling her companion that she would swear by the man!"

Maggie roused herself, looking at Cecilia and Mireau. "Perhaps . . . dear God! Perhaps this man is real." She slumped back down. "But we've no room to have the chap!"

"All right, all right, listen!" John said. "I happen to know where 'e's going to be, this very night."

Mireau groaned this time. "You're going to spend the rest of what we've left!"

"Bah! There is a pension!" Cecilia said.

Her friend was wild, but she did have a touch of genius, Maggie decided. Cecilia should never have had status and position. She should have gone on the stage, traveled to America, and had wild affairs all her life, and be acceptable as outrageous because she was an actress!

"If it will help Auntie!" she said, pleading as she looked at Mireau.

"This man is not a fake—you swear it?" he demanded of the man.

John raised a hand. "By me poor mother's grave, I swear it!"

"But how do we reach this man . . . Will the people let us in?"

"Aye, it's at the home of a cigarette maker, a modest man. He'll be glad to have ye—hoping, of course, that ye can help out a bit?"

"What have we got on us?" Maggie asked weakly, pulling away from Cecilia's shoulder.

"About seven pounds sterling," Mireau whispered.

"Seven pounds sterling!" John said. "Near wot those fellows, Burke and Hare, got for the bodies they snatched, eh?"

The four of them stared at him dumbly and he quickly said, "Sorry, it was the amount ye said! Ah, now, now, don't be worrying none! We'll see that Auntie leaves happy as a clam. Wot was her good man's name, did ye say? Frank, was it? Hanbury Street, then, the big white house with the broken stone wall in front. Be there . . . well, soon. It's getting late."

He stood then and left them.

"Seven pounds sterling!" Cecilia swore to Mireau. "That's a fortune in these parts. We'll be set upon by thugs before we get there!"

Maggie shook her head. "I don't think so. I think they're going to be after the pension. Remember, whatever they do tonight, we believe. We have to find out if Arianna is with them!"

Mireau finished his gin and shuddered. "We'd best get going. The hour is growing very late. We're already past midnight, the 'haunting' hour!"

Sounds of music still rose above the screams and shouts beginning to fill the night. A working-men's educational club took residence in one of the houses, and apparently, all those carousing that night had not yet realized that just beyond their lively talk and dance, a woman had been murdered.

There was mass confusion on the scene when Jamie arrived. By trying to talk to the individuals around, he discovered that a fellow named Louis Diemschutz—who was a tinker of costume jewelry as well as steward of the club—had brought his cart along the street and into the court, and his pony had shied. He'd investigated the large mass in the shadows, and discovered it to be a woman. And even with the atmosphere of death pervading the streets, he had at first assumed her to be drunk. He'd gone into the club for a candle, a few men had come out with him, and they tried to lift her.

Then they'd found the blood. And the police had

been summoned. They were then trying to gain control of the streets, and creating a great deal of resentment as they went into the club, searching it for clues, and questioning the men. As Jamie listened to the explanation, he saw Dr. Bagster Phillips, police surgeon, arrive.

Jamie, milling with the crowd, noted the blood running to the door of the club, but it had sluiced down the cobblestones, and it was apparent that the murderer had not entered the door—footprints would have remained. He was certain as well that the murderer did not remain in the vicinity. Though the body might have been warm when discovered, Jamie would bet that the fellow was now long gone.

By then, a number of constables had been summoned. It was difficult to get close to the body, but he wedged his way as near as he might. Near enough to hear Bagster talking to one of the policemen.

This woman's throat had been slashed, ear to ear.

But she'd not been mutilated.

Jamie stood where he was for several long seconds, listening. One of the constables started to come toward him, ready to investigate him, to demand to see his hands, and check his clothing for blood. But luckily, it was a fellow named Quinn Hardaway, an officer he'd met once awaiting Maggie by St. Mary's. He looked at him with a curious frown for a moment, then nodded his way, and moved on.

As he stood then, with the melee going on around him, the curious now jostling with those being questioned and searched, he had a sudden uneasy thought.

The murderer had been interrupted.

He turned quickly, shoving his hands into the pockets of his coat, and moving along.

"This is insane! We need the police," Mireau whispered as they headed up a small walkway toward the house of the cigarette maker. "What if this fellow is Adrian Alexander going by another name. And what if Arianna really is with him, and wants you dead?"

"I don't recognize myself, Mireau. How would she recognize me?"

"She'll know me, and think I'm a traitor," Fiona said.

"That's true. We've got to get Fiona back to the carriage; she'll be safe with Clayton," Maggie said.

"She could recognize me," Mireau said.

"No," Fiona said.

"She saw me at the funeral, and at the wake, and—"

"No," Fiona said, and flushed furiously. "I saw you at the funeral and the wake."

"Why, you little minx!"

"We grew up together; I'd served her forever," Fiona explained.

"If we're any later," Maggie said, "this cigarette maker may not let us in his house. Mireau, see Fiona back to the carriage."

"You're not going in there without me!" Mireau protested.

"Yes, I am," Maggie said. "I have to find Arianna. I owe Charles something! Hurry—once we're in, they'll let you. Now, move!"

He glared at her, but he knew her, and knew that arguing at that moment was going to be futile. He set an arm around Fiona's shoulder, nearly running her along the street.

"Cecilia, you don't have to come with me," Maggie told her friend.

"I have never felt so alive!" Cecilia said.

"Good, because if this man is Alexander, he's deadly."

"Bring him on. Or, rather, Auntie, you come along with me!"

They headed on up the walkway. Maggie got a moment's start when a man stepped from the shadows at the overhang of the house. He was young, like the fellow who had called himself John. He was dressed in light trousers and a dark coat as well. He had no waistcoat, but wore a white cotton shirt.

" 'Ello, there."

Cecilia stepped forward. "We've . . . we've been told we might have a chance to see Jeremiah Heath here this evening." She said the words with reverence.

The man nodded but looked down the walk. "What happened to the pair with you?"

"Our little serving girl has taken sick. My husband will be back in just a few minutes. We were afraid that we wouldn't be allowed in, were we to take any more time. It's so late," she said apologetically.

The man watching her nodded, then stepped forward and opened the door. "They've not started as yet. Mr. Heath has been detained. Come in."

They stepped into the house. A rather worn-looking woman in a worn black dress, yet surely her best, came forward, wiping her hands on an apron. "I'm Mrs. Hennesy." She looked Cecilia and Maggie up and down, and must have approved them. She extended a hand. "Welcome to our poor abode. I hear that you've lost your dead husband, missus," she said, looking at Maggie.

"And you've lost a child," Maggie said, the sorrow in her voice real.

"This is Sissy, my niece," she said, indicating Cecilia. "I'm Mona. We're so very grateful to you." She didn't quite manage to bring a tear to her eye, but she dabbed at her face convincingly with her handkerchief.

"Do come in, Mona. We've a very small parlor, but I've been assured, size means nothing."

They walked into the parlor, and Maggie's jaw nearly dropped. Arianna was indeed there, sitting in a chair at a round table set before the hearth.

Jeremiah Heath might be late, but his "controls" were awaiting his appearance. There were three young men surrounding Arianna, one directly behind her, and one on either side. They were neatly dressed, but still had the hardened appearance of street toughs.

Arianna looked exceptionally drained, thin, and white. She offered a weak smile when they walked into the room. She was clad in something like a white robe, and her black hair streamed down her back.

Maggie knew, at that moment, that Adrian Alexander was indeed making his way back into his game. Arianna had taken the place of his "Jane," still rotting at Newgate, if news reports were to be believed.

"This lovely dear little thing is Ally," Mrs. Hennesy

said, introducing the new arrivals. "Ally, Mona and Sissy. Dear Mona has lost her husband—"

"Yes, her husband, Frank," Arianna said. She appeared almost to be drugged. Her voice was listless, yet the intonation was right. It was as if she had become a trained seal.

Cecilia nudged Maggie. "Frank, yes! Dear, my husband was Frank!" she said. An idiot could deduce that John might well have told her the name. But people who wanted to believe would be in awe that the stranger had known the name. They wouldn't bother thinking.

"Ah, here's my husband, George!" Mrs. Hennesy said.

A portly man of stocky build had come in. He kissed his wife on the cheek and apologized. "There's more mayhem out there tonight."

"Another murder," Arianna said.

"Another poor unfortunate!" George agreed. "Perhaps a different killer, though. Of course, the talk in the street is wild, but they're saying as this one wasn't chopped up. Lord, forgive me, ladies. I don't mean to speak so crassly."

"Another murder!" Cecilia exclaimed. She stared at Maggie with real alarm and discomfort.

"Now, now, a woman like you will certainly be fine."

"Of course." Cecilia let her hand flutter to her throat. "My—my husband will be right along as well."

"It's the same murderer," Arianna said dully.

They all stared at her.

"Well . . . I've bit of brandy. Perhaps we all need a swallow," Mrs. Hennesy said.

The toughs standing behind Arianna heard the word brandy. She smiled. "You dear young men! You are most certainly welcome to a wee sip, as well. Come along!"

The house was small and poor, but they were heading for the kitchen. Cecilia went to slip her arm through Maggie's, but Maggie quickly shook her head. "Go!" she mouthed.

Cecilia looked worried, but did so. Maggie hurried over to the table, taking a chair by Arianna.

"You have to come with me!" she urged the girl. "You are with an evil man, and you must come away."

Arianna turned her dazed look on Maggie, and stared at her for several long minutes. Then she gasped, and clapped her own hand over her mouth. "You've got to get out of here!" Arianna told Maggie. "You're the one who doesn't understand. He'll kill you. They kill anyone who crosses them. They kill for sport, for fun, for a few shillings."

"Yes, yes, I'll get out! You must come with me."

Maggie was startled to see a glaze of tears coming to Arianna's eyes. "No! You say a word, I make a move . . . they'll kill me. If he even hears who I am . . . that there's anyone out there who might care for me . . . I'm dead. Please, Maggie, I'm begging you . . . we'll both be dead. Do nothing, nothing!"

She heard the slight swishing sound of fabric. "There you are, Mona!"

It was Mrs. Hennesy, bringing a bit of her special brandy to Maggie. "This is special, we've saved it, but . . ."

"We intend to help with Jeremiah's fee, of course!" Maggie said, flashing a smile to John, who had returned to the room, and taken up a position behind Arianna once again. "And I know already that he will be worth it! This sweet young Ally believes that my Frank is near!"

"Ally is priceless!" Mrs. Hennesy assured her.

They all turned as the door opened. Maggie held her breath, frozen, waiting.

It was Mireau. "Our young maid was ill," he explained. "Lord, I don't know that she won't become far more ill, poor thing, don't know if we'll be able to afford to keep her . . . I'm sorry, I didn't mean to trouble you with our woes!" He reached into his pocket, looking at George Hennesy. "My good man, you are the head of the house?"

"George Hennesy," the portly man said, reaching out for the coins, counting them, and looking very pleased. "Give this fellow his sip of brandy, Ellen!" he told his wife. She nodded his way, and her eyes had a knowing look. *See!* She seemed to say to her husband. *Other good people are willing to give their last few coins up in honor of such a man as Jeremiah Heath!*

Mireau was brought a brandy, and Mr. Hennesy turned the coins over to John, who smiled pleasantly. "Jeremiah, 'e'd help ye out from the goodness o' his heart, 'e 'ould!" John said. "But a man's got to live, and such a man, well, 'e needs a decent bed for his sleep!"

"Of course, of course," Mrs. Hennesy said. "But oh, dear, oh, dear, he is coming, isn't he? I have such hopes set in this evening!"

" 'E's coming, Mrs. Hennesy, don't you doubt it."

"He's held up in the streets; there's mayhem out there," Mireau said.

"Aye, another murder," Mr. Hennesy said.

"Another murder?" Mireau said. He shook his head. "Two murders, I'm afraid." He stared straight at Maggie, his eyes filled with warning. "A double event, so they're shouting."

Sadly, Jamie's intuition had been right.

His sense of direction had been wrong.

The shouts and whistles had been going on for some time when he finally found Mitre Square at last. And already, people were milling and crowding, and the police were in vast confusion.

Some of it, Jamie ascertained immediately. The other body had been found off Berner Street while this one was in Mitre Square.

For the first time, the killer had struck in an area that was within the actual square mile that constituted the City of London. And so, officers belonging to the City of London police were running around, claiming supremacy, while their comrades from the Metropolitan force were out in abundance as well—they'd been chasing clues, chasing a killer.

Sadly, a number of policemen would still be in the Berner Street area, canvassing the homes there, searching for any small clue.

It wasn't yet two A.M. Jack the Ripper had indeed been interrupted so it seemed, and he had walked less than a quarter of a mile to strike again.

The police were desperately trying to hold people back, to control the crime scene, and again, to find what evidence they could. There was a lieutenant apparently in charge, and Jamie excused himself through the crowd, pulling his papers from his pocket to produce for the lieutenant.

"Lord Langdon!" the officer murmured with surprise. He studied him a minute and knew that his appearance was not to be questioned. He lowered his voice. "Some of the Metropolitan fellows aren't happy with me, but Lieutenant Colonel Henry Smith hasn't arrived yet, and . . . this is his jurisdiction. He was spending the night at the Cloak Lane station, but . . . he'll be here soon enough."

"I don't intend to touch anything or get in the way. If I might just take a look . . . ?"

"Of course."

Jamie wished that he had not felt obliged to do so as he hunkered down to view the victim.

The woman was on her back. One leg extended straight out, the other was bent and open. She had been ripped open from the groin to the chest, and her organs had been ransacked. In a horrible display, pieces had been strewn around the body as if the killer had intent in the design. But the madman had not stopped there. Her face had also been mutilated.

Whatever fervor had been interrupted in Berner Street had been given free rein here. He stared at her a very long moment and wondered if he had ever seen her before, in one of the pubs, walking the street, or listening to Maggie as she spoke. It was sad to say, that with her nose clipped and the blood all about, he would have no idea.

The officer buckled down beside him. "He worked quickly, he did. Officer on duty came through here

at one thirty A.M., and found her at one forty-
five."

"He gets around like a wraith, and works quickly,
indeed," Jamie murmured, and rose.

As Jamie stood, he saw two men being let through
the crowd. "Doctors . . . Brown and Sequira," the officer said.

Jamie nodded absently, looking around the
square. There were three entrances to it. There were
warehouses to one side, and what looked like a few
empty houses to the other, along with one that had a
light shining within.

"A policeman's house," the officer told him. "And
there's a night watchman at the factory . . . and no
one heard a thing."

"No, of course not," Jamie murmured, and he
wondered in what direction the killer must have
gone.

"Which way does the officer's beat go?" he asked.

"Well, he would have arrived here from the
street—there."

"Thanks," Jamie said, and walked in the opposite
direction.

"You poor people don't get much sleep around
here," Mireau said, stifling a yawn.

It was very late, past 2:30 in the morning.
Discomfort among the group was beginning to grow.

Then, the door burst open once again. One of the
boys had opened it for a man in a long back cape and
deerstalker hat.

Maggie had to stare at him very hard.

He'd grown facial hair—artistically, at that. And hair atop his head. It was short, and strange, but dark. He had a mustache. With hair, and rather astonishingly, he resembled Eddy, the Queen's grandson.

But for Maggie, there was no mistaking the man. He might be calling himself Jeremiah Heath now, but he was Adrian Alexander. She felt a freeze settling over her, and one look at Mireau, and she knew that he recognized the man as well.

She suddenly prayed that he didn't recognize Mireau.

But though her friend hadn't been disguised to appear elderly, as she had been, Cecilia had also done a wonderful job with Jacques Mireau. He was a redhead tonight, and his handlebar mustache was red, as were the heavy muttonchops on his cheeks. She forced herself to find confidence in their masquerade. If they only behaved as they should, he would not know them.

And she had to pray, of course, that he would not, because she had come to understand Arianna's terror. She tried to count the amount of young cutthroats around them, and decided that, with "Jeremiah" they equaled a group of seven. Seven men, and they were armed. She, Mireau, and Cecilia would be able to walk out tonight—leaving Jeremiah and his thugs eager to have them again, and more of their pounds sterling. But Arianna . . .

Arianna was their prisoner. And if she tried to get the girl out tonight . . .

They would all end up dead.

"Good evening," the man said.

"Oh, Jeremiah!" Mrs. Hennesy fluttered out, obviously so pleased to see the man that it didn't matter what the hour.

"I do apologize for my lateness. Traveling the streets tonight is mayhem. You may not be aware, the monster has struck again."

"Oh, we know!" George said, "I just came through the streets myself. As did this gentleman," he said, indicating Mireau.

"Horrible business, horrible," Mireau said.

"Ah, yes!" The man calling himself Jeremiah Heath brought his hands to his heart and looked heavenward. "Perhaps, in time, the spirits of those poor unfortunates will speak to me, and I'll be able to help the police. God knows, the fools have done little. Whether they mock my powers now, they'll seek them soon enough."

"Oh, Jeremiah! Just think. Perhaps you could help!" Mrs. Hennesy said.

"Alas, I have not been able to contact any of those wretched, departed sisters!" he said, and came closer to the table. "You are Mona," he said, taking Maggie's hand. She forced herself not to wrench it away. She nearly screamed. He was not wearing gloves, and his hands were uncomfortably . . . damp. Wet, actually, as if he had just washed them, and not dried them.

"And you are Jeremiah Heath!" she breathed.

He nodded, pleased, looked around and met the others with a nod.

He took special note of Cecilia, who blushed prettily.

He then looked around the room, and Maggie saw that his men nodded in return, and disappeared, as if they were taking up their guard positions.

"Ah, and I have kept you waiting long enough," Jeremiah said, and now he took a position opposite Arianna. "Mr. and Mrs. Hennesy...next to dear Mona here. And you, my dear sir," he said to Mireau, "down there, and you, my lovely lady"—this to Cecilia—"next to me."

Soon they were all seated. One of the "boys" lowered the gaslight. Arianna began to speak, just as Jane had previously, and soon, Jeremiah Heath was in a trance.

For the second time that night, Maggie thought that someone had missed their calling.

This man, too, should have been on the stage. He might have made his fortune that way, and not through murder and intrigue.

He spoke in a child's voice, and Mrs. Hennesy was in tears, speaking back, telling her beloved Billy how she missed him. Then, he fell silent. After a while, Arianna began to say softly that she was sorry, apparently Jeremiah was hearing from no more spirits.

But then, his head jerked, and his eyes rolled again.

"Mona!"

The voice this time was deep, raspy, and that of an old man.

"Dear, dear, Mona!"

Arianna involuntarily jerked her hand.

"Frank?" Maggie said hesitantly.

Then Jeremiah Heath's head fell forward.

"I'm so, so sorry!" Arianna apologized, again, as if her lines were learned by rote, and she was already half dead herself. "There is only so long that such a state can be maintained. Jeremiah is exhausted, and has lost the connection. I'm certain, however, that your Frank can be reached again. Of course, you heard his voice. It's certain you were loved, Mona. This must be very painful. Perhaps there would be no need for you to reach him again."

"No, oh, no!" Maggie whispered. "No, please, Mr. Heath must allow me to see him again! He must." Her voice was desperate, as well it should have been. There would be no way to get Arianna tonight, and yet, she would go mad if she wasn't able to rescue the girl soon.

Jeremiah Heath opened his eyes and stared at Maggie. He slumped, as if he were truly in a state of exhaustion. "Water," he whispered.

"Oh, dear, yes, of course, of course!" Mrs. Hennesy gasped, leaping up. Tears were still streaming down her face. Tears of gratitude, Maggie realized, and she was angry suddenly, so angry she could scarcely endure it. But she must. All of their lives depended on it. She had met with this man before, and she knew for certain what they faced.

Mrs. Hennesy raced back with the water. Jeremiah drank. "Mona, dear woman, did I fail you?" he asked.

"No, no . . . but . . . I'm ever so happy for the Hennesys. Their Billy stayed with us quite some time. But Frank . . . I didn't have time to tell him . . . to say that I'm sorry, that I loved him so. Oh, please, please, Mr. Heath, you must agree to see me again!"

"My dear woman, you mustn't be so distressed. Certainly, we can arrange to meet again in a few weeks' time."

"A few weeks' time!" Her dismay was very real.

"I'm afraid, my lady, that I and my helpers must earn

a living as well. This takes so much from me that . . .
well, I have business affairs that I must manage as well."

"No!" Maggie said, stricken.

"Dear lady, I understand that you are in financial
straits as well, and that, I believe, you were in this
area tonight looking for a home that was . . . afford-
able."

"Please, please, put your affairs on hold. There's a
pension . . . I need only get to the bank. I can draw
an advance, enough to get you and your people
through the next month. I know that you don't require that kind of payment, but I am so desperate. I
cannot live if I cannot come to peace with the way
that my dear husband died!"

He sighed and looked down. "I am gifted, madam.
I hate to live off this kind of a gift. It is something
that I should give away."

"No one can live without an income," Cecilia ventured.

"I am begging you, Jeremiah. Money is nothing—
except a bed and food," Maggie said. "Let me give
you that in exchange for the peace of my soul."

"Oh, dear."

"Please, in the goodness of your heart!" Mireau
said. "My poor auntie is impossible to live with, as it is
now. She needs your help so desperately." He indicated
Cecilia, his "wife." "We must all move on, and so, we all
need your help."

"All right, then. Think we can do it, dear?" he
asked Arianna.

Listlessly, she shrugged. "If you wish, Father, of
course."

"Then it's settled," Jeremiah said.

"Ah, but we're not, as yet," Mireau reminded them.

"Oh, please! You're welcome here again!" Mrs. Hennesy said. "Perhaps my dear Billy will have just a word to say again, too. George, that is all right with you, isn't it?"

George was evidently thinking of the fact that he would owe very little for the night, since Mireau had given him such a fine stack of coins.

"Naturally," George said.

"Well, we've certainly imposed upon your hospitality enough tonight," Cecilia said, rising. The others did the same.

Maggie was desperate to get a word to Arianna. As they all headed for the door, she hung back, throwing her arms around her and proclaiming, "I didn't thank you, my dear. You blessed, blessed, wonderful girl!"

Ahead, they all stopped. But Maggie dared whisper, "Tomorrow night, you'll be out of here. Take care, just until then!"

To her amazement, Arianna hugged her back. And whispered in return, *"No, you fool! I won't come with you, he'll kill us all. He can do it, he'll kill us all. Even a hint of the police, and anyone in his way will die! Try to take me, and I'll scream, do you understand? He'll not think I was a part of it. Somehow, sometime, I'll get out of this!"*

Aloud, she said, "I've done nothing for you, Mona, but . . . I know that tomorrow night, Jeremiah will give you the solace that you need."

"Yes, yes, of course!"

There could be nothing else said. The man had returned. His huge hand was on her shoulder.

"Until tomorrow!" Maggie said, and then, Mireau was dragging her out of the house and she could only look back and see the sadness in Arianna's eyes.

A sadness like . . . death.

Chapter 16

The papers ran headlines that screamed across Britain and beyond.

Jack the Ripper had struck again. And again.

The first victim in the wee hours of the morning had been Elizabeth Stride, Long Liz, as she had been known, and the killer had evidently been interrupted, because the lady had lost her life, but not, as one article so crudely put it, her innards.

The second victim had not been left in one piece. She had been cruelly vivisected. Many of the newspapers were gruesome in their detail.

And speculation was running rampant. There was a gang, there was one madman, there was rumor that someone of influence and money was surely doing the crimes, entering into the district with horse and carriage, and thus disappearing without signs of blood upon his person. There was even speculation in a few of the papers that suggested there might be a conspiracy, reaching to very important persons in the country. Considering the behavior of some members of the highest of the high in society, God alone knew just what might be happening.

There were those who suggested that it was a midwife gone mad. Jill the Ripper.

It was someone with an extreme knowledge of anatomy—a doctor.

It was someone with a crude knowledge of anatomy—a butcher, a hunter, perhaps even a housewife who knew what to do with a chicken.

It was a late in the morning, nearly noon, when Jamie awoke at last. He had attended the autopsy of the second victim, Catherine Eddowes, also known as Kate Kelly, among a few other names, and he had left the mortuary feeling weary and ill, shocked. In all his days, and some of those in India, facing the continued threats of the Thugees, despite the fact that India was now part of the Empire, he had never seen such heinous butchery perpetuated upon one human being by another. But the autopsy had not been the most dismaying part of his night out on the Queen's behest.

Far worse had occurred.

The police must have been right on the trail of the killer. They had found a piece of the woman's bloody apron. And near it, on the black dado of a wall on Goulston Street, there had been a written message. Chalked by the killer? No one knew.

And there was not even a photograph of what might have been crucial evidence.

There was chaos over that fact. Detectives had guarded it, had pleaded with their superiors to leave the writing for daylight, so that it might be photographed. But Sir Charles Warren—of the Metropolitan police—had ordered that it be wiped down before it was seen by people in the area. He claimed that he was afraid there would be a riot. Englishmen were up in arms about foreigners, and there was a hotbed of hatred and fear in existence.

The Juwes are not
The men that
Will be
Blamed for nothing

Warren had sworn that leaving the message would create a riot.

The papers clamored for Warren's resignation. Jamie had to wonder if it would be forthcoming.

Inspectors had crawled over the buildings; they had spent the night questioning people, and looking, ever looking, for any possible clues. But Jack had struck twice—and walked away, leaving a mass of confusion and accusation that shrieked across the land.

There were those working the streets of Whitechapel, Spitalfields, and the neighboring areas who might have ignored the first two murders.

No more.

The streets tasted of fear, sounded of fear.

No woman could consider herself safe.

There was far too much horror, and far too much speculation.

Jamie lay in bed after he woke, staring dully at the ceiling, still feeling exhausted. His first course of action, once he had returned home, had been to soak in a very long bath. It had seemed to take forever to breathe in what did not seem like the stench of blood.

And with it, the stench of poverty and disease.

The Queen would be sending for him, he knew. She was, despite the many years she had secreted herself away, a very kind and caring person, and felt her sense of duty keenly. She was going to be appalled, and horrified, and she was going to wonder how these things were happening, when so many people who were supposedly so qualified were in charge.

He dreaded seeing her. How to explain that he had been there, been on those streets, and seen nothing? He groaned aloud, and then fell silent, listening. There had been a tap at his door.

He was surprised. Randolph had known of his exhaustion. He would not awaken him.

"Yes?"

"My lord?" It was Randolph, but he wasn't alone as he cautiously opened the door. Maggie burst in around him. He'd been sleeping in the nude, since he'd crawled from the bath into a towel, and straight into bed from there.

"I explained that you had a late night, my lord, but Lady Maggie is rather insistent," Randolph explained.

"Maggie," he breathed, sitting up in the bed, chest bare, sheet to his waist. "Well, do come in. Be forewarned, I had a very bad night."

"A bad night!" she exclaimed. "You cannot imagine."

"You cannot imagine," he snapped back angrily.

She flushed then, realizing that she stood with Randolph, and that Jamie was in a state of complete undress. But then again, Randolph must be very aware of certain things that he kept entirely to himself.

"I'll just leave the two of you," the man murmured, and stepped out, quietly closing the door behind him.

Jamie rose then, his temper truly vile, heedless of her being there. It was not as if she had not seen him so before, and she'd had the rudeness to push her way in.

He walked into the bathroom and splashed cold water on his face, calling back to her, "Lady Maggie, I really don't give a damn about your petty problems this morning. Don't you read the papers?"

"Of course I read the papers. And it's appalling. But—where are you going? I need you to listen to me."

He wrapped a towel around his waist and walked back out to the bedroom. He was annoyed to realize that despite his anger, despite the sense of tempest raging in him, the sorrow, the horror, she could take him away.

She was standing there in a day dress of blue, skirt embroidered elegantly, bodice beautifully fitted. A shawl of a darker shade, cobalt, like her eyes, was cast around her shoulders. Her hair was pinned back, but gold ringlets of it curled about the length of her throat. She was breathtaking, and he felt the urge to sweep her up, and hold her. Hold her, and believe that he could always keep her safe, that nothing so horrible as what he witnessed could be real. He suddenly wanted assurance of life, be that in the strength of the way that he would put his arms around her, or in the oblivion to be found when he drowned in the depth of her eyes, in the sensuality of her flesh.

Except that . . .

He had to keep his distance from her. The other day . . .

He had behaved abominably himself. She was Charles's widow, no matter what the circumstances. Every step he had taken with her had been wrong. And now, she was proving to be a thorn in his side. He'd had to chase her down in Whitechapel, of all places. He'd burst into her bedroom then, and now . . .

Now, he gritted his teeth. There was business at hand, and he could neither forget himself by seizing her up with or without her consent, nor could he allow himself to be waylaid by any silly domestic situation.

"What?" he barked.

"It's Arianna."

"Lord above us!" he raged. "Arianna, Arianna! Madam, the girl was left to your guardianship! What, are you jealous of the lass? What is your problem with her! Sit down, have a heart to heart talk. You married Charles, you rule a fortune, and you have every possible luxury at your disposal. Don't come to me. You have no desire, ever, to be told what to do. Therefore, madam, you're on your own! Whatever it is, deal with it yourself!"

He turned again, leaving her there, staring at him openmouthed.

This time, he slammed the door to his bathroom.

And instantly, he felt regret.

No one else could understand what he was feeling this morning—unless it was one of the men who had witnessed the discovery of the body last night. No one could understand his sense of failure and helplessness—except for those who walked the streets as well, and came up empty-handed.

And still . . .

He was sorry. So very sorry. She had enraged him because of the night of sadness and horror he had just endured. . . .

And because he was so very much in love with her, and it was simply so very wrong.

He swung the bathroom door open, ready to step out and apologize, beg her pardon, try to explain, even if he couldn't really tell her everything.

But when he stepped out that time, Maggie was gone.

Maggie paced the library, staring at Mireau. "He was awful, horrible! I couldn't talk to him."

"Maggie, in this situation, you simply have to behave in a very mature manner. Whatever your problems are—"

"Mireau, you're not listening. He refused to talk to me. He just started screaming at me, and slammed the door."

"But Arianna's life is at stake."

Maggie stopped dead-still and nodded grimly, her arms folded over her chest. "That's why I decided, after I left, that what happened was the best possible thing."

"What?"

"Mireau, we don't dare bring Jamie in."

"Now you've really lost your mind."

She shook her head. "You don't understand just how frightened Arianna was. I know she believes that if anyone so much as reaches for her, she'll be shot or stabbed on the spot."

"But you just explain that to Jamie and—"

"I'm afraid. Afraid that she'll panic. Don't you see, Mireau? We can go in there with big guns blazing . . . a half dozen policemen, good heavens, we could get the military! But it wouldn't help anything because Arianna might well be dead before we could even begin to attack."

"You're losing me," Mireau said. "What on earth are we going to do then?"

"I'm still working on it. But honestly, it will be best if Jamie is not involved."

"Um, sounds best to me. We'll just go in and get ourselves killed."

"No, you see, what we have to do must be incredibly clever and—subtle."

"All right, Maggie, go ahead—explain to me how we're going to subtly handle a pack of thugs and murderers."

"We have to make it appear that Arianna is dead."

"Maggie—"

"No, no, hear me out! Remember how we all had a sip of brandy last night? Well, we'll have to do the same tonight. And into Arianna's brandy, we'll slip enough laudanum to cause her to pass out."

"Great—what will that do?"

"Keep her from fighting us, for one. Because we'll have laced all the rest of the brandy as well. Then, once we're out on the street . . . I can't tell Justin exactly what I'm doing, but I will ask him to be in the street, and be wary—there's so much going on, that he should bring a few friends, and my cousin Tristan, who has decided that he wants to be a police officer."

"Maggie, why not just explain it all to your brother?"

"Because he'd stop me, and I know what I'm doing makes sense, and that I can make it work."

"It doesn't make sense to me."

"Mireau, it does! And believe me, I've gotten to know laudanum very well. We can do this. Listen to me! Once those hoods are under, we carry Arianna out. We have help waiting, warned that they need to be armed. We send them in for the thugs, once we've gotten Arianna and ourselves out, and we're all safe."

"You're scaring me, Maggie."

"Why?"

"Because, in a very bizarre way, you are making sense. But, what if . . ."

"No! We can't deal with any 'but, ifs . . .'! We have to make it work."

"What if we can't get them all to drink brandy?"

"They drank it. They all drank it last night."

"Except for 'Jeremiah.' "

"Don't worry. I'll think of something."

There was a knock on the door. Maggie jumped. "It's probably just the oh-so-charming Mrs. Whitley," Mireau said with a smile.

It wasn't, and no permission was needed to cause the caller to open the door.

Jamie was there.

"Lord James!" Mireau murmured uncomfortably. "Good afternoon."

"Jacques," Jamie said, glancing his way, then giving his attention to Maggie. "I'd like to speak with you. Forgive me, Mireau, but I'd like to speak with Maggie—alone."

"We were in the middle of a discussion," Maggie said stiffly.

"Ah, now, that's all right. We can speak again later. I was just leaving."

"You were not."

"Maggie?" Jamie said politely.

"I'm on my way!" Mireau said cheerfully, rising. He mouthed the words, *"Don't worry, I'll be back."*

And then he left her. She wanted to throw something after him, and call him a deserter.

But he was gone, and the door was closed, and she was left standing there, staring at Jamie. And he looked wonderful, dark hair smoothed back, crimson waistcoat, dark trousers, and matching cravat. Freshly shaven, sleek, tall, imposing, immaculate . . . entirely handsome, completely powerful, suave, and seductive.

"What?" she said quietly, not daring to move, her voice very low.

"I came to apologize."

"Apology accepted," she said simply.

Her hiked a dark brow. "That easily?" he said skeptically. "Maggie, I slammed a door in your face. I cannot believe that you're just standing there so sweetly."

She shrugged. "You were right. I need to deal with Arianna on my own."

He sighed. "Listen, I haven't been fair to you. I have an appointment in about an hour, but I can take a few minutes to talk to her. It's just I know that, if you two give it a chance, you'll get along fine."

"It doesn't really matter, does it? In a few months she'll reach her majority . . . and you two will be together."

He frowned. "She'll reach her majority . . . and we'll remain relations, and I rather hope we'll always be close."

"How much closer could you be than man and wife?"

"Man and wife? You want me to marry my cousin?"

"I don't care what you do. Isn't it what your uncle wanted?"

Jamie stared at her, honestly puzzled. He shook his head. "No."

"But I thought—"

"He did have someone in mind for her."

"But I thought . . . it was someone rather . . . in the family."

"Maggie, Charles was very fond of Justin. Oh, your brother made some mistakes, but most of us make a number of mistakes. I was nearly thrown out of the service. Justin got into gambling. Seems he's taking politics very seriously though, now. He is going to prove to be an asset to the Empire one day, I'm certain."

Her knees suddenly felt very weak. He was not going to marry Arianna.

Of course, that didn't mean he had any really serious feelings for her. . . .

She suddenly had to moisten her lips to speak, nonetheless. "Arianna isn't here," she told him.

"Oh? I'm sorry I missed her. But I will speak with her."

Maggie nodded.

He frowned. "Are you all right?"

She nodded again, hesitated, and said, "So . . . you have an hour."

"Yes, just about."

She smiled wistfully. "Would you talk to me for that time, then?"

For a very long time, he was just as still as she was. Then he walked to her, where she stood next to the old oak library desk. He brought his knuckles to her chin, and drew them slowly against her flesh. "Maggie, honestly, I'm very sorry. I was there, last night, you see."

She leaned against him, cradling his hand against her face. "In Whitechapel?"

She didn't dare look at him.

"Yes. I saw them, both of the victims."

She drew back from him. "Why? What were you doing there?"

"Trying to catch the man," he said ruefully.

"Hundreds of policemen are trying to do just that," she said.

"I know, but . . . the Queen is truly a good woman, and of course, worried about the monarchy as well, but . . . honestly, there's no one who can remain untouched by these terrible events."

She nodded gravely. "But, Jamie . . . the policemen there know that area. They know the people. They could arrest the prostitutes many times, and don't. They could charge them for drunkeness, but they don't, they know the poor women can't pay the fines."

"Do you know, that was one of the saddest things

about last night was that they had Catherine Eddowes in a cell at a station for being drunk. She sobered up, and they let her out. And she met the Ripper."

Maggie nodded. "She was one of mine," she said softly. "She came, for bread, really, not because she was fascinated to hear me talk. I saw the sketch in the paper this morning. Poor woman, truly. She was a sad creature, so sad!"

"And quite out of her misery now," Jamie said, closing his eyes for a minute. "Well. I should go."

She shook her head. "No."

"No?"

"You said you had an hour."

"Yes. But I *should* leave."

"I wish you wouldn't," she told him.

"Oh?"

"I wish that you would just hold me," she told him, and though he was close, so close she could almost feel the texture of his coat, she didn't move. She gazed into gray eyes as deep as the mist at night.

He reached out and pulled her against him, his hand cradling the base of her skull, fingers moving through the length of her hair. She laid her hand against his chest, and felt the beat of her heart rise to an erratic pulse. For a moment, she felt his tenderness. And it was very sweet, something to be cherished. She felt, as well, the deep depression and futility that had assailed him, and experienced a tremulous moment of fear herself. Life was fragile, no matter whom one might be, from the most noble lord to the poorest, most pathetic of humanity.

Fragile, and precious, and she was learning that

there were moments that must be taken, and savored.

"An hour . . ." she murmured.

"An hour, and I am glad to hold you."

She leaned back her head, smiling very slowly as she looked into his eyes. "Well, to be quite frank, I rather wish you would do more."

A grin crept to his lips. "In the library? I don't believe you're referring to the enjoyment of a good book."

She shook her head. "It's a large house, and offers other rooms. Such as mine."

"What will the servants say?" he asked her.

"I haven't the least idea. Nor could I care less."

"Ah, but people could talk."

"Talk about *me?* In any scandalous way? Imagine!"

"Well, then . . . I can admit, a few moments of a very tight hold upon you would be a delightful moment of bliss in an otherwise agonizing day."

"I'll go first. Then, perhaps the servants won't notice."

"The ever present Mrs. Whitley won't notice?" he queried.

"Ah, well, so she will. But we won't let her in. Then, all her gossip must be pure conjecture," Maggie told him, and she swept by him, exiting the room.

She ran up the stairs then, wondering at the frantic beat of her heart. She was behaving quite insanely. Like a young girl with a first crush. Emotions tumbled through her with a drastic edge. *He was not intended for Arianna, or she for him, or any such thing.*

And what did that mean? Nothing! This was scan-

dalous behavior, at the very best. She had indeed married Charles, and he had been gone now for so very short a time. And yet . . .

She was in love. As she had never thought that she could be again. The world was a place where so much right now seemed to be horrid and ugly, tragic women had died more tragic deaths, and the mood of the people was thus that the very foundations of the country could come tumbling down around them. As the picture became smaller, more intimate, her very personal world was in the midst of crises. She had determined her course of action, and he really had merit, and still, she had never known a time when life had seemed more infinitely precious, and more fragile.

And the next moments seemed like a final breath to take, something of ultimate wonder, to be savored now with abandon, before the night could come.

She flew into the bedroom, swore that she would think no more. What she had then was meant to be seized with all abandon, and reflection could come later.

She had scarcely entered the room before he came behind her, carefully locking the door, and turning back to her. She felt her heartbeat, still racing at her pulse, and then, again, watching him, it was as if she froze. As he walked toward her, she met his eyes, with everything that was open and honest in her own, and in the seconds it took for him to walk to her, she thought of all that had combined to make her fall so heedlessly and hopelessly in love. Definitely, those eyes, gray, misting, light with laughter upon occasion, so very grave at others. His voice, the same, gentle in tenderness, deep in passion. Hands . . . the way they could move upon her, and the strength they offered when needed. All that was within his heart and soul, vibrant, never easy, volatile . . .

He reached her, and their eyes continued to meet for the longest time, infinite heartbeats, and then, his lips touched down upon her throat where that heartbeat raced. She leaned into him, craving ever more, and he obliged. Fingers upon the ribbons of her bodice, catching the tiny buttons of her skirt. And when those had fallen, he came to his knees, intent upon the removal of shoes and hose. The brush of his fingers created minute sensations that electrified and multiplied, streaking in hot little lines up her thighs. The pressure of his lips against her kneecaps seemed the most intimate and erotic stroke that ever existed. And yet, he proved that such a touch could be greater still, for his touch and kiss moved on, and she began to shake until her knees gave, and she came down before him, falling into his arms, finding his mouth with her own, and igniting a fire where they knelt there on the floor, so aware that she was alive, that she was in love, and that this touch was the ultimate luxury she had ever known.

Somewhere soon, they were up together, and his clothing became strewn, and their passion and hunger were as volatile as ever. And yet it was all the sweeter, for there were those moments when urgency was staved, and their eyes would meet again, wonder would fill them, and if not the desperate love she felt for him, at least he returned something of the simple awe of the fire that raged between them. Then time became of the essence. Simple need raced raw between them, and still, the need between them to touch everywhere, elicit the greatest hunger, know the total diving into the flesh and soul of another, the drowning there. Until, at last, they came together, he gloved within her, she filled with him, and the last fever rose in a frenzy, climax like lightning, and the slow sweet reality of drifting downward, flesh cooling, the tangle of sheets and limbs, and the awareness again of the world, and the fact that he must go.

They remained entwined together for some time before he stirred at last, his arms closer around her, pulling her tight, and then he released her and rose.

Maggie remained where she was, watching him, his every movement.

He walked to her at last, gently brushing her lips with a kiss, and saying, "It is another woman dragging me away. The Queen," he told her.

"You owe me no explanations of your time," she said softly.

He smiled. "I wish that there need not be such explanations for my time." Regretfully, he rose, dressed, and headed for the door. He paused there.

"Maggie, please, at this time, stay out of Whitechapel."

She held silent.

"Maggie?"

"I know what's happening there, Jamie."

He seemed satisfied that her grave words meant that she was in total agreement.

The Queen was naturally and visibly distressed.

"Two, Lord Langdon. Two women horribly butchered in one night!"

"Your Majesty," Jamie told her, "I was there, throughout the night. I watched the police work the streets. There are plainclothesmen in abundance; despite their differences, the head of the City and Metropolitan forces have every available man working the district."

"So. The greatest city in the world is just to be held hostage by one maniac?" she said, and didn't await an answer. "And what do you make of this writing on the wall! Sir Charles Warren was afraid there would be horrible riots, that common folk, and maybe others, would blame it all on our Jewish population. But others are saying that it gives reference to the Masonic lodge, to the rites they practice, and therefore, there must be some government conspiracy, that the highest in the land are protecting a heinous killer!"

She was outraged, so indignant, that she was shaking.

"They are going so far," she said softly, "as to suggest that Eddy is responsible! That he had some silly affair, and government officials are killing women who might know about it! Next, they'll be saying that I'm out there as a Jill the Ripper, doing these deeds myself!"

"Your Majesty, no one would ever suggest such a thing."

"But they will blame Eddy, or his tutors, or his friends—they are looking for a scapegoat."

"Unfortunately, Your Majesty, people will talk, and we are the greatest country in the world, and therefore, they have their right to talk. But you, madam, with your upright life and fever for the plight of the poor prove that you are a great and good Queen."

She flashed him a wise and angry look. "Don't try to soothe me! Do you know that Eddy is not even in London? He is in Scotland, hunting!"

"Then let that be known."

"Some have said that the police officials are Masons—and therefore protecting the killer!"

"It's to my great indignation that the words on the wall were erased, no matter what they said," Jamie told her. "They were evidence."

"Perhaps they weren't even written by the killer."

"Perhaps not. We may never know. They were erased."

"And yet, what does it matter! Every Tom, Dick, and Harry on the streets knows exactly what was written! Just as they know the truly wretched and ghastly details of what was done to the one poor woman. Jamie, this lunatic must be stopped."

"Yes, Your Majesty."

"Get back out there, and don't fail me. You uncle would not fail me."

He lowered his head for a moment. No, Charles had never failed her. But here she was, expecting him to go out and accomplish what hundreds of trained police had not managed to do. The only real encouragement in his mind was the fact that she was probably planning on having this exact same conversation with many of the lords and sirs and gentlemen of the realm that day.

By the time he left the grandeur of the palace, the afternoon was already waning toward the evening.

Newspaper boys were on the streets, everywhere, hawking, and selling their papers.

"Murder! Murder most foul."

"Murder! Gruesome murder!"

"Murder! Jack the Ripper strikes again. And again!"

"War on Warren."

"Is the monarchy dead as well!"

He bought the papers, all of them, thinking that he had a fine project for Mireau at last. What was written could form opinion. Opinion could be fought with the pen, as well as with angry words and fists.

He returned to the carriage, pausing on the street, then looked at his coachman.

"Home to change?" Randolph called to him.

"No. I'd speak with Abberline first. To the station, Randolph, please. You can just bring me some clothing to change into. I'm feeling a strange urge to get to Whitechapel as soon as possible. Have you ever had a strange feeling like that, Randolph? That you just need to be somewhere—and it's quite urgent . . . except that . . . ?"

"Except that what, my lord?"

"Except that you really have no idea just exactly where it is that you're supposed to be."

"Well, my lord—"

"It doesn't matter, Randolph. I'm running around blindly in the dark. But get me to Whitechapel, and I'll . . . I'll just walk in the dark until I find out what it is exactly that I'm looking for, and why . . ."

"Why?"

"Why I feel so desperate," Jamie said grimly.

Chapter 17

Maggie wrote the last of her notes, sealed the envelopes with her signet ring and wax, and looked at Mireau. Cecilia was due any minute.

"Well? Have I missed anything?" she asked.

"No."

"Then why are you staring at me so?"

"Someone has to be brought into it. What if we are able to drug all these people, and carry Arianna out of the house into the street, and there is no one there to meet us? No one to get us out quickly, no one to go in for the culprits?"

"I've written a note to the police, as well, suggesting that they might catch the Ripper on the street, right at two o'clock A.M."

"And what if Jeremiah Heath is late, as he was last night."

"We'll have this managed by two o'clock!" Maggie said. "If he's late, we simply get Arianna out, and then worry about the man himself at a later date."

"Have you any more arguments?"

"Yes. We need someone to know."

There was a knock at the library door. Maggie rose and walked to it. "Lord and Lady de Burgh," Mrs. Whitley announced, her tone showing her disapproval.

"*Lord* and Lady?" Maggie said.

"Thank you so much, dear woman!" Cecilia said, sweeping in behind Eustace, and closing the door on Mrs. Whitley.

Maggie and Mireau stared at Cecilia blankly.

"Um . . . Eustace. How are you?"

He smiled, a very handsome-looking rake. "Maggie!" He kissed both her cheeks, and she tried a weak smile, but stared at Cecilia with reproach. *What were they going to do? Eustace could not accompany them! In their cover, Cecilia—"Sissy"—was married to Mireau!*

"Don't look so panicked," Eustace told her. "I know what is going on. Cecilia wisely came to me. And if all else fails, I will be in the street." She looked at him doubtfully.

"Maggie, I may be what many consider deviant in my thirst for pleasure and entertainment, but I'm a fair man with both pistols and daggers. I, like most others of my station, have served in the Queen's army."

"Eustace, I'm sorry. Forgive me. You all gave me quite a start."

"We should get going with our disguises," Cecilia said.

"After we leave, he'll bring the letters I've written to Father Vickers, Justin, Jamie, and the police."

"All right, then, let's get going," Cecilia said. "Is your girl coming? Fiona?"

Maggie shook her head. "I'm afraid that someone will recognize her from having been with Arianna at an earlier time."

"All right, then . . . you've brought your bottle of brandy?"

"Oh, yes, we're quite prepared."

"Then, come on, Auntie! Time for me to make you into an old crone!"

Detective Inspector Abberline had aged ten years in a month, Jamie noted. The man was so harried that Jamie was surprised he agreed to take time to see him, but then, he'd had no sleep and taken little time for food. Even a man as pressed as he had to take a few moments.

"The people are crying out in fury," Abberline told him with a sigh. "And it's not that I blame them. They believe that the East End fiend has now struck six times. I don't. I believe that this lunatic has now killed four. I need every man, but the forces are now called upon to keep order in the parks, where citizens are gathering to protest Warren, to mock the police, and generally, cause disturbances when we need order more than ever!"

"What did you think of the writing on the wall?" Jamie asked him.

Abberline was quiet for a moment, stroking his chin. "Already, I have heard every theory and supposition out there. 'It is a cover-up!' 'Someone in a high place is being protected!' 'The killer is an educated man.' 'It is a well-known and respected doctor.' 'It's Prince Eddy, it's one of his servants, it's a cover-up!' 'It's a reprehensible Bohemian artist seeking the truth of human suffering for his work.' Or, 'It's the anarchists, trying to make sure that the world sees the sorrow and degradation of the East End, and thus, the great Empire, and the monarchy, would fall.' I've heard them all, Lord Langdon. Frankly, I think they're all wrong."

"What do you think?"

"I think that people are in horror, and reaching, and that they actually want such an answer to such a terrible puzzle. Perhaps they're even trying to romanticize what is happening. My opinion? Perhaps this man has some kind of an education. I don't think he needs to have had medical training, though he surely knows something about animal butchery, through hunting, perhaps, or through his work at a butcher's . . . such knowledge would not be difficult to come by. Perhaps he's even had a copy of *Gray's Anatomy!* In the end, this killer will prove to have a name we've never heard before; he will be extremely sick, mentally, and perhaps have the ability to appear almost normal at other times. Perhaps he is a petty criminal. I don't think we'll ever discover that it was a great artist, a nobleman, or a doctor. Just a madman as sad in his life as his victims were in theirs. If you walk these streets long enough, it becomes difficult to weed the sane men from the lunatics. And God help us, all we have to do is chase any petty thief these days, and a crowd rushes forward, ready to lynch him as Jack the Ripper! And, my God! You cannot begin to imagine the letters we have received from families, rich and poor, convinced that one of their kinsmen is Jack the Ripper." He shook his head. "The coroners talk about the evidence, and how the police are failing. The evidence! Look for a man covered in blood? Do you know how many men work for the slaughterhouses, or work for butchers? A live chicken does not last long in these parts; indeed, one woman had blood on her hands the other day—she had slaughtered a rat for a meal! Ah, we read every letter, and there are hundreds . . . thousands. We look for every clue. We follow up on leads. We listen to people rant and rave about royal conspiracies. And we are no closer to catching this man. Indeed, we've brought in a few lunatics, and we can have them committed—and pray that the killing stops. But we've no proof against anyone. Oh—among those lunatics? I think we've had a good ten confessions, but all are false. Witnesses knew where the men were at the time of the killings!"

"Where do you go from here?"

"Back to the streets," Abberline told him.

"I'll be around," Jamie said. "If there's anything you think that I can do . . . ?"

"I'll ask. And if there's anything I can tell you, I'll see that you're notified."

Jamie left a sadly discouraged Abberline.

Then, he took to the streets himself.

"How am I?" Maggie asked Mireau anxiously.

He stared at her, then at Cecilia. "Quite incredible. I'd swear you were sixty, if you were a day."

Cecilia smiled, and reached out to assure that one

of the muttonchops was securely set upon Mireau's face.

"Eustace . . . the coachman needs to let us out here. Then you must spend some time a distance away . . . Those ogre-dwarfs, or whatever you want to call Jeremiah's ruffians, are all about, watching all the time. And I believe every one of them is lethal."

"I don't like being too far, my dear," Eustace said. "What if something should go wrong?"

"It can't go wrong," Maggie said.

"Ah, if only all life could be so positive!" Eustace said, smiling. He looked at Mireau then. "And, my good fellow, you are armed?"

"I have the knife you gave me, and I'm not a total weakling."

"Didn't mean to imply that you were," Eustace said.

"Maggie?"

"I have the little pistol. And I do know how to use it."

"Ah, yes! You did marry a policeman. She's awfully busy for her tender years, isn't she, my love?" he said to his wife.

Cecilia grinned back at him. Whatever their diversions away from one another, they were a remarkably happy couple, Maggie noted. She was sorry that she had mocked Eustace in the past.

"Eustace," she said.

"Yes?"

"Thank you."

He smiled, shrugging casually, his hands resting upon his dapper cane. "Think nothing of it. All right, you had best get out here . . . the street is empty. Maybe all the little whores are staying home tonight."

They piled from the carriage. They were several blocks away from the Hennesy's house, and as they briskly walked the distance, they were stopped by a policeman.

"Hey, there! You . . . where are you off to, at this time of the night?"

"Visiting friends," Mireau said. "My auntie's cousin."

"At this time of night? Are you daft? Could you not have heard of the double event last night?"

"We're traveling together, and tight. And this is my wife, this our auntie. My good fellow, we are not soliciting on the streets!"

The officer nodded then, and shook his head, as if with disgust that folk just seemed to have no common sense. "Fine, then. Go on where you're going!"

Maggie quickened her pace, very afraid that they might be waylaid again. She was so desperate to reach Arianna.

"You should have brought Jamie in on this," Mireau breathed.

"I couldn't."

"Because he was so angry?" Mireau asked. "How amazing . . . he stayed a very long time after asking me out of the library! And in your room, at that."

"How delightful!" Cecilia said.

Maggie glared at Mireau.

"Surely, you weren't arguing all that time?" Mireau said.

"Don't you understand? He would have tried to

stop us. He would have been convinced that there was another way."

"Well, there is another way. We could just have police surround the house," Cecilia said.

"I'm just really afraid that they do have orders to kill Arianna the second that anything looks out of the ordinary," Maggie said. "Once we have her out of that house . . ."

"What do we do if Jeremiah is late again?" Mireau asked.

"Tonight, it just doesn't matter. We just get them drinking, and get Arianna out. And we'll hope that the police are able to find him, once we have Arianna out of the house."

"They haven't been able to find a maniacal killer," Cecilia pointed out.

"What matters most is Arianna. If Jeremiah is not there, we still bring out the brandy. We are here for Arianna. Agreed?" Maggie said.

"Obviously, it's most important that we get the girl out," Cecilia said.

"We'd best pray that your notes reached their intended destinations!" Mireau said.

"Darby will see that they do."

"Eustace will not fail us," Cecilia said. "He does know where the house is, and he'll be ready to assist us."

"One problem," Mireau noted.

"And that is?" Maggie asked.

"All the fellows are never *inside* the house. They stand guard outside."

Maggie nodded. "Yes. You're the strongest, you must take Arianna. She will be dead weight. Cecilia and I will have our weapons ready."

"His thugs carried guns before," Mireau reminded her. "And you've made sure that Jamie will not be here to come to our rescue tonight."

"We know that they are armed, and we will be ready to shoot first," Maggie told him.

"Oh, God!" Mireau moaned. "I cannot believe that we are doing this."

"Eustace will be outside as well, and he is a crack shot!" Cecilia reminded them proudly.

"Shush!" Maggie warned. They were on the walk and might well be overheard.

They reached the house. Maggie felt a crawling sensation of fear streak up her spine. She was suddenly entirely uncertain about dragging Mireau and Cecilia into the fray.

"I should go alone," she said.

"Never!" Mireau told her. "And ridiculous. How are you going to carry Arianna out, and keep the two of you from being shot?"

"Maggie, you did not force either of us into this. We're on the walk. Let's go—before we do look suspicious!" Cecilia said.

They were right. Squaring her shoulders, Maggie headed toward the house.

John was at the door. "Ah, ev'ning! Come in, come in. The Hennesys await ye!"

They all greeted John cordially and entered the house. Ellen Hennesy was there, dusting her hands on her apron once again, greeting them warmly. This night, George was home already as well, and just as she had been the night before, Arianna was already at the table. She allowed no spark to come to her eyes. She spoke as one dead. "Perhaps Jeremiah will reach Frank for you tonight, mum, perhaps he will."

"Not to be indelicate," George Hennesy said, "but . . . were you able to get to the bank?"

"Indeed!" Cecilia said.

"I didn't think my good friend, Mr. Thayer, our banker, would keep me from an advance on the pension," Maggie said. "Please give Mr. Hennesy the money, Sissy," she told Cecilia.

"Of course!"

Ten pounds sterling were handed over to Hennesy, who then passed it on to John. "Jeremiah will be grateful," he said.

"He is late again?" Maggie asked.

"I'm afraid so," answered the fellow standing behind Arianna. Maggie counted.

Four of them inside. Jeremiah to come.

Two of them were outside, somewhere, keeping an eye out.

"Well!" she said. She smiled warmly at the Hennesys. "Since you were so kind in your offerings last night, I thought that I should return the favor." She pulled out her bottle of brandy. "An excellent year! A gift to my husband from one of his clients, a landed gent, who got it from the royal family, so we were told. I've saved it for a very special occasion. It should have a truly wonderful taste."

"Lovely!" George Hennesy said, beaming. "My dear . . .?"

"Everyone must have some," Maggie said. "I'm so very grateful to you all."

"Of course, of course, I'll get glasses," Ellen Hennesy said.

Soon, they were brought. The brandy was poured. "Cheers!" Maggie said, lifting her own glass. She pretended to drink.

Thankfully, Jeremiah's "boys" all liked their liquor. They drained their glasses quickly. "Oh, do finish the bottle!" she said. "If I can reach Frank tonight, it will have been the most special occasion ever. I'll have felt that I enjoyed it with some new but very good friends, and my dear Frank himself!"

She gritted her teeth and forced a smile as George Hennesy was the first to reach for more. But the "boys" were ready for a second round, and she, Cecilia, and Mireau were able to offer up empty glasses for a refill, all having managed to toss their first rounds beneath the table.

Only Arianna had ignored her glass.

"You're not enjoying this wonderful warmth!" Maggie said to her.

Arianna shook her head, eyes filled with warning as she looked at Maggie. "I'm not much of a drinker, mum."

"Don't insult the woman," John said, and Maggie felt her jaw harden as she watched the way the young thug bit his fingers into the girl's shoulder.

Arianna picked up her glass, and drank. She swallowed down the brandy in a gulp, set the glass back down.

Mireau saw that it was quickly refilled.

"Definitely a special taste," John commented. He'd probably never had good brandy before in his life, but he pretended to study the color. Maggie smiled, then frowned, looking Arianna's way again. Her serious concern brought John's fingers to Arianna's shoulders once again. Before he could touch her, the girl swallowed down the second glass-ful.

It was not, however, Arianna who went first.

Ellen Hennesy was simply sitting one minute, en-joying the taste as they awaited Jeremiah, then, with-out word or whimper, she crashed forward, head downward, onto the table.

Jamie chose to keep out of the City of London, and walked the surrounding streets. He had split up three couples, earned two beatings about his head by way of the prostitutes' poor reticules, and angrily offered up doss money for the women him-self thus far. One woman ran straight into a pub, and he felt his aggravation rising. This was not an easy task.

It was near one-thirty when he saw the suspicious fellow in the deerstalker hat and sweeping black cape walking along the side of the road. He was keeping deep to the shadows, and his every movement seemed furtive. Jamie watched him, following at a distance, then saw an opportunity to duck into one of the alleys, leap a gate, and come at the fellow from the opposing direction.

He slipped into the alley, ran the length of it. A cat let out a horrid screech. In the mist-shrouded night, it sounded like a glaring alarm.

He leapt the fence at the end of the alley, and came around.

His quarry had apparently heard him, and stopped. For a moment, he remained still against the fencing, waiting, listening. No sound of footsteps. Indeed, he'd been betrayed by an alley cat.

Still, he forced himself to wait. At last, he heard a furtive movement. But he was certain his quarry knew that he was on the other side of the fence.

Indeed, the man knew. He burst out into the night suddenly, a walking stick with a wicked blade at the end of it poised for the fight. Jamie burst into motion, knotting his muscles, racing forward, catching the man in his midriff with a violent tackle.

They both went down into the mud of the street. Jamie had the edge, and was able to sink a knee into his opponent's middle. The man caught his jaw with a solid punch, and he nearly staggered from his position. He gained his balance and prepared to strike.

"Jamie!"

He hesitated, peering against the poor light, staring down.

"Justin!"

"What in God's name are you doing, man?" Justin demanded. There was suspicion in his voice.

"What are you doing?"

"Stalking the Ripper," Justin said.

Jamie rose, dusting the mud of the road from his clothing. He reached out a hand to Justin, helping the fellow leap to his feet.

And for a moment, rumor, talk, fear made them both stare at one another. *Anyone might have been the Ripper. A rich man, a poor man, uneducated, well tutored, they just didn't know right now. The killings might be part of a conspiracy; they might be perpetuated by a fel-*

low capable of walking the streets as an ordinary citizen by day . . .

"It's a strange place for you, Justin," Jamie said.

"And stranger for you, Lord Langdon."

"I've been asked to look into this matter," Jamie said.

Justin studied him, then shook his head. "And I came down because I've been made to realize recently that I've not led a very useful life. And sadly, I am familiar with these streets, because some of the company I keep is fond of the most tawdry amusements."

The sound of a carriage crashing along the street at a dangerous speed, caused them to leave off their focus on one another, and stare in the direction of the sound. "Out of the way, or we're both dead men!" Jamie warned, shoving Justin.

But Justin stood in the street, staring at the approaching vehicle.

"It's Darby!" he said.

"Whoever it is, we're about to be run down!" Jamie warned him, and, grabbing him by the collar, dragged him to the edge of the road.

The carriage jerked to a halt just past them. They'd been seen.

Darby jumped from the carriage. "Sweet Mary, Mother of God!" he exclaimed. "I've been looking for the two of you for hours!"

"Why?"

"Letters for you. I tried my hardest to eavesdrop, that I did. But Lady Maggie has been very secretive since last night. I tried to stay with her, but she was going off with Lord and Lady de Burgh, and their coachman was taking them . . . wherever it was that they were going, and I've got my suspicions!"

"She's down here somewhere!" Jamie said, taking the letter offered to him. "Damn her! She promised that she wouldn't come around here!"

Justin had ripped open his own letter by then. "There's a street name here. But no number! And the letter says that we need to be there by two o'clock, a matter of life or death."

Jamie pulled out his pocket watch. "We've about three minutes," he said grimly, and started for the carriage. "Three minutes! Let's go!"

"What is wrong with her!" John called out, alarmed.

And then, Arianna went as well.

"Oh! The poor dears!" Maggie cried, leaping up. She went straight for Arianna. Frowning, John started to come around for Arianna. He came to the table, staggered back, and then fell. Slowly. But he could not prevent himself from doing so.

"What have you done?" the one called Matthew grated out. He drew a pistol from inside his jacket and took aim, straight at Maggie. She caught hold of Arianna's shoulders and dragged the girl from her chair, and to the floor.

The gun exploded. The shot went wild. Matthew lay flat out on the floor beside them.

"Maggie!" Mireau called.

"I'm fine!"

He and Cecilia came around beside her. She

stared at them. "They're all down, they went in order, smack, smack, smack!" Cecilia said.

"We must be quick! Whoever is outside will have heard the shot!" Mireau warned.

"Get Arianna," Maggie said, struggling to her feet. Cecilia helped Mireau struggle up with the girl's dead weight.

George Hennesy had collapsed over his wife. One of the thugs was lying in the archway. Cecilia leapt over him. Mireau followed.

Maggie was about to do so when the fellow stirred. He, too, had a pistol out.

He didn't aim it at Maggie, but at Arianna's lifeless form.

"No!" Maggie screamed, and she stepped forward, giving the man's arm a lethal kick. The gun went flying.

His fingers wound around her ankle.

"Maggie!" Mireau called, blinded by Arianna's body draped over his shoudlers.

"Go, I'm fine!" she called.

But she wasn't. She tried to wrench free, and sprawled down on the ground herself. The man halfway rose, eyes on fire with fury as he fought to keep his mind alert. His hands reached out for her throat.

She couldn't reach the little pistol in her reticule. She struggled for balance and knotted her hand into a fist, slugging him as hard in the jaw as she could manage. She heard the sound of the crack of her blow against his face. But still, he kept reaching for her . . .

Then fell back.

She shoved his weight off her and made it to her feet. She raced then for the door, bursting from it.

Eustace was there, as he had said he would be, his carriage in the street. She could see that Mireau was stumbling forward, bearing Arianna's weight. Cecilia was following him, her back toward the carriage as she fired shots randomly at anyone who might follow them.

She heard police whistles; bless Darby! He had gotten her letter safely to one of the station houses.

And there was the sound of a runaway carriage racing toward their location. Jamie, her brother . . . they'd both yell at her, of course. But it wouldn't matter. Arianna was safe, and Jeremiah's thugs were out, and if they didn't have the murdering fake himself, they would surely find him this time.

She started to open her mouth, to cry out to Cecilia to quit firing so that she could reach the carriage herself.

But even as she opened her mouth, she felt the sharp pain against her nape. A blow struck hard, one that caused her to stagger instantly, one that seemed to add to the mist of the gaslight and the fog that filled the streets.

"Bitch! I thought it was you. But you are a clever thing. And a pretty one. We'll have some fun . . . before you die."

The carriage that had been racing down the street was coming to a halt. The Langdon carriage, Darby driving. She thought she saw Jamie leaping from it. It all seemed to be spinning before her eyes, and yet it all seemed to be playing out in slow motion.

"Maggie!" She could swear that she did hear her name shouted. Cried out in anguish.

Jamie. Jamie's voice . . .

Then the mist and the gas-lit fog turned to black, and she crashed down into a state of ebony oblivion.

Chapter 18

There was bedlam on the street.

The police had arrived, and their whistles were blowing. They were running around like chickens because they knew that they were looking for something amiss, but they didn't know what they were looking for. The gunfire had ceased. Mireau had gotten into the de Burgh carriage with Arianna, and Cecilia was standing with her husband by the carriage door, and there was no sign of Maggie.

"What the hell is going on?" Justin demanded. "Where's my sister?"

"Right behind us!" Mireau said. "But careful . . . the guards left at the outside are armed . . . Cecilia and Eustace were firing back and they might have taken them down, but . . . ."

One of the police inspectors was there as well.

"Guards? For who? What is going on here?" he raged. "There will be pandemonium any second now, people spilling out on the streets, thinking we've got Jack the Ripper!"

Jamie caught hold of Cecilia's shoulders. "Cecilia, who was in there, what is going on?"

"A fake spiritualist," she gasped out. "Arianna . . . ran away, wound up kidnapped, really, and we brought laudanum to knock them all out and . . ."

He didn't wait for any more but went streaking toward the house. A shot blazed, so close that for a moment, the buzzing sound cost him his hearing in his right ear. He heard the bullet embed in the fence post behind him.

There was a man half fallen against the front wall of the house. His smoking pistol was still raised, aimed at Jamie. His hand was shaking; he had a bullet wound in his shoulder.

Jamie instantly calculated the risks, and flew at the man, bringing him down. The gun fell with the man's hand to his right side. Jamie rose, kicking the gun away, reaching for the injured man and dragging him up.

"Where's the woman?" he demanded.

The fellow grinned eerily. Then slumped into a dead faint. Jamie realized that he was covered in blood.

He dropped the man and burst into the house. People were splayed about everywhere, so it seemed.

Justin came running in behind him. "Where is she? My sister?" He saw one of the fellows, prone of the floor, and tried to drag him up. "Where's my sister?" he raged.

But the man couldn't answer. He lolled in Justin's hold. Disgusted, Justin dropped him.

By then, Jamie had made a cursory inspection around the small house. Everyone in it was out cold. There was no help to be had here.

Time, Jamie was certain, was of the essence. He ran to the carriage and dragged Mireau from it. "Maggie's gone."

"He came back, then, he's got her," Mireau said.

"Who?" Jamie raged.

"Alexander. Adrian Alexander. He's calling himself Jeremiah Heath now."

Justin burst forward, reaching for Mireau's lapels in a fury. "You let her come here! Jesus, I should kill you here and now, on the spot—"

"Stop it!" Cecilia cried. "She forced him to keep silent. They had Arianna, don't you see!"

Perhaps Justin didn't. Jamie did.

He'd had his chance. When she'd come that morning. And when he had raged so . . .

She had decided on her course of action.

"Justin, take the north, I'll head east. Mireau . . . you, go south, and Eustace, head down there in a westwardly fashion. Cecilia, tell the police what you can—get them moving as well. Then, take your coachman, please, get Arianna home, and get the doctor for her. Not Sir William Gull! Get Dr. Mayer, and stay with her, please! Stay at Moorhaven."

Cecilia nodded, jumping into the carriage. She caught Jamie's hand briefly. "It was the only way she thought that she could save Arianna!" she said softly.

"It doesn't matter now! He has her—we have to find them."

"I know, but . . ."

"What?"

"You know she loves you," Cecilia said.

"All that matters is that I find her now," he replied, and freed his hand. Time. He had to hurry. He'd seen Adrian Alexander in action before.

And he believed that the man was capable of anything.

Maggie woke because of the water being thrown on her face.

For a moment, all she knew was that it was cold and startling. Then she realized that she was lying on a hard stone floor, that her cape and wig had been snatched from her, and that someone powerful and very angry had not just sluiced her face with water, but was then nearly suffocating her, scrubbing away with a vengeance at the theatrical paint she had been wearing.

Instinct made her fight. Fingers wound into her hair, pulling so hard that tears came to her eyes. Then the hold eased, but as she fought to get the cloth from her face, she became aware of another, far more terrifying sensation.

There was a knife at her throat.

She held very still, barely breathing.

"There, there! I knew you weren't a stupid girl. You're not about to scream, are you, Lady Langdon? You're quite fond of living. Who wouldn't be, in your position. Funny thing is, I didn't get who the girl was right off. But, after our little debacle, I naturally tried to discover just who you might be. And when I looked back, I found the newspaper reports, and . . . I honestly didn't recognize you last night. But then, something warned me . . . some spirit, maybe! So I waited tonight, and watched."

It was almost completely dark. Maggie thought that after he knocked her out, he must have dragged her into an empty house or factory. It was damp, and freezing, as well. Only a pale illumination seeped in through broken windows from the streets beyond.

Alexander seemed to have the eyes of a cat, or else he was accustomed to the darkness and the shadow of the East End. He knew her discomfort as well, knew that he held all the advantages.

"You thought that you would strike a blow against me tonight, eh? Good heavens, woman, what on earth is wrong with you? Haven't you heard—there's a madman out there. Why bother with a spiritualist?"

He started to laugh. The knife edged closer to her throat. If she took a breath at that second, her flesh would be cut. She remained dead still. Chills swept through her as she remembered how he had come in the night before.

With his hands wet.

As if he had just washed them.

Washed away . . .

Blood.

She fought the rising panic within her. *Whether this man was actually Jack the Ripper or not didn't really matter—since his intent was to kill her!*

"You know, though, m'lady, you actually make many an *unfortunate* in this area look like a saint. Ah, well, perhaps that's pushing it. They're whores, wretched whores, wanting their alcohol more than there own silly little lives. If Jackie weren't taking his knife to the bitches, they'd die soon enough anyway, rotting to pieces from pickling their own innards! But then, that's the likes of them. And there's the likes of you. What a high price to be paid for your companionship! But then, not a few pennies, eh? For your favors, you'd have a marriage license, and lots and lots of riches. Then you're all supplied with a coachman, or several coachmen! And you can buy disguises. And set out to attack people who had no argument with you!"

Maggie remained very still, tensing only as she heard the police whistles and footsteps that suddenly broke the quiet of the night.

"Look at the commotion you've caused! Alas, pity, I really must get going tonight. There would be no way to do you any true justice . . . but, then again, you'll help me to slip into the darkness."

The knife was suddenly gone. Maggie breathed in and out, desperate to see in the night. Then she gasped out involuntarily as a noose was slipped around her neck. "They'll have to let you die to take me!" he said cheerfully, and she was dragged up to her feet. She felt the coarse rope around her throat. "Let's see . . . a doorway or window . . . or the lamppost. The lamppost, and quickly." He dragged her to a doorway. She struggled to find the reticule she had brought, the braided handle of it held on her person through the black sash that tied around her waist. As he pushed her forward, she struggled to find her little pistol.

He had a grip of steel. She was tight against his body as he held her, looking out. "One sound and I will gut you like a pig!" he warned.

Then . . .

The little square, with the gaslight that was out or broken, was empty again. No sound of footsteps. No shrill of police whistles.

He forced her out. She kept attempting to slip her hand into the reticule.

It was difficult, for he dragged her through the street, with the strength of his hold, and with the ever tightening pressure of the rope. She worked her fingers into the bag . . . curled her hand around the pistol . . .

Then gasped, choking, as he threw the rope over the lamppost, and used his weight and strength to jerk her up.

She fired . . . quickly, desperately, in the split seconds before she dropped the gun, drawing both hands instinctively to the stricture around her neck.

She heard a scream . . . police whistles again . . .

But they were fading. No matter how she tried to slip her fingers beneath the rope and stop it, it was strangling the life from her; she was dying . . .

"Maggie!" She heard a voice. His voice. Once again.

Maybe she would always hear it. Maybe there really was such a thing as true spiritualism. Maybe she would hear him, envision him, see and feel and need him, far beyond the grave. . . .

"Maggie!" It was a shout again.

Then, she heard a shot crack through the night again. And she was no longer choking, but falling . . .

Hard upon the cobblestones below her.

There was no mist, no fog. Rockets seemed to explode before her eyes.

Then her shoulders were lifted, cradled gently

into a lap. "Maggie, oh, my God, Maggie! I'm sorry, I had to shoot the rope . . . I couldn't wait, you were kicking and strangling. Is anything broken . . . can you move?"

Jamie. Brows knit in a frown of desperate concern, cradling her on his lap, in his embrace. At first, she couldn't talk. She moistened her lips, nodded. Croaked, "I'm . . . I'm all right."

"Take her!" Jamie said. She was dimly aware of footsteps hurrying toward her. Someone else was there. Her brother. Justin was taking her. Mireau was there, too, at her side.

"I've got to go after him!" Jamie said. And then he was gone.

"I have her," Justin said firmly, and she was lifted into her brother's arms.

"Sorry, Lord Graham," someone with a voice of authority said. "We've got to talk to her for a few moments."

"I don't think she can talk right now!" Justin said, outraged.

"We need her help," the other man said quietly.

And so, she was taken first to a police station, and she tried hard, with Mireau's help. Finally, what seemed like hours later, they were free to leave.

In the carriage, Justin supported her. And partway home he said to her, "I could actually strangle you myself! Maggie, what were you thinking? You need to be locked away in a tower somewhere. Of course, I am your brother. And I've let you play these dangerous games. Well, I didn't exactly let you." Then he quit trying to sound so stern. "Maggie, thank God, oh, thank God!" And he hugged her.

He was still so protective as they made their way into the house at Moorhaven. She was actually able to walk somewhat, with him supporting her, Mireau at her side.

They came into the grand salon. Mrs. Whitley, Dr. Mayer, and Cecilia came rushing forward.

"Arianna?" Maggie said, her voice still a bare scratchy whisper.

"She'll be fine. She'll come out of it soon enough," Dr. Mayer said.

Maggie was stunned when her brother suddenly gasped. "*That's* Arianna?"

The girl was lying on the settee by the hearth. Pale, stretched out, black hair streaming behind her, porcelain skin as white as the snow, she lay in a state of suspended beauty.

"Of course," she murmured, frowning.

"Arianna!" her brother breathed.

And then, to Maggie's chagrin, her brother almost dropped her flat. In fact, she would have fallen if Mireau had not been at her side.

"Delighted to see that you've fared well enough!" Cecilia said dryly.

Justin was oblivious to having left his sister. Long strides brought him across the room. He fell to his knees at Arianna's side. "Arianna!" he breathed again.

"He knows her name," Mireau commented.

Justin took the girl's hand reverently. He stared, fraught with worry, at her still face. Then, delicately, lightly, he kissed her lips.

The girl stirred. Her eyes very slowly opened. "You!" she breathed.

"But they've met, haven't they?" Mireau said, confused.

"They have now," Cecilia said. "How darling!"

"Indeed, just adorable." Maggie grinned, and then the night proved to be just too much, and she sagged into Mireau's arms in a dead faint.

She awoke much later, sometime the following day. She heard birds, and the sounds of their chirping seemed a miracle. Her eyes opened very slowly. Her throat hurt terribly. In fact, she had pains everywhere. She remembered the cobblestones that had embraced her when she had fallen from the lamppost.

"Maggie?"

She turned her head. Even doing so hurt.

Jamie was there. He was a mess. He had been up all the night, she knew.

"Maggie . . . I . . . I should give you a sound thrashing!" he said.

She tried to smile. "I'm not sure it could hurt much worse than what I'm already feeling," she told him. And he smiled and shook his head, touching her cheek very tenderly. "We didn't get him. You wounded him . . . you did get him with a shot . . . but he didn't die. He escaped. We looked all night."

"But . . . Arianna is home."

He nodded. "Charles would have been very proud of you, you know."

"I'm glad."

"I'm still ready to thrash you! You should have told me."

"I couldn't tell you . . . I had to get her out first, or you would come there ready to be shot yourself and you both might have died. You hadn't been there, and actually, I was going to tell you, but—"

"But I behaved like the biggest ass in the world," he said ruefully.

"But . . . it didn't really matter. Honestly, it didn't work out quite as I had planned it, but we are all alive, and Arianna is home, and . . . Jamie?" she asked, suddenly wincing in pain. "Do you think that . . . that he might be the killer as well? I tried to tell the police everything he said. And I told them that he'd come to the séance the night before after the murders had occurred, and when he took my hands, his were wet. All wet, as if he'd washed them."

"I don't know, Maggie. I do know that he's still on the loose out there, somewhere, and that we've got to find him." He leaned forward, kissing her forehead. For a moment he paused there, and she felt him trembling. "You're all right," he said softly. "Dr. Mayer says that, amazingly, you've not got a single broken bone. You'll not feel great for a few days, but . . ."

He sat back again. "I've got to change. I've got to have a bath, change . . . get some sleep myself. You, rest. If you even think about getting out of that bed, leaving this room—I will beat you to within an inch of your life!"

She tried not to smile. He'd saved her life. He'd never hurt her, and she knew it.

But she hadn't the strength to argue. Not then.

And so she nodded, and her eyes closed again.

The next time she awoke, it was to Arianna's face.

The girl sat by her side, watching her so anxiously. And when her eyes opened, Arianna cried out, "Oh, Maggie!"

The hug that she gave her hurt. Maggie managed not to cry out. It was far too precious a hug to refuse.

Three days later, her throat no longer hurt, her voice seemed just fine, and even the little aches and pains that had plagued her had subsided.

She hadn't seen Jamie again, and she was concerned, except that her brother had taken up residence at the house, and told her that Jamie had asked about her, but that he was busy. He had gotten Mireau to write some articles and see that they were sent to the paper; they were calming articles, saying as how the entire community must learn to fight terror together.

Hearing this, Maggie decided that she could aid the cause, and she got Mireau to sit with her while she had him write up her version of her particular story, claiming that the police, along with Lord James, had certainly saved her life, that they were a city with a massive population, learning to fight crime. She made certain to stand up for Prince Eddy, pointing out clearly that he had been in Scotland during the murders, and she had urged other men and women of any financial prosperity to help those who were so in need. She made sure that the byline was that of a fictitious member of the Salvation Army, and therefore, she didn't add any of the scandal of her own life to what was written.

The days ahead were hard, though—horrible. The

entire city indeed lived in fear. A piece of kidney, proved to be human, was delivered to Mr. Lusk, head of the Whitechapel Vigilance Committee, and the police and the citizens had to grimly accept the fact that it might well have been taken from one of the victims.

The story was printed, and Maggie was glad to see that there were people who talked about it, and rather than drag down the monarchy or continue to ridicule such hardworking fellows as Abberline, they began to form their own watch committees.

And to add aid to those in the East End.

A week after the night when she had gone to Hennesy's house and possibly had her own encounter with the madman, Jamie came to the house. He was in a tense and dire mood, and she was surprised when he said that he wasn't ordering her about, but if she cared anything for him, she would go away for a while.

"Where?"

"Go visit Clayton's sisters. Visit the baby," he told her.

Mireau was there, and she glared at him furiously. He lifted his hands helplessly. "He . . . has a way of making me say things!" Mireau said.

"Just for a while, Maggie, please. Just for a while. Alexander is a madman, whether he is the East End fiend or not, and he wants you dead. I can't worry about you and do the things I should be doing."

She wanted to argue. She didn't. She had to admit that she wasn't feeling her usual strength as yet. Except that she didn't want to be away from him. First, everything had been so volatile, and then, when she had finally discovered a taste of real tenderness . . .

"All right," she told him.

So she went up to the woods, and met Clayton's sisters, and spent time playing with the absolutely precious little girl called Ally.

Arianna came for the first week, which made Justin come, too. They were waiting, of course—her period of mourning for her father was long from over, but as she told Maggie, Justin was her prince in shining armor, and she wanted to be with him more than anything in the world.

Cecilia came to visit as well, bringing with her news from London. Sir Charles Warren had buckled to pressure and resigned.

Actually, he resigned again, and then again, but the whole of the police departments were in a state of flux. Maggie's cousin Tristan had joined with the Metropolitan police, and was very pleased to be working.

Cecilia announced that she had done some investigating, since they really didn't know much about their little Ally.

"There is definitely a woman named Annie Crook now escaped somewhere to the North. She had been in and out of many of the relief houses. She is not supposed to be a prostitute, but, well, women make their money where they can! And she has borne a few children. One whose name is Alice, but that baby is with her, alive and unharmed. Whether this is a woman with whom Eddy had an affair . . . I do think that our Ally is his child. Annie Crook may have had several, or maybe she isn't even the mother."

"It doesn't matter now," Maggie told her. "Ally belongs here, in this lovely cottage, being raised by gentlewomen who adore her. You're not supposed to know who she is, or that she's here. Mireau can't keep a secret!"

Cecilia was offended at that. "Maggie! I would go to my grave with the secret! After all we've been through together!"

And, of course, she was right.

"No one must ever know about her, though. Really, truly," Maggie reminded Cecilia.

"Of course!"

And they progressed to talk about other matters.

There was other crime in the City of London. As accusations and arguments climbed, so did the fear. More and more letters poured into police stations.

But time passed . . .

A month, and the murderer did not strike again.

Then, he came back with his most savage rage of killing yet.

And naturally, the papers were full of it. For once, he didn't kill his victim on the streets, or leave the body there, exposed.

But what he did surpassed any evil previously seen.

His victim was different as well in that she was young, and pretty. Once.

But not when the killer finished with her.

He attacked her in her room, in Miller's Court. She was very late with her rent money, and hadn't had the money to repair a broken glass pane in her window. That was how those who discovered her body came in the next day.

Mary Kelly. Twenty-five years old, not yet worn down by the life she had come to lead. Not being on the street, the killer had taken his time, and his frenzy had seemed to know no bounds.

It was in the afternoon, two days after the killing had taken place, that Merry had brought the papers back to the cottage. She had been deeply disturbed to do so, but there was no way out of the fact that it *was* deeply disturbing.

Maggie couldn't help but wonder if she hadn't known the killer. Jamie had talked to her about his conversation with Abberline. People wanted to make something different of the killer. They wanted a conspiracy, a political movement; indeed, they even wanted to be able to say that the killings had been committed by a demented person among "the highest of the high." No one wanted to accept the fact that the killer could be a simple criminal, a man capable, at times, of appearing completely normal when he walked on the streets.

Arianna, Justin, Cecilia, and even Mireau were back in the city, and she sat up late that night, chilled, tending the fire. The baby was peacefully sleeping, as were her "aunties."

Maggie wrapped her shawl tightly around her shoulders, musing over the state of her life. The murder of Mary Kelly had made her feel that, whatever her worry about her life, and with the scandal that always seemed to surround her, with her love for Jamie, and his true feelings for her, she was blessed. She had never had to live in the East End. She had never known that kind of desperation.

She had learned a taste of fear.

And it appalled her to think of what the women

had gone through in the hands of the man becoming known to history as Jack the Ripper.

It was as she sat there thus that she heard the snap of a twig outside the window.

London was in a frenzy such as it had never seen before.

The last murder was bringing about a state near chaos. People protested the police action in the streets. They shouted accusations.

Everything had been tried.

A fiasco with bloodhounds.

Handwriting experts.

Dreams.

Psychics.

Mesmerists, spiritualists.

The police were bombarded with those who had dreamed of the Ripper, with those who had seen him when they were hypnotized. A woman claimed that the ghosts of the victims came to her each night, and that if she was to stand on a certain street on a certain date, the Ripper would appear.

Jamie decided his best assistance to the police and the situation would be to follow up some of the more bizarre leads given to the police. Someone was certain, having seen some of his work and his strange behavior at times, that the artist Walter Sickert could just be the murderer. But friends stated that he had been in France at the time of several of the murders, and so Jamie had taken a ferry across the English Channel. He had found not just a few, but several people who swore that yes, Sickert had been there, and so, it seemed that he might be eliminated.

Two foreign men, both totally erratic in their behavior, threatening people with knives, getting into brawls, and making other certain statements, were taken into custody and jailed. The police became convinced that one of the them was the murderer—only to find out that he had been in jail already on the night of the double event.

And so it went. There were whispers among those who believed in a royal conspiracy—that since Eddy had been proved to be in Scotland on certain dates, Sir William Gull, the steadfast physician, had done the killing for him.

One had only to look at Sir William and know that the man had been incapable of the killings and the mutilations in the amount of time in which they had occurred. He could scarcely move on one side of his body.

Jamie was also convinced that fine carriages were noted in the East End. He watched for them constantly himself.

And, of course, he was left to wonder if he'd nearly had the murderer in his grasp, only for the man to escape. It was a bitter question, and a frightening one.

He spoke again with Abberline the day after the discovery of Mary Kelly's body.

"What now?" Abberline asked woefully. "Such a terrible blood bath, good God, man! If I live to be one hundred, I will never forget what I saw in that room. So, where does a man go from there? Would a man's sanity snap entirely?"

"I wish I could say," Jamie told him.

When he returned to the town house that night, he frowned, noting that a letter had been left at his door.

There was no postmark on it.

When he opened it, he found only the words, *"Catch me when you can,"* written in a crude scrawl. They had been written in another letter that had made its way to the police. Originally, the letter had been sent to Mr. George Lusk, chairman of the Whitechapel Vigilance Committee.

The letter had been accompanied by a piece of human kidney.

The killer knew him. Personally, Jamie thought.

And then he was seized with a sudden terror. He still had no proof. But Adrian Alexander was still at large. He had disappeared back into the bowels of the East End as if he had never existed.

He knew Jamie, and . . .

He turned the letter over. More words were written on the back of the paper.

I like the woods.

Maggie seized hold of the fire poker, and stood, listening. She knew that she had heard a rustling in the bushes.

But now . . .

Silence reigned.

For an endless amount of time, she simply stood her ground. Seconds passed, then minutes, and still, she stood perfectly still, listening.

Finally, she eased down the poker. Her nerves

were rattled, she told herself. She was far away here. Far from the city. Jack was holding his reign of terror in London.

Still, as she walked into the kitchen, determined to make herself some tea, she took the fire poker with her.

The mullioned-glass windows that bordered the sink were closed. A gas lamp had been turned low, causing shadows to flicker on the walls. Outside, the autumn weather was growing crisp and chill. She shivered, and pumped up water, filling the kettle. As she set it over the stove and lit the flame, she wondered just what she was going to do. Jamie cared for her, she was certain. But since that day . . .

She had been here, and he had remained in London. Perhaps he had felt the pressure of his position. Perhaps he had felt that they needed time. Perhaps he didn't mind at all having her as a lover, a mistress, and had no intention of anything further. That didn't mean that he didn't care. Nor did it mean that he wanted a life together.

And if not . . .

What was she going to do about the child? Not the beautiful little Ally, happily living here, beloved and adored. Her own child. She was almost positive . . .

She knew she could never, in a thousand years, give up a babe. And her heart bled with a greater concern for those poor women she had known, so often forced to the streets, and turning to gin as their only escape from unbearable lives.

Perhaps that was what suddenly gave her chills again. Thoughts of the East End . . .

She was staring at the stove, the fire poker leaning against it. She reached forward, picking it up.

And turned.

And he was there.

She didn't know he had gotten into the kitchen, if he had made his way into the cellar and come silently up the stairs, or if he had jimmied the back lock.

It didn't matter. He was there.

He had changed considerably once again, since they had met. His face appeared sucked in; the cheekbones were very prominent. His chin appeared sharp, and his hair had grown out more and fell in a strange, mousy way, in a single length covering a skull that seemed too large for his body. He had grown a shabby, untrimmed mustache, and his sunken cheeks looked all the worse for the scraggly growth of beard upon them.

His eyes burned with a peculiar glow.

He smiled. His teeth had gone very bad, and the stench of him seemed to suddenly reach her. She almost fell back. He smelled like something dead. As if he had been rolling in the carcasses of rotting animals.

He wore a long open coat, and dark, mud-spattered trousers. His appearance in itself was enough to bring terror to her heart. But there was more. His hands were at his sides. In one, he carried a very long blade. A hunting blade. He moved it back and forth, almost convulsively. It had cut through the fabric of his pants. It was cutting flesh, as well. A smattering of blood could be seen against his leg, where he continued to scrape the honed blade.

"You were easy to find," he told her. "Your house

was easy to find . . . and his house was easy to find. Your friends were even easier to find. Following them here was very easy."

"What do you want?" she demanded. She tried to keep her voice bold. *If he was, indeed, the Ripper, he was accustomed to women easily giving in to his demands, practicing their trade, being pliable. Perhaps if she tried to show that she was ready to fight, and able to do so . . .*

"What do I want?" he said, and appeared to be very amused by the question. "What do I want?" And he laughed aloud. "You. Dead. But I want to hear you scream first."

She held her stance, feeling the poker in her hand. At least he didn't seem to be interested in the aunts—or the baby.

He only wanted *her* dead.

She raised the poker, ready to swing. "I don't want to die. Or scream," she told him.

He seemed to be amused still further.

"But you will. Die and scream," he assured her.

"Not easily," she promised.

He took a step toward her. She tried quickly and rationally to weigh her fight. Swing the poker . . . if he caught it, and held it, and his strength was anything up to what it had been, he might well wrench it from her.

Stay where she was, and the knife would soon come against her throat.

She felt the steam rising from the kettle behind her.

She swung around, snatching up the kettle, splashing the scalding water at him. She drew a scream from the man, and dared to step closer, swinging the kettle. He let out a howl again, crashing against the cellar door.

As he righted himself, she gained a better grip on the poker, thinking that she would attack, and stand a better chance than if she just waited for him to recover.

But then she started, hearing a sleepy voice. "Lady Maggie?"

Merry. Come to the hall from the bedrooms, her nightcap and robe in place.

She came to a dead standstill, and Alexander, hands clenched into fists, suddenly made a lunge toward her.

"Lord! Lord have mercy!" Merry shrieked.

He might be in agony, but he would wrest hold of her, seize her . . .

And the knife would come against her throat. And she would be dead, because of Maggie's determination to stop the ills of the world.

"Here! You want me? Come and get me!" Maggie called. She threw the poker down and stared at him defiantly.

He turned away from Merry.

And Maggie purposely flew at him, veering just at the last minute, sliding around him with a slap to his injured face, and bolted to the front door of the cottage. She wrenched it open, and fled out into the night.

To her relief, she heard his bellow of pain and fury.

And the thunder of his stride as he came after her.

* * *

Jamie hadn't bothered with the niceties—or the slowness—of a carriage ride. Nothing could bring him more quickly across country than Newton.

Still, it had been a long, hard ride. And much of it had been in near-dark. At last, he had neared the cottage, and to his dread, he had found light blazing from the cottage and Merry standing at the open doorway, rocking, tears burning brightly in her eyes.

Jamie reined in on Newton, but didn't dismount. "Merry! He came here, right?" he demanded, leaning down. "Alexander?"

She looked at him, focused. "His name . . . I don't know his name!"

"Where are they?" Jamie demanded.

She shook her head. "She ran . . . she hit him and ran. He went after her . . . she was trying to stop him from coming after me. She led him away. He could have . . . he could have butchered the whole house while we slept!"

He could have, Jamie thought with horror, and a truly sinking feeling. But he wouldn't have done so. He wouldn't have done so, because it wouldn't have been enough.

"Which way?"

She pointed straight, out into the darkness.

"How long ago?"

"A while!" Merry said, catching back a sob.

"Get back in. Lock the house up, everything, check every window, Merry."

The woman nodded, and a shot of steely reserve seemed to come to her. "Yes, yes, there's the baby, and my sisters!"

She walked back into the house, and Jamie swung Newton around.

Luckily, there had been some rain. And he could see the tracks before him. He nudged the horse on.

The tracks went down the trail to the road. He was able to cover that ground quickly.

Then, at the road, the tracks were harder to read.

He dismounted, moving closer to the ground.

He straightened. Maggie had run across it, and into the foliage beyond. He threw the reins over the horse's neck, and gave him a slap. "Go on, boy, back to the cottage."

He moved into the foliage himself.

Maggie could scarcely breathe, and she was afraid that if anything gave her away, it would be the sound of her desperate breathing.

She knew that she was ahead of him by a good thirty feet. It had taken him some time to realize that she hadn't circled back around the house, that she had opted for the overgrown wealth of trees and brush on the other side of the road. She realized that she was buying time, and then she wondered why she was bothering.

Then, of course, she knew. It was instinct. Simple survival.

But as she drew him from the house, she knew that she was going to have to do much more if she really wanted to survive.

She watched from the rear of an oak as he came across the road and found where she had crashed through the foliage. There was a low, young branch on the tree, and as he moved, she grasped hold of it, pulling it back.

"Hide and seek, Lady Maggie?" he called. "Hyde . . . Jekyll and Hyde!" he called, and laughed. "That's me . . . I might have been a Dr. Jekyll, but in all of us, there's a Mr. Hyde!"

He came closer, and she knew that he hadn't discovered her exact whereabouts yet.

"Ah, my lady! I can head back for the house, you know!"

She allowed herself a small noise, and he crept toward her. She had to force herself to wait. Wait until, in the misty moonlight, he saw her there. He lengthened his stride, grinning. She pulled back the sapling as hard as she could . . . waited, and let it go.

It slammed him dead center in the chest, and his feet went out right from under him, and he screamed in fury and pain. He must have been winded, because, he went down, and stayed down.

For several long moments. She looked about for a weapon, any weapon, aware that she didn't dare leave him to rise and come after her again.

Or go back. For the sisters, and baby Ally.

But she could find no handy rock or log, not quickly enough, and so, she took off again. As she ran, she heard a bubbling sound. There was a stream or a brook ahead.

A stream. She burst out from the bushes and saw that there was a rickety little wooden bridge ahead of her. She raced for it. As she started over it, a log beneath her feet gave. She almost cried out, but caught herself in time.

He was coming, and coming fast. She ducked

down, and began ripping at the old rotting planks. The first fell into the rushing stream and rocks below. The second came apart in her hands.

She could see him, then. He was coming out to the thin strip of embankment that bordered the bridge. She wrenched hard at a third log, then looked at the gap she had created.

"Maggie, Maggie, Maggie! You're just what I needed, you know? There was that instant's gratification at first. The look in their eyes as my fingers wound around their throats. Then, there was one— she was choking, couldn't breathe, but she squealed a little. Still, got to see her face as my knife went across her throat. Had to shut them up. Then there was more. Of course. And it was so much fun. Destroy me, would you? I almost brought down all London!" He was staring at her, then, from the embankment. She had one of the planks in her hands, and he would have to attempt quite a leap to get to her.

He started to laugh. "Do you believe all that? Ah, should I tell you the truth or not? Are you wondering if you're going to fall prey to a man who's an animal—*because you made him one!*—or am I Jack the Ripper, a fiend to the utmost degree?"

He started toward her once again. She waited. And waited.

He walked slowly, assessing the situation. He seemed totally in his right senses, no longer worrying the knife, but keeping it firmly in his right hand.

"Ah, can I leap that distance?" he asked her, and smiled.

He walked to the base of the bridge.

"Are you Jack the Ripper?" she asked him.

And he grinned, taking his first step upon the bridge. Then another, and another. He was about five feet from her. The span she had broken was perhaps four.

He started to laugh suddenly. Then, he turned, walked back, and started to run.

He *was* going to try to leap the distance.

Jamie broke out onto the embankment just in time to see the man running.

He tore out after him.

Alexander leaped . . . and fell, but caught the last plank, just beneath Maggie's feet.

She screamed.

The bridge gave entirely, and crashed into the stream.

She was in the water, and he had her ankle. She had so little breath, and was so blinded by the rush and the darkness above. He was trying to drag her back.

Had he lost the knife?

Her fingers curled around a rock in the streambed. She kicked out furiously.

Suddenly, his face appeared before hers in the water.

She screamed again, and choked on water, and struck out with the rock. Her hand moved slowly . . . so slowly through the water.

The rock connected with his face.

He stared at her.

His arm rose as they both kicked and struggled in the depths.

Then, just as she saw the knife rising above her arms, his wrist was wrenched back, and the man was ripped away from her.

Her ankle was free. Desperate for breath, she kicked her way to the surface. Gasping and screaming, she clawed her way to the embankment.

She saw a man rising from the water, and she backed along the damp, cold earth. "No!"

"Maggie!"

That voice . . .

"Jamie?"

She hadn't the strength left, but she found it. She came to her feet, and leapt forward, into his arms. Then she drew away.

"Alexander?" she said desperately.

"He's dead."

"Are you certain?"

"I'm certain,"

She looked around his shoulder, and she saw him. Blood oozed from the slash against his throat. He was in the water, caught between two boulders in the stream. Eyes open, he stared up unseeingly at the night sky.

"Dead?" she whispered again.

"Dead," he promised her.

She leaned against him, fell against him. Her knees gave. He held her. He lifted her chin, and searched out her eyes. "Maggie, was he . . . Jack the Ripper?"

She started to shake. She couldn't laugh, and she couldn't cry.

"Maggie?"

"I don't know. I don't know. I wonder if . . . if we'll ever know!"

She couldn't walk. He picked her up in his arms.

"Jamie?"

"Yes?"

"I love you," she said, and touched his face, and waited.

"I love you, too," he told her, and said no more, but made his way back to the cottage in the woods.

Epilogue

There were two books written about the whole affair.

Mireau's book, unpublished I thought, was far superior to the one which was published just days after we had returned to London. Of course, reading Mireau's, I was pleased. I *had* done everything in my power to save Arianna, I *had* seen to it that Prince Eddy had been defended in the press with the facts of his whereabouts, and *I* might well have met with the infamous and savage butcher who had all but brought London to its knees.

But in the other story . . .

I had blatantly murdered Charles. I had attacked a true spiritualist, a man of God, who had come to warn others of what was about to happen in the city. I had seduced anyone who had come my way, and consorted in the worst dens of iniquity in the city to seek out those that I might harm further. I had lured an innocent man to his death, and brought about the destruction of seven young men who had only needed jobs, and were seeking a way to go straight. I had gone to a home where my stepdaughter was working, and I had poisoned her, preferring to kill her myself rather than let her lead a life I didn't control. I was a horrible, wicked, cruel stepmother!

Of course, my name wasn't actually in it, not at all. It had been very cleverly written. Since I had been the object of scandal several times, there was no doubting, though, just whom was meant by the Lady Evelyn Quinn. And, of course, the gorgeous stepdaughter, Lady Bianca. Cecilia had been the one to first bring the book to my attention, and naturally, it had infuriated me. Especially since I had just returned to the city, and gotten to spend a single blissful night with Jamie before he had gone on to meet with the authorities . . . and sent a message that he would not be returning that night. At first, I understood. There hadn't been another murder, but the last had been a crescendo, and the city remained in an uproar, as it would for weeks, months, and even years to come. At that time, though, we could only tell what we knew, what had been said.

And speculate. I realized that until the day I died, unless a madman was caught in the act at a future date, I would never really know.

Had the man been the heinous killer?

Or more frightening still, just another of his ilk?

So Jamie's days with the authorities, inundated with meeting after meeting, detail after detail, went on and on. I could bear it. I could wait.

But then the next thing I knew . . .

The officer had come from Scotland Yard, and I had been informed that Lord James Langdon would be coming for me, and I would be taken to the Queen. So, here I was—held at Scotland Yard! All I could think was, *that book! That awful book! People have read it, and believed it! Because they are looking for monsters now, they must have a monster, or a witch, as in my case!*

I heard a noise behind me, and I spun around. Rather quickly. I still jump at the least sound.

Jamie had come.

Oh, he was imposing as he stood there! A tall hat upon his ink-dark hair, handsome fawn breeches accenting the length of his legs and the power within them. His waistcoat was a brocade crimson, and his overcoat was black, as was his cravat. He looked so respectable, every inch the lord. And stern, as I had seen him as well. For a moment, my heart fluttered. He could not have changed! He had been there the night of the séance, and the night the crazed killer had come to the cottage in the woods. He had spoken with Arianna, he . . .

Could he still wonder if I had killed Charles?

Then he smiled. "Maggie . . . are you quite all right?"

I frowned, afraid suddenly, keeping my distance. "Let's see . . . I was twice accosted by a killer, and now I am under arrest! Am I all right? Quite frankly, no!"

And then he laughed, sweeping the hat from his head as he stepped into the room. "You're not under arrest!"

My eyes widened. "I was escorted here by a burly police fellow I've never met. I was told you were coming for me—that I was to see the Queen."

"Maggie, Maggie, Maggie!"

"Jamie, Jamie, Jamie!"

He shook his head, stepped forward, and his eyes were pure silver and mist as they stared down into mine. "The Queen is outraged for you. She wants to assure you that you have done her a tremendous service. And—"

"What?" I breathed. And as I did so, I thought that I would never fall out of love with his smile. With his eyes. With just the sound of his voice.

"She found out who wrote the book. The published book."

"Who?" I asked cautiously.

"One of the misguided 'dwarfs'—you know, one of Adrian's young fellows, who is now rotting away in prison. Says he really does want to turn a new leaf, and the story is made up with names and notions he got from the papers."

"Really?"

"The Queen intends to see that Mireau's version finds an excellent publisher immediately."

"Thank God," I said, and yet remained a bit uneasy, for even in Mireau's version, some things were a bit too personal.

"Are you ready?" he asked me softly.

"For . . .?" I breathed.

"Tea. With the Queen."

"Oh! I . . . I, of course."

He took my arm. "She sends her congratulations, as well."

"Her congratulations?"

He nodded. "On our marriage."

This time, I caught my breath, went dead still, and stared straight at him. I was still in widow's weeds.

"We're getting married?" I asked him.

"Scandalously soon," he advised me. "But . . . I admit to feeling something of a sense of . . . an extra sense, perhaps. I thought that they might talk about us far less if we rushed the wedding . . . and had the child within the bounds of wedlock. Well, either way, they're going to talk."

"You're going to marry me?" I said to him.

"And soon, yes. There *will* be talk, you know that?"

And I started to laugh. "Whenever wasn't there talk!"

"Um, I guess I'll have to get used to it. Actually, it's rather fun, in a way!" He had led me from the room, and out to the center of the station where there were many police officers about. "We'll give them a bit more, shall we, eh?" he asked.

His eyes were silver with humor.

And then he kissed me . . .

And kissed me . . .

I didn't hear any talk at all.

Only the applause.